'[A] rip-roaring seaborne adventure thriller . . . absolutely terrific. *Dead Rich* provides thrills and spills in abundance'

Shots Magazine

'An all-too-topical thriller with some wonderfully gripping maritime set-pieces'

Daily Mail

'Timely thriller . . . The two of them are well drawn and attractive, and there is plenty of action to keep thrill-seekers reading'

Literary Review

'Timely thriller *Dead Rich* is G. W. Shaw's gripping new tale which explores what happens when oligarchs fall foul of Putin'

Sun

'G. W. Shaw delivers a superbly crafted, adrenalin-charged thriller that engages the reader fully from start to finish'

Irish Independent

'*Dead Rich* is a cleverly crafted and suspenseful locked room thriller set against the backdrop of the high seas and the world of the super wealthy'

CultureFly

'This cleverly constructed adventure thriller, set on a Russian oligarch's mega yacht in the Caribbean, makes entertaining reading'

Choice Magazine

D0599814

DEAD RICH

G. W. Shaw

riverrun

First published in Great Britain in 2022 by riverrun
This paperback edition published in 2022 by

riverrun

an imprint of

Quercus Editions Limited
Carmelite House
50 Victoria Embankment
London EC4Y 0DZ

An Hachette UK company

A CIP catalogue record for this book is available
from the British Library.

Paperback 978 1 52942 006 7
Ebook 978 1 52942 004 3

10 9 8 7 6 5 4 3 2

Typeset by CC Book Production
Printed and bound in Great Britain by Clays Ltd, Elcograf S.p.A.

MIX
Paper from
responsible sources
FSC   FSC® C104740
www.fsc.org

Papers used by riverrun are from well-managed forests and other responsible sources.

To Karolina, with thanks.

They arrive at luxury marinas, slipping up the Thames, shadowing the pink mansion houses that fringe the shores of Portofino, edging slowly into fat moorings off Brooklyn Marina. From the hills of Monaco, you see them crowding the harbour below.

Each one is different; each special. The cheapest cost mere millions. Sheikh Mohammed bin Rashid Al Maktoum, the ruler of Dubai, spent four hundred million on his. Roman Abramovich has a fleet of them, several costing as much as Sheikh Mohammed's. He paid over a billion for *Eclipse*.

Most of these floating palaces are gleaming white, though some are grey or even black. Their owners like their exteriors to say something about them. There is one you often spot cruising in the Mediterranean that has been painted in rich geometrical shapes of yellow, pink and blue by the artist Jeff Koons.

But more impressive is what you can't see. Yachts are secretive, like their owners. Their gleaming hulls conceal dance floors, fireplaces, spas, underwater observation windows and swimming pools with glass floors, under which you can see the fish moving. Many have what their designers call toy garages, with doors in their hulls that open to launch other smaller versions of themselves, tenders and sailing boats, even mini-submarines.

The bigger, the richer. Compared, say, to the fragile carracks that took Columbus to the Americas, these are huge, fantastical monsters. Like castles, these vessels become symbols of power, created to inspire awe; a physical projection of wealth and power and internationality. Like their owners' money, they can slide silently in and out of any port. Like castles, too, they are defended.

They are an entire world, separate from the rest of us. They are fabulous.

ONE
2021

The house cleaner is Romanian. Her name is Mihaela and the first time she hears the phone ping in her handbag she does not look at it because she is under the bed in an apartment off the south end of Paris's Rue de Vaugirard trying to retrieve a pair of knickers that she has discovered there while vacuuming.

The second time it pings she doesn't pay it any attention either, because she is examining the knickers more closely; they are black, flimsy and not the kind that would belong to Mme Caron, who is a tall, broad-hipped woman. Mihaela is fond of Mme Caron; she tips Mihaela whenever they meet, much to M. Caron's annoyance. Mme Caron also remembers Mihaela's son's name, despite the fact that she has only met him once, when Mihaela had to bring him with her to work because he had an upset stomach.

'And how is poor little Florian?' she asks each time, as if she imagines her son to be perpetually ill.

Mihaela considers returning the knickers to the place under

3

the bed where she discovered them; or innocently putting them into one of Mme Caron's own underwear drawers where she can find them and confront her husband about who they might belong to. Mihaela very much dislikes the idea of his infidelity. However, she is a cleaner and depends on M. Caron for her work.

Not just an ordinary cleaner, like so many others in this city. She cleans for a very exclusive class of client. The agency she works for boasts of their reputation for discretion, and lecture their workers on the importance of it. Confidentiality is of the utmost importance. So she puts the knickers in the pocket of her jeans and carries on with her work.

It isn't until after she leaves the apartment over an hour later, setting the alarm and locking the door, that she finally takes the phone out of her bag and looks at it. The message that arrived when she was under the Carons' bed is there on the lock screen.

Returning from Orly now will need to sleep today. No cleaning today. DB.

The colour vanishes from Mihaela's face. She clutches the dark wood banister of the staircase and sways.

It was Kiki's fault. Kiki works at a gay nightclub in the Quai d'Austerlitz and carries her sense of excess with her wherever she goes. It was Kiki who suggested they hold Daria's twenty-first birthday party in David Bullimore's apartment in the sixième arrondissement.

Though maybe it was Mihaela's fault as well, for boasting to Kiki about David Bullimore's hot tub. 'It has a built-in stereo and a TV.'

4

The neatest feature of the Englishman's apartment is a secluded roof garden from which you can see the Eiffel Tower, plus the six-person jacuzzi that he has installed up there. Sometimes, she cannot resist telling her friends the details of her clients' lives, just to remind them that though the hours are long and the pay could be better, her job is superior to theirs. She has told them about the woman who had a Swarovski-studded catflap; the couple with the vitamin-C-infused shower; the chain-smoking academic who appears on TV and who has a genuine Mondrian in his toilet.

'David's jacuzzi has really cool lights,' Mihaela said, like she was a friend of his.

'I bet *David*,' Kiki mocked, 'would like to get you in there one day.'

Mihaela wouldn't mind if he did. She harbours what she knows are adolescent fantasies of a man like him taking her and Florian away from a life of short-term contracts. 'The water is always kept hot so he can use it whenever he wants.'

Kiki goes on Extinction Rebellion protests and thinks that kind of squandering of resources is unforgivable. 'Somebody should use it,' she declared. 'Otherwise it's a waste.'

Plus, Daria has been feeling miserable because she has no work and knows nobody in this foreign city. The Englishman David Bullimore was supposed to be away in Tel Aviv on business until next Tuesday.

There were a total of five of them up there last night dressed in their bikinis, drinking strawberry jalapeño mint juleps under the June stars, smoking weed, listening to hip hop and giggling, all except for Mihaela, who hated every minute of it. The breeze splashed candle wax all over the decking. She sat in the pink-lit bubbling water, fingering her crucifix, anxious about the babysitter she had hired to look after Florian, worrying that one of them would break something, or spill pink drinks on his white stair carpet, or that David's neighbour would spot them on his security cameras.

Unlike all her other clients, David Bullimore doesn't have a burglar alarm. He boasts that he doesn't need one because his neighbour, who owns the top three floors of the eighteenth-century building next door, is an ultra-paranoid Russian billionaire called Stepan Pirumov – *the* Stepan Pirumov – who has security cameras overlooking the front and back of his apartment. Having such a wealthy neighbour is good for the neighbourhood.

'Relax,' Kiki told her as she sat in the brightly illuminated tub. 'The Englishman isn't back for a week. I'll help you tidy up. It's not a problem.' For some reason, Kiki was wearing a black nylon wig like the one Uma Thurman wore in *Pulp Fiction*, and whenever Mihaela complained about the mess she said, in English, 'Don't be a . . .' and drew a square in the air.

But by the time Mihaela told them the party was over, Kiki was so drunk she had thrown up takeaway pizza into the frothing water. When they hauled her out, she could barely walk. She and Daria had to guide her cautiously down the back stairs to the servants' entrance in the narrow Rue de Nevers behind the house.

'What about my coat?' complained Kiki, loudly. 'I left my coat behind. It's Zadig and Voltaire and it cost me five hundred euros. Six hundred. I don't remember.'

'I'll get it tomorrow.'

'But I'm cold.'

The Uber driver refused to take her home unless they accompanied her, so Mihaela had no option but to leave the mess upstairs for another day.

She reads the message on her phone again, hoping she has made a mistake. She hasn't. It is an hour old. The Englishman will be on his way back from Orly now and the sixième arrondissement is at least twenty minutes away on the Metro. She fumbles with the key for her Piaggio scooter.

The Englishman is a neat freak. He has hundreds of vinyl records which he keeps in strictly alphabetical order. He sends her texts if the toilet roll has been installed the wrong way around, or if there are smears on the mirror above the fireplace, but as a cleaner she respects that. When she has her own apartment, she will be the same. She knows where she stands with him, and he with her; now she feels as if she has betrayed him. At Saint-Placide she cuts in between a cyclist and a braking car and the cyclist yells at her.

The Rue Guénégaud is close to the Île de la Cité. She dodges pedestrians on crossings on the Rue de Rennes. David Bullimore will already be there, she thinks. She will have to admit everything. He will tell the agency that she held a party in his flat and she will lose all her work. In this country good work is so hard to find. She has been an idiot.

The Rue Guénégaud is a one-way street. It's quicker to park at the south end and walk up. She has just made it to the junction on Rue Mazarine and is locking her bike when she looks up and she sees the black Mercedes rounding the corner at the top. Somehow, she knows that will be Bullimore's car. She watches in horror as it pauses right outside number 15 and the door opens.

A uniformed driver in a peaked cap emerges. The passenger door opens.

It is him.

It is her fault for giving in to Kiki. She should never have listened to her. Now there is no way she can make it to the apartment before the Englishman to try and tidy the worst of it. To reach the servants' entrance from here – the only door she has the key for – she would have to walk all the way past the front of the house up to the Quai de Conti and then turn right into the narrow back street, and there is David Bullimore already ahead of her, taking his bag from the driver and reaching into his pocket for the front door key. Any second now he will be inside, calling the lift.

She picks her phone out of her bag. She will send him a note of apology right away before he sees the mess, and throw herself at his mercy, knowing that it will make no difference. Tell him she would work for nothing, perhaps. Of all her clients, he is the one who would be most outraged by the mess they had left. *I am most sorry, Mr David*, she begins to write in English.

As she hesitantly presses the keys, composing her message, she barely notices the noise, a dull *crump* that came from somewhere up the road.

She hears a man next to her gasp, but she doesn't look up. The screaming starts a second later. Finally she tears her eyes from the phone.

From where she is standing, she has a clear view up the pavement on the right side of the road. A man appears to be lying on the ground barely a metre from where David Bullimore is standing. There is something strange about the shape of his body.

The woman who is screaming is on the far side of the man;

she was pushing a child in a buggy. The man lies just in front of the little boy's dangling legs. Now David Bullimore's voice joins the woman's in an inchoate wailing, his voice deeper, but just as full of shock.

She watches, puzzled as her client staggers backwards now, tripping over his own suitcase, falling, then scrabbling up again, pushing himself away on his elbows.

A man has emerged from the gallery on the opposite side of the street talking on a mobile phone while pointing upwards.

It takes Mihaela another second to realise that the man is not just lying there; he must have fallen. There is blood, she sees now, on the grey of the pavement. He has landed between the woman and David Bullimore, missing both of them only by centimetres.

In no time the gendarmes seemed to have arrived too, blocking the street. Not just ordinary *flics* either, which is strange. They are RAID, a tactical unit, in full body armour, automatic weapons not just slung over their shoulders, but grasped in gloved hands. They hustle Bullimore and the others back from the prone body, away from the apartment's front door. A SAMU car arrives, blue light flashing, and two paramedics leap out. She watches them as they close off the whole street.

Looking up, she mentally traces the line between the pavement and the balcony he must have fallen from, and realises that it is the one next to Bullimore's – the Russian's. She glances again at the paramedics and the man they are busying themselves with and then turns away.

Through all of this Mihaela is strangely calm. She recognises the opportunity for what it is. God-given. Pushing past the shocked

9

faces that have gathered around her, she walks the long way back until she reaches Rue Dauphine, turning left again into the back alleyway.

She guesses the front entrance will be blocked for at least half an hour, maybe more. That will be enough.

She is pulling out her key for the servants' door when she notices something strange, and her skin goes cold.

The black door is not properly locked. To any passer-by it would look closed, but she can see a couple of centimetres of white door frame. She was an idiot getting drunk with friends here last night. In her hurry to get Kiki out of the building she must not even have closed the door behind her properly.

If David discovered that she had left his back door unlocked, she would be sacked on the spot. Another stroke of luck; another chance to set things straight.

Closing the door behind her, she climbs the stairs quickly. In the living room, Kiki's Zadig and Voltaire faux-fur jacket is lying abandoned across the back of a leather sofa, along with her Uma Thurman wig.

Mihaela tuts; she doesn't even hear the footsteps behind her. Not until the hand is clamped firmly over her mouth.

In horror, she sees the other hand holds a kitchen knife.

She thinks of the body on the pavement below her; that this is all Kiki's fault. She thinks of her son Florian and how he will be alone here in a strange country without her.

TWO

Zinaida was moored in Yacht Haven Grande in St Thomas, in the US Virgin Islands. She had been there for over a year. On the bridge, Captain Marius Falk pressed a button and said, 'First Mate, come to bridge please.'

Falk sat back in the plush white leather captain's chair and waited for the reply. None came; all he could hear was the reassuring hum of electronics, a noise he never noticed when he was at sea.

'First Mate, come to bridge please,' he said again. 'I have an urgent question.'

The first mate was a woman, and she was standing right behind him in shorts and T-shirt; she didn't find the joke particularly funny.

Falk liked to do things like this when they were alone together aboard *Zinaida*, which, until today, was most of the time.

Captain Marius Falk was in uniform; she was not. On board, he always wore the white shirt with gold on its epaulettes. He

11

ironed his own shirts. A compact, muscular man, he had a Master's in Marine Science from Ålesund University and over twenty years' experience at sea. He had taken massive cruise ships to the Arctic, captained huge oil tankers in the Persian Gulf and even, as a younger man, steered comfortless Baltic ferries through terrible storms. On those vessels he had worked much harder, but for much less money.

The first mate wore scruffy shorts and a faded Miami Dolphins T-shirt. Marius disapproved, but when the family who owned the boat were not on board, the first mate didn't see the point in dressing up.

'First Mate. I think we should have sex.' The intercom message rang out through the whole boat.

'Not funny,' said the woman, punching him hard on the arm.

'Ow.' He grinned at her.

'There are other people on the boat.'

'Only engineers. Workers don't count,' he said dismissively.

'Asshole,' she said. 'In case it escaped your attention, we are just workers too, Marius. It's not like this is our yacht, is it? We have urgent work to do.'

'You may be a worker, but I am the captain. So that's Captain Asshole to you, OK?'

For most of the last year it had just been the two of them on board *Zinaida*; Erin Wade, first mate, and Marius Falk, captain. Local hotel services came aboard daily to clean and polish; maintenance crew came on board just as regularly, but mostly it was just Erin and Marius. The billionaire who had commissioned the boat, and had her built at a cost of 256 million dollars, seemed

12

to be losing interest. According to what Erin read about him in the newspapers Marius brought on board, he did not enjoy vacations. Or maybe the novelty of owning her had worn off. He was rich enough not to have to bother to charter her, so most of the time she had just sat in harbour; except for when Captain Falk took her out to run her engines.

'What about it?' He raised his eyebrows. 'It will be our last chance.'

Erin shook her head. 'I'm too busy even if I wanted to and I don't, asshole.'

Tomorrow, the billionaire and his family were arriving, at short notice. Just yesterday Yuliya Pirumova had called, telling Marius to prepare the boat. The mother would be flying in from Moscow, the daughter from London and the father from Paris. Marius was excited. He liked it when the billionaire came aboard.

Erin was not. She preferred having the yacht to herself.

The extra temporary crew were flying into the island tomorrow before the family arrived; a head chef from Puerto Vallarta, a second chef from Bremen, a chief steward from Miami, a steward from Sweden, a chief engineer from Lagos, an electro-technical officer from Poland, a second mate from Taipei, a security officer from London and a personal fitness trainer from Los Angeles to supplement the locals. In the past Marius booked people they knew and trusted. There was no time for that. However, there were specialist agencies who understood the type of worker Marius required, people who were diligent and who, most importantly, were aware of how to behave around the very rich.

13

After so many months of inactivity, there was much to do. As far as Erin was concerned, this was a relief. She hated doing nothing. This morning, Erin had tested the safety gear, the life jackets, the rafts, the firefighting equipment, the flares, the first-aid kits, the torch batteries and the emergency beacons and communicators in each raft. She had refilled the spare petrol tanks for the outboards and checked the spare mooring lines. Right now, two local marine engineers were aboard, checking over the twin MTU diesels. On other ships, an engine would need to be serviced after running for a given number of hours. On *Zinaida*, it was never like that. Underuse was the risk. A stationary engine was not a happy one.

Erin sympathised with the engines. It felt wrong to be so idle. Once a month they and a small crew took the boat out overnight to gun the engines and keep them alive. Idleness, rather than passion, had made her and the captain lovers.

The sex was convenient. Marius Falk made love conscientiously, which was how he did his job, and that meant it was better than most of the sex she had had.

She was not his type. She was short, stocky and muscular. She had seen him on shore with the willowy blondes in expensive clothes, pointing out the boat in the bay to them as if it was his own. He was not her type either. Though she liked him and respected his knowledge of the sea, had it not been for *Zinaida*, they wouldn't even have been friends. When docked, he spent his time on land; she spent her time here on the boat, as close to the water as she could be. After all the privations of a seaman's life, he had fallen in love with this luxury. He enjoyed the jealous glances from onlookers at the dockside. He was saving up to buy an expensive waterside property on the island of Husøya. She was saving for something much simpler; a boat of her own.

A woman in her thirties, Erin had long given up the idea of finding someone who would love her for who she was.

The yacht sung its own low song; the thrum of pumps and engines and air conditioners. It was alive. It was a beast. No expense had been spared. It was not a boat you were ever truly in control of because it was in control of itself. The truth was, Erin believed, any idiot could sail a ship like *Zinaida*, because it did most of the work for you. It was not, in Erin's critical eyes, a real boat.

She leaned past Marius Falk to press a button and checked the weather. She longed to be away from the shore again and didn't want high winds to keep them in port, which was always a possibility in the Caribbean. She selected a tab on the touch screen and watched the forecast movement of the depression from the open sea towards the islands. A deep purple blob, 0.95 bars of pressure, creeping over the ocean. 'Seen this?'

'Yes, of course.'

The forecast showed the storm passing hundreds of miles to the north of them, but weather here was fickle.

'It won't be a problem,' he said. And she believed him. He had far more experience of these waters than she had. 'I've been thinking,' he continued. 'We should take the boat out tonight, once the engines have been checked. A one-night run.'

Erin was holding a worn pulley block that needed replacing. 'There's no need if the engineers have already done it. I need to go over to the chandlery and replace this – the bearings have gone. Can we get the outboards serviced too?'

15

He grinned and slipped his arm around her waist, lowered his voice. 'I just think we should give the boat a real going-over.'

She was, he reasoned, having her period. He was an excellent judge of people. And he was about to say, 'Suit yourself,' when the humming stopped.

Not just the humming. Everything stopped.

The screens in front of him all went dark. The air conditioning that kept this glass box at the top of the boat cool in all heats ceased blowing. The green, red and white LEDs that decorated the knobs and on every panel all blinked off.

There was silence.

'What the . . . '

' . . . actual fuck?' she completed his sentence.

And then, before they could even register that it had happened, the screens switched back on, the lights blinked and the cold air was blowing onto his face again.

Instead of being annoying, the hum was now oddly reassuring. The navigation system began to reboot itself.

'Bloody engineers,' he muttered.

'Was it them?'

'Of course it was.'

A minute later the two engineers were on the bridge. 'All good, sir,' they said.

'Why the hell did you switch off the electrics, without checking with me first?' he demanded.

The two men looked at each other, puzzled.

'No, sir. We didn't do that. We thought it was you.'

'Don't lie to me,' he said. He snatched the newly completed certificates from them.

The men stood silently. They were locals, well-paid, used to deference.

'Well?' said Marius. 'Why are you still here?'

They didn't answer.

'Get the hell off my boat then. I will be reporting this.'

The two men stood awkwardly, not going anywhere. 'May we have our phones, sir?' they asked, eventually.

Captain Falk yanked the drawer beneath the chart table open and pulled out the two phones he had taken off them when they had boarded – visitors were not allowed to use their own mobiles on this private boat in case they took photographs – and thrust them at the men.

'Typical local workers,' he said to Erin later. 'They never take responsibility for anything.'

THREE

That evening, when the police finally allow David Bullimore back into his apartment, even he is surprised at how tidy it looks.

It seems different, though, but he is too tired and upset to think about it.

This morning, a man died at his feet. If he had been a second earlier, he might have died too, crushed by the man who fell from his neighbour's apartment. The violence has scarred him.

At first, the gendarmes were convinced it was his neighbour who had thrown himself to his death. The moment they realised the apartment belonged to a well-known Russian oligarch, they had shut down the entire area, sent in SWAT teams and forensics experts. They even sent in a hazmat team. These days, with Russians, you never know.

David tried to tell the *capitaine* that the man who had died was not the owner but another man who sometimes visited, but he and his colleagues were too worked up by then to listen to him. They had set up a mobile command post in the street and were refusing to tell him when it would be safe to return to his home.

He retreats to sit at the Café Dauphine around the corner and drink pastis to calm himself. His hands are shaking as he drinks.

Back in his flat, he showers, orders a takeaway he doesn't eat, and then tries to sleep but can't.

At five in the morning he wanders barefoot around the apartment. Eventually he realises what it is that was different. His Mashad rug is in the wrong place. Instead of being in front of the sofa, it is behind it.

The cleaner must have misplaced it.

Rolling it up to put it back where it had belonged, he is shocked to see a large dark damp circle; his cleaner, Mihaela, had obviously spilt something there. The moisture has stained the parquet beneath it. The stupid woman has had to cover it up by moving the rug.

He will have to have words with her. It is a shame, because as a rule she is an excellent cleaner.

But he doesn't ever have words with Mihaela, because she does not come back next week. Instead of Mihaela, the agency send a Latvian student.

'What happened to Mihaela?' David demands, upset. He does not like disruption of any kind.

'She left,' says the cleaner. 'Unexpectedly. She didn't tell anyone. She just disappeared. The agency are very angry with her.'

Unlike Mihaela, the Latvian leaves water stains on the bathroom mirror and, within two weeks of starting, breaks a Lalique vase of his mother's. It's ridiculous, he knows, but this seems to disturb him almost as much as the death of a man at his feet.

However, on the plus side, the stain on his parquet fades and in a few weeks he will barely notice it at all.

FOUR

'Perhaps you're right,' said Kai. 'A proper job. That's what I need.'

'Exactly,' said Marley. 'A proper job.'

At around the same time as a man fell to his death in front of David Bullimore, two brothers were dining in Clerkenwell. The restaurant was called Bone. Kai was the younger, grateful that he and his brother were nothing like each other. Kai had gone into the music industry. Marley was the more responsible one; he was in advertising and was senior VP of a company that had adapted to embrace the world digital media when others had gone down the pan. Kai wore loose-fitting trousers, an orange cotton pullover and had not shaved. Marley dressed well but conservatively, entirely in shades of blue; he had recently begun to shave his head to disguise his hair loss.

Marley peered over the menu. 'You were so mopey the other day, about how you didn't get the royalties you used to and how Covid had wrecked the live circuit.'

'Perhaps I was a bit drunk,' said Kai.

'So I thought I'd ask around.' Marley looked up at the waiter who had appeared. 'I'll have rib-eye steak with bone marrow gravy.'

It was one of those restaurants that made a point about vegetarians by only putting a single item they could eat on the menu. 'And me, the celeriac,' said Kai.

'Turns out this CEO pal of mine called Trevor is a massive fan of the stuff you did back in the day. Has all your records. Do they call them records? Anyway. I put a lot of work his way.'

'Who's Trevor?'

'It's a sound design company. Every brand has its own particular sound. The Apple chime. That Intel thing. Even your microwave makes noises. All that's very hot right now and that's what Trevor does.'

'And he wants to see me?'

Marley raised his hands. 'It would be a trial period, obviously, to see if you get along. But I told him what a genius you were and he's really keen to meet.' Marley had always believed in his younger brother; had always supported him, even if he had lived in a different world.

'That's very generous,' said Kai.

'I know it's not what you're used to.'

'But maybe it's time I grew up?' said Kai.

'No. No. Not at all. Not grow up, exactly,' said Marley. 'But it couldn't go on for ever, could it? Maybe this whole Covid thing was a blessing in disguise.' Marley delved inside his jacket pocket and pulled out an index card on which he'd written a name, an address and a date and time.

21

Kai took it; read it. 'Thursday?'

'Strike while the iron's hot.'

Kai looked up again at his brother; his eyebrows were raised, expectant. 'You probably had to call in a favour or two.'

'No,' said Marley unconvincingly. 'Course not. He's dying to work with you. Like I said, big fan.'

'Right.'

His brother looked out for him. He always had. Since their parents had died it was just the two of them. When the food arrived, Marley chopped up his steak into little pieces before he started to eat it. His brother had always done that, thought Kai, watching him.

'Any prospect of some gigs coming up?' Marley asked, though gigs were now largely a thing of the past. Kai never asked about his brother's work. He didn't know where to begin.

He imagined himself at a desk, maybe with a Herman Miller chair and an iMac. Maybe it would be a positive change, having some structure in his life. The music business was necessarily chaos. A regular life would be a healthier one. He could do yoga in the morning; go out to the cinema in the evening.

'Gigs? No. All that's gone, really.'

'It's not in the bag yet, but I think you're in with a good chance.'

They talked genially for half an hour until Marley looked at the time on his phone and announced, 'All this is excellent, but I better get back to work.'

It was like a bell chiming in Kai's head. His brother had to leave now because he had to get back to work. He, however, could stay here, maybe drink a glass of wine, see an exhibition

22

or wander down to the Thames for a while until the light started to go, and then maybe head home and work on a mix.

'What's wrong?' asked Marley, a look of concern on his face.

'No . . . Nothing.'

'Good.'

Marley insisted on paying. 'You paid last time, didn't you?'

'No. You did.'

'I'm sure you did.' The usual white lie hung between them, awkwardly as Marley held out his credit card to the waiter. He knew how Kai's finances were these days.

They stood outside to say goodbye. It must have rained while they were having lunch; the pavements were dark and dirty.

'Forgot to say. Charlie sends her love,' said Marley. Her name was Charlotte, but when they became a couple she became Charlie and they became Charlie and Marley, a single corporate entity – as Kai always thought of them. Charlie was a good person. She worked for a charity that dug wells for people in Africa.

'You still seeing that photographer from New York?' asked Marley.

'She got engaged,' said Kai. 'To someone else, obviously.'

'Oh. I'm sorry to hear that. But she was quite young, wasn't she? Maybe it's good to be single for a while.'

'I'm seeing an art student right now in fact,' said Kai.

'An art student?' The girlfriends had come and gone. Marley tried to keep up.

'She got in touch because she wanted to use some of my music for something she was doing. An installation for her Master's. Then she invited me to come and see it.'

23

'And one thing led to another?'

'Don't be cynical, Marl.'

'I'm not. I'm sure she's lovely. Do bring her over. We'd love to meet her. What's her name?'

'Zina.'

'Sexy.'

'It's Russian. It's short for Zinaida. Zinaida Pirumova. She came over here to go to school and she stayed on.'

Marley frowned. 'Pirumova?'

'You know her?'

'As in the daughter of Stepan Pirumov?'

But Marley's car arrived before Kai could tell him he didn't know who he was talking about. 'Don't forget,' said Marley, opening the door. 'Next Thursday.'

FIVE

Erin waited in Arrivals at Cyril E. King Airport, flicking through a copy of a yacht magazine she had picked up at the news stand. Marius had asked her to buy the *New York Times* and the *FT*.

Marius Falk was obsessed with news. As far as Erin was concerned, it was pointless reading about things that you could do nothing about. Between pandemics, populism and climate change, the world was a mess and she didn't need to know any more than that. Alone, at sea, the rest of the world could do whatever it wanted.

There was a nice enough 35-foot Beneteau advertised in Miami for 78,000, which was way, way out of her bracket, but she tore out the advert anyway, and put it in the pocket of her shorts. When she found the right boat she would be done with all this.

The first arrivals started to come through, so she held up the sign she had bought that read, simply, *Zinaida*.

The crew started to emerge into the baggage claim area one

by one. The chief steward turned out to be very pretty, but then they always were on luxury yachts. She had long black hair and very even teeth. 'Hey.' She greeted Erin like an old friend, though they had never met before. 'I'm psyched about this trip. You know where we're going?'

The chef came next, followed by the engineer, then others. Erin ticked them off her list one by one, until there were only two names left. 'Where's the security officer and the ETO?'

The engineer, a Nigerian, said, 'Security is in security.'

'Anything wrong?' Erin asked.

'Nah. He is just collecting his guns.'

When the yacht went out with guests on board, they travelled with weapons; Erin had become used to this. 'What about the ETO?'

The engineer shrugged.

A thick-set man emerged after another fifteen minutes holding two bags, one of which, Erin guessed, contained whatever had delayed them. There would have been special paperwork to accompany them too. 'Tommy,' he said, holding out a muscled arm to show her his ID. He seemed young, she thought, and perhaps a little nervous. Normally they were men in their forties, ex-forces. There was still no sign of the electrical officer. The trickle of passengers into the arrivals lounge slowed and finally stopped. Erin checked at the airline desk and they confirmed that all passengers had got off the plane so she called up Marius.

'Yes,' he said. 'I've just had a text message. The ETO missed the flight from Krakow. He'll be on the next plane.'

The next plane didn't arrive until the early afternoon. He was cutting it fine but crewing the boat at such short notice was not easy. Erin led the rest of them out of the air conditioning onto the hot strip of tarmac that lay between the airport building and the ocean, to the waiting minibus. The chief steward, whose name was Marissa, went to get in the front next to Erin, but the security officer pushed in and said, 'My seat.'

'Excuse me?' Marissa's accent was pure Miami.

'I always sit in the front.' Tommy's was pure South London. 'That's how it works.'

'Jesus. It's, like, a ten-minute drive,' complained Marissa. 'What are you expecting? An ambush?'

The security officer ignored her and stepped into the seat.

'Well, you're going to be a lot of fun on this trip,' said Marissa from behind him.

'Yes,' he said. 'I am.'

It wasn't until they were out of the van and the others were waiting for golf carts to take their bags to the yacht that the security man said, 'You're the first mate, right?'

Erin nodded. He looked her up and down, raised his eyebrows. She ignored him because she was used to that.

'Wow,' hooted Marissa, approaching them. 'Is that her?' She was pointing through the forest of aluminium masts to where *Zinaida* lay on her pontoon. 'She's a total monster.'

'Yes she is,' said Erin.

'I'm loving this trip already. That's one big frickin' boat. Just three guests too, right?'

'That's all.'

'Whoop-de-doo. Best trip ever.'

'One thing,' said Tommy. 'I want to check people's bags before they go on the ship.'

27

Erin stopped in her tracks. 'Check crew bags? Did Mrs Piru-mova request that?'

He shook his head. 'I requested it.'

'Oh my God,' said Marissa.

Erin looked at him. 'Can't we do it on board? It's thirty-five degrees out here.'

'Not much point in checking if they're taking anything they shouldn't aboard once they're on,' he said.

In all her time on superyachts, she had never done this before.

'And I'll need all your phones please. I have instructions that the family's privacy on this voyage is of the utmost importance.'

Marissa groaned. 'No way.'

Out on the wooden quayside, Erin asked the new crew to line their bags up and watched as Tommy the guard worked his way through each one. A few messaged their lovers or families before surrendering their devices. The Nigerian seemed to have brought mostly DVDs to watch on his breaks; he had hidden a Garmin satellite phone at the bottom of his bag. Tommy picked it out and put it into a black tote bag without comment. Seeing that, the second mate sighed, pulled his phone out of his backpack, and handed it over too. The chef had a bag of weed, which the security officer picked out and put into his own pocket. He pulled out a knife and pocketed that too. Marissa had a bottle of vodka stashed in hers, wrapped in her pyjamas. 'Don't you frickin' dare,' she said.

The security officer smiled, put the bottle back.

'Hey,' Marissa said when he'd zipped her bag back up. 'Who gets to check your bags, mister?'

Tommy ignored her and turned to board *Zinaida*. Erin

followed him over the gangplank. In any crew there was always one pain in the arse.

The boat had been silent for so long. Now it was suddenly busy. Erin preferred it when she had it all to herself.

SIX

Kai liked it when Zina spoke Russian. It sounded like a tape being played backwards.

She sat on the side of his bed, her naked back to him, a cigarette in one hand and her iPhone in the other, arguing angrily with her mother. She had a mole on her left shoulder blade that he had never noticed before. It was the shape of Africa.

When he had met her, a week ago at her private view, he had been drunk; she had looked very beautiful. Sober, she was still beautiful. It would not last. He should grow up. Get a proper job.

He stood, put his underpants on and went to the kitchenette. It was not a big flat. He could still hear Zina's voice from there.

The sink was full of the dishes they had eaten last night's takeaway on. He had let the cleaner go a month ago. Kai opened the sliding balcony door to look out at the uneven London skyline. It was early afternoon. The June sun was thin and weak.

A manager told him to buy this flat when the money was

coming in. It had been his only good investment, but it was dull and soulless. He liked living high above the city but he had always hated lifts because any small space made him uneasy. It had been a convenient place to retreat to after tours, when there had still been tours, and now that world had gone, it felt like a trap. It didn't help that he had furnished it in a single afternoon; the chairs were grey, so were the blinds and the carpet.

Maybe he could afford to redecorate it, if he had a job.

When he returned to the bedroom with two mugs of coffee, she was still talking.

Zina looked up. '*On prines mne chashku kofe*,' she told her mother. She took a last suck from her cigarette, dropped it into a wine bottle by the side of the bed, where it hissed as it hit the dregs, and then reached out and took the coffee from him.

'Say hello to my mother,' said Zina, holding out the phone. 'She's driving me fucking insane, but I told her you've brought me a coffee and now she thinks you're a nice boy.'

'Hello, Zina's mother.'

Kai got back into bed and picked up a book of short stories that he had started months ago, but read so infrequently he always forgot his place.

Zina took the phone back. 'Mum, this is total bullshit. I'm perfectly fine here. I don't want to go anywhere,' she said, then lapsed back into Russian.

He and Zina had been going out for a week. For her art show, Zina had made a gigantic sculpture out of old electric cookers that she had painted gold. They were piled on top of each other. Every few minutes a nozzle above them released a fine spray of

31

water which turned to steam when it hit the glowing rings and hotplates. Lit by projectors, the steam became the back drop for films she had made about women cooking. He had liked it a lot, he said, and asked if it was about global warming. She had told him that of course it was because it was impossible to make art that was not about global warming.

'My bloody father,' she muttered, when the phone call ended. 'He has gone insane. He says London is not safe.'

'Why ever not?'

Zina pulled the duvet around her and sat looking at herself in the wardrobe mirror. 'He just wants to control me always. I already told him yesterday I don't want to go. He's insisting. I want to stay here in London.'

'With me, obviously.'

'Obviously. Or just in London. My family is so fucked up.'

He turned the page. 'Tell him you're perfectly fine here. After all, he can't make you go, can he?'

But she didn't answer that. Instead, she threw off the bedding and marched naked to the bathroom, still muttering. The phone she had left on the bed buzzed and the home screen lit up, and he couldn't help noticing that it was a reference for a British Airways plane ticket.

Kai knew nothing of her family. She never talked about them and that was fine by him because if he was honest about it, he preferred the kinds of girlfriends who didn't talk about their parents and their brothers and sisters. If they did, it usually meant that an invitation to lunch at their house was coming soon.

When Zina returned, she pulled on a T-shirt, picked up the

32

phone, looked at it and, gathering the rest of her clothes from the floor, scowled. 'I have to go. I don't have any choice. It's so messed up.'

'That's a pity.'

'You could try sounding like you meant it, even,' she said.

'I do,' he protested.

'Well, come with me then. My mother will love you. She will say you are very handsome.'

He thought of the appointment he had made. Thursday with Trevor. 'I'm busy.'

'Bullshit. You sit around in here all day doing nothing, playing computer games, feeling sad. You don't even bother to pick up a guitar. You're supposed to be a musician.'

'I have a business meeting.'

She wrapped a towel around her wet hair. 'Postpone it. Seriously. You should come.'

'Really. I can't.'

'Please. I don't want to go,' she said. 'I would rather be here. But we could make it fun. Please come. I'll be so fucking bored on my own. I'll tell her I'll go but only on condition I can bring you.'

He looked out of the window. A thin summer drizzle was falling.

'To Russia?'

She laughed. 'Jesus, no. Not Russia. To the Caribbean. They want me to go on their stupid yacht and sit in the middle of nowhere on the yacht, just me and my father and mother and nobody else.'

He looked at her, blinked. 'The yacht? Definite article.'

33

She was texting. 'My father has a yacht.' She smiled.' Did I not say?'

'You did not say.'

'I don't like to talk about him.'

'Just how rich is he?'

She ignored the question. 'It doesn't mean anything, me asking you. I just want you as my on-board entertainment, that's all.' She leaned forward, kissed him. 'It will do you good,' she said. 'You've been cooped up here licking your wounds because nobody wants you any more and you are doing nothing.'

'I have not been licking my wounds,' he said. 'And I'm not sure I like the idea of being cooped up in a little boat with your mother and father . . .'

She laughed. 'It's not a little boat. It's huge. Like a giant white penis.'

'How giant a penis?'

'A huge penis,' she said. 'A gigantic fat white penis.'

He thought about it. 'Listen, Zina. I have a job interview. It's something my brother set up. What if I come after that? Say, at the weekend.'

'By then we will be at sea, my mother says. My dad is in some kind of weird hurry. If you don't come now there's no point.'

'Your father will hate me.'

'I will tell him you are a very famous musician. He will think that means you are not after my money. Come on.' She thumped him hard.

'You mean, now? What? Today?'

'Yes, now. The plane is tonight.'

'But I don't have tickets.'

She rolled her eyes.

Kai thought about the idea of being on a yacht with Zina. He thought of the index card sitting in the pocket of his trousers. The meeting on Thursday; the job. The desk and the thought of regular hours.

SEVEN

Zina had taken a valium and slept all the way through the night flight to Florida. From there it was a three-hour journey from Miami to the Virgin Islands. A white Chevy Tahoe picked them up at the airport, shiny chrome and tinted windows. They waited inside in an air-conditioned chill while the driver went back to fetch their bags.

Kai was used to being supplied with itineraries by tour managers, used to foreign travel as something organised for him, but this was something else. Jet-lagged and a little hazy from the plane, he settled back into the soft leather seats. There was a selection of newspapers and magazines, neatly folded, in a rack at the front of the passenger compartment; the *New York Times*, the *FT*, *Monocle*. Zina opened a cooler in the armrest between them and picked out still water.

'So what? My father owns some companies. Do you care?'

He had looked up her father on his phone on the plane and read that he was more than just rich. Stepan Pirumov. No wonder his brother had recognised the name. 'It says he's worth four point eight bloody billion dollars.'

'Maybe. I don't know.'

'He's on the Putin list,' he said. He looked it up on cnn.com. Zina's father was right there on the list of ninety-six oligarchs the White House had compiled in response to Russian meddling in the 2016 US election; they were the men who were supposedly close to Russian leader Vladimir Putin.

'That list is total bullshit. It was made up by Donald Trump when he was President, for Christ's sakes. It's fake. You really actually trust something like that?'

'I'm just surprised to find that out, that's all I was saying.'

'I am a student. I'm an artist. I'm at Camberwell College of Arts. We're going to have fun for a few days. What is your problem?'

'It's like you were pretending to be someone else.'

'Shut the fuck up. I wasn't pretending to be anybody. I just don't want to talk about my super-messed-up family all the time. Seriously. If this was your family you would never want to talk about it either. And besides, what's wrong with pretending to be someone else? You pretend to be a rock star.'

'Ouch,' he said.

'If you don't want to come to be with me and my family, just say it. I'm serious. I would understand. Believe me. I will get you a ticket back home. Go back to your flat and play computer games. We're about to get on a boat and once you're on it, the only way off will be to swim.'

'I'm not saying that,' he said.

She pulled open the door. Warm tropical air flooded in. 'Go. Get lost. I don't care.'

37

The driver, a limber young Hispanic man with thickly gelled hair, peered into the car. 'Is everything OK, sir?' He had the bags behind him on an aluminium trolley. He looked from Zina to him and back again.

'Yes, it's fine,' said Kai. 'Everything's absolutely fine.'

'I'm really super tired,' complained Zina.

The marina was a short distance from the airport, down a clean, tidy-looking dual carriageway.

Zina said, 'This is my father's idea, OK? He's a control freak. He always wants us to be like a family.'

'*Like* a family.'

'Exactly.'

The marina looked more like a country club than a harbour. Palm trees had been planted close to the waterline. Red-roofed villas crowded along the shore. 'There are no other guests?'

'No.'

'I just assumed there would be other people. Did you even tell them I was coming?'

'There are other people. It's just that they work for my dad.' The driver pulled up at the dockside. The door opened and sticky air crowded in. 'My mother and father married before my father got lucky. I think he stays with my mother because he's a traditionalist. He's religious, Russian Orthodox bullshit. And maybe because he doesn't want to give my mother the money she'd ask for if she divorced him – though he could afford it.'

'Does she want to?'

'Jesus, no. She'd be too scared to be without him. Actually she loves him, I think,' she said, sounding puzzled by the fact.

'Here is your transport,' said the driver, pointing to a small, white golf cart rolling across the concrete dock towards the car.

'Is my father here yet?'

The limo driver answered, 'I'm picking him up at ten tonight. Your mother is already on board. She's waiting.'

The first cart pulled up next to the car; the driver loaded their bags into it. A second cart arrived a few seconds later. A smiling young man in a white T-shirt beckoned them to get in.

'I'm not going in that stupid thing,' said Zina. 'We'll walk.'

The man shrugged, got back in, and the vehicle departed with a gentle electric whine.

The blue water was full of white boats. To the left, huge cruise ships were tied up along a dock. Straight ahead, sailing yachts crammed along the pontoons, and beyond them lay the superyachts.

Each superyacht was different; each was a bit the same – the tinted windows, the white curves and the thick cluster of communication masts and domes above the bridge.

'So? Which one's yours?' Kai asked, gazing at their profiles against the green islands beyond.

'It's not mine,' muttered Zina, setting off in the direction their luggage had gone.

He walked after her down the pontoon. The sea around them was a rich aquamarine. Crews, working on the moored boats, paused to watch them as they walked past in the morning heat.

'That one?' He pointed to an old-fashioned ship with cabins made of varnished wood with polished brass portholes.

'I wish,' she said, and turned right down a second pontoon, the one that the bigger boats were moored on.

'This one?' He pointed to a huge boat with blue-tinted glass called *Le Grand Bleu*.

'Horrid,' she said.

Soon there were only a couple left ahead of them. Kai realised which one it was when he got close enough to read the letters on its stern.

'Shit. It's even named after you,' he said.

'Yes,' Zina said darkly. 'It is.'

In big black letters on the back, her name. Of all the boats moored on these pontoons, the one named after her was the biggest and shiniest by far.

EIGHT

Kai said, 'I'm the stowaway.'

Zina's mother didn't smile. She either ignored the attempt at a joke, or didn't understand it. Wearing a one-piece bathing suit, dark glasses and a big black hat, she kissed her daughter on both cheeks and said something in Russian, then glowered at Kai for a while. Zina answered, turned, still holding her mother's hand, and said a few more words that were clearly about him. The woman looked at Kai. 'My daughter says you are a very famous English rock star.'

'Your daughter is exaggerating in order to try and impress you.'

'I know,' Yuliya Pirumova said. 'We were not expecting you.'

'He's my boyfriend, Mum. For God's sake, I invited him.'

Inside, the yacht was as dazzlingly white as it was outside. The main cabin they were standing in had white settees arranged on three sides, covered in huge white cushions. Glass doors at the rear opened up onto a huge covered outdoor space filled with more white chairs and tables that surrounded a small pool. At the bow end of the room was a large bar, upholstered in white leather.

Zina took Kai's hand to pull him away. 'Where you going?' her mother demanded.

'I'm tired, Mum. We drank too much on the plane. Now I need to sleep.'

'You've only just arrived. Stay a while, my darling.'

'What is all this about? Why does he insist on us being here?'

Her mother sighed. 'I expect he will tell us tonight. He is worried about something. It will blow over.'

'He's always worried,' said Zina.

Yuliya returned to speaking Russian, asking her daughter a question that clearly irritated Zina.

'Of course I didn't get him a present. What's the point in getting Papa a present? He has everything already.'

Her mother finally removed her huge black sunglasses. She had sad eyes, Kai thought; they seemed to curve downwards at the edges. 'You have not seen him in months. I have bought you something to give to him,' Yuliya said. 'I think he will like it very much. Come. Let me show you.'

'Later. I'm going to show Kai his cabin. Then I'm going to sleep.'

Her mother was about to argue, but then she held up her hands and nodded. 'You know which is his cabin?'

'Yes, Mama. The same as always.' Zina kissed her mother on the cheek, then tugged Kai to a vast pale-wooded spiral staircase behind the white bar. 'I'm going to show him around the boat first.' One flight led down, the other up; Zina went up. He followed.

42

When they arrived on the next floor, she said, 'What do you think?' It was another living space; smaller, but plusher and darker, lit by low lights. This time the settee was upholstered in gold; a gold chandelier hung from the ceiling above a gold coffee table. This was a more private space. 'Hideous,' she answered her own question. 'Isn't it?'

At the bow end of the lounge, spotlights shone on a family portrait in oils.

Kai stood in front of it, looked from the portrait towards Zina and back again.

'Don't,' she said.

'You actually look like a Mormon,' he said. Zina was barely recognisable in the frame. The artist had painted an obedient daughter with long pale hair and a plain, smiling face, and a pristine white dress that reached to her ankles. 'A weirdly sexy Mormon.'

'That's perverted. I was, like . . . fifteen.'

'You look about thirty in it.'

'I cried the first time I saw it. I wanted to burn it, but it was a present for my mother.'

It was framed in plain gold. In the painting, Zina's mother Yuliya knelt on an imagined beach with a pale moon behind her, wearing a low-cut floral dress. Sitting in a wooden chair above them was a serious-looking man with dark eyebrows, trying to smile. 'My father commissioned it for their twentieth wedding anniversary. He hates all art, as you can quite plainly see.'

'Which is why you are an artist.'

She smiled. 'You're smarter than you look.'

At the far end of the room a small perfume bottle sat in the middle of a low table as if it too was a work of art. It had a purple cut-glass stopper. Zina picked it up, took off the lid and sprayed some on her wrists, then sniffed it and wrinkled her nose. 'It's my mother's. She says it is her favourite. It costs about five thousand dollars a bottle or something stupid.' She raised up her arm for him to smell, then aimed the bottle at his groin and sprayed again. 'That's about two hundred pounds' worth,' she said.

The scent was very floral, of roses and jasmine.

'Zina, *myshka*. Have you shown your friend his room?' Yuliya called up from below.

'What do you mean, his room? Not our room?' whispered Kai.

'Come,' she said. She led Kai towards the bow into an enormous dining room, surrounded by a vast C-shape of tinted glass that looked forwards, over the front of the boat. A long white table sat in the centre of the room. Gold-handled cutlery lay on either side of white plates. It was laid and ready, as if always ready for a party. Then she pulled him through another wooden door onto another landing, off which lay several cabins and an enormous spa room, tiled in tiny dark green and gold mosaics, with a massage table and a sauna room. The taps were all gold. 'My mother designed this.'

'Jesus,' he said.

'Actually, my favourite bit of the boat. I chose the green.'

She pointed to two doors. 'This is my cabin,' she said. 'That one is my parents'.'

'Your cabin? We sleep in separate cabins?' he said.

'Of course.' She kissed his cheek. 'This is my mother and father's boat.'

'So where is mine?'

44

'You are two decks down, lover boy. Lower deck, number one. The guest floor.'

'You're kidding me?'

'My parents like to pretend I'm a virgin.'

'Well, I don't,' he said.

'Papa's ship. Papa's rules.'

'Terrific.'

She had already taken him by the hand again and was leading him up another, narrower staircase. At the top was a door; when she opened it, they were back in the bright daylight again, on the bridge. The decor here was more obviously nautical; a shinily varnished wooden floor; wooden chart tables and chests. A long sofa, upholstered in a navy and white stripe, filled the back of the room, presumably so the family could sit and watch the crew at work.

There were two expensive-looking adjustable white leather chairs, each facing a small ship's wheel, also trimmed with white leather. Above the chairs sat a bank of six computer screens, all blank. Ahead, a window looked over the massive white prow of the boat.

Kai sat in one of the white chairs. It sank slightly under his weight. 'Stardate 2021. We have been sucked into a bizarre parallel universe.'

'You know, everyone does that, the first time.'

'Will your dad let me drive it?'

'Do you know how much this is worth?'

'Millions.'

'Times ten. More maybe. I don't know. I don't care about all that. Come on. I have to go to sleep. I'll show you your room.'

She led him back down the first stairs and then back down the spiral staircase, past the Pirumovs' floor, and back to the main cabin. Her mother was still standing in the middle of the lounge room, watching her daughter. 'You like the *Zinaida*?'

'It's remarkable,' he said, because there seemed to be no other answer to give.

'There's more. I'll show you it some other time but I'm so fucking tired,' said Zina, continuing down to the floor below; these were the lower decks. There was a sign on the landing: *L1*. This landing was less ornate. There were five doors off it. Four were wooden; the fourth was metal. Zina opened the metal door and beckoned him to look inside as the lights blinked on.

It looked, at first, like a prison cell. Brightly lit, there was no window to the outside world, just four metal bunks inside and what looked like a row of cabinets behind them.

'You're actually kidding me?'

She pushed him inside and closed the door behind him.

'Wait,' he said. There was an ominous clunk of metal and when he tried the handle, it was stiff. The door had been locked from the outside. She had shut him in. 'Very funny, Zina.'

He banged on the door.

From the other side of the metal came muffled laughter.

NINE

'Do you love me?' Zina's voice came from the far side of the door. 'Or are you just going out with me because I'm rich?'

He called through the door, 'Let me out.' He thumped angrily with the side of his fists. No answer. He strained to listen, to see if she was still there.

Confined spaces made him anxious. He turned, looked for another door at the far side of the room, but there was only a wall of steel lockers. One of them was marked *Toilet*. It was like being trapped in the galley of an aeroplane.

Her voice came again. 'Answer my question.'

He was tired; he was too old for this. 'OK. Just for the money.'

There was a pause before he heard the lock moving. She stood on the other side of the door, unsmiling.

'Was that the right answer?'

'Obviously,' she said, sullenly.

'Very funny,' he said, when he was out.

'That's the brig. Where the captain locks up prisoners who misbehave.'

'You have prisoners?'

'It's also what they call the citadel. Everyone has to have them these days. We can stay for forty-eight hours in there. It has food, water, its own electrical supply, its own air. Once you lock the door with the right security code, no one can get in – or out.'

'A panic room? You actually have a panic room?'

'All the best people do. Come,' she said.

His room was on the same floor as the brig, on the starboard side of the yacht. 'This is your real room. It's much more boring.' They went in together and he looked around. It looked like some of the hotel bedrooms he used to sleep in when he was on tour. The walls were panelled in pale wood. The bed was large and covered in white linen and had a white leather bedhead; a huge TV screen hung on the wall opposite it. There was a bar. Three windows looked out towards a boat moored next to them. On a large luggage stand, looking battered and out of place, sat Kai's small suitcase.

She leaned forward and kissed him. 'I'm going upstairs to sleep.'

'Sleep here,' he said. 'With me.'

'No.' She brushed his lips with her tongue. 'You don't love me.'

'When you spoke to your mother, you said, *The same cabin as always*. You do this a lot then?'

'Why do you care?' she said. 'You're only here for my money.'

'I didn't know you had money until yesterday.'

'It seems to be quite the aphrodisiac though, doesn't it?'

She pulled away and closed the door, leaving him alone with the low hum of air conditioning.

He sat on the bed for a while trying to make sense of this.

As far as he was concerned, the panic room had been aptly named. He had not wanted to show it in front of Zina, but the idea of being locked up held an unnatural horror for him. It was a phobia he found hard to understand. Nothing bad had ever happened to cause it; he assumed it was his free-spiritedness, a horror of any confinement. His brother Marley had no such fear, though he was terrified of flying bugs and thunder; again there was no particular cause for either.

He took a breath, unzipped his suitcase, then opened drawers and cupboards. He could have had five suitcases and there would have been enough room for all his clothes.

A note on the desk gave a password for the wi-fi. Though he didn't want to disappoint his brother, he knew he should contact Marley and tell him he was going to miss the meeting. He tried to connect his phone, but it rejected the login. He tried a second time and the same thing happened.

There was cold mineral water in the fridge. He opened a bottle. The bathroom was white marble; the shower was behind a sheet of glass. He stripped, glad to be out of the clothes he had been wearing since London. With a towel over his shoulder, he emerged from the cabin in swimming shorts and a T-shirt.

Up on the main deck, Yuliya had vanished. The main cabin was empty too. He walked out of the back of it through glass doors to the pool deck. There was a discarded towel and a foreign paperback left on one of the loungers.

'Hello?' he called. No one answered.

The afternoon sun was sweltering and the air was thick. He looked around. Such luxury demanded you take notice. He was from the English middle class who found such obviously boastful wealth ridiculous; the English middle class, however, were just as ridiculous themselves, he believed. While he was here, he might as well enjoy it.

Towards the stern of the boat there was another covered seating area. Kai walked towards it, his T-shirt already damp with sweat.

He leaned over the rail at the back. Below him he saw that a door had opened up in the side of the boat. It was extraordinary. Half the door lifted up; the other dropped down to water level to form a kind of small dock. It was like something from a Bond movie. Below him a young woman was standing in a large RIB boat; it was moored against this small dock, and she was attaching the prow and stern to a pair of davits that extended from somewhere inside the yacht.

She was young, medium height, heavy-set, olive-skinned, neck red from the sun, and she wore a black T-shirt and black shorts. The boat she was working on looked as expensive as everything else, with pale wooden boards underfoot, white leather seats, and shiny chrome railings around the outside. As he watched her tying off the lines, she stopped; looked suddenly up at him.

'Hello.' He gave a friendly wave.

Unsmiling, she just lowered her head and went back to her task. Maybe she didn't speak English, he thought. He watched her for a while longer. There was something very satisfying about the way she worked; the way she was coiling rope in the boat and

50

tying it off was purposeful and practised. Then she stepped off the side into the yacht and, with a quiet whirr, winches pulled the boat into the hull, and then the two doors closed, like the jaws of some animal, and the opening disappeared.

This yacht has just swallowed another boat, he thought. Luxury within luxury.

Zina was asleep; he guessed her mother had retired to her cabin too. He stood a while looking down at the water, clear as gin, where silver fish with yellow fins darted about.

At the rear of the boat below him was a swimming deck. The woman who had just put the boat away appeared there now, lowered the passerelle and descended onto the pontoon carrying two red metal jerrycans, walking back towards the shore.

Sweat prickled his back. He descended to the swimming deck, which extended out over the stern, just above the surface of the water, and dived in.

The salt water was delicious and warm. He swam along the side of the spotless boat for what seemed like the length of at least two swimming pools, and then headed straight out into the open water until his arms were tired. There he lay on his back squinting up at the sun as the small waves bobbed around him.

The town lay in a natural harbour, protected from the open sea by a densely wooded green island with a few private houses fringing the shoreline. In the other direction, behind the marina, the rest of the town rose haphazardly up the curve of hillsides around it.

Luxury was something you had to get used to. He felt he could try. He was not a greedy man, but Covid had come from nowhere and taken his livelihood away. It seemed only fair that the universe should right itself in some way. And so it had. He had fallen in with this rich family. He couldn't help thinking that maybe something would come of this. In his charmed life, it always had. Just as his body felt a little lighter in salt water, so did his spirits.

Far away, close to the islands he could make out at the bay's mouth, a small fishing boat chugged out to sea, finding a passage to the south of the island.

Only when he turned back towards the marina did he realise how far the current had taken him away from the boat.

TEN

It was almost as if Erin felt it, that she was being watched as she prepared to clip the launch onto the davits. It may just have been his shadow that gave him away, but when she looked up, there he was, smiling down. 'Hello.' He waved.

She pretended she had not seen him.

The smiling was by far the hardest part. When she and Marius were on their own, she could be herself. Now the family were on board, she had to smile. You were expected to do it all the time, especially if you were a young woman. Mrs Pirumova told her, 'You would be prettier if you smiled more. Not that you will ever be pretty. Not conventionally pretty . . .'

She had studied navigation, maritime information systems, pilotage, seamanship, she had worked hard to get her Yachtmaster's Certificate and her Chief Mate Certificate, she had learned everything she needed to sail a boat in the most hazardous conditions, but nobody had ever taught her about smiling.

She recognised the man who was leaning over the deck above

her, still watching as she worked, as one of those well-connected people who cruised through life easily, leaving little mark on it. In the five years she had been on superyachts, she had come to know them well. There were some in every port they visited, hanging around wherever there was money. Few of them had proper jobs; they just partied, absorbing the wealth around them as if it was their due. They had never had to do real work.

The grey rubber of the RIB was hot on her hands. She reached into the compartment in the back of the boat and took out the spare petrol can, and then stepped into the dark void of the garage deck with it and pressed the button that closed the doors. She had emptied the can into the tank earlier today to burn it off. In hot climates, petrol went off fast. If you didn't use it, it could be dead after two or three months. Running a safe ship was about eliminating as much risk as you could.

It was hot, but she didn't mind. She needed to refill a pair of the jerrycans that were stored on the garage deck, so she loaded them onto a trolley on the pontoon and tugged it away from the yacht towards the fuel station.

Behind her, she heard a splash.

The new guest had jumped off the swimming deck and was heading straight out into the water beyond the pontoon.

She watched as the man filled the first can. 'I saw you got new crew on the boat.' He was a young man, long-limbed and athletic, who had grown up on the island, and never travelled much beyond it.

'Oh yes. New crew. New passengers.'

'New journeys,' he said. 'Man just jumped off your boat, I see.'

54

'Yep,' she said.

They turned and watched him doing the front crawl. 'Be halfway to St John before he knows it.'

'Let's hope.'

The man giggled.

'Put it on *Zinaida*'s account,' she said.

'Food delivery arrived last night OK?'

'Yep. All good. We're off early tomorrow morning. Heading for St Croix. Be there for tomorrow night.'

'Get in before the weather comes.'

'You think there's going to be storms?'

The man looked around at the clear blue sky. 'Maybe.'

It was never wise to predict weather in the Caribbean. Systems could come out of nowhere. It was safer just to be prepared for anything it might throw at you.

He finished the first can and moved on to the second. 'Man's gone quite a way already.'

'Hasn't he?'

They watched him as the second can filled. She snapped the cap back on and hauled it into the metal trolley again.

'Wish you a safe trip, Erin.'

The guest seemed to have been swimming out towards Hassel Island at the far end of the bay, but the current that ran east was pulling him towards Rupert Rock and out to sea. He had not thought to ask whether it was safe to swim here. He had just jumped in.

Zinaida was quiet above deck. Mrs Pirumova and her daughter were both taking a nap. Below deck the new crew were getting used to their surroundings. In the galley, the chef had ordered ingredients for the next few days. He was reading the items off the list.

'Butter. Salted. Ten.'

'Yeah.'

He was Mexican but sounded American. Marius said he had trained at La Dame de Pic in London. It would be nice, at least, to eat proper food again.

'Butter. Unsalted. Ten.'

'Yeah,' Marissa with the perfect straight hair and immaculate dark eyebrows said. She was removing items from the cold box and putting them into the fridges.

'Caspian Beluga caviar. Four times fifty grams.'

'Can't see it . . . hold on. It's here. Yeah. I adore Beluga caviar.'

The first full day with the new crew was always like this. People worked with a nervy excitement, getting to know their stations, getting to know each other. Erin looked out of the porthole as she listened to them work. She couldn't see the swimmer any more, not from down here at least.

The chef and the chief steward were trying to find the chocolate tart shells when the second mate had turned up. 'Ma'am? Was wondering if you can spare some time today to talk me through the bridge?'

She pushed past him, up the stairs and onto the port deck. The guest can't have swum far. She had only had her eyes off him for a couple of minutes. She scanned the water to the south.

'Ma'am?' He was next to her now again, eager to get on with things on this shiny new boat.

'You're not actually going to call me Ma'am for the whole trip, are you?'

'Not if I don't have to.'

'Can you see a swimmer out there?' she asked.

'No.'

'Shit,' she said.

Between the bay and the island the sea was light blue, lit by the white sand beneath it, but to the east, where the water became deeper, its colour darkened and the waves became bigger.

ELEVEN

Kai swam again, harder this time, until his arms began to cramp. Away from the land, the sea became choppier. Salt water splashed into his face and into his throat. When, after several minutes, he paused for breath and looked again, he was still no closer to the marina. If anything, the current had taken him further out. He looked around, hoping to spot one of the small fishing boats he had seen earlier, but there was nothing. He was being pulled out into open water and there was nothing he could do about it. Were there jellyfish below? Or sharks? He had no idea how deep the water here would be. The only person on board who would notice that he had gone was Zina, and she was asleep in her cabin.

He was not going to die, he told himself.

For a few more minutes he kicked hard, put his head down and pulled himself through the water but he could not keep it up for long. He stopped again, gasping for air. There was no point swimming against the tide, he thought. It was a waste of energy. He should just lie in the water and see where it took him.

In this warm water, he did not feel like a drowning man, even if he was. Humans were the only species who could understand what death was, but who always refused to believe that they themselves were the ones about to die. He was no different.

He was not going to die, he told himself again. He wondered how long he could float. Hours probably. But he had looked at the map on the in-flight magazine. This island was a speck of dust.

He should have swum harder against the current before it was too late.

As a boy growing up in North London, he had drifted. His brother had been the one who had always studied hard to pass exams, or struggled to learn guitar, spending hours taking lessons. Kai had picked up guitars and keyboards and found it easy to create tunes on them. He hadn't understood what his brother had found so hard. While his brother studied, he had hung out with friends, truanted from school to lurk in record shops, but still seemed to do as well.

Most of the time Marley hadn't minded. Though he worked hard for everything he had, he was proud of his younger brother's achievements. Kai had accepted this, too, as his due.

In his teens Kai drifted into music. He had made a few dubstep tracks in his bedroom and put them onto Myspace back in a time when the site was still a novelty. At seventeen and underage, he was blagging his way into Shoreditch nightclubs like FWD and Shape and the older clubbers indulged him.

He played them his music. They found it amusing to let him onto the turntables and he accepted his position as their mascot. Soon he was more than that. He started adding his own creations to the ones he played, and in no time it seemed perfectly natural to have managers approaching him, asking him to make tracks for their artists.

Life unfolded easily. Ambition puzzled him. The people who he met in the clubs or in the record company meetings seemed to want success so badly it was painful.

There was the record producer in his thirties – ancient – who wore a string of wooden beads around his neck. 'You know the secret of being cool? The more you want it, the less you are it.' To a teenage Kai, just saying something like that was proof of trying too hard.

He was young; he lived in a great city, and it felt he knew people in every club or bar.

People used his tracks. They sold records. At eighteen, he found himself with a manager and a publisher. Life unfolded with ease. The pop stars who sang over his tracks, who had to tour and make videos, were the ones who had to work the hardest. Royalties arrived in his bank account and he spent money on clothes and trips to Goa.

Inevitably, finding girlfriends had always been much easier for him than it was for his more studious brother. Girls were probably his only real source of stress. He found it hard to reject advances, even when there were others already in his life. It wasn't that he didn't understand the rules; he just found it hard to apply them. If people wanted to love you, that was a blessing. He was willing to accept it. He had never thought of himself as lucky.

But now he realised that he should have tried to swim harder against the current, though in life he had never had to, and it was too late now.

Lying on the water, he extended his arms and legs wide, and floated. The thing he felt saddest about was that he wished he had told his brother that he loved him. Because he did. Marley had always been a much better man than him. A much kinder, more decent, more hardworking man who had always looked out for him.

At first he thought he heard a plane, but there was nothing in the bright sky above him.

He set himself upright in the water and looked around and saw, bouncing through the waves, a grey RIB. It was heading off to his right.

He raised an arm and waved, but the boat did not see him.

He shouted, 'Hey!' realising that no one in the boat would be able to hear him above the engine noise, but at that moment the engine slowed and the boat turned towards him.

When it was closer, he recognised the young woman he had seen on *Zinaida* tying up the launch. When she was alongside, she killed the engine and he grabbed the side of the boat and tried to raise a leg onto the hot rubber.

'Wait,' she ordered. 'Just give me your hand.'

He did as she said and she hauled him halfway up, pulling on his arm, then, leaning over, she grabbed the waist of his swimming shorts and tugged him firmly into the boat, like a parent yanking a child from a swimming pool.

'Ow,' he said.

'You're welcome.'

He lay on the bottom of the boat panting. 'The current was too strong.'

'Yes. It is.' Her accent was English; northern, he guessed.

Now he was safely in the boat, she turned away, pushed the throttle up and roared back towards the yacht. Limbs still weary from swimming, he hauled himself up into one of the white leather seats. 'I can't thank you enough,' he said, above the noise of the engine. 'I think you saved my life.'

'So do I,' she said. Slowing the throttle, she turned to face him. 'Just a tip, sir. If you're swimming anywhere new like this, spend a minute looking at the shoreline and seeing where the water is taking you before you go too far out. OK?'

'Right.' He nodded. 'Stupid of me. My name is Kai.'

'Pleased to meet you, sir,' she answered. He waited for her to give her own name, but she didn't.

Her eyes were curiously pale. Though she was young, maybe his own age, her skin had the kind of leatheriness of someone who spent long hours in boats.

'I was lucky. You might not have noticed me.'

'I saw you jump in.'

'So you were keeping an eye on me all that time?'

She nodded, turned back to face the direction of travel.

'You knew it was dangerous out there?'

'Yes.'

'And you waited for me to get that far out before you came and rescued me?'

'I could have left it longer,' she said.

Given how long he had been in the water, struggling against the current, it appeared to take them no time at all to reach the boat again. She held the launch alongside while he clambered out onto the sea deck, legs rubbery from fatigue, feeling like an idiot.

'Who is he?' said a voice.

Kai looked up. There was a man, also dressed in black, above him.

'Zina's guest Kai.'

'He isn't on the passenger list.' His black T-shirt was lifted slightly. Beneath the hem, tucked into the waistband of his trousers, nestled against his skin, Kai realised with a shock, was the unmistakable shape of a small gun. Kai had been supposed to see it; a subtle signal for anyone not on the list.

'Last minute thing, apparently, Zina brought him along.'

Still exhausted, Kai grabbed a towel and started drying himself. 'Yes. Last minute thing.'

'Welcome aboard, sir,' said the man unwelcomingly, looking him up and down. 'My name's Tommy. I'm security. Have you known Zina long?'

'Is that any business of yours?' Kai asked.

Kai turned to speak to the young woman again, but she had already turned her back and was back in the boat, loosening the lines.

'Can I get you a beer or something? To thank you?' he asked her.

'She's crew, sir,' said Tommy. 'Crew don't drink.'

'Right. You the same?'

'You'd hope, wouldn't you, in my line of work?' said Tommy, putting his hand on where he had tucked the gun. The security guard squinted at him in the sunlight.

'You're here to guard the boat?' Kai asked.

'And you, sir.'

Kai looked around at the blue water around them. 'What from?'

But the man had already gone. Kai went to his cabin, showered briefly, then lay on his bed, a single sheet above him. He had been stupid; he had almost drowned. Even a couple of years ago, that might have made an item on the news.

TWELVE

Kai was woken by Zina's voice: 'Apparently you almost drowned.'

He was in darkness. He had gone to sleep in daylight, exhausted from his misadventure. It took a while for him to remember where he was. How long had he slept for? He fumbled for a light switch, put his underpants on and opened the door.

Zina was outside. 'Is it true? The crew had to rescue you?' He looked her up and down. His girlfriend was unrecognisable as the boho art student he had met in London. She was wearing a long black dress and what looked like diamond earrings. She had been transformed into someone much richer.

'A little embarrassing,' he said. 'How do you know?'

She laughed. 'The new security guy. He's a weirdo. He started giving me a lecture about how none of us should get off the boat without letting him know. He's going to make this a fun trip. Were you scared?'

'Of course I was.'

She kissed him on the cheek. 'Oh, poor baby. I'm sorry.'

It seemed ridiculous to talk about, standing in this cabin alive and well, but the terrible sense of hollowness he had felt out there in the water sat inside him still. He felt out of his depth here and out of place. He was still tired, he reasoned. Jet-lagged too.

'Get dressed, lover. Dinner on the island. My father is landing at ten. He's meeting us at the restaurant.'

He looked at the earrings Zina wore. 'Am I supposed to dress up too?'

'No. You're an artist.' She sat on the bed and watched him putting his clothes back on.

'I thought you were the artist?'

She shrugged. 'Not as far as my parents are concerned.'

'Am I here to play the part of the inappropriate boyfriend?'

'My father hates all my boyfriends. He thinks they're all inappropriate.'

He pulled up cotton trousers, picked up his phone. 'Do you know what the wi-fi password is? This one here doesn't work.' He wanted to get in touch with Marley, to apologise because tomorrow was Thursday and he had no intention of taking the job his brother had so generously persuaded a friend to create for him.

She sighed. 'The new security guard, Mr McFun, has changed it. He says we have to change it every day. He says he's worried about hacking. He's a fucking asshole.'

'I met him too. His name is Tommy. He carries a gun, you know,' said Kai, pulling a crumpled shirt from his bag.

'Of course he does. I would be disappointed if he didn't.' She stood. 'Don't shave,' she said. She approached him and mussed

66

up his hair even more than it already was. 'That's better.' And she left, closing the door behind her.

Standing in the main cabin with a large orange-coloured cocktail in one hand and a pink mobile phone in the other, Zina's mother Yuliya was dressed in a large, loose, yellow dress. 'He could borrow something of Stepan's I suppose. Tomorrow we can maybe buy him some clothes in St Croix, though the selection there is very poor. We could ask one of the shops here to open up this evening.'

'Leave him alone,' said Zina.

Yuliya wrinkled her nose.

'He's not my papa's boyfriend. He doesn't have to dress up for him.'

Yuliya wrinkled her nose again. 'Your father is in a terrible mood. I was just speaking to him. I don't know why. Please don't put him in a worse one, darling,' she cajoled.

Zina was sprawled on a white sofa, a cigarette in her hand. 'It's not my fault he's in a bad mood.'

Kai had heard somewhere that Russians were more deferential to their parents than the British. Zina appeared determined not to be.

Yuliya took a sip from her glass. 'This week, though. You have flown here specially for him. Be nice.'

Zina said, 'What's he got to be in a bad mood about anyway?'

'He never talks to me about business. Oh, Zina, you should see the present we have bought him before he arrives.'

'So I don't look surprised when he opens it?'

'Try and be nice. Please.' She turned and called out. 'Marissa?'

Almost immediately a young woman with long black hair appeared. She was dressed in a black tube skirt, black blouse and black tights. Black seemed to be the staff uniform. Yuliya spoke to her in Russian and she disappeared again.

'Jesus, Mama. What is it?'

'You'll see. It's very special.' She grinned, pleased with herself, and sat down on one of the white sofas.

'She does this.' Zina turned to Kai. 'She buys presents so I can pretend I bought them for him.'

'It'll make him happy,' her mother said.

The young woman returned with what looked like a black leather attaché case and laid it carefully on the table.

'That looks like something a drug dealer would carry,' Zina said.

Her mother arched an eyebrow. 'You would know that, I suppose.'

Yuliya put her drink on the table next to it, flipped open gold locks and opened it, revealing a backgammon board made of black and red alligator skin. It shone in the cabin lights. The points on the board were alternately in gold and silver. Only when Kai peered closer could he see that each was dotted with tiny stones that sparkled in the light. 'Do you like it, *myshonok*?'

'Mum, it's absolutely hideous. How much did you pay for it?'

'Are they diamonds?' asked Kai.

'Yes,' said Yuliya, pleased. 'And look at the dice.' She rolled one from the shaker, picking it up between her red fingernails and holding it up so they could inspect it. The number dots were picked out with the precious stones. 'Twenty-one diamonds on each. See?'

'Does Dad actually play backgammon?'

'Of course he does. He likes it very much,' said Yuliya, offended.

'I've never once seen him playing it.'

'It's a very special item, made by Jewish craftsmen. Only one of its kind. I bought it in New York and now you can give it to him.' She put the shaker back in the box and snapped the gold clasps shut. 'You don't think he will like it?'

'He'll love it, I'm sure,' Zina reassured her mother. 'I mean. Why wouldn't he?' She stood, walked over to where her mother was sitting, took her face in her hands and kissed her on the cheek.

Yuliya smiled again, relieved. 'Yes. I thought so. He will like it. You must be the one who gives it to him.' Yuliya took a sip from her cocktail.

'No, Mum. You chose it. You bought it.'

'Yes. But you are special to him. He will like it more if you give it to him.'

'He'll know you bought it.'

Yuliya ignored her. She stood, picked up the case and held it out towards Kai.

'Feel it,' she said.

Kai took the case. His arm drooped the moment he held it.

'See? Real quality.' She took it back from him. 'It will be fun. We will buy oysters in St Croix so they will be super fresh. Then we spend the day together. You, me and Stepan.' She looked over at Kai. 'And your boyfriend,' she added, in an attempt to mollify her daughter. 'In the evening we will be off Canouan. We can have fireworks.' She beamed. 'A huge display. It will be

69

wonderful. Everything will be fabulous. Let me see if that girl has got the boat ready.'

When she was gone, Zina said, 'She loves fireworks. She loves it. When she was a small child in Yekaterinburg she used to love the Soviet fireworks. Every celebration must have fireworks.'

'What are we celebrating?'

'I don't know. That we're not living in Yekaterinburg, probably.'

'Will your father really like the backgammon board?'

'He will pretend to because she gave it to him. Marissa, can you do something for me?'

'Sure,' said the chief steward.

'Something special?'

'Like . . . ?'

Zina beckoned her closer by crooking a finger. When she was leaning over her, she asked, 'Can you get me some coke?'

The dark-haired woman cocked her head to one side and smiled. 'You mean – not the drink?'

'Not the drink.'

'Okey-doke. I'll see what I can do,' the steward said, without batting an eyelash.

'But I would like a drink too, while you mention it. Can you do an espresso Martini?'

'Coming right up. And you, sir? We haven't spoken. My name's Marissa.' Her smile was dazzling.

'Just a beer for me,' said Kai.

'How very proletarian,' said Zina. 'You should drink something like a daiquiri, or a mimosa.'

'Why?'

70

'Despite all this –' she waved her hand – 'my father approves of proletarian things. He sees it as a sign of honesty.'

'You really do want me here just to piss him off, don't you?'

'Duh,' she said.

He looked at her, slouched on the sofa, more accustomed to all this than she pretended. 'Cocaine? Honestly? You expect her to do that for you?'

'For my sanity,' she said. 'Besides. It's free. Everything is fucking free. Don't you get it? Don't be so judgey.'

'What if she tells someone?'

'She wouldn't dare.'

'You trust her . . . because you pay her?'

'My father pays her. And you would be insane to mess with him. Nobody would ever dare do that.'

And in a while the chief steward was back with their drinks, and then before they knew it, the boat was ready and Kai remembered he still hadn't called his brother.

THIRTEEN

Yuliya insisted that Kai drive the boat. 'He's a man,' she said simply.

Zina was no help. 'Go on,' she said. 'Big, strong man.'

The woman who sat behind the steering wheel and had saved his life was now beside him. Behind them sat Zina and her mother. In the front section Tommy sat on his own, looking out of place. 'First time driving one of these?' asked the young woman.

He nodded.

'Put this on your wrist,' she said, offering him a red plastic cable, wound tightly into a spring, like an old-fashioned telephone cord. 'It's the kill cord.'

'The what?'

She looked at him. 'If you fall out of the boat it stops the boat killing you. Hence the name. If a boat like this runs over you, you're meat.'

'It stops the engine. You don't have to put it on just because she tells you to,' said Yuliya. 'It's our boat.'

Kai put it round his wrist all the same, then the woman showed him the throttle. 'Just use a little. Don't push it too far forward. This boat has two hundred-horsepower engines back there. It can go up to about fifty knots – fifty, sixty miles an hour – flat out.'

She got up again and began loosening the ropes, fore and aft.

When she was back, sitting beside him, he tipped the lever forward and the boat inched forward. 'So. Where are we going?'

She pointed to the far side of the bay. 'Those lights over there. It's about a half-mile to Frenchtown. Straight line.'

When they were clear of the superyacht he increased the throttle a little and soon they were coursing towards the bay. Behind, Zina was chattering to her mother in Russian.

'My name's Kai,' he said to the woman next to him.

'You said.'

'And yours is?'

There was a significant pause before she said, 'Mine is Erin, sir.'

'Sorry. I was just trying to be . . .'

'Friendly?'

He sighed. 'And obviously you get that quite a lot from guests.'

She didn't answer.

'I thought I was going to die out there for a minute,' he said. 'Weirdest thing. Everything I'd ever done in my life counted for nothing.'

They were almost there at the shoreline now. He could make out coloured lights strung out over it, reflected in the still water, a red light on a marker buoy just ahead of it.

'I just wanted to thank you again, that's all. I didn't think anyone had seen me.'

73

'You're welcome. Pass to the left of that light,' she said, instructing him to slow the boat.

'I was stupid and I got into trouble.'

'Just a touch of reverse now.'

He bumped gently against the wooden piles and thought he'd made a pretty good job of it. He looked to see if she approved, but she had already turned her back on him to step out and take the mooring lines.

The restaurant was above them, tucked into the slope of the hillside.

'Had a nice chat?' Zina said as they walked up the steep wooden steps towards it. They reached a landing, then zigzagged up again. 'I didn't think she was your type.'

'I was trying to thank her for saving my life.'

Unsteady on heels on the stairs, she grasped his arm. 'It would have been pretty bad to lose you on the first day.'

They reached the deck and Kai looked back. Tommy was behind Yuliya, making sure she made it to the top OK, looking to the left and right as he walked, like he was in a movie, like he wanted everyone to know he was guarding them.

The staff had been expecting them, and led them to a table at the edge of the verandah; the table with the best view of the bay. Yuliya and her mother ordered sweet tea margaritas. Kai stuck to beer. Yuliya ordered lobster, and Zina the yellowtail snapper. Kai asked for the vegetable pasta.

'Be a man,' said Yuliya. 'Eat something real.'

'I told you, Mum. He's vegetarian.'

Yuliya scowled. Kai noticed Tommy had occupied a table on his own in a dimmer spot towards the rear of the restaurant.

The drinks came almost at once, along with a plate of olives. 'Kai has tried to strike up a friendship with the first mate,' teased Zina.

'The captain speaks very highly of her,' said Yuliya, 'but I don't like her at all.'

'She saved his life, Mum. He got into trouble this afternoon swimming off the boat. He almost drowned.'

'Oh my God. The poor baby. Bring me bread,' she told a waiter. 'It better be fresh.'

Kai excused himself, took his beer and pulled his phone out of his pocket. His messages told him that he would be charged £1.80 to make a call. He tried anyway, but couldn't get it to connect. 'Is there wi-fi?' he asked a waiter.

He moved to a dark corner of the bar, out of Zina's earshot, and called his brother. The first time it rang out. The second time, he picked up. 'Marley. It's me.'

'It's two in the morning, bro. What's wrong?'

'About tomorrow . . .'

Marley sighed. 'Just tell him how keen you are to start work. There's nothing to worry about.'

He tried to interrupt, but there was a delay on the line and each time he did his brother was talking again.

'Is there something wrong with your phone? I can barely hear you. You sound strange.'

'Listen, Marley. I'm sorry. I've made a really terrible mistake . . .' But the call had already dropped. The line was dead and when he tried calling again the connection failed.

Back at the table, Zina and Yuliya were arguing in Russian. Kai walked to the balustrade and looked out over the bay, its shape defined by the electric lights of houses on the waterfront. Only yesterday he had jumped at the chance of running away from a London summer.

The trouble with distance is it allowed you to see the whole of things. It was not a welcome perspective. The virus which had meant the end of paid live work wasn't the end of his career; it had been ending for years. He had tried to tell himself that smaller fees simply reflected an industry that was struggling, or to blame the loss of income on his management, but it was impossible to ignore the way his name had become smaller on the billing for years, slipping down from top ranking to somewhere near the bottom. The disappearance of his career had left him feeling untethered. He should not have come. He should have stayed in London and taken the job.

The air was muggy and hot. Dinner was being served at his table. He drank a little more beer and realised there were small bugs biting his legs. He slapped at one, then returned to sit opposite Zina.

Yuliya was tapping angrily at her iPhone. Zina looked pale. Neither of them had touched the food in front of them. Kai looked from one to the other. 'Is anything wrong?'

Zina leaned forward. 'Mama had some bad news.'

'Is everything all right?'

'A family friend is dead. A close colleague of Dad's. They're saying he committed suicide the day before yesterday. He was staying at my father's apartment.'

Yuliya muttered unintelligibly.

76

'How awful. I'm sorry,' said Kai.

The two women sat in front of their plates, eating nothing.

'It's not possible,' said Yuliya.

'You don't know anything yet. Papa will tell us everything.'

Yuliya nodded uncertainly. 'Maybe. Maybe not.'

It was after midnight when Yuliya got a message to say that Stepan Pirumov had finally landed on the island, two hours late.

'Finally,' said Yuliya.

Kai looked around. Tommy had vanished, presumably to meet the billionaire at the airport. All the other diners had left the restaurant too, but the management had kept it open for the Pirumovs.

Yuliya stood, summoned a waiter. 'He will have a steak. Rare. And a green salad,' demanded Yuliya. 'Nothing more. Open a bottle of the burgundy. Have it ready in fifteen minutes.'

Though he had stuck to beer, Kai realised he was a little drunk. So was Zina; her pale face had turned pink. Yuliya, who had been downing cocktails followed by red wine, now seemed remarkably sober, ordering the waiters to bring a clean tablecloth and a fresh setting.

She had insisted on the meal being ready in fifteen minutes. It took Stepan Pirumov just ten to arrive from the airport.

FOURTEEN

Kai had been expecting someone bigger. He recognised Stepan Pirumov from the photographs he'd seen online, but now he was dwarfed by the men who towered on either side of him. On his left was Tommy; on his right an even larger man in a leather jacket, fair hair shaved close.

Between the two, Stepan stood, small, neat, and dressed in a pressed white shirt and navy blue trousers. Only his five o'clock shadow suggested it had been a long and trying day for him. He might be another commuter, were it not for the fact that just by arriving, he had become the centre of attention in the restaurant. It was as if a magnifying glass was concentrating all the energy in the room at a single bright point.

He made a direct line for Yuliya, kissed her on both cheeks, then went to Zina, smiled broadly and did the same. Then he sat at the table while the staff scurried around.

'And this is my friend Kai,' said Zina, taking the chair between her father and him.

Kai, sitting at the newly laid table, half stood, extending his hand. Stepan Pirumov looked him in the eye, then spoke with quiet formality: 'Pleased to meet you.'

'I thought you were coming alone, Stepan?' Yuliya looked at the huge man in the black leather jacket who had taken a chair at the bar. 'Why did you bring Dimitri?'

But Stepan's attention was still fixed on Kai. 'So you have come to join us,' he said. Stepan's English was excellent. Unlike his daughter, he spoke with an accent, but he seemed totally at home in the language.

'Yes.'

The billionaire picked up a napkin and flapped it, then spread it on his lap. 'My daughter tells me you are a pop star.'

'Former pop star.'

'Former?' Stepan frowned.

'I am no longer in fashion, exactly.'

'How unfortunate,' said Stepan. He picked up his knife and fork and started to work on his steak.

The chewing was Kai's opportunity to answer. 'I don't think I was ever that much in fashion, to be honest. I just had some luck.'

Stepan lifted a small lump of meat to his mouth and chewed. When he had finally swallowed, he said, 'The same with me. I just had some luck.'

'Poor Martin,' interrupted Yuliya. 'What is going on, *milyy*?'

Her husband nodded. 'Yes. Poor Martin.'

'Do you know what happened?' Zina said.

Around the table, they waited for his answer. Stepan took his time. He carved another piece of meat, took a sip of red wine, kept his eyes on his plate. 'He had been drinking, the French police said.'

'Oh my God,' exclaimed Zina.

'That's crazy,' said Yuliya. 'He drinks a little but he doesn't just fall over. Was there something wrong? Why are we here, *milyy*?'

Stepan reached out across the table and took Yuliya's hand. '*Mne zhal' moya dorogaya.* I just wanted us to be together.'

The expression on Yuliya's face was sceptical, but she said nothing.

'Martin's death was a shock.'

'Were you with him?'

Stepan looked away. 'He was staying at the apartment for a couple of nights. We had business to discuss but . . . we never did.'

Zina turned to Kai. 'I was at school with his daughter. We are friends.'

'I'm sorry,' said Kai. 'That's awful.'

'What happened?' Yuliya was saying. 'They say he jumped from your balcony. That is absurd. Why would he do that?'

Stepan paused, fork in hand, a mournful expression on his face. 'Can you let me eat?'

'People don't just jump from balconies,' said Yuliya.

Stepan took a sip of wine, lifted a napkin and dabbed his mouth. 'Not often, no.'

Yuliya's voice was suddenly angry. 'It's ridiculous. What was he thinking?'

Her husband didn't answer.

'I have been saying for months we should spend time on the

yacht,' complained Yuliya. 'And then you call and say hurry, hurry, hurry, and now you are here you won't tell me what is wrong.'

Stepan's voice was gentle. 'I know, *lyubimaya*. Martin is dead. But don't worry. We will have a wonderful trip. Have you ordered fireworks?'

'Of course I have.'

He smiled. 'Then everything will be beautiful. Do you like fireworks?' He turned to Kai.

Before Kai could reply, Yuliya interrupted again, 'But why did you bring Dimitri?'

'To be on the safe side,' he said.

'The safe side of what?' Yuliya's voice was sharp. 'Is something wrong, Stepan?'

'Ssh, my darling. Nothing is wrong,' he said, reassuringly, taking her hand.

The waiters cleared the plates. The family lapsed back into Russian. Kai relaxed in his chair and tried to figure out what was being said. Zina's mother took Stepan's hand and murmured something to her daughter. Zina rolled her eyes. Her father shook his head, lowered it a little, as if he was looking over glasses that weren't there, and said something else that Zina clearly didn't like. The conversation went on like this for a few minutes. Kai might well have not been there. In the end, Zina said angrily, 'This is ridiculous,' pushed her chair back and stood.

Her father shrugged and called after her as she walked away to the top of the steps down to the jetty, but she ignored him, stopped, and pulled out a cigarette. She had left her lighter back on the table. Instead she just held it up, to the main bar, and one of the waiting staff walked over to her with a lighter.

Kai followed her to the top of the steps. 'What's going on, Zina, between you and your family?'

'I'm so angry. I should never have come.'

Kai looked back at the table. Stepan had put down his knife and fork, laid the napkin on his plate and was taking another small sip of wine.

'My family is a fucking circus, that's what's going on. My dad wants me to go back to Russia. He says it's not safe in London any more. That's ridiculous. He is going to cut off my money.'

'Why do you need money? You could do some waitressing, maybe.'

'Are you fucking kidding me?' she muttered.

'You live in a housing co-op. You're a student. You don't need money.'

She looked at him like he was an idiot. 'I don't actually live in a co-op. I just told you that because it was cooler than saying I live in my dad's house in Pimlico. I have friends who live in a co-op. Sometimes I stay over, but it's a shithole. I just don't want people to think everything is easy for me because my daddy is a gazillionaire.' She snorted. 'I hate my father. I mean . . . when was the last time your family went on vacation with two bodyguards?'

'You know that guy?' Kai looked over at the big fair-haired man, who was sitting with his back to the bar, elbows propped on the counter.

'Dimitri? Sure.' She waved at him. 'He is former special forces in the GRU.'

'I don't know what that means.'

'It's like the secret police. They are military spies and killers. If Dimitri is here, it means Papa is scared of something,' murmured Zina.

On cue, Dimitri caught Kai's eye and stared at him. The gaze was unnerving.

'So why is he here?'

Zina had kicked off her heels and was standing barefoot on the boards facing away from the restaurant. Below, down at the bottom of the steps, the grey RIB boat bobbed on the water. 'I don't think it's to help with the laundry.' And she blew smoke out into the darkness.

FIFTEEN

Erin sat in the boat below, her legs over the side of the launch. She had checked the water temperatures on her phone and the early June average was already half a degree warmer than it had been last year. Warm water brought bigger storms.

Early tomorrow they would be casting off to head south. After months tied up on the quay she should be happy. Instead she was nervous; probably because it was so long since they had taken the yacht out on a proper voyage. She had checked all the safety gear. Everything she could see was fine; there was all the stuff you couldn't see, though.

The weakness of superyachts was their sophistication. So much was automated. From navigation to propulsion, everything could be managed by dynamic positioning and collision avoidance systems. Because it could be done, it was. Rich clients always wanted the latest and the best, which meant that there was always more that could go wrong.

She had picked up the new ETO that afternoon, an affable

Polish man, who had only half a day to familiarise himself with *Zinaida*'s electrical systems; she had watched him sitting on the bridge going through the manuals, lips moving as he struggled to translate the English text.

None of this felt like proper sailing.

The RIB bobbed gently in the water. Every boat had its own dance.

The first boat she had ever sailed in was an Enterprise dinghy. It was wooden and beautiful. It was her uncle Ben's boat. It was from him she had first got the bug, sailing it on Kings Mill Reservoir, near her home in Nottingham.

She had been an only child, raised by two parents who loved her so much it often made her want to scream. They had had her late, after trying for a child for years, and inevitably, despite the force of their love for her, she knew she disappointed them. When her friends became tall and willowy, she remained solid.

Uncle Ben never minded her borrowing the dinghy and sailing on her own on the reservoir. Though Enterprises were supposed to be two-person boats, she handled it single-handed without much difficulty, holding the mainsail sheet between her teeth while she sorted out the jib. Older sailors marvelled at her ability. Ben was always there watching from the shore, sitting on a bench, smoking cigarettes, talking to the men from the rugby club whose grounds were next to the sailing club's.

When her parents finally discovered Ben was letting her sail on her own, they were furious. 'It's much too dangerous,' they scolded. 'It's irresponsible.' They wanted to keep their precious daughter safe. At home Erin argued, slamming her bedroom door, calling her parents idiots. In the end, they bought her proper sailing lessons, which she took, privately seething at having to sail in an Optimist, a tiny training boat that was much too childish for her.

In her early teenage years she stopped being jealous of her friends and their cliques who met daily at the shopping centre after school or bitched on Myspace. They were more lost than she was. At fifteen, after many more arguments, she persuaded her parents to send her on a Tall Ships adventure, sailing around Arran and the Isle of Bute. It was then, on night watch, Arcturus shining just above the horizon ahead of her, feeling the wind pressing at the huge boat's sails, that she became conscious for the first time of the exact texture of pure happiness. Happiness for her, she decided, was directly related to blistered palms and winds that stung your skin. Happiness was work, the power of nature, the sea and boats.

She may have found the days on the ship hard; the boat was full, and privacy was scarce, but moments like that made her more sure of who she was and who she wanted to become.

The next year Uncle Ben chartered a boat; they planned to sail around the coast of the UK, but that May he was diagnosed with a brain tumour and, for a while, lost movement in his right leg. She suspected her parents were secretly pleased that she had to cancel the journey, but by next year he had been successfully operated on and the trip was back on. By now she had passed her shore-based Coastal Day Skipper exams. Ben spent the weeks sitting in the cockpit, giving orders only when needed. By the end of a week she was taking the boat onto a pontoon single-handed and, if the weather and the approach were good enough, doing it without the engine on. When they saw her stepping on shore to tie up, other sailors nodded approvingly. One or two applauded. She would load the dinghy up with provisions and return to the boat with them. When Ben wanted whisky, she had rowed around the other moored boats, asking if someone could buy a bottle for her.

'At home, you're so sulky and dull,' Ben had said. 'Out here on the water, you're like a lion.'

She realised it was true. She felt at home in a boat in a way that she never did within brick walls.

That was the year she started telling people she wanted to sail around the world. At sixteen, she had no idea how difficult it was going to be to make that come true. She worked in Primark at the weekends, saving money, but it was slow going. On her seventeenth birthday, Uncle Ben gave her £200 and, with her earnings, she was able to afford her own Wayfarer dingy; second-hand, it came with its name already hand-painted in bright blue on the stern: *High Hopes*.

That's what she had had back then. High hopes.

A little way off, there was a splatter of stones falling into the water.

In the darkness someone was moving across the rocky foreshore towards her. There were no other boats on the private mooring. She reached onto her utility belt and unsnapped a torch, then pulled her knife out of her belt.

Crime on St Thomas was not as bad as some of the other islands, but you always had to be careful. There was no time to shout to the security guard on the patio above; besides, she lived by the rule they all lived by aboard *Zinaida*: discretion. Never draw attention to the family. The man was trying not to be seen or heard as well, keeping low on the uneven ground. He reached the edge of the jetty and saw her with the knife, then hesitated. He was an islander dressed in a dark T-shirt and combat trousers. 'Your name is Erin?'

'Who are you?'

'I have a little something special. The woman on the boat asked me to fetch it. Mauricia, her name is.'

Erin thought for a second. 'You mean Marissa.'

She put the knife away and he dug in his pocket and extracted something. It was a small, carefully wrapped plastic package, and she understood what she was supposed to do with it. This was not what she had learned to sail for.

She heard voices from above. The breeze brought snippets of conversation. The man was already disappearing the way he had come. She hoped it would not be a late night; she would be up at dawn preparing for departure. Zina was leaning over the wooden balustrade above her, talking to someone.

'My family is a fucking circus, that's what's going on . . . When did your family last go on vacation with two bodyguards?'

This puzzled Erin. She knew there was one bodyguard on board; there had been no information on a second.

'Why is he here?'

She watched Zina blow out smoke into the air above her.

And then the party broke up and there were people coming down the stairs. She started up the engine, went to stand on the jetty, ready for them. Stepan would want to drive; he always did.

88

She hadn't seen her boss for over a year. He looked thinner somehow, and more worn.

He ignored her. Zina and her mother stepped into the back of the boat. The boyfriend joined them. Tommy stepped into the front section of the boat; *I always sit in the front*, she remembered. The last person to emerge down the steps was a huge man with cropped fair hair whom she had never seen before. He was carrying a holdall, just as Tommy had. There would be weapons of some kind in it. She frowned.

The new man took the bow seat directly facing Tommy. She cast off and stepped aboard; Stepan had left the kill cord dangling by the side of the dashboard as he always did. She picked it up and slipped it over her own wrist instead. And all the way across the bay she was conscious of Tommy staring forwards at the new man, and of the new man, whoever he was, looking warily back at Tommy from the bow, each trying to get the measure of the other.

SIXTEEN

To Kai, the yacht seemed even bigger when they boarded it this time. Its whiteness glowed in the dark.

Yuliya and Stepan said goodnight and went straight to the family's floor. Kai followed Zina to the main cabin, where she threw herself on one of the white couches and asked Marissa where the remote for the TV was.

'I put what you asked for in your room,' Marissa said, handing it to her.

'You're an angel.' Zina pressed a button and an enormous screen rose slowly out of the coffee table.

'Christ,' said Kai, watching it appear.

'You like that?' said Zina. The screen finished its ascent with a subtle click and came on automatically.

'Can I do it?'

He sat down next to her and she leaned in close, handed him the remote and said, 'Go crazy.'

Kai sent the screen back down again and then brought it back up. It moved with a barely audible whirr. Marissa returned with a tray, glasses, an ice bucket, a jug and a bottle of Black Label, lowering them to the table in a sideways squat. 'Do you guys want snacks? You want me to pull the blinds?'

''K' sake. Go to bed, Marissa,' Zina said.

'Just call me if you need anything, OK?' she said as she descended the stairs. Her default setting was chirpy.

'Wait, Marissa,' called Zina.

Marissa came halfway back up until her head was just above floor level. 'Hey,' she said. 'You wanted me?'

'Did you know anything about Dimitri joining the trip?' Zina asked.

'The Dolph Lundgren kind of guy? Nobody told us he was coming. He just turned up with you on the boat. The security guy that Captain Falk hired is a little pissed. It's like a bitch fight going on there downstairs about who's top dog,' she said, disappearing again.

'No question. Dimitri's the top dog. That other guy is going to find that out pretty quick,' said Zina, settling into the cushions.

Zina had taken the remote back, switched on YouTube. She pressed PLAY and let one video just follow another, seeing where it led, head on his shoulder. Every now and again she leaned forward, topped up her whisky and added a single cube of ice.

'See?' she said after a while. 'All of this. The yacht. The servants. You see what I mean now?'

'It must be hell.'

'Fuck you,' she said, still staring at the screen. 'Poor little rich girl,' she muttered, wriggling free of his hands.

'I didn't say that.'

'You didn't really have to. You really don't understand me at all. You don't understand how toxic this all is.'

'I've just never been on anything like this boat, that's all.'

She picked the remote off the sofa and muted the TV. 'My mum and dad announced that they are going to set me up with a nice tasteful little art gallery somewhere so I can sell other people's corny paintings to their friends. They don't like that I live in London. My life is basically over.'

'I'm sorry,' he said.

'My dad is going to get a lease on a gallery. That's what he was telling me in the restaurant. That's what they want me to be. He wants me on a leash. I have no say in it any more.'

She picked up the whisky and poured herself a large glass, then held out the bottle towards him. He shook his head. 'They're making you move back to Russia?'

'You know what? We should take this boat out onto the middle of the ocean and just sink it. That would be beautiful. That would be an artwork.'

After that she lapsed into silence. At around three, she was still drinking, so Kai left her to it and went down the stairs to his cabin.

Kai was not sure when he became conscious of the motion of the boat. They were under way. It was morning and, in the gentle swell, he had slept surprisingly well.

Opening the curtains, there was only sea and sunlight. He picked up his phone, but there was still no connection, so he got dressed and went upstairs.

The main cabin was empty and spotless. The sofas looked

92

like nobody had ever sat on them. He walked to the back of the boat, by the swimming pool, leaned on the wooden top-rail and looked at the lines of the white wake behind them. The island they had started from was already far away.

He would make it up to Marley when he was back in England. Marley would forgive him because he always did.

'The family is upstairs in the dining room having breakfast, sir.' He looked around. Marissa was standing at the entrance to the main lounge.

'You American?'

'Yes, sir.'

'You speak Russian, don't you? I heard you yesterday.'

'Sure. Russian. Mandarin. You get the best gigs with those. You want to join them in the dining room?'

He followed her up the staircase, and then into the large, light room. Stepan, Yuliya and Zina were sat at an oval table facing the panoramic windows that looked out towards the bow.

A fourth chair was placed on the opposite side. 'Coffee? Orange juice?' said Marissa.

There was music playing; Kai recognised 'Beyond the Sea'. He sat in the fourth chair, feeling a little like he was facing an interview panel. 'Morning,' he said. Zina was wearing dark glasses and a sullen expression.

'How you feeling?' he asked her.

Zina remained silent.

'So,' said Stepan, looking up from the screen of an iPad. 'You are still here.'

'I apologise for gatecrashing,' Kai joked.

'No apologies necessary,' said Stepan, deadpan. 'Any friend

93

of Zina's is welcome. Though the last man she brought with her to meet us was a drug user. Are you?'

'Papa,' said Zina, slumping in her chair. She picked up a cup of coffee in front of her. 'Of course he's a drug user.'

'Are you?'

'Mainly paracetamol this morning,' said Kai.

Stepan laughed, finally, then returned to his iPad. The sound system, Kai noted, was extraordinarily clear, equalised perfectly for the room. The brass stabs of the chorus kicked in. Added sixths, Kai told himself, never having really noticed them before.

He liked sixths. A sixth chord had nowhere to go. It wasn't like a seventh chord that was itching to resolve somewhere. It was kind of a louche thing, with a lack of clear purpose.

'Men date my daughter because they want her money,' Stepan said, not looking up from his screen.

'Stepan!' protested Yuliya. 'He has not even ordered breakfast yet.'

'Don't worry. Kai is only after my beautiful mind,' said Zina.

Music filled the silence. The song was sung by Bobby Darin, thought Kai, a singer everyone had forgotten about. Hearing it today, people thought they were listening to Frank Sinatra.

Granola arrived, with fresh fruit and oat milk. The next song was 'Into the Mystic' by Van Morrison, a song about the ocean as an unanswered question; then 'Sail on, Sailor' by the Beach Boys. Kai understood it now. There was a theme; all the songs were about the sea. This was a playlist curated for a luxury yacht. Stepan had presumably paid for it, like he paid for decor.

'Will you be joining us for yoga, Stepan?' Yuliya asked.

'No,' he answered, not looking up.

'What about your boyfriend, Zina?'

'He's just across the table from you, Mama. Ask him.'

'If that's all right,' said Kai. 'I'd enjoy that.'

Conversation dried again. Above the music, there was only the sound of cutlery and china. 'I'm sorry about your friend,' said Kai eventually.

Stepan looked up again. 'I beg your pardon?'

Kai repeated himself.

'Yes. Thank you,' said Stepan. 'So am I.'

'Do you know what happened to him exactly?'

Stepan didn't answer, instead lowering his head to his iPad again. Kai noticed Yuliya and Zina exchanging a glance, but neither spoke. After a few minutes Stepan stood. 'Will you excuse me?' he said. 'I have some calls to make.' And left the room.

After breakfast, Zina put on a bikini and joined her mother by the pool. Kai was not a fan of lying in the sun.

On the same level as his cabin, L1, he found a gym, complete with a treadmill, cycle, leg press and a bench press. He turned on the treadmill, set it in motion and looked at it for a while but decided against getting on it. He wasn't in the mood. He switched it off and was listening to the slow whirr winding down when, out of the corner of his eye, he thought he saw someone at the half-open door, but when he looked again, there was nobody there. He abandoned the gym and went out onto the landing. 'Hello?'

Upstairs, the main cabin remained empty. There were fresh flowers in a crystal vase on the table. Where did you find fresh flowers when you were at sea, he wondered? He hadn't brought anything to read. The only books he had seen were Yuliya's, and they were in Russian. There were small drawers along the side of the table. He started opening them in the hope that one of them might contain an old paperback he could read, but they were all empty.

When he looked up this time, he was conscious again of someone standing halfway up the staircase, just where Marissa had stood the night before. It was Tommy, the security man. 'Looking for something?' he asked.

'Something to read. Have you been watching me?'

'I'm watching everyone,' said Tommy. 'It's my job.'

SEVENTEEN

Zinaida was on autopilot on a course of 183 degrees. Up on the bridge, there was nothing for Erin to do except sit and gaze out at the big sea in front of her, because every vessel must at all times maintain a proper lookout. The weather was calm, they were in open water; the radar showed no other vessels for ten miles. Sailing in a vessel like this was a kind of drudgery requiring none of the attention that it takes to sail a real boat, but at least she was at sea again.

She and Marius were alternating six-hour watches. He had taken the boat out from St Thomas. Now it was her turn.

At eleven, the Polish ETO appeared on the bridge dressed in the black uniform that all the crew apart from Marius wore. The ETO's name was Aleksander and he said he wanted the inventory of EPIRBs and PLBs – the emergency beacons and communication devices that were stowed around the boat and in the various life rafts. 'I should check them,' he said.

'I already checked them before we left port.' On boats, everyone spoke English.

'Oh. You're good,' he said with a grin. 'I should still look though. It's in my manifest.'

'If you hadn't missed your plane, you could have done it yesterday.'

He smiled like a boy caught stealing something. 'You want to know why I missed my flight?' He actually winked. 'It is because I was in bed with a girl.' He spoke good English, but with an oddly sibilant accent. 'It *isss* because I *wass* in bed with a girl.'

She laughed.

'She was very beautiful. Like you are.'

'Oh please.' She was not beautiful; she knew that. She pulled out a drawer in the chart table and handed him the inventory.

'I asked her to marry me, as a matter of fact.'

'You did? Congratulations.'

'I always ask them to marry me,' he said, looking down the list. They sat together and she explained how he'd access all their locations. 'I will look because I should, but everything on this boat is perfect. I can see. It *isss* impressive.' A thought occurred to her. 'One thing. We had an electrical outage when we were moored. There were mechanics on board checking the engines. Marius thinks they switched something off by mistake.'

'Probably.'

She nodded. 'Except the instruments and the air con went off at the same time.'

'Huh. Yeah, that's a little kind of strange,' he said.

'I thought so too.' Ships' electrics were a complex mix of generators and batteries, inverters and differing voltages. There

98

was a myriad of systems, mostly entirely independent of each other. That's why yachts like this had electro-technical officers in the first place. 'The instruments and the air con, they're separate, yes?'

'They both went out?'

'And came back on again at exactly the same time.'

He nodded. 'Very strange. I get you. I'll look into it,' he said.

He had gone by the time the door opened a second time. The sound of New Age music drifted in through the door. Staff had set up the awning over the helicopter deck. Yuliya Pirumova did yoga every morning when she was on board. Erin looked around expecting to see Marius, but it was Stepan, with the larger of the two security men. His name was Dimitri, she had learned. She sat a little more upright. 'Morning, sir,' she said.

He nodded at her, said, 'Ask Marissa to bring two coffees,' then the two of them went to sit on the huge sofa at the back of the bridge, talking together intensely in Russian, their voices low. Erin had no idea what they were discussing, but Stepan's voice had a tension in it she had not heard before.

Until the last few months, when *Zinaida* had lain idle at St Thomas, Stepan Pirumov had come on the yacht often. Six years ago he had been excited about owning such a huge, cutting-edge boat and had wanted to understand how to sail her. On her first ever trip on *Zinaida*, he had spent hours behind the wheel. He enjoyed being the one in charge of her. Today, though, he seemed too preoccupied to pay any attention to what Erin was doing.

She thought she should look busy, though, so she toggled the view of the radar in front of her a couple of times and zoomed in on the weather system out in the mid-Atlantic. The yellows and greens of the storm she had discussed with Marius were still far to the east of them, still heading west-north-west. It seemed that Marius had been right. It looked like it would pass to the north of them. It was surprisingly intense though, for this time of year. Hurricane season didn't really peak until October.

Marissa arrived with the Turkish coffees and placed the tray on the table in front of the sofa, served them, then went to stand next to Erin. 'Hi,' she said quietly. 'First woman first mate I've ever sailed with. You must be so clever.'

Erin didn't really have an answer for that. 'You want a go?'

'Steering?'

Erin stepped back. 'Sure.'

'Wow,' said Marissa. 'Can I?'

Erin switched off the autopilot and let her take the helm. Like everyone who took the wheel, she was hesitant at first, turning it cautiously to port and then starboard. Marissa laughed delightedly. 'This is so fun.'

'Steer it to one-eight-three,' said Erin.

Marissa spent some time trying to get the knack of keeping the boat on the right heading, concentrating hard on the electric screen in front of her. She turned to her boss. 'How's your coffee, sir?'

'Good.'

Stepan was not interested in conversing. He was still deep in some kind of discussion with Dimitri. Erin guessed that with this few guests on the boat, Marissa too didn't have much to do. There were two chefs to produce lunch. Marissa would have made the beds and cleaned the bathrooms already. People who crewed boats knew how to work hard; Erin liked that.

'I could do this,' Marissa joked, quietly, so as not to disturb the men's conversation. 'It's easy.'

Marissa chewed her tongue as she concentrated, looking down at the screen, then up at the bow, then at her fingers on the small wheel, then up again. The sea around them was curiously empty. A couple of years ago it would have been full of markers of other ships, but now there were only a few vessels within fifty miles of them; mostly container ships. The cruise ships that had once crowded these waters had all but vanished.

'What are you saving for?' Erin asked.

'What do you mean?'

'Everyone I've ever met in this job is doing it because they're saving for something else. Marius wants to buy a big house. How about you?'

She shrugged. 'I just think it's really frickin' cool going on yachts.'

Erin waited for Marissa to become bored, but she didn't. She kept her hands tightly on the wheel, but Erin noticed she didn't seem to be paying attention to the direction any more. The boat was turning slowly to port. Erin waited to see if Marissa would notice, and realised she wasn't concentrating on steering the boat at all. Instead, she appeared to be listening intently to the conversation the two men were having, chewing on her tongue again. Erin was puzzled.

And then Stepan and Dimitri, too, seemed to become conscious of the fact that they could be overheard. They stopped talking.

Marissa snapped to life again. 'Oh, shoot,' she exclaimed. 'I'm miles off.' And swung the boat round hard.

101

Erin reached over her and corrected the wheel so that the turn wouldn't be too sharp. They were in no hurry, after all.

When the men finally stood and left, Erin asked, 'So. What were they saying?'

Marissa coloured.

Erin waited for the boat to come slowly round to the right heading again, then said, 'You were listening, weren't you?'

She shook her head. 'Not really. I mean, only I couldn't help it.'

'You were. I could tell. Should I be worrying about you? How come you speak Russian, Marissa?'

'It wasn't like I was doing it deliberately. I mean . . . They were just talking.'

'And you happen to speak Russian too?'

She smiled. 'Sure. It's why I was hired.'

Erin held her gaze for a second longer, then said, 'What were they saying, then?'

'It was kind of creepy.'

'Well? Is it something I should know?'

Marissa whispered. 'I don't know. That feels like spying. He's our boss, right?'

'If it's important, tell me. Or maybe you should tell Marius.'

Marissa nodded. 'OK. But don't say I said this, right? I'm serious. I could lose my job . . . and you know, word gets around.'

It was true. Everybody knew the crew agencies kept blacklists. If one employer complained about you, you'd never get work in this sector again.

'I promise I won't say anything.'

'You know Tommy? Dimitri says he doesn't think he's legit.'

'What do you mean, legit?'

'He said he thinks he's *fal'shivyy*.'

'What's that?'

'It's like . . . a phoney.'

'A phoney? Like he's not a bodyguard?'

'Or maybe he's not even supposed to be on this ship. Like he's a spy or something. That's what they were antsy about.' She looked around, nervous now.

'The bodyguard is an impostor? Jesus.'

'I don't know. I might have misheard. I need to go,' she said. She picked up the tray and pulled open the door and was gone, leaving Erin alone on the bridge. Erin needed to talk to Marius about what she'd just heard. She paged him: '*Important!*' He messaged back: '*Busy.*'

It was supposed to be his break; she wondered what he was busy with.

After Marissa had left to set up for lunch on the pool deck, Erin was alone.

She saw someone emerge onto the front deck and recognised Zina's boyfriend. It had been a long time since she had had a real relationship, and then she wondered why she was even thinking about that while looking at Kai, because he was the definition of everything she wouldn't want in a man. Just as she had that thought, he turned, smiled and waved in a friendly kind of way.

Out of politeness, she waved back. The trouble with boats like this is they gave you too much time to think about what you didn't have.

Then, at around three, Marius Falk called her up and said, 'Do you mind staying on watch? Something has come up.'

'Of course not,' she answered. 'Is something wrong?'

'No, no,' Marius said. But his answer was a little too hasty and there was an edge of nerviness in his voice.

'You sure? Because . . . Can we talk in private? I think there may be an issue with one of our crew.'

'I am dealing with it,' he said. 'Everything is under control.' He sounded tense. 'Everything is fine,' he said.

Through the warm sea air, St Croix was visible now as a dark shape low on the horizon dead ahead. It would not be long before they docked. Christiansted was a shallow harbour. They would moor a little way off the dock and use the launch to take the family ashore. It was a scrappy little town, nothing like the millionaires' playground of St Thomas.

A couple of minutes after Falk had hung up, the door opened again. She expected Falk, but when she turned she saw it was Dimitri again. He looked around the room. 'On your own?'

'Yes.'

'Good. I need to talk to you in confidence. I need to know I can trust you,' he said, 'to do something extremely important for me when we get to Christiansted.'

He had worn an easy smile the first time she had seen him. Now his expression was serious. He approached her until he was so close she could see each individual bristle on his chin and smell the vinegariness of his aftershave.

EIGHTEEN

Under a pale canvas awning on a hot flat deck, the personal trainer led Kai, Zina and Yuliya through simple sequences. Kai wore swimming trunks and a T-shirt, which was all he had with him; Zina and her mother both wore yoga leggings and sports tops.

Their mats had been laid within a large black circle marked on the white deck. Rugs and brightly coloured cushions had been scattered around the edges. They were doing warrior pose, right arm stretched forward across the deck. The Californian trainer had cultivated a quiet, reassuring voice.

'Let your hands float,' he said, 'as if they were on lily pads.'

He was good; he didn't push them hard but worked with a quiet confidence. Kai was looking out over his arm towards Zina when he realised that the black circle had a purpose. He asked, 'Is this where the helicopter lands?'

'Ssh,' said Yuliya.

'Breathe into your arms,' the trainer said.

The white vinyl awning was held on silver poles placed into holes around the edges of the deck and lifted at the centre by a steel guy rope that ran up to the main communications mast; the result was a kind of brilliant-white marquee.

'I don't know why Dad had a helipad. He thinks helicopters are a waste of money.'

'Superyachts, on the other hand . . .'

'Yeah. Right.'

'OK. Now reverse warrior,' said the trainer. 'Raise your right arm over your head and slide that left arm down . . .'

Kai shifted pose.

'He has a point. You can party on a superyacht,' said Zina. 'All you do in a helicopter is feel sick.'

'Ssh.' Yuliya glared.

'I'm too hot for this,' said Zina, dropping her arms and slumping down onto her mat.

'OK, Zina,' said the Californian. 'You go into savasana.'

Yuliya and Kai continued the session. Zina lay on her back on the mat peering up at Kai through half-closed eyes.

'OK, and if you can, warrior three.'

Yuliya stayed where she was in warrior two; Kai lifted a leg and balanced on one foot, chest parallel to the ground. He had thought it would be harder to balance on a moving yacht; to his surprise he maintained the pose, as if he was somehow already in tune with the motion of the boat on the water.

'Excellent,' said the teacher. 'You do a lot of yoga?'

'Most days.'

'Cool,' said the teacher. 'You want to try something harder?'

106

And, though her eyes still looked closed, Zina murmured, 'I can see right up your swimming shorts.'

'Ssh,' said her mother.

When Kai made it back to the room to shower there were three paperbacks on his bed. No note explaining why they were there. They were thrillers; not the kind of thing that he enjoyed reading normally. He wondered who had put them there.

After the shower, he picked up one and went to the pool with it. Zina was already lying on her back in the water. He stood and watched her floating.

'Is this what you do all day?' asked Kai.

'All fucking day.' Swimming over, she crossed her arms on the edge of the pool and squinted up at him. 'Luxury is pretty dull, most of the time, to be honest.'

He was bored, it was true. How could you be so bored on a yacht that seemed to have everything on board? 'How long till we're in St Croix?'

'A couple of hours maybe.'

He moved one of the loungers into the shade of an awning and picked up the book but didn't open it.

'What are you reading?'

He held up the cover. 'It was in my room. I think Tommy put it there.'

Zina wrinkled her nose. 'It looks like trash.'

'Have you seen Stepan?' Yuliya called from the far side of the pool.

Kai told her he hadn't.

'He's supposed to be on holiday. He's probably in our cabin doing work,' Yuliya grumbled. 'He'll make himself sick.'

'He's preoccupied,' said Zina. 'Upset about Martin. I mean, a man doesn't throw himself off a fourth-floor balcony for no reason.'

Yuliya grunted. 'Can't we just forget about that for now?'

Kai read the blurb on the back of the book. The President of the United States had gone missing from the White House, it seemed, but nobody had seen him disappear. The premise was ridiculous, he thought. When he looked up, Zina was sleeping again, laid out on another of the sunbeds.

He got up and walked along a gangway to the next sun deck, on the Pirumovs' private level, then inside, past the room with the gold chandelier and the family portrait into the next landing, where Zina's bedroom was. He paused for a second. Behind one of the doors, he could hear Stepan Pirumov talking. It sounded as if he was on the phone to someone.

He was about to move on when he heard a small cough behind him.

Kai spun round. Dimitri was sitting in a chair behind him, one leg crossed over the other. He hadn't even seen him when he'd walked onto the landing.

'Y'all right?' Dimitri said. It was the first time Kai had heard him speak English: he had a faux cockney accent.

'I was trying to make it onto the foredeck.'

Dimitri smiled. 'That way.' He nodded towards the dining room.

It had looked like he was eavesdropping. 'I wasn't . . . I just . . .'

'Sure,' said Dimitri. He laughed. 'Of course you weren't. Go on. Straight ahead.'

The dining room was deserted. There were doors on each side that led out to a narrow companionway that in turn gave on to the front deck. It was wide and dazzlingly white out here. He walked towards the bow and looked back up the superyacht.

Behind the darkened glass of the bridge he could just make out the silhouette of the first mate, Erin, looking down at him. He waved up at her. This time she gave him a little wave back. He looked forward and could see a dim shape on the horizon straight ahead of them that he guessed was St Croix.

Before they arrived at the island, the staff served a light buffet lunch at the poolside. There was a chicken salad with wasabi dressing and a shrimp and noodle salad with ginger, but Kai managed to find a couple of things he could eat.

Stepan joined them, dressed in crisp light blue shorts and a white T-shirt. He served himself, sat on a lounger next to his wife, then looked up at Kai and said, 'Dimitri said you were listening outside my door.'

'Was he?' Zina looked up from her plate.

Kai coloured. 'No. I was just passing through. I was trying to get to . . .'

Stepan ignored him and turned to his daughter. 'I have a question. How long have you known your boyfriend, Zina?'

'Like . . . I don't know.' She frowned, as if in thought. 'Maybe a week?'

'A week?'

'And do you know whether he is who he says he is?'

Kai looked from his girlfriend to her father disbelievingly. 'Of course I am,' said Kai.

Yuliya had stopped eating now and was watching the conversation, a worried look on her face.

'It's convenient that he meets you just before our family holiday,' said Stepan.

Zina nodded. 'I suppose so,' she said slowly. 'I never really thought of that.'

'I was trying to find my way through to the foredeck,' said Kai. 'That's all I was doing.'

Stepan stared at him, then looked back down at his plate. 'I have reason to be concerned that not everyone on this boat is who they said they are.'

'*O chem ty, chert voz'mi, govorish!*' protested Yuliya, looking shocked. 'What do you mean, Stepan?'

'This is ridiculous,' said Kai. 'I didn't even know who you were when I agreed to come on this trip.'

Apart from the humming of the engines and the slapping of water against the hull, there was only awkward silence.

Until Stepan burst out laughing.

'What's so funny?' demanded Kai.

'That you have never heard of me,' said Stepan. And now Zina and Yuliya were laughing too. Stepan leaned across from his seat and put his arm on top of Kai's. 'Don't worry,' he said. 'I was only messing around with you. You're not the problem on this boat.'

Kai was laughing too now, though nervously.

'You're such a fucking kidder, Dad,' drawled Zina.

When Yuliya stopped laughing she stared at her husband. 'Is everything OK, Stepan?'

'It is now,' he said.

'What are you talking about?'

'Nothing to worry about, my darling.'

Stepan lowered his head to his plate and skewered a lettuce leaf with his fork and placed it carefully into his mouth, chewing slowly.

After lunch, Kai got into the pool and swam for a little while. Zina sat on the edge, kicking her legs gently.

Kai approached her. 'Well, that was hilarious.'

'Don't be so defensive.'

Stepan had stretched out on one of the loungers in the shade, with an iPad and a wireless keyboard.

'Did you know he was kidding?'

'Sure,' she said.

'Really?'

'Jesus, Kai. No one's ever going to seriously mistake you for a threat.' Marissa and the second chef were clearing the plates away. 'Plus Dimitri looked you up on Wikipedia. He listened to some of your music. Honestly, I don't think he liked it much. Dad's in a really dark mood though,' said Zina. 'Something's going on.'

Marissa called from the table, 'Hey. I heard you were, like, some big musician?'

'Like some big musician,' mocked Zina.

'So cool. What are your records? The ones that I would know.'

'She's flirting with you,' Zina said quietly. 'She thinks you're rich.'

He listed a couple of titles of songs that he'd been part of; Marissa smiled blankly. 'Wow,' she said. 'That's amazing.'

'Stop pretending,' said Zina. 'You haven't actually heard of any of them, have you?'

Marissa flushed. 'Yeah, but I bet they were huge in Europe or somewhere.'

'It was a while ago,' said Kai.

'Very cool.' Marissa smiled benignly.

When Kai looked again, the island was a little closer.

He went down to his room for a shower and was opening his door when he heard a knocking noise from close by, the muffled sound of something hitting metal.

He looked around, saw no one.

The noise came again. Three regular bangs, then a pause, then three more.

It sounded as if the noise was coming from the panic room.

Still dripping wet from the pool, he laid his hand on the door. The next time the noise came, he could feel it through the metal.

'Hello?' he called.

The banging stopped.

'Are you OK?'

'Who's there?' It was unmistakably Tommy's voice, though he sounded faint.

'It's Kai.'

'This is Tommy. Get me out of here, Kai.' His voice was muffled by the thickness of the secure door, but it was clearly audible.

Kai tried pressing down on the main door handle but it didn't move. 'I think it's locked.'

There was a second, smaller knob above it, which he figured

must be the lock that Zina had used to lock him in there. He twisted it, and it moved, but it made no difference to the handle.

'Of course it's locked. Get the key code.'

'Who did this?'

'Just get the code. Let me out. Please.'

'Where is it?'

Tommy's voice was angry. 'I don't know. Find it.'

Kai turned away, then paused. 'Who locked you in there?'

There was no answer.

'What are you doing in there anyway?'

There was a long pause, then Tommy's voice came again. He sounded very tired. 'Get me out and I'll explain everything.'

NINETEEN

Kai stood outside the locked door for a second longer.

'Wait there,' he told Tommy, which, he realised, was a really stupid thing to say.

Back at the pool, Zina was in the water now, down at the far end, looking over the stern with a bottle of beer in one hand. He dived in and surfaced next to her.

'Want a beer?'

'Tommy the bodyguard is in the panic room,' he said quietly. 'Something's going on. Somebody's locked him in.'

'What?'

'Seriously. He's locked in there asking me to get the keycode. He sounds . . . kind of scared.'

She gave Kai the bottle to hold, turned and said, 'Papa? What's with the bodyguard in the panic room? The annoying one. The Englishman.'

He didn't look up from his screen. 'It's nothing,' he said. 'Don't worry about it.'

'What do you mean, nothing?' Zina asked.

Placing the iPad on the seat next to him, he said, 'I wasn't joking earlier. I have reason to be concerned that not everyone on this boat is exactly who they said they are.'

'That's a bit fucking dramatic, Dad.'

'It's only a drama if you want to make it into one,' said Stepan.

'You're kidding, right? What's going on?'

'Did you talk to him?' Stepan asked Kai.

'He wants me to let him out,' said Kai.

'Of course he does. Do not talk to him. At all. He's not trust-worthy. Nothing he says is true.'

Yuliya sat up too. 'Is something wrong?'

'Not any longer,' said Stepan, and he lifted up his screen again and placed it back on his lap.

When Kai returned below, Dimitri was sitting in a chair outside the panic room with his big arms folded. He smiled when he saw Kai. 'You again?' said Kai.

'Hi,' the big man said softly.

'You standing guard at this door now?'

Dimitri nodded. 'Sitting. Standing. Same thing.'

'Why do they need you to guard it? I thought you couldn't get out of a room like that anyway.'

'Pretty much. Only, I heard that he has been asking for you to let him out. He might trick you, or someone else, into doing that.'

'Why is he being held in there?'

'I am not supposed to tell you,' said Dimitri. 'Stepan does not want to worry his family.'

115

Kai hesitated at the door of his cabin. 'I don't like the idea of being on a boat where people get locked up.'

Dimitri beckoned him over. 'Me neither. Just this, OK? When I arrived on the boat last night, we told him he could go home. I was here instead. He wasn't needed. He refused. He insisted he come on the boat. Why is that?'

'Because it's his job?'

'The man gets paid whether he stays on the boat or not. Think about it. He could have gone home. When he wanted to stay on the boat so much last night, I thought, yeah, maybe he's just keen on getting a free ride on this nice boat. Like you.' He smiled at Kai. 'Who wouldn't? But I am here to keep you safe. Then one of the staff told me he found her cleaning his cabin and threw her out, which was not very nice at all. Apparently, he searched everyone who was coming on board. So I thought I should do the same to him. When I did I found something in his room that was a little concerning.'

'He has guns. You have guns. Both of those are pretty concerning, if you ask me.'

Dimitri considered for a while. 'You are a pop musician, yes?'

'Close, but . . .'

'I am in security. I know my business. You must not tell her or any of the family this because only Stepan knows. You may feel sorry for this guy, whoever he is, but when I searched his room it turned out he had two four-hundred-milligram cans of carfentanil-based aerosol spray hidden under his bed. Know what that shit is?'

Kai didn't answer.

'It's the stuff our security services used in the Dubrovka

116

Theatre siege twenty years ago when Chechen militants took over the place. Remember? We accidentally killed one hundred and thirty hostages with it. If you're lucky it knocks you out. If you're not, it kills you. Tell me. Why would a security guy from London have something like that?'

The horror of this sank in. 'He was trying to kill us?'

Dimitri shook his head. 'Christ, no. Of course not. He wasn't trying to kill you. Just Stepan.'

'Why?'

Dimitri shrugged. 'I was hoping he would tell me. He said nothing. Whoever he is, he's getting off at St Croix. He's lucky we didn't just throw him overboard. That would be much simpler.'

'What is going to happen to him?'

'We've called the police. They're meeting us at the dock. They will hand him over to the US authorities who have promised they will investigate it for us. Everything above board.'

'He was the one who checked everybody's ID before he allowed them on board.'

Dimitri nodded. 'It's a technique we were all taught at military school. Accuse others of being the thing you are. It's remarkably effective. Why does the Kremlin accuse Ukraine of attacking Russia when everybody knows the reality is the other way around?'

Kai hesitated, opened the door to his cabin, but didn't go in. 'So who is he?'

'I sincerely wish that I knew. It would make my job a great deal easier.'

From inside the room came the voice of the man who had called himself Tommy. 'Who's there? Kai? Is that you?'

117

Dimitri held his finger to his lips.

'Kai?'

Kai said nothing.

In his bathroom, Kai splashed water over his face, unsettled and confused.

He became conscious that the motion of the boat had changed somehow. Emerging into his bedroom, he looked out of the window and saw they were stationary in a bay dotted with much smaller moored boats.

Dressing quickly in shorts and a T-shirt, he emerged from his room, but Dimitri had gone. He knocked on the door.

There was no answer. He tried the handle; this time it gave. The door opened and he peered inside. The small room was empty.

Upstairs on the deck, the Pirumov family were huddled at the rear of the pool deck. Kai joined them. Erin already had the launch out, tied to the cleat at the stern of the yacht. He couldn't see what they were all looking at.

They didn't need to tell him because just then Tommy emerged out onto the swimming deck below them; right at his back was Dimitri. It took a second to register that Tommy's hands were clamped behind his back with cable ties. There was a longer one around his elbows, trussing them together.

'What the hell . . . ?' Kai said, looking around, but the family didn't appear to be as shocked as he was.

Erin was standing on the gently rocking boat and holding out a hand towards him. Dimitri grabbed Tommy by the upper arm and forced him forwards until Tommy had no option except to

118

step onto the edge of the waiting boat, where Erin steadied him until he was ready to sit in one of the seats.

As he sat, he looked up at the back of the boat. Kai was shocked to see his left eye was swollen and there was a bloody wound under his hairline.

'What happened to him?' Zina asked.

Nobody answered.

'Well?' she demanded. 'Isn't anyone going to tell me?'

'He resisted,' said Yuliya eventually.

'What the fuck is going on?'

Stepan turned to his daughter and said, 'I understand you find this upsetting.'

The man below said loudly, 'All this is bollocks.'

'Please don't talk,' said Dimitri, stepping into the boat after his prisoner. Kai was shocked to see that Dimitri was holding a handgun. 'OK, boss?' he called up. Before Kai could even process this, the boat was roaring away from them, churning white water as it sped towards the small harbour, where an untidy cluster of colonial-era buildings hugged the shoreline.

'I've cancelled the reservation tonight,' announced Yuliya. 'We shall stay on board the *Zinaida*. It is not safe out there.'

Kai looked out at the little town of Christiansted. It looked like the sleepiest place in the world.

'What do you mean, Mama, not safe? I just want to go and hang out at a dirty little bar somewhere and drink beer.'

'Not safe.' Yuliya turned around and went back inside the lounge.

'Not safe from what?' demanded Kai. 'Not safe for whom?'

Stepan said, 'That's not your concern,' and turned to join his wife.

'Control, control,' muttered Zina. 'It's all about control.'

They could see a police car, a large four-wheel drive, parked on the dockside. Kai watched the boat moving towards the quay, spraying water from its bow; a warm trade wind was blowing across the bay, whipping up small waves.

'Do you know what's going on?' Zina asked Kai.

'Me? No,' he said. The boat had reached the dock now. In the distance he could see officers pulling Tommy out of the boat. 'Is it always like this?'

'Actually,' she said, 'no. Even by our standards, this is super creepy.' The boat, with Dimitri and Erin in it, was already heading back towards them.

Zina turned her back on the scene. 'I need some beer. Hey. Marissa? Can I get something?'

By the time Marissa had returned with two bottles of Sierra Nevada, Erin was back tying up the boat onto the rear cleat again.

'Wait,' he called down. 'Can you take me to the port?'

Erin straightened, looked up at him, then at Stepan.

'No,' called Stepan from the other side of the pool. 'You stay on board. We're all staying on board *Zinaida* tonight. All of us. I don't want anyone going ashore. Dimitri says it is not safe for us on the island.'

'I am not sure I want to be on a ship where people are assaulted, locked up and marched off at gunpoint.'

There was a shocked silence, as if Yuliya and Zina were unused to hearing people talk like this in front of Stepan.

120

Stepan nodded. 'I understand your feelings. But you don't know who this man was or what he was planning to do.'

'That's not the point. I don't want to be on a boat where these things happen, whatever the reason.'

The two men looked at each other.

'You want the launch any more?' called Erin from below.

Yuliya walked to the back and leaned over the railing. 'No. He doesn't.'

'I am genuinely sorry,' said Stepan. 'I know this is unusual for you. But I have to ask you to stay on board.'

'Why?'

'Right now, *Zinaida* is the safest place in the world.'

'Safe for who?'

Stepan raised his eyebrows, as if he did not approve of the question. He did not answer. For a second Kai thought he was going to lose his temper. Instead he softened. 'In fact, we should celebrate.' He looked around. 'We are here together. As a family. And you are a friend. We'll have some good food and drink together and, you and I, we'll talk. OK?'

He clapped his hands and servants appeared; Yuliya started giving them instructions. It was as if they were on stage, watching the set being changed around them.

TWENTY

Erin had been shocked to see that when Dimitri emerged with Tommy, he was holding a gun at the man's back. More so that Tommy had a bruised eye socket and a wound on his forehead. Dimitri had said he was in custody, but Tommy must have put up a struggle. Automatically, she stood in the boat and steadied Tommy as he got into the launch. Because he was tied, he had no free hands to stop himself falling if the boat wobbled. She was aware that the whole family were watching over the stern; Stepan, Yuliya, Zina and her boyfriend.

As an employee of the family she had attended security briefings in London. They had felt like a necessary but abstract process, rather than something that was real. They had gone through piracy and hijack procedures, as well as enhanced dock security. She had taken notice of everything she had been taught, but never expected it to be a thing she actually did. Weather was real; hidden reefs were real. Men with guns were from movies.

Tommy heavily sat in the seat behind Erin. 'You're making a big mistake here. It's not me.'

'No talking please,' said Dimitri calmly.

'Erin. You're the first officer. Listen to me. You don't have to do anything he says,' said Tommy, his voice slurred. 'You are still in command. Don't believe what anyone says.'

Dimitri spoke. 'I have already explained the situation to Captain Falk and his first officer. Now we are going to take you to Christiansted and hand you over to the police. You have nothing to worry about from us.'

'All this is bollocks.'

'Please don't talk,' said Dimitri. 'We've had enough of this now.'

Erin had sailed boats through Atlantic storms in seven-metre waves, but this was new to her. She hesitated.

'It's OK,' Dimitri said, calmly. 'It's what he does. He wants to spread distrust. Fake news. OK, boss?' he called up at Stepan Pirumov.

Stepan nodded. Dimitri loosed the mooring line and pulled it on board. 'Go,' he said.

It was a short journey to the dock. There were two officers of the US Virgin Islands police standing on the dockside, behind them a blue SUV with flashing lights.

The officers jumped down into the boat as she bumped against the quayside, and hauled Tommy out.

The officers had the rear door of their vehicle open and were pushing Tommy's head down as they ordered him to get in. When the door was closed, they turned and spoke to Dimitri.

The last thing she saw of Tommy was the expression on his

face pressed against the glass door of the SUV. His eyes were wide. He looked terrified.

She took her time on the way back to the boat.

'Are you going to tell me what the hell that was about?' she demanded.

'There are some . . .' Dimitri paused. 'Some concerns around Mr Pirumov's security right now.'

Erin didn't like the sound of this. 'What kind of concerns?'

'I cannot say. I came aboard as a precaution. It turns out it was fortunate that I did. That man was an impostor.'

She switched the outboard to neutral, so they bobbed on the water. 'Why do I have to take your word for that?'

'Because I am in charge of security on this boat. Please take us back to *Zinaida* now.'

'Was it an attempt on Mr Pirumov's life?'

'I could not say.'

Erin thought out loud. 'Tommy insisted on changing the passwords. He said it was for security reasons.'

Dimitri frowned. 'I am aware of that too. I've asked the ETO to look into this. I will require him to check all the communications systems you have there in case there is anything that may have been interfered with or hacked. He will need access to the bridge to check satellite systems, communication systems, all the control technology . . . anything that might be vulnerable.'

'What about everyone else? You're sure it was just him?'

'We cannot be sure. We will remain vigilant.'

'So if you hadn't arrived with Pirumov . . . this man would have been able to do whatever he intended to do?'

124

'There appears to have been an oversight. It was not your fault. You are the first officer. It was Captain Falk's responsibility to make sure everyone who comes aboard this boat is who they claim to be. He failed. I understand Stepan is very angry with him. He will remove him from his duties after this journey.'

'Remove him? You mean, sack him?' Erin took this in. Falk had assumed he would captain this ship for a few more years, making a fine living, then retire early to the house he planned to buy in Husøya.

'It was a basic mistake. It is the captain's responsibility. This is obviously worrying. We need to be sure that he was not acting in collusion.'

'That's ridiculous.' Erin was shocked. 'He's an excellent captain.'

Dimitri raised his eyebrows and scrutinised her. 'Why do you think it's ridiculous? You are very close to the captain, I believe.'

Erin felt uneasy; how much did he know about her relationship with Marius? 'I know him. I work with him.'

'Yes. Of course you do.'

'What? And I am under suspicion too?'

'Should you be? You tell me.'

'Of course not. Neither should Marius be.'

Dimitri shrugged. 'I have looked at Captain Falk's records. He has an interest in expensive things. Maybe he thought that Stepan was not paying him enough. Take us back to the boat now please.'

Erin stared at Dimitri as if he was insane. If Marius had made a mistake letting Tommy on board, he would be distraught enough. He liked everything to be right on his ship.

'You can't treat Marius like he's a criminal. It's not fair.'

'It's not about being fair. It is about being safe. Believe me, I carried out checks on everyone. I have my concerns with Marius.' He leaned forward. 'If you have any concerns about him, now is the time to share them with me.'

She folded her arms. 'I have none at all.'

Dimitri nodded. 'OK.'

'So what did you find out about me?'

Dimitri smiled. 'You are an only child. Both your parents are dead. You have a driving licence but you don't have a car. You have a Facebook account but you never use it. Your credit history is good. Unlike Marius, your tastes are modest. You own no property and as far as I could see you are not in any relationship and have not been in one for way, way longer than you should be—'

'OK. That's enough,' she interrupted. She switched the engine back into gear and headed for the yacht.

'Captain Falk was very adamant that you were trustworthy as well.' The boat bumped gently against the rear of *Zinaida*. Dimitri stepped onto the swimming deck, turned and said, 'Do not interfere with my job and everything will be fine. OK?'

She was just wrapping a figure-of-eight round the cleat when she heard Kai call down. 'Wait. Can you take me to the port?'

She looked up. Stepan was looking down at them too.

They seemed to be having some kind of argument up there.

TWENTY-ONE

One moment the sky was light, the next it was dark and filled with stars and the glint of electricity from the bay around them. The tropical sunset was very sudden. So was the change of mood. Kai sat with a beer.

'Come on,' said Stepan. 'Let's bring some champagne. We'll have dinner out here.'

Staff had already started moving tables and putting up strings of lights, transforming the deck. Zina put Doja Cat on the stereo at full volume and Yuliya didn't object. The family seemed determined to forget the surreal scene of someone being escorted off their boat at gunpoint.

Kai longed to be in a grubby pub in London, or some dirty bar in the town whose lights shone onto the water. The noise of the boat's stereo crowded out the sound from the modest beach bars, but he knew where he'd rather be. They looked ordinary and suddenly very appealing. It was not far to the shore. He could swim there easily.

Zina was dancing alone next to the pool. 'Switch on the pool lights,' she shouted, and they came on, just because she had ordered it. They were pink at first, but then, as Kai watched, the colour slowly changed to blue, then to green. 'Cheesy as shit, isn't it?'

Marissa brought him a glass of champagne so cold that it almost hurt, and he felt it prickle as it went down his throat.

It was as if they all knew something was very wrong and were doing their best to persuade themselves that it wasn't.

Dinner was lobster with coconut, which smelt amazing, even to Kai. The chef had made a papaya and cashew salad for him. The family chatted in Russian most of the time, leaving him to eat his food alone. He watched them. He understood nothing of what they were saying, but for a little while they looked and sounded like a normal family. In their presence, Zina was suddenly a child again, looking from her mother to her father as if seeking their approval. Marissa stood back a little way, in earshot, ready to step forward if summoned.

He ate in silence, feeling like an intruder. He didn't want to be here at all. He would like to have just got out onto the island and found a small hotel maybe, stayed for a few days on his own before making his way home.

Perhaps it was harder than it looked, being so rich. After a while, you trusted no one, except the people who were like you. So it was no surprise, perhaps, they talked so much more easily with each other, grinned and scowled in tandem, laid their hands on each other's with a kind of tenderness.

The conversation faltered. The plates were taken away. Afterwards, Zina and Yuliya lit cigarettes and Stepan stood up, walked

128

purposely to where Kai was and pulled up a chair to sit next to him. 'May I?' he asked, as if this was not his boat at all. 'Are you OK? After what happened?'

Kai looked at him. 'I might be more OK if I knew what was going on.'

Stepan nodded. 'I promised we would talk. What are you drinking?'

Kai was on beer; he held up his bottle.

'Do you want something stronger?'

Kai was not much of a drinker but now seemed the right time.

'Do we have Teeling's?' Stepan asked Marissa.

'Sure.' She ducked behind the bar and reappeared in no time with a bottle of Irish whiskey, a couple of plain tumblers and a bowl of ice. She set about removing the seal.

'I think you're the kind of person who would appreciate it.'

'The kind of person?'

'It's an ordinary whiskey, but very good, I think. I've been watching you. You think all of this –' Stepan waved his arm – 'is bullshit, don't you?'

Kai hesitated a little too long.

Stepan laughed. 'You can't help it. The English look down on the rich. It's a national psychosis.' Marissa placed the open bottle on the table in front of them and Stepan picked it up, poured two whiskeys. 'Please don't get me wrong. I am very fond of England. I like the culture very much. It's why I sent Zina to be educated there. And there are many times when I thought I would move there too. Money is so much safer there. You may look down on the rich, but you will do anything to make sure we give you our money.'

129

It was an odd, one-way conversation. He was conscious of Zina observing them from the corner of her eye. This seemed to be Stepan's way of making friends.

'Lots of my friends live in London. I have places there, and in New York, Paris. But I believe maybe we should live in Russia. It has been pretty good to us, after all.'

He took a sip from his whiskey.

'The thing you need to remember, Russia is a mess but it will get better. In England things will only get worse.'

Kai said, 'I quite like our old, dying culture myself.'

Stepan smiled. 'It's only natural. We love where we're raised. I am the same. But I worry that political systems like yours are too weak for our times. Today people are restless and afraid.'

'They want strong leaders, like yours?'

Stepan shrugged. 'Maybe they do.'

'The trouble with your system is it can't change. At least ours tries to. You have elections, but the same guy always gets in.'

Stepan sat up. 'Zina's boys do not normally like to talk politics with me. She usually likes the stupid ones.'

'She always brings a boyfriend?'

'Every time a different one. She picks the ones she thinks I will not like. This time maybe she slipped up.' He grinned. 'Besides, you are wrong. You have elections and a different guy gets in, but it's always the guy we choose.' He laughed abruptly, then was serious again. 'It is an important question though, is it not? In the post-democratic world, how to move on without destroying everything that went before?'

'I wasn't aware that I was in a post-democratic world.'

'That's because you're English and you haven't realised it

yet.' He dug in the pockets of his chinos and pulled out an iPhone, opened it. 'You're a musician. Please choose some music. Anything you pick has to be better than what my daughter is playing.'

Kai looked at the iPhone. It was open at Spotify. 'Do you like jazz?'

'I don't know. I never have the time to listen to it.'

'Poor little rich boy,' said Kai.

Stepan laughed and, with his fingers, picked up an ice cube and dropped it into his whiskey.

Kai searched for his profile and found a Spotify playlist he had put together of Scandinavian jazz. It was music with the kind of clean lines you'd expect on a superyacht.

'But you have hit on a very relevant point,' said Stepan. 'In our system, the same guy always gets in. Our system works well enough until we need it to change. That is the issue. And then the only way to effect change is through force. It's not just in government. Force becomes the only thing that's important. Which is why Dimitri is here.'

Cautiously, Kai tasted his whiskey; it was rich and smooth. 'Are you talking about your friend? The one who died.'

Stepan looked at him. 'I may be, yes.'

'What are you two talking about?' called Zina. 'And what the hell is this shitty music? Did you let Kai put it on?'

'Leave us alone, sweetness. We have important things to talk about,' said Stepan.

Kai looked at him. 'He didn't fall from his balcony, then?'

Stepan shook his head. 'Most certainly not. Not without help.'

The silence of the moment was broken by a shout. 'Look out.'

It took Kai a second to realise that it had been a man's voice, coming from the deck above.

Stepan was already up, a worried look on his face.

'Everyone inside,' the raw same voice shouted. 'Quickly.'

The calm of the moment had vanished. Stepan was already retreating back to the interior of the boat. Kai looked around, unsure of himself.

Then the shock of seeing the captain, Marius Falk, clattering down the outer staircase from the bridge, shouting incomprehensibly, face red and with a gun in his hand.

132

TWENTY-TWO

'Everyone inside!'

Erin had been alone sitting on the bow watching the lights of the town when she heard Marius's shout, then the others screaming in alarm. Leaping up, she ran back through the boat and out onto the empty helicopter deck.

She was shocked to see Marius below standing with a pistol in his hand, shouting. And in that second, she realised Dimitri had also pulled his own gun from his waistband and was raising it to aim at Marius.

'Stop!' Erin shouted.

Taking no notice, Dimitri levelled his gun at Marius, not looking where the captain was pointing. Erin had quickly followed the line of Marius Falk's finger: lit only dimly in the darkness, the pale shape of a much smaller yacht was heading straight towards them. It was under sail; though it was dark, the boat was showing no navigation lights.

She shouted, 'Dimitri, no!'

He looked up at her finally, seeing her from below, clearly pointing too towards the oncoming boat. It was already so close that she could make out that the jib was fluttering and the reefed mainsail badly set, but nevertheless it was heading straight for them and would collide soon. It was difficult to see past the boom, but as far as she could make out it looked like there was no one at the helm. It was already less than fifty metres from them, she calculated, and closing.

Dimitri looked round, lowered the gun.

Erin ran down to the next deck.

'Maybe it's nothing,' Marius was saying. He was still holding his gun in his hand, looking sweaty and anxious. He had been wrong once before; this time he seemed keen to prove himself.

'Put the stupid gun away now. I almost shot you. It's safer if I'm the one with the gun, OK?' Dimitri took Marius's pistol from his hand and stuffed it into his own pocket.

'Where's the family?' asked Marius, looking around. 'Should they be in the secure room?'

Dimitri was remarkably calm. 'No. Not yet.' He turned to Marius Falk. 'You're the captain. Your job is to stay alert, OK?'

'Of course,' said Marius. 'But what if this boat has a bomb?'

'A bomb?' said a voice. Erin turned and saw Kai standing there, mouth wide.

'Go inside, sir, please,' said Dimitri.

Erin ran for the companion way to the swimming deck and was in the boat, throwing off the mooring lines in a few seconds.

The oncoming boat was only ten metres away now. Starting the engine, she looked up and saw Dimitri training his pistol on the boat, ready to fire.

Curving away first to port, she turned sharply back to starboard and smacked into the front of the oncoming yacht about two metres behind her bow. The rubber nose of the RIB flattened and she felt the bang of the metal pulpit against the other boat. Flush against the vessel, she pressed the throttle forward, the powerful engines nudging the rogue sailing boat away. The bowsprit swung a metre wide of *Zinaida*'s immaculate hull but didn't touch it.

As the sailing boat turned into the wind coming off the shore, the sheet slackened and the boom swung over its cabin. For the first time she saw the helm clearly. There was no one standing behind it. Now the sail caught the breeze and the boat started to turn back the other way.

'What the fuck is wrong with them?' Dimitri was looking down from the deck above, gun still in his hand.

As far as Erin could see, the boat looked totally deserted. As the sails filled, it heeled a little, picking up speed. Erin read the name on the transom: *Crazy Lady*.

She had averted the collision but had set the runaway boat on a heading towards shallow water behind *Zinaida* where it would ground if it didn't crash into other moored boats first. Erin sighed. No sailor wanted to see a boat damaged. She pushed the throttle again and quickly ran up alongside the yacht, standing, one hand on the wheel, to throw a line around one of the boat's mainsail winches. When the launch was secure she pulled herself up onto *Crazy Lady*, which was gathering speed again, and dropped into the cockpit.

As she stood, she heard applause drifting across the water from *Zinaida*.

Someone had lashed the helm to keep the rudder straight. She freed the wheel and pointed her into the wind. Down at her feet, the cockpit was an ugly tangle of lines, hard to make out in the dark, as if someone had been struggling with the boat and had not had time to tidy the ropes. Had they gone overboard, she wondered? She pulled a torch from her pocket. Looking down, it didn't help that the lines weren't colour-coded. The flapping mainsail was a mess too, fraying on the leech, with stray threads flicking in the wind. Tracking the path of the lines, she found the topping lift and tightened it, then jumped onto the cabin roof to start lowering the mainsail, tugging the cloth down by hand. Halfway down it stuck, caught in the luff track. She yanked hard until it was free, leaving the untidy bundle of sail folded loosely over the boom.

The boat slowed to a standstill and began drifting backwards. Back in the cockpit, she searched for the switch for the windlass, found it, and pressed it, but it was dead. She guessed the boat's batteries were empty. Making her way to the bow, she pulled up the lid to the chain locker and lowered the anchor by hand.

The boat drifted backwards for a little while longer, then stopped in the water. She stood for a while on the gently rocking boat, clutching the forestay. Looking around, the boat she was on was a mess. It wasn't just the mainsail that was in a poor state. She could see without touching them that the shrouds were not tightened enough. The cross-trees were at a crazy angle. The forward hatch was missing and had been replaced by a tarp, tied with rope. *Crazy Lady* was not seaworthy. Back on *Zinaida* she would have to call up the harbourmaster and let them know. At least the boat was anchored now and couldn't do any more damage.

She needed to find the logbook, or any papers, so she pulled the cabin door open and was met by the strong smell of cannabis.

'Shit,' she said.

Shining her torch to the left, the galley showed signs of a recent meal; plates lay in the sink.

Walking through, she pushed open the door to the forward cabin, shone the torch inside and gasped.

In the triangular cabin there were two bodies, a man and a woman, naked in the darkness. Her first thought was that they were dead. But then the naked woman groaned.

'What the fuck?' she mumbled. She sat up, blinking in the torchlight. 'Turn that off.'

'Whose boat is this?' Erin demanded.

The woman pushed hair out of her eyes and she shook her sleeping companion.

'Jacob,' she said. 'I think there's someone to see you.'

An unshaven man with sun-browned skin and sun-bleached hair opened his blue eyes and smiled. 'Hey,' he said.

TWENTY-THREE

Kai joined them clapping again as Erin tied up the boat. Erin didn't look back up at them, as if a little embarrassed by the attention.

It was as if the weather had broken. Everyone's mood had been lifted by the comedy of the incident. It gave everyone the opportunity to forget about Tommy.

'Come up. Have a drink with us,' called Yuliya.

'Thank you, but . . .'

'No. I insist. You were magnificent – wasn't she, Stepan?'

In the end Erin joined them at the table, pulling up a chair to sit awkwardly next to Kai. 'When the man woke up, he said they'd been sold some grass that was much stronger than they'd expected,' she explained.

'Priceless,' said Yuliya.

'They had just set the boat on any heading and gone down to the cabin and got stoned.'

'I'm kind of jealous,' said Zina quietly.

'They don't know what they are doing. They were lucky not to hit rocks or run aground.'

'You were magnificent,' said Stepan. He passed her a glass of champagne. 'Did you see her? You should employ her, Dimitri.'

'Like Napoleon said,' agreed the security man, 'action is all that matters.'

'It was Captain Falk who spotted the threat,' Erin piped up, loyally. Falk, she noted, had not been invited to join them for drinks. After Dimitri had taken his gun he had watched the incident, then looked foolish when the threat had turned out to be simply incompetent sailors.

'It was you who acted on it,' said Dimitri, smiling at her. 'And I'm grateful.'

'It was just a loose boat,' she said. 'It's nothing. Happens all the time.'

It was true. It was just a loose boat. But for a minute, after what had happened with Tommy, all of them had imagined they were under attack. That's how nervous they all were. And now they could all laugh at themselves for being so silly. 'Would you have opened fire on the boat if she hadn't done that?' Kai asked Dimitri.

'Not unless there was an obvious threat,' Dimitri said quietly. 'It wouldn't be good to draw attention to Mr Pirumov unnecessarily.'

'But if you'd decided there was a threat?'

'Of course. That's my job.'

'She said they were both naked,' said Zina. 'Naked and stoned. I wish.'

'Zina,' scolded Yuliya.

'His name is Jacob. He's twenty-three, an app developer,' Erin was saying. 'He's just sold a company he set up when he was eighteen. He told me he bought the boat in Sarasota for eleven thousand dollars. He thought it was a bargain. I told him he should take it to the local boatyard now and see what they'd give him for it and be happy with whatever they offered. It's an old Island Packet. Nobody sells a boat like that for that price unless there's something seriously wrong with it.'

Zina said, 'What about the girl? You said there was a girl on the boat?'

'Yes. Lucy. She's nineteen. He'd persuaded her to join him. *Hey. I got a yacht. Aren't I a big man?*'

'Is that what I'm like?' teased Stepan. 'Hey. I got a yacht. I'm a big man.'

Dimitri laughed.

'Sorry,' said Erin. 'I didn't mean . . .'

Stepan joined the laughter. 'I'm joking.'

She coloured again.

'Marius tells me that's all you want to do – have your own boat like those two and sail around the world by yourself.'

'Yes,' she said, simply.

'Naked,' added Zina.

And everybody but Kai laughed, because the laughter was crueller than he liked. They thought the idea of the short, muscular, slightly masculine Erin, the one who wore unflattering shorts and T-shirts, naked aboard a boat was somehow funny in itself.

'Priceless,' Yuliya said.

Kai looked at Erin sitting among them, clearly embarrassed

140

by the attention but unable to leave because her employer had insisted she join them. 'You know what's really funny?' he said, breaking through their chatter.

The laughter stopped and the entire table looked at him, smiling, expectant.

'A boat with a couple of stoned hippies on it comes up to us and people are brandishing guns at them.' They looked at him, unsure what the punchline was going to be. 'All of us imagined something bad was happening, didn't we? The captain was carrying a gun. How come everyone is on tenterhooks? Will you tell me what's really going on now?'

Conversation stopped. The mood had changed. Yuliya fiddled with the stem of her wine glass.

'What do you think Tommy was planning to do? If I'm going to stay on this boat, I've a right to know.'

He looked at Stepan.

'Actually, no,' said Stepan. 'You don't have a right.' Stepan reached out and took the bottle of whiskey, and poured himself a glass.

'When I hear of a Russian businessman who happens to be a friend of yours falling off a balcony, I kind of assume things,' said Kai.

'Kai,' hissed Zina. 'No.'

'And today I see someone being escorted off the boat with a gun in his back. Seriously? If you're in danger, so is your family. Am I in danger? Is she?' He pointed at Erin.

Stepan put down his glass and spread his arms wide above the table. 'Relax. The danger is over. The man is in custody. We are safe now.'

'So why is everybody so jumpy? Why was everybody freaked out by a little boat that came a little too close?'

There was a pause, then Stepan laughed. 'You're right. We should be calmer. Please. Have a whiskey. It may help.'

'I don't think this is a suitable conversation,' said Yuliya. 'I don't want to hear about any of this.'

All eyes were on Stepan now. Kai was conscious of Erin next to her, trying her hardest to pretend she wasn't there. 'It's true. Martin is dead. Sometimes I wonder if we have gone a little out of fashion with the in-crowd. Like you,' he said eventually.

'People don't usually kill musicians when they go out of fashion.'

'Not yet,' said Stepan with a smile.

Music suddenly blared out of the stereo, making him jump. Zina had cued up some Tupac and had started playing it at full volume. Kai recognised the track: 'Life Goes On'. 'Let's get very, very drunk,' she said, reaching over and taking the whiskey from him.

TWENTY-FOUR

'Get up.'

Someone was banging on Erin's door. Years of single-handed sailing had made Erin a fast waker; she sat straight upright in her dark cabin.

She shook her head, still fuzzy from the whiskey.

'I need you on the bridge immediately.'

Erin snapped fully awake. That was Marius Falk's voice outside her door on the level two landing.

'Up, please. We need to leave.'

She turned on the light, checked her watch and frowned. It was 2 a.m. She looked around. Her cabin was simple. A small shelf of books, mostly about sailing, and a desk with a laptop on it, alongside a framed photograph of her sailing *High Hopes* on Kings Mill Reservoir. She opened her door in a long T-shirt. 'What are you talking about, Marius?'

'We weigh anchor right away.' In the light from her cabin she could see the darkness under his eyes. He looked exhausted.

'Are you OK, Marius? I'm sorry about your job . . .'

'Not now,' he said, flushing. 'It's not about that.' He was a proud man; he didn't like his feelings discussed. 'Just come to the bridge,' he muttered, and he was gone again.

She dressed quickly, then headed up the exterior gangway to the bridge in the dark, pausing to look out at the town. A few street lights were reflected on the water; the place was asleep. So was everyone else on *Zinaida*.

'We need coffee,' was the first thing Marius said when she opened the bridge door. 'Wake up that steward. Strong coffee.'

'Let the kitchen staff sleep. I'll make it.'

Marius scowled.

'Tell me what's the problem first? Why do we need to go?'

Marius was sweating. There were already dark patches under the arms of his freshly ironed white shirt. 'I let someone on board who is a danger to the family.'

'I know. He's in police custody. Listen, Marius . . .' She was struggling to put it into words. Something about that situation with Tommy did not feel right.

But Marius shook his head. 'Not now. He tried to escape, Dimitri had a call from the police station just ten minutes ago to warn me. I don't fucking believe it. The police shot him.'

Erin was shocked. 'Tommy's dead?'

'*Ja*. They think he had accomplices here on the island. They attacked the station. We must go. We have to be safe.'

She was having trouble understanding. 'Tommy is dead? How?'

'His name was not Tommy,' Marius said angrily. 'Some armed

144

men appeared at the police station, Dimitri said. There was a gunfight.'

'Wait, wait, wait,' Erin said. 'He had accomplices?' She looked out of the window, over the bow, into the small town.

'Yes. Accomplices. The police said they were armed. They got away. That's why we have to go. They may be coming to the boat.' He engaged the automatic engine-starting sequence. A moment later she felt the gentle hum beneath her feet.

'Where's Dimitri?'

'He's on deck keeping watch to make sure no boats approach us.'

Shaken, she looked at him a while longer, then said, 'I'll fetch the coffee.'

The galley was deserted, but still warm. It smelt of freshly baked bread. Rather than wait for the coffee machine to be ready, she made instant; three cups. By the time she was back, Dimitri was also on the bridge. He nodded at her, looking grim, took the coffee gratefully.

'You think there are armed men coming for us?'

Dimitri said, 'Let us hope not. But we have to be prepared for an armed attack on this yacht at any time.'

'You're not serious?'

'Of course I am.'

'How could that happen? An armed raid on a police station?'

'A lot of guns in this place,' Dimitri said. 'Crime is pretty bad here.'

Marius had turned slowly to port, away from the town. A light wind was whipping up small waves in the bay. The crests caught the light from the boat, luminous in the darkness. She stared out of the port window into the darkness. Picking up the binoculars she scanned for the silhouette of a boat, first one way and then back again. Their wide arc was taking them close to where she had moored the runaway yacht, but *Crazy Lady* was not there. Lowering her eyes, she checked the radar screen, adjusted it. Nothing. Had she dragged her anchor again, she wondered? Erin had been sure she had left plenty of chain.

'Did you see when the Island Packet left?' she asked Marius.

'What?'

'The hippie boat. She was moored just over there.' She pointed to the eastern side of the bay and then back down at the radar.

He squinted into the light and shook his head. 'You sure there's not just a mast sticking up out of the water? I hope they drowned. Idiots. Are there any boats following us?'

Still looking at the radar, she adjusted the sea clutter setting. Small boats could be hard to spot. Using a radar was like looking at tea leaves at the bottom of a cup; you had to make sense of the pattern. 'Nothing I can see,' she said. 'You should see this though.' She pointed to the next screen. 'The weather's not so good.'

'*Ja.* I've been watching it too.'

The weather system she had been tracking from St Thomas had become messier. It had a name now. Tropical Storm Cora was heading towards Bermuda. It was still twenty-four hours away and they would miss the worst of it. They had plenty of time to make it to Canouan before it made any impact, but the tiny island was not a great anchorage in a storm. It offered little in the way of shelter, but they would be fine. If the storm turned further south, they'd have to head straight out to ride out the bad weather at sea.

146

'What if they do send a boat after us?' asked Erin.

'Just keep looking,' said Dimitri.

She stared at the screen, looking for anomalies. When it came to small boats, radar was not a reliable tool. Weather, wave size and interference from other radars made smaller vessels hard to identify.

'What is this actually about?' demanded Erin.

They were out of the bay now. Marius increased speed, putting distance between him and the island. Dimitri said nothing.

When they were safely out of harbour and putting miles between them and the island, they slowed. Dimitri left them to it to stand on deck with binoculars. There had been no sign of any following craft. She turned to Marius and asked, 'More coffee?'

'Your last one was shit. Make proper coffee this time.'

'You OK?'

He took his cup out of the cup holder on the arm of his chair and handed it to her. 'Stepan told me he is terminating my contract at the end of this voyage. After yesterday you're their golden girl now. They even invite you to join them for drinks. They will probably make you captain.' He was sounding like a child, she thought. 'I call an emergency and it's just a sailing boat. They think I'm a joke. You on the other hand did cool stuff. Round of applause for Erin.'

Unlike her, he genuinely loved this monster of a boat. He resented being thrown off it.

'But you're staying for the rest of the voyage?'

'Who else knows this boat as well as I do?' he answered. 'Even if they think I'm an idiot.' He looked straight at her. 'Were they talking about me? At the dinner table.'

He'd been stewing on it, she supposed. 'No. Not at all. It was just awkward being there, that's all.'

He snorted, adjusted the course, slowed again. 'Still nothing behind?'

She checked again. 'Nothing,' she answered. 'This is crazy . . . right? What are we even running away from?'

The island was falling behind them now, the night ahead was a deep black. There were no navigation lights on the horizon, just empty ocean.

'Remember Martin Artemyev?' Marius said.

She remembered Martin well. He had been a guest on the boat the first time she had gone out on *Zinaida*, a trip around the Mediterranean; a good-looking man with a Parisian model girlfriend who sunbathed nude, smoked cigars and ate nothing. Martin had been an enthusiastic chess player and had challenged Erin to several games because nobody else on the boat played. Though he had always beaten her easily, he had complimented her on her game. 'Of course I remember him,' she said.

'They're saying on the news that he might have been assassinated.'

'Martin is dead?'

'Don't you ever listen to the news, Erin? At first they thought it was suicide. Now some people are saying that maybe he was pushed off the balcony of Stepan's flat in Paris. And if someone was out to get Martin, maybe they're out to get Stepan too.'

'You're kidding. That's insane.'

148

'They were involved in business together. Martin's dead and some fraud bodyguard turns up with a bag full of poison . . . Now this.' Marius was talking fast. 'What I don't understand is why Stepan? Why Martin? I mean . . . Alexander Litvinenko, Boris Nemtsov, Anna Politkovskaya, Alexei Navalny . . . These were people who got in the regime's way. They were the opposition.'

Erin looked at him. She was not interested in politics, but some of the names were familiar.

'It is like a signal,' Marius continued. 'In cases like these there is just enough evidence – so that you can see it is murder, or at least an attempt. Enough so it is a warning to others. But not enough so you can prove anything. It is not just a murder. It is a performance. Am I boring you?'

'No. You're scaring me,' she said.

He nodded. 'You know Sergei Skripal? The Russian intelligence officer who they tried to poison in England? It didn't matter if he died or not. It didn't matter that we all knew it was the Russians' doing, even if they denied it. That was the point. It is a message. A show that is put on for anyone else who is watching, to make them nervous.'

'You think Martin was killed as some kind of message to Stepan?'

'To Stepan? It has certainly made him nervous, hasn't it? It makes me nervous. But I don't understand it. Stepan is not one of these people. He is a friend of the regime. He is on the same side.'

'We're just here to sail their boat,' said Erin. 'You shouldn't be sacked for this. It's not our concern.'

'I'm the captain. Everything that happens on this boat is my concern.'

She did not want to think about it. She did not like the people who came on board this boat; she did not like what they did and how they made their money. People who made this kind of money never did it by being good. In the past she had always told herself that as long as she did her job, what they got up to was nothing to do with her.

'You look tired,' she said.

'A little.'

'You should sleep. I'll do this watch.'

'No,' he said. 'Out of the question.'

She kept her eyes glued on the radar, but there were no boats anywhere near them. She went down to the empty galley and made more coffee. At four in the morning she left Marius to it. One of them should sleep, at least.

TWENTY-FIVE

When Kai woke, the boat was on the move.

In the dining room, Yuliya was complaining to Captain Falk. 'We were supposed to collect fresh oysters before we left.'

The captain looked exhausted. There were dark rings under his eyes. 'Sorry, madam,' he said. 'We had to leave in a hurry.'

'I don't understand why. It was supposed to be fresh oysters and champagne for dinner. We were to collect oysters this morning from St Croix. It was absolutely crucial. Now you have ruined it. Can we get some delivered to us?'

'I'm sorry,' the captain said again, looking at his polished black shoes.

Stepan was at one of the breakfast tables, already at work on a computer. 'Don't worry, Marius. I'll live without oysters.'

'*No ya khotel, chtoby eto bylo osobennoye, Stepan,*' his wife complained.

'It will still be special, I promise, darling. Even without oysters.'

Marissa appeared with coffee. 'Hi there, sir,' she called cheerily up at Kai. 'The chef made coconut milk pancakes. You want to try them?'

'He can't eat too many,' said Yuliya. 'He's about to do yoga.'

'Am I?'

They were setting up yoga on the swimming pool deck. Out at sea today it was too windy on the deck above.

The sea was rougher than it had been the day before, waves slapping against the hull, and the boat was starting to roll gently, but nothing woke Zina. Sitting outside on the pool deck, after the yoga session, Kai drank coffee to try and clear his head and watched the pool water as it sloshed lazily from side to side in the swell. Kai thought about reading the books that had been left in his cabin, but knew it would make him seasick.

He walked around the boat a little aimlessly. *Zinaida* had seemed huge when he had first seen her. He already knew his way around her too well, above deck at least. Below his own level were two more; L2 seemed to be crew cabins, hidden from view. 'Are you lost, sir?' a man dressed only in loose shorts demanded as he passed his half-open door. His voice seemed almost hostile, as if Kai had broken some rule by coming down here. One floor lower, the corridors of L3 were crowded with ducts and wires. He opened a door and found himself in a large workroom, surrounded by computer screens.

A young man looked up from his screen. 'Can I help you, sir?' His accent was East European.

Beyond him, through an open door, Kai saw the engine room, thick white pipes and silver insulation. It looked surgically clean.

There was a man in there dressed in white overalls. He had seen neither of them before; it was as if part of their job was to be invisible.

'Just looking around,' Kai said. In the swell, being in the windowless belly of the boat made him feel sicker. Their smiles were polite, but unwelcoming. This was not his world. He retreated.

After wandering around for another twenty minutes, he found himself on the bridge. Erin said exactly the same as the man in the engine room. 'Can I help you, sir?'

There was no one standing behind the ship's wheel. 'Shouldn't there be someone steering?' he asked.

'Autopilot,' she said.

'Really? Hey. Can I try?'

'Sure.'

She came and stood at the wheel and explained they were on a course of 104 degrees, heading eastwards towards Canouan. 'Just hold it steady on that.' She switched to manual and stood back.

Kai squinted at the small numbers, spun the wheel. The boat moved to the left.

'A little goes a long way,' she said.

'Isn't that the truth? So you don't even have to steer this thing?'

'We only really use manual when mooring. What about you? Nothing better to do, sir?'

'Here in paradise?'

She noted the sarcasm in his voice, but didn't respond.

'You're drifting,' she said.

Kai pulled the boat back to the left. 'So very, very true,' he

153

said. They stood, side by side, and he suddenly felt self-conscious that they were awkwardly close. He concentrated on the needle on the readout: 104 degrees.

All around them, uniform blue sky; even blue sea. Behind them a straight white wake.

'What's that? Radar?' He pointed at a screen above the compass.

'You can set your course on that too, if you prefer. It's a radar display and chart plotter.' She leaned past and pressed a button. A line emerged on the screen. 'That's your course.'

The screen was filled with information, green numbers on the left, white dots within green rings.

'Don't worry. There's nothing closer than twelve nautical miles away right now. You won't hit them, however hard you try.'

'Can I try?'

'No.'

'Can't I wiggle a bit? Go left and right. A figure-of-eight.'

'Waste of diesel.'

'I think Stepan could afford it. What do all these buttons do?' There was a row of half a dozen joysticks, beneath it rows of buttons lit by green LEDs. He lifted a finger, hovered over the buttons.

'Don't.' She looked unamused.

'And what's this?' To his right another screen scattered with small arrows, coloured in red, green, grey, magenta.

'Those are the satellite positions of other vessels.'

'Other boats, right?'

She leaned over him and tapped a green shape on the touch screen. Information appeared: *Black Eagle [US] at 8.3kn / 145°.*

'It's an American container ship,' she said.

154

He pressed another grey shape. *Unidentified Ship. Position received via satellite.*

'It doesn't have an automatic identification system. Probably something small like a local fishing boat. Don't worry. It's miles away and stationary.'

He pressed more shapes on the screen. 'All these ships. It's a bit like trainspotting,' he said. 'Which one is us?'

'We're registered as a yacht.' She pressed the screen. 'There we are.'

He looked at the screen. *Status: Active. Length overall x Breadth Extreme: 90 x 16m. Speed/Course: 12kn / 110°.*

He read the figures and realised it was showing his exact speed and course. 'Shit. One-ten degrees.' He steered a little back to port. 'That's kind of uncanny.'

Now he looked, he saw that this empty sea seemed full of ships. He flicked through container ships, oil tankers, sailing yachts and fishing boats. Mostly, it was larger vessels in open water. Yachts and sailing boats clustered around the islands.

'Up until thirty years ago people had to sail using compasses and keep their eyes wide open,' she said.

'You sound like you disapprove.'

'For the last five thousand years you had to understand the sea in order to sail on it. These days, any idiot can helm a boat.'

'You're welcome,' he said.

For the first time, she laughed. It was a deep-bellied, rewarding sound. 'Exactly. Before GPS you had no idea about all this other stuff around you. It felt like you were alone out here. Look at this . . .' She pointed at the screens in front of her. 'These days it's like being in a shopping mall.'

155

He carried on pressing the symbols and looking at their names. Erin left him to it and moved on to the chart table, writing some notes on a clipboard.

'What if it all went wrong?' she said. 'Half the sailors at sea these days would be lost without it. What if the satellites went down? What if they had to rely on dead reckoning and celestial navigation? It would be chaos out there.'

'There are musicians like you,' he said. 'They want to go back to acoustic instruments.'

She laughed again.

He smiled. 'You would want to be out here on your own, then?'

'God, yes.'

He tried to imagine it. 'Isn't that scary?'

'Absolutely.'

'Scarier than being on a boat with this family?'

'I really couldn't say,' she said, but she was definitely smiling.

He steered a while longer because being up here looking out at the horizon had stopped him feeling seasick and because this felt like the sanest place on this strange ship.

'I can switch it back to automatic pilot, if you like,' she said.

'No. I'll stick to acoustic instruments for now. I'll be honest. The family is doing my head in.'

'What about your girlfriend?'

He changed the subject. 'Is that a storm?' He pointed to yet another screen that was showing the weather radar.

'Yes it is. The edges of it are going to hit us in about twelve hours, the rate it's travelling. Don't worry, we'll be safely at Canouan by then.'

'A bad one?'

She shook her head. 'Not by Caribbean standards. We'll have thirty or forty of these this year. Gusting to fifty-mile-an-hour winds at worst. You'll feel it but it won't do much damage. More than likely it's going to bring a lot of rain with it. We'll probably ride it out at sea, just to be on the safe side.'

'That's the safe side?'

'Safer at sea than being near land. There's nothing to hit when you're at sea. We were off St Thomas when Hurricane Dorian passed through here. There were seventy-five-mile-an-hour winds around us and that was fun. Over in the Bahamas they recorded one-hundred-and-eighty-five-mile-an-hour winds.'

'You'd have liked that even better, I expect.'

'Maybe I would,' she said. 'It's pretty cool to feel what nature can do, sometimes. Puts you in your place.'

It was good talking. Maybe it was that they were both Brits. The next thing, she was telling him all about about how she had sailed around Britain with her uncle Ben as a fifteen-year-old, and how she'd bought a dinghy called *High Hopes*. When she was telling him about sailing, she was a different person from the frosty, awkward woman he had talked to before.

'When I was seventeen, I got this job in a boatyard. I loved that job so much, but—'

'Hey. Funny thing,' he said, interrupting abruptly. 'You know you said that stuff about what happens if these instruments stop working?'

'What?'

'Come and look at this.'

'Are you messing about again?'

'No. Seriously. Have I done something wrong?'

She stood and approached the wheel. 'See,' he said. 'That's us there, right?' He clicked on a boat on the screen in the middle of the pale blue sea. *Zinaida. Yacht. Status: Active. Length overall x Breadth Extreme: 90 x 16m. Speed/Course: 19kn / 104°.*

'Yes.'

He clicked on another boat shape, to the south. 'I was just flicking around and I saw this one.'

He clicked on the symbol. It read. *Zinaida. Yacht. Status: Active. Length overall x Breadth Extreme: 90 x 16m. Speed/Course: 28kn / 352°.* 'Two of us. I mean. That's not right, is it?'

She leaned past Kai. He watched her click back onto their boat, and then to the other one. And back again, frowning.

'That's crazy,' she whispered.

'It wasn't there a second ago. I'd swear it. It just appeared, so I pressed on it to see what it was, and . . .'

Erin stared a while longer, then nudged him out of the seat and pressed an intercom button. 'Marius? Are you there? Can you come to the bridge?'

She sat there in the chair, hunched over the screen, flicking from one boat to the other. And then, with them both looking at it, the second boat simply disappeared again. Where it had been there was nothing. It was as if it had somehow sunk in the pale blue ocean of the screen, or as if it had never been there at all.

TWENTY-SIX

'That's crazy,' Erin had said, trying to figure out what had caused this spectre of a ship to appear, then disappear. She had always believed that trusting instruments was a mistake, but they always told you something. The difficulty was working out what. She had seen the two identical markers with her own eyes. She was struggling to understand how a glitch like that could have possibly happened.

Marius Falk arrived, red-faced, from the cabin at the back of the bridge where he had been sleeping.

'What this time?'

Erin explained that there had been a double of their own ship on the screen, but it had disappeared.

'Show me.'

But however long they looked at the screen for, the boat didn't show itself again.

'*Det er umulig,*' breathed the captain. 'Impossible.'

He summoned Aleksander, the ETO, to the bridge as well. The Pole arrived looking wary. 'Is something wrong, Captain?'

Erin explained what she and Kai had seen and the man frowned. 'Are you sure you didn't make a mistake?'

'We both saw it.'

Kai nodded in agreement. The ETO said, 'I have no explanation.'

'Maybe the weather?' said Falk. The tropical storm was to the west. 'Or could there be a problem with how we are encoding our own position?'

This made sense to Erin. Each ship recorded its own position and broadcast it to nearby vessels using VHF. If the ship's own instruments were malfunctioning, it could be sending out the wrong signal.

The ETO seemed to be thinking this through. 'Possible. Maybe there is an issue in our own navigation software. I must look.'

'I mean . . . we can't be in two places at once,' said Marius.

Erin glanced at him. 'Do we need to tell Dimitri? Just in case . . .'

They both turned to the ETO. 'Sure. It's a mirage. We just need to know what caused it.'

'A ghost ship,' Marius suggested.

'If you like.'

'Sort it out. As soon as you can. I don't want any more alarms,' said Marius. He turned to Kai, suddenly aware that he was not one of the crew. 'I'm sure it is nothing to worry about,' he told him, with as reassuring a smile as he could manage.

'Everyone is jumpy,' said Kai. 'What are you so worried about?'

160

They all looked at him, but nobody answered. Erin realised the guests had been told nothing about why they had weighed anchor so early from St Croix.

'Well. I should probably go,' said Kai.

'Not at all. Guests are welcome here all the time,' Marius said, unenthusiastically, looking from him to Erin. 'Though your girlfriend is downstairs on her own.'

'She's awake?'

'She is downstairs by the pool drinking coffee, I think.'

'Thanks for the navigation lesson,' Kai said, smiling at Erin, and then left. The ETO followed him out of the door.

'Navigation lesson?' Marius repeated, now he was gone, his voice heavy with sarcasm.

'He was bored. I talked him through the GPS navigation and the AIS.'

Marius looked disapproving. 'He must have been very bored.'

'You're jealous?' she said.

Marius raised his chin a centimetre. 'Not at all. He has a very beautiful girlfriend, after all. Why would he want you?'

And with that, he too left her. 'Captain Asshole,' she said to the empty bridge.

She thought about her boat *High Hopes*. She had loved that dinghy. It was the absolute opposite of the ship she was on now, and it had taught her a lot.

At seventeen, she had taken a job in a boatyard in a town called Coningsby, east of where she had grown up, far enough away to feel like she had left home. It wasn't the ideal job. Erin had a contempt for the kind of cruisers they worked on there.

They were more like floating caravans than real boats, and the coyness of their names annoyed her; *Ice and a Slice*, *Living the Dream* and *Bjorn Free* were all moored up in the old canal dock, gathering bright weed on their hulls. But the job gave her a chance to learn diesel engines and electrics, which she knew she would need to know if she was going to sail around the world.

She was free of her suffocating parents. She lived in a bedsit above the main boatyard workshop, with a tiny Baby Belling cooker, a single bed and a small square window with four panes, looking out onto the river. It was the smaller of two rooms, tucked under the eaves.

Erin returned home every weekend of her first month to face the tight-lipped disappointment of her parents who had expected her to go to university. On the fourth weekend home, her father told her he had arranged an internship for her with a local office supplies firm. After that she made excuses and started spending her weekends in Coningsby and not going home at all.

The man who owned the boatyard was called Marshall and he was in his early thirties, fair-haired, handsome and kind. He was married to Jill, a plain-faced woman who brought him lunch every day, and who, upon learning that Erin had nothing to eat herself, started bringing a second lunch for her wrapped in silver foil. There would be a different sandwich for every day of the week and a single boiled egg already shelled with a small wrap of salt. In a separate compartment within the foil, tucked up in greaseproof paper, were three digestive biscuits and a slab of homemade cake. The package, so carefully and lovingly constructed, seemed superior to anything her parents had ever given her to eat.

Jill had all the warmth Erin wished her own mother had had.

She understood that Erin was sometimes homesick and lonely but she never once mentioned it. 'You can always come and have dinner with us, if you like. We get so bored, the two of us, rattling around together,' she said.

Erin accepted the invitation. And soon she was going round there two or three days a week. 'Why do you only let Erin have that poky little room? The other bedroom is much nicer.'

'I'm fine, honestly,' said Erin. 'I like my room. It looks out on the water.'

'Or she could stay here sometimes. No. You like it on your own, don't you?'

Erin nodded.

'I think you're amazing,' said Jill. 'You're so brave. Your parents must be so proud of you. The things you're going to do . . .'

She loved Jill, though sometimes she found it hard to escape her hugs at the end of an evening. In truth, she liked more than anything to be up in the small room, with the smells of grease and penetrating oil rising from the workshop below.

On *Zinaida*'s bridge, she could smell it now and wished she was back there.

In the early winter, Ben drove up to visit in an open-topped Saab.

She was thrilled to see him, giving him a hug as he stepped out of the car.

'Your hands are filthy. Get off me,' he said, only half in jest.

It was true. Her hands were black with oil. She and Marshall had been stripping down a very old BMC Diesel engine that was suffering from condensation; many of the parts had become so seized up it had taken them the whole morning to dismantle it.

Marshall emerged from behind the workshop's big wooden door in a white T-shirt smudged with grease. 'And who is this?' demanded Ben.

'This is Marshall. He's my boss.'

'Hello, Marshall,' said Ben with a smile, and when he held out his hand to shake, Erin noticed that he didn't seem to mind that Marshall's hands were even dirtier than hers. 'I was thinking pub lunch. Is there anywhere nice round here?' The question was directed towards Marshall, not her.

Marshall suggested the Tattershall Park, a five-minute drive away, and when they'd all cleaned up he drove them, top down, Marshall and Ben in the front seats, Erin perched in the back, freezing cold but not minding it at all as Ben accelerated down the dual carriageway towards the pub.

Ben and Marshall both drank pints of lager. At seventeen, Erin didn't like alcohol at all. Ben plied Marshall with questions about boats and engines. The two men seemed to form an instant friendship. After a lunch which Ben insisted on paying for he offered to drive them back to the yard.

'You can't! You're drunk,' said Erin.

'It's only a few minutes,' protested Ben.

He backed out of the parking space fast, snapping her head back, then drove straight out into traffic, oblivious of car horns, speeding through a red light on the Sleaford Road, Marshall laughing beside him and Erin thinking she was going to die.

'Are we going to finish the engine?' she asked as she climbed out over the side of the Saab.

'Nah. Let's do that tomorrow. Why don't you start sanding down *Rest-A-Whyle*.' The owner had delivered her the previous week. The boat had been smashed into while on its mooring and when they had winched her out of the water, they had discovered a long crack in the GRP hull.

When she had emerged from the workshop with the electric sander on a long cable, protective goggles ready on her forehead, and looked up at the window of the other bedroom, the one next to hers, she saw that the curtains had been pulled shut.

She knew gay men; she just had never realised Uncle Ben was one of them. The friendships he had struck up on their trips together suddenly came into perspective.

Marshall was a surprise though.

When Jill had appeared the following morning with her shiny pack of sandwiches, she was conscious of Marshall watching her closely. Erin blushed as she accepted them, not knowing what to say. Jill's husband had cheated on her with another man and she was expected to keep that secret.

'What's wrong?' asked Jill. 'Don't I get a hug this morning?'

She worked through the early winter at the boatyard. She never talked about what had happened with Uncle Ben, or with Marshall. Several times more Jill invited her round to their house for supper, but after that Erin always refused, staying alone in her room.

When she went home at Christmas, Ben didn't come around as he had done every year. He said he was a little below the weather. When her dad asked her when she was going back to the boatyard, she said, 'I'm not.' She never called Marshall to tell him she wasn't coming back. He never called her either, to ask her why she had not come.

She was angry at Ben. She had liked working at the boatyard and he had ruined that for her.

People were so messed up. Her mum, her dad, her uncle Ben, her schoolfriends who talked endlessly about boys. It was around then that she decided she would prefer to make her voyage around the world completely alone.

By the afternoon there were still no boats chasing after them; nothing showed on the radar. There had been no other AIS glitches. Marius seemed to relax a little. Erin took a break in her room. She would be on duty again at midnight for the next watch.

She lay on her bunk and tried to rest. Up until now she had always felt safer out here in open water, miles from land. She thought about the expression on Tommy's face the last time she had seen him. It was as if he had known he was going to die.

For a while she slept fitfully. She dreamed of the terrible things that happen at sea, of uncharted rocks, of faulty keels that sheered, of being tossed overboard without a line, but the dreams didn't feel like sleep.

At ten she sat up, wide awake, because something had occurred to her. Marius Falk had said Tommy had been killed in a gunfight at the St Croix police station. They kept a twenty-four-hour watch. How come nobody aboard had heard it? The police station was on the east side of the small town, not far from the water, and they were moored close enough to shore to have heard any gunshots. They only had Dimitri's word for it that the gunfight had even happened.

She was wide awake now; anxious. She dressed and went to

the galley. The kitchen smelt delicious, warm and reassuring. The chef was there kneading dough for the morning's bread.

'Where is everybody?'

'They went to bed. The guests are all in their rooms. Last night they all drank too much. Tonight they sleep and I work. Yesterday Madame Pirumova wanted Wagyu beef for lunch tomorrow. Today she wants Ayam Cemani chicken,' he said, smiling.

She made herself a cup of cocoa and left him to it. Not wanting to go to the bridge until she had to, she took the mug out onto the swimming deck at the stern of the boat and sat watching the pale wake behind them for a while, thinking.

The evening was close. She would have time for a shower and a change of clothes before her watch. She checked the time, stood, and took the service door behind the stairs, towards her cabin on L2.

Inside, she noticed that the door at the top of the next stairs – deck level – was swinging open. Cup in hand, she went up to close it in time to see a shape moving on the spiral staircase. A glimpse of bare feet on the subtly illuminated treads. Someone was trying not to be heard.

She pushed open the door and followed up the stairs. It was none of her business, she thought, but she went up anyway.

Her head was just at the level with the floor above in time to see Kai disappearing into Zina's cabin. He had taken the rear stairs to avoid going past the Pirumovs' cabin, she guessed. From inside, she heard a suppressed giggle.

None of her business, she thought darkly. He was just another asshole too. She headed back down to L2.

167

TWENTY-SEVEN

Dinner had been a subdued affair. The family ate *pelmeni* with *smetena* – Russian dumplings made with lamb and soured cream. The chef had filled some with mushrooms for Kai and made a vegan cream from cashew nuts. After dinner Stepan and Yuliya had gone to bed. 'Everything is fine,' Stepan said, smiling.

When they had gone, Zina lifted up her purse onto the table and took out a wrap of coke. 'Want some?'

Kai shook his head. 'I don't do it.'

'You're duller than I expected, you know?'

'Can I get you guys anything else?' Marissa had been in the room all the time, Kai realised.

'You want some coke, Marissa? I hate taking drugs on my own. It makes me feel like I'm some low-down dirty addict. Which I'm not.' She wiped her nostril clean.

Marissa laughed, but didn't answer.

Zina stood and picked a paper straw from a glass on the table and held it out towards her. 'Come on, Marissa. Have some.'

The chief steward hesitated. 'I don't know. Your dad wouldn't like it.'

'You bought me it, Marissa.'

'I mean. I'm kind of working here.' Marissa laughed a little more awkwardly this time.

'It's an order, Marissa. You have to do it. Come on. This is all your fault. You got me enough coke here to sink the United States Navy. Please.' Marissa looked at the line Zina was preparing, using a table knife to mash and separate the powder. In a sing-song voice, Zina cajoled, 'I can tell you're tempted.'

Kai watched the steward hesitate. 'Don't, Zina. It's not fair.'

Zina ignored him. 'Your job is to keep us happy. Think of this as your job, Marissa.'

'Don't,' said Kai again.

'Jesus, Kai. You are such a spoilsport. Come on, Marissa. I can tell you're a party girl at heart.'

'Just one itsy-bitsy line, OK?' Marissa took the straw.

'Attagirl, Marissa.' There was something triumphant about Zina's smile. She picked up her phone and changed the hip hop music up a notch.

Kai had seen enough. 'I'm going to bed.'

'Go then,' said Zina, not looking at him.

He walked down the stairs to the main cabin, then out onto the pool deck.

The wind had come up. There was a steady roll to the boat as she moved through the water now. Down on the deck below, he saw Erin; she was sitting on her own, drinking something from a

169

mug. He considered going down and talking to her, but he was in a black mood. He wished he was in London.

In his own cabin he sat in the armchair, switched on the TV and flicked through films. It didn't help that there were over six hundred titles to choose from; mostly blockbusters from the last decade. The choice was stifling.

He was not tired. He switched off the screen and looked around the room. His eyes lighted on the books Tommy had left for him, lying on the floor by his bed. He sighed, picked one up, sat down again, opened it and tried to start at the beginning. It opened with an American major having a heart attack in a seedy North Carolina motel. He turned the page. The hero was being called up to investigate.

Pouring himself a fizzy water from the fridge, he returned to the chair and noticed a small rectangular card of paper on the white armchair. Strange. It hadn't been there when he'd sat down.

It must have fallen out; someone's bookmark, he guessed. There was printed writing on it. *Thomas R. Scadder. Private Security Consultant.* Tommy. There was a number, too. Kai wondered if it had belonged to the man who had been taken off the boat in Christiansted, or to the man he had impersonated.

He was about to put it back into the book when he saw that there was some tiny writing on the reverse of the card. He read it.

Dear Sir. Here are some books you might like to read. If you have any concerns about your safety or the safety of others on this boat, please share them <u>directly</u> with me or Captain Falk. Faithfully, Tommy.

Kai wondered why the word 'directly' had been underlined. It was disturbing to receive a message from the man who had been sent to kill them. And there was something disturbing about the message itself. What did he mean, 'directly'?

He sat up in the armchair. If the security guard had not been an impostor, this would have been a perfectly innocent message; instead, the message appeared to implicate the captain in the plot too: '*share them directly with me or Captain Falk*'. His skin prickled.

If Tommy had been part of the plot, then Captain Falk was too. Dimitri had suspected that Tommy had not acted alone. Kai needed to share this information.

The staff were on the deck below him; he didn't know which cabin belonged to Dimitri, but the other staff would. He left his room bare-footed, closing the door and tiptoeing up two floors. The boat seemed dead; the hallway lights were dimmed. Ahead of him, the dining room where he'd last seen Marissa was empty, the table already cleared. The crew seemed to have gone to bed.

Returning to the landing he saw a light visible through the peephole in Zina's cabin door. She would know where Dimitri was quartered. He approached and knocked gently.

There was no answer. He hesitated. Zina could have fallen asleep with the lights on, or be in the shower, or be listening to music with her headphones on.

He knocked a little louder. The light in the peephole dimmed. There was someone looking back at him. The door opened.

'Well, well, well,' said Zina. 'Goody two-shoes. Come for a little candy?' From behind her came a giggle.

She opened the door wide to let him in. Marissa was sitting cross-legged on the floor, a cigarette in her hand.

'Hi there.' Marissa smiled sweetly. 'We've been talking about all sorts of stuff. Your boyfriend has a cute face.'

'Turns out Marissa here is quite the party girl.' Kai went to close the door behind him, and as he did, thought he caught a glimpse of someone on the stairs behind him and shut the door as quietly as he could. 'What are you doing here anyway, boyfriend?'

'I should go,' said Marissa, checking her watch. 'You guys need to be together.' She grinned goofily at them. She stood unsteadily as the boat rolled. 'Bye, cute face. I feel real hot. Does anyone else feel like it's way too hot in here?' she said, and burst out laughing.

'Marissa. Which is Dimitri's cabin?'

'Why?'

He hesitated. 'I just need to know.'

'L27,' she said. 'I wouldn't try him now. I think he's sleeping. Hey, I should really go. I have to be up at five. Jesus. I'm going to pay for this.' She laughed. Kai opened the cabin door for her as she headed out into the corridor.

'Don't look so disapproving. Jesus. You're such an old man sometimes. What do you need Dimitri for?' she demanded.

He was about to tell Zina about the business card he had found and the note that had been written on the back when –

The room went black.

'What the fuck?'

Pitch black. All the lights in the room had gone out.

'What the actual fuck?'

Kai pulled his phone out of his pocket and fumbled to find the torch function, but by the time he had, the dim green glow of the emergency lighting had begun to cut through the blackness. The screen showed the time as 11.50.

'That has never, ever happened,' said Zina.

'What?'

'Jesus. Seriously. This is not supposed to happen.'

'Hush,' said Kai. 'Listen.'

The strange thing was that there was no noise at all, apart from a distant slapping of water against the hull of the boat. The engines had stopped.

'What is going on?'

They were not the only ones awake now. They heard noises of people moving elsewhere in the boat, though it was hard to tell where they were coming from.

And then the clear sound of a single gunshot.

Kai was not a man familiar with violence, but the noise was unmistakable. It was impossible to tell where it had come from, whether it was on this deck, above or below.

'Lock the door,' shouted Zina, her voice suddenly high.

As Kai stumbled towards the door there was another shot; and then a short sustained burst of automatic gunfire. He turned the lock on the handle, then looked round and saw, in the dim green light, Zina's white face, hands over her ears, eyes wide with fright.

TWENTY-EIGHT

None of her business, Erin had thought, as she saw Kai disappear into Zina's cabin. Just another asshole.

But not wanting to disturb the family, she had crept as silently as she could back down the three floors to where the staff cabins were.

Her cabin was L21, down on L2. Odd, she thought as she reached that floor. Something was off. It took a second for her to realise what it was. She was sure she had closed her cabin door, but perhaps she hadn't. It was swinging open now and closing again in the boat's slow roll.

There was the mug she had just drunk from, and a plate she had eaten her dinner off on the small desk. She shrugged, checked her watch. Quarter to midnight. She still had time to wash off the evening's tropical sweat. She ran a cool shower and stepped in it just for a minute and thought about Kai going to Zina's cabin and what would be happening there. Not that she gave a damn at all.

*

She had never been successful with relationships. At eighteen she had moved south to the Hamble and worked in a boatyard there, crewing for anyone who would have her. If you wanted a boat of your own, you needed money or sponsors, and to get sponsors you needed to make your name racing. She checked the online bulletin boards where people posted messages when they were were short-handed and hung out in pubs where the weekend racing teams hung out. During her first winter she sailed eight days in a row in the Hamble Winter Series in some of the worst weather she'd sailed in, and word started to go around about her skills. After races there was always time in the pub. A few fellow crew members made passes at her. The sex was short-term, just as her time in their boats was.

The next year she heard Uncle Ben was dead. He had driven off a road in his open-topped Saab; it had rolled and crushed him to death. When they checked his blood he was three times over the limit. It was a shock to realise, looking back, how unhappy he had always been. He had always joked he was going to leave his fortune to her, but he had never made a will and there was no fortune anyway.

At twenty, a thirty-four-year-old marine engineer she had slept with twice proposed to her. When she turned him down he took it badly. When crewing opportunities started to dry up, she found out later that he'd been posting messages about her on the bulletin boards, warning other crews that she was temperamental, selfish and hard to work with.

When she dreamed of sailing, though, it was all about sailing alone, competing in the Mini Transat single-handed across the Atlantic, or better the Vendée Globe, around the world. The single-handed racing scene was small, with more people wanting to be part of it than there were chances to sail, and financially it was always just out of her reach. She was awkward, spiky and bad at making the right connections.

That was the year she got a place crewing on the Istanbul Europa, which was to be her longest race yet. Skippering the boat to Istanbul to deliver it, she hit a rogue wave in the Bay of Biscay and the boat was knocked down, damaging its mast, so it missed the start. It wasn't her fault, and the owner never blamed her. If anything, the incident increased her reputation as an up-and-coming sailor who could cope with whatever the sea threw at her. Offers started to come in. Finally there was talk of sponsorship for the 2004 Québec–Saint Malo. It was her chance to make it onto the ladder.

At the time she was dating an Austrian sailor called Eric, who was good-looking, seemed to be caring and kind, and was talking about the two of them moving in together. That winter, her mother had a stroke while she was gardening. Her father found her lying between the raised beds. When she came out of hospital it was in a wheelchair; her speech was difficult to understand. Her father didn't cope well. Her disability angered him. Erin moved home to look after her. A month later, when he posted a new relationship status on Facebook, she found out Eric was dating another woman. She wrote to her sailing team and told them they would have to find someone else for the Québec–Saint Malo.

At the start of it, she assumed that the stay at home would be temporary, but she ended up looking after them both for the next seven years. It was hard work. She didn't go near a boat, nor

176

men, all that time. She got over the disappointment. It had never happened for her, but there was nothing she could do about it.

She dried herself quickly and put on fresh black shorts and a black T-shirt, and when she checked her watch she saw it was still only just after quarter to twelve. She had time to take her crockery back to the galley on the way to the bridge.

This time she tugged on her door to make sure she heard the lock click, then, plate and cup in hand, shook her head, and set off towards the front of the boat.

The corridors were dim, but the galley shone with bright light ahead of her and the smell of cooking wafted into the corridor. When she entered the cabin this time, it was strangely silent. She looked around. There was no one here, though the kitchen still looked occupied. The dough lay rising in a bowl. A leek lay on the counter, on a white board, half chopped into tiny fine rings. On the hob, a stock pan sat on top of a gas flame. The chef must have gone to the bathroom, or gone outside for a cigarette.

She opened the dishwasher and added her plate and cup to the shelves and then paused.

She sniffed the air. It took a second to realise that something was burning. Above the sound of water on the hull and the low hum of the engine, she could hear a faint crackling sound too. She looked back at the pot. Black smoke was starting to drift upwards from it.

She looked around again, called down the corridor, 'Chef?'

Receiving no answer, she stepped past the stainless steel island that sat in the middle of the galley to switch off the pot before it set off the smoke alarm, and as she reached to twist the dial, she slipped on something on the tiled floor, her right leg sliding forwards in front of her. She kept her balance only by grabbing the side of the cooker. She looked down. The floor was slick and red.

The chef must have spilt some kind of meat *jus*, she decided. That thought was gone in a fraction of a second.

To her left, between the island and the big fridge, the cook lay face down on the floor, still, fresh blood circling from beneath his chest. As the boat rolled, the blood flowed a little further across the floor towards her until the boat rocked back the other way and it retreated.

She must have screamed briefly, she realised afterwards, but she cannot have made much noise. Mouth wide, she squatted down to get a better look at him, but she didn't need to go any closer to see that he was dead.

His eyes were open, staring at the floor tiles below him. The cut the knife had made across his throat had been deep and vicious. Even face down, the gaping edge at the side of his neck was clearly visible. She hadn't known him – she hadn't really had time – but he was crew, and she and Marius had been responsible for him. Heart thumping, she stepped over the blood, switched off the gas, grabbed a fire blanket from a case that hung next to the cooker and put it over the smoking pan –

And then the lights went out.

Suddenly dark, the room was lit now only by the dim green of the emergency lighting.

Seeing the dead man had been a jolt, but now her heart was racing so hard she could hear the thumping herself.

Her first thought was that there was someone else in the galley and whoever had killed him could be anywhere in this darkness.

'Hello?' she said, nervously.

The intercom was next to the door, she knew. She looked towards it and saw it in the blackness; the buttons were luminous, designed to be found in emergencies just like this.

She stepped back across the blood, reached the intercom, pressed the button and called loudly, 'Marius.' There was no answer.

'First mate to the bridge. Urgent. Please answer.'

Still silence. She strained her ears. A third time she tried, more desperately. 'This is Erin. Urgent. Respond now please.' It was impossible to tell whether the intercom was dead too, or whether there was just nobody on the other end.

It was then she realised how profound the quiet was. Alongside the lights going off, the ship's engines had cut out. It wasn't that someone had switched off the lights in the galley; the whole boat was dead. She felt the shift in motion as the ocean swell started to take control of her.

The silence was broken by a gunshot, then, a few seconds later, a second, followed by a quick burst of fire.

179

TWENTY-NINE

There was a banging on the door to Zina's cabin. '*Skorree! Zina. Otkroy dver!*'

Zina's mother was outside screaming.

'What's going on?' Kai shouted. He opened it. Yuliya stood in a dark nightdress; she didn't have time to look shocked by finding a man in her daughter's bedroom.

'To the safe place. To the safe place,' she urged.

Stepan, behind her, dressed in a T-shirt and sleeping shorts, pushed past his wife and grabbed Kai's arm to yank him out into the corridor. 'Fast. Fast.'

'What's going on?'

'I don't fucking know. We must be under attack,' said Zina. She grabbed Kai's hand and pulled him, following her father down the stairs.

'Hurry,' shouted Stepan.

Attackers must have boarded them in the darkness. Kai

remembered Dimitri's nervousness when the yacht had almost collided with them off Christiansted.

Stepan ran on down the dark stairs, towards L1.

'Here. *Zdes.*'

Stepan was already holding the door to the citadel open for them. Though the rest of the ship was dark, inside, it was dazzlingly bright. Yuliya and Zina entered; Kai followed, blinking in the light, Stepan close behind. The moment all four were inside Stepan pulled the door closed and pressed a button on the keypad to the side of it. Kai could hear the carefully engineered mechanism locking the door.

'Safe,' breathed Yuliya.

'Papa. What's happening? Where is Dimitri?'

Stepan pushed past Kai to the opposite end of the room. He opened the door to one of the stainless steel lockers and pressed a button in what looked like a communications panel. 'Captain Falk?' There was no answer. 'Captain,' he called again. Still nothing. *'Kakogo chyerta!'*

'What's wrong?' Yuliya demanded.

'There's nobody on the bridge. They are not answering.' He stood still, staring at the board.

'Where is Dimitri?' wailed Zina.

'He is outside fighting the pirates,' declared Yuliya.

'Are there pirates? Did you see pirates?' Stepan demanded, turning towards them.

And then they were all shouting. 'I saw nobody . . .' 'I heard guns . . .' 'I went to get our daughter . . .' 'Who saw what? What did you hear?'

'Shut up,' cried Zina. 'Shut up. Shut up. Listen.'

181

The shouting stopped. They listened. For a second the boat was silent, until another burst of gunfire rang out. 'Who is out there?' Stepan raged. 'What happened? Why didn't the captain warn us?'

'What if the captain is one of them?'

'One of who?' Kai demanded. He thought of the note Tommy had left him but said nothing.

Zina was sobbing now. Yuliya put her arms around her daughter. Stepan quietened finally. He looked pale. 'Everything is OK,' he said, eventually. 'We are safe here. Nobody can harm us. We have to do as we are instructed. There is the alarm. We are supposed to activate it.'

Kai watched him turn back to the communications board and lift a small plastic cover and press the red button that lay beneath it. Kai had expected an alarm to sound throughout the ship, but there wasn't anything.

They looked at Stepan expectantly. 'I can't hear anything,' Yuliya said.

'It is silent. It doesn't alert the attackers. Just a satellite transmission to shore stations. Except . . .' He frowned. Pressed the button again and again.

'Except what, Papa?'

He looked at the panel, leaning a little close to it. 'The light is supposed to come on when you use it.'

'Maybe the light is broken,' said Yuliya.

He pressed it again and again. 'Maybe,' answered Stepan, dubiously.

'Is it working, Dad?' asked Zina.

'Of course it is working!'

Kai looked around. The room they were in was basic. There were four bunks by the door and, beyond them, two small sofas facing each other. Beyond that was the bank of lockers in which the communications panel sat, and to its left, the door to the toilet. Mounted on the ceiling was what looked like a large air-conditioning unit.

'They cannot get at us. This room is bombproof,' Stepan announced. 'It has its own air and its own water. It is completely sealed off from the outside. It runs off its own emergency power system. We can last forty-eight hours in here. Everything will be fine.'

'Jesus,' said Zina. 'What is going on, Dad?'

'People will come and rescue us soon.'

There was another gunshot. The four looked at each other.

'Where is Dimitri?'

'He is out there protecting us,' said Yuliya.

'Who from?'

Stepan looked uncertain. '*Ya ne znayu.* I don't know.'

'What did you do, Dad? Why is this happening to us?'

'Zinaida,' scolded Yuliya.

'Seriously? They killed Martin and they're trying to kill us. What did you do? Why is this happening?'

Her father didn't answer. They listened for more gunfire, but could hear none.

'Tell us, Dad. What do you think is going on?' asked Zina.

'Leave your father alone,' said Yuliya.

Stepan lowered himself onto one of the couches. 'We wait.'

There was a bang on the door that made them all jump.

'Who's there?' Yuliya called.

Then another bang.

'Shit,' said Zina. 'Is that them?'

'They cannot get in,' repeated her father.

Then, from the other side of the door came a quiet, 'Hey!' Then a knock.

'Is it them?'

The voice was plaintive and frightened. 'Guys. Can you please let me in?' It was Marissa.

Kai looked at all three of them, one after the other. None of them moved. 'Well?'

Still they did nothing. He pushed past Zina and went to the door. To the left there was a green button that said OPEN. He pressed it but nothing happened. 'Is it down, too?'

'No. It's locked,' said Stepan. 'You can't open it without the key code.'

'Hey.' Another bang on the door.

'Give me the key code then.'

Stepan looked at him. 'We don't know if she's alone. It may be a trick.'

Kai put his eye to the peephole in the door. In the fish-eye lens, Marissa stood on the other side, on her own, looking very small. He could see her face wet from tears; her lower lip was trembling. 'There's no one else there. I can see. Quick,' he said.

'They may be hiding,' said Stepan. 'Using her to persuade us to open the door.'

'Guys. I'm real scared.' Through the thick metal door her voice was muffled, but the words were still easy to make out. As Kai watched, there was another burst of gunfire and the woman

184

flinched down, out of sight now. When she stood again, Kai could see she was trembling in fear. Her mouth was forming the word 'please', repeatedly.

'Are you on your own?' called Kai.

There was no answer.

'You can't just leave her out there.'

'It's a trick,' said Yuliya.

'She's on her own. Give me the fucking code.' He turned round to look at Zina. 'Christ's sake, Zina. Come and see for yourself.'

Zina said nothing.

'The boyfriend was in Zina's room when I went to fetch her.' Yuliya spoke quietly.

'That's the single least important thing in the world, Mama.'

'Zina. Tell your parents to let her in.'

'Procedure is clear,' said Stepan quietly. 'When the door is locked you don't open it until the ship is safe. That is it. End of story. When Dimitri tells us it is safe, we open the door.'

'And what if he's dead?' Kai said.

'Then we wait for the special forces to arrive.'

'Of course he is not dead,' said Yuliya. 'He is trained for this.'

Kai must have looked incredulous. 'And if the special forces don't come?'

'We wait,' insisted Stepan.

There was another burst of gunfire and a scream. Everyone in the room flinched, including Kai.

'Jesus. Let me in. They are killing everyone.'

Shaking, Kai walked over to Stepan and leaned his face close to his. 'Open the door,' he hissed.

Stepan remained calm. 'Sit down,' he said. 'You are in here. You are with us. You are lucky. But there is absolutely nothing you can do.' He leaned his head back against the wall behind the sofa and looked up towards the ceiling.

THIRTY

After the first burst of gunfire, Erin knew the place she needed to get to was the bridge. If Marius was not there, someone needed to be. Two choices: she could go up through the heart of the boat or go by the external gangways.

'Think, Erin. Think,' she whispered to herself. They must have been boarded. The boat the attackers come on would still be alongside *Zinaida*. If she left by the wrong door, she would expose herself to whoever was on deck. The question was, why hadn't Marius raised the alarm? He had been on watch. Rogue boats might be difficult to spot until they were close but they would show up on radar eventually.

He had not responded to the intercom. She glanced again in the direction of the dead chef, hidden in the darkness. She blinked, confused. Was it possible that Dimitri had been right and Marius was the other traitor on the boat? The thought was terrifying.

Going outside, she risked being seen; taking the internal route had other dangers. There were too many blind corners on the only way up to the bridge. Neither option was good, but she felt safer in the open, even in the darkness.

Cautiously she left the galley and walked to the rear of the boat, past the other crew cabins, doors swinging open, past the door to the electrical room, then up the small stairway to a staff door that was concealed behind the stairs on the swimming deck. She opened it just a crack and peered aft.

There was nothing moored behind them, at least, though that was strange, as the rear of the boat would be the simplest point from which to come aboard. Emerging onto the low deck, her body still shaking with shock, she peered back up the starboard side of the boat. Nothing there either.

The stairs up to the next level were on the port side; when she reached them, she was shocked to see nothing there, either. So where was the attackers' boat?

She stepped back, looking up towards the mast. Her view of the bridge was blocked by the decks above, but as far as she could see in the starlight, the staircase to the swimming deck was clear. Taking a breath, she made her way up it, pausing when she was just high enough to see onto the next deck.

Water splashed at her head. It was as if a bucket had been poured over her. She gasped.

To the right of her head was the pool. Stationary, with engines off, the big boat had started to roll awkwardly from side to side; a swell had thrown the pool's contents out onto the surrounding deck and sent it cascading down the staircase.

She wiped her eyes. Ahead of her, the main cabin, with its

armchairs and coffee tables visible in the pale emergency light, seemed to be empty.

Crouching, she reached the top and scurried for cover at the base of the next staircase, and had taken a few steps up it when she heard a man scream. Someone was pleading. She flattened her body low against the stairs. The noise had come from the main cabin, below her to her right.

A second later came a burst of gunfire and the simultaneous sound of shattering glass, fragments spinning over the deck she had just run across. A man stepped heavily out of the ruined glass door, putting one leg in front of the other with what looked like considerable effort before he fell among the shards.

It took Erin a second to understand what she had just seen. The shots that had smashed the glass had hit the man too.

He was lying on his side now, naked in the moonlight, save for a pair of white underpants. Whoever it was was moaning quietly, uttering words in a language she did not understand. She recognised him eventually as the third mate, the sweet, nervous one who had called her 'Ma'am'. In the dim light, the blood on his torso shone black.

Before she could move, another figure emerged, stepping through the shattered doorway, shoes crunching on the diamonds of safety glass. He was carrying a semi-automatic rifle of some sort. He lifted it, put the butt against his shoulder and fired, just once, at her colleague's head. The third mate had not even tried to defend himself.

Whoever the killer was, he was taking no prisoners; he was eliminating everyone who was on *Zinaida*. She guessed the third

189

mate must have been asleep in his bunk when he too had heard the gunfire.

She was crying now, she realised, and tried to stop the gulps of air from giving her position away.

To her horror, the man with the gun stopped and looked around as if looking for the source of the noise, and as his head turned towards her she recognised him. It was Aleksander, the electro-technical officer; the one who had joked about his girlfriends, who had puzzled over the ghost boat with her.

He seemed to look straight at her and she waited for him to raise the rifle and fire. Instead he craned his head the other way again, scanned the sea as if looking for something, then turned and disappeared back inside.

Erin raised her head to look up the stairs towards the helicopter deck, and realised she was shaking so hard she was not sure she could make it any further.

Just a few minutes ago she had been tiptoeing around a peaceful, silent yacht, about to start her watch. Out of nowhere had come chaos, violence and murder.

It seemed to take an age to get her breathing back under control. She began crawling upwards, again, limbs like rubber. She paused once more near the top to check that the helicopter deck was empty. The moment she emerged onto it she would be exposed, with nowhere to hide. Ahead of her she could now see the dim lights of the bridge above her. There was just one more set of stairs to go.

She flinched as another burst of gunfire rang out, this time from somewhere in the heart of the boat. Aleksander was below her now, presumably eliminating any other survivors one by one.

With horror, she realised there had never been an attack boat. Aleksander had struck at night when the fewest crew were on duty, when most were asleep or relaxing in their cabins, methodically killing them, one by one. She wondered how many would have made it into the citadel. If they had, they would have already triggered the Ship Security Alert System, but she knew she had to check and she couldn't know for sure until she made it to the bridge. She guessed that the chef had been one of the first to die. He was one of the few who would have been awake. Aleksander would not have wanted to rouse people with gunfire until he knew he had the upper hand; he had cut the man's throat with a kitchen knife.

She remembered how her own cabin door had been open; she had not been there when he had come looking for her.

More gunfire from below. Aleksander's attention was elsewhere at least. She took a breath, stood and ran as softly as she could across the deck towards the final gangway, then took the stairs two at a time up to the bridge.

She couldn't help herself from crying out loud when she opened the door. 'Oh . . .'

He was there, on the floor, in his own circle of blood, just as the chef had been.

Marius had not been part of the plot. He was face up, as if he had been pulled backwards from the captain's chair even as the blood had left him. There was no sign of a struggle. He had known his attacker as a fellow crew member and had not been expecting what was about to happen. Hand at her mouth, she took in a gulp of air.

191

Poor Marius. He had never made it to the luxury house he had so badly wanted. He had been a pompous man, but they had kept each other company.

She bit her lip, punched her thigh just to snap herself out of it. There was no time for sentiment. Later, if she survived, she could cry over him.

She looked around, swore.

On the instrument panel to the left of the wheel, she could see the SSAS had not been activated. The red light beneath the plastic cover was still dark. Marius had been caught by surprise. No one had activated it yet from the citadel, either, which was worse. Maybe nobody had made it there. She flipped over the protective plastic cover and pressed the button.

It didn't light up. Confused, she pressed it again. And again.

Then groaned. It was suddenly obvious. Aleksander was a communications specialist. There was a reason why he had not struck until now, the third day of their trip. He had needed time to prepare this attack and he had done so at some length. He had deliberately disabled the emergency device. She went to grab the VHF transmitter. That too was dark; the power had been cut. She looked around in horror and realised that all the instrument screens were dead. It wasn't just the lights that weren't working. Aleksander had put the boat into total darkness.

They had given him access. Dimitri had insisted Aleksander check all the equipment in St Croix.

Aleksander was not acting alone.

Shit.

It was Dimitri who had arranged everything; she saw it now. Dimitri had removed Tommy from *Zinaida* so that no one could stand in their way. They had left St Croix for open water because Dimitri said it was not safe.

She looked around. Ships were full of communications equipment these days. There had to be another way to call for help. She hit her thigh again. Think. She remembered there was a satellite phone in Marius's cabin behind the bridge.

As she turned to fetch it she heard footsteps on the stairway. Heart thumping, she ducked down behind the side of the big striped sofa.

'Help me. They're killing everyone.' The voice of whoever it was running up the stairs sounded desperate.

She ran towards the door. Whatever the risk, she had to help him. Then stopped, suddenly unsure.

'*Isss* there anyone there?' the voice came again. 'Please help me.'

Time slowed.

She was already in motion, making for the door on the port side, when the first gunshots came. There was no time to think, just to vault over the handrail and drop over the side into the black water below.

THIRTY-ONE

'Are you even fucking listening to me?' Marissa's voice came from outside the room.

'What's going on out there?' Zina called to her. 'Tell us.'

'I don't know. Oh shit. I think I heard someone going overboard. There was kind of a splash and then all these guns and stuff.' Kai could hear she was trying to hide the panic, to lower her voice. 'They're shooting again. Guys. They're going to kill me. All you have to do is open the door. Please. It's all you have to do.'

'Who have they killed?'

Marissa wailed, 'I don't know. You think I'm going to go up there and look? I don't feel well.'

People were dead, Kai thought. 'Please,' he pleaded with the Pirumovs. 'Just open it. I can close it straight away.'

'Procedure is clear,' said Stepan. 'Once the door is locked, we don't open it until we are rescued.'

'I can see her,' said Kai.

'Precisely. But you can't see them,' said Stepan.

Up until now the chief steward's voice had been pleading. Suddenly it was full of indignation. 'Let me in before they come down here, you selfish bastards.' She was no longer the young woman who had brought food to their table, pretty and servile. 'You think you're fucking invincible. You're the worst people. The worst people ever.'

'Can you see Dimitri?' Yuliya shouted. 'Is he still alive?'

'Please. Just open the door. I'm going to die. I know I'm going to die. Please save me. I won't let anyone else in, I promise, you selfish bastards.'

'Go to your room. Lock yourself in,' said Stepan. 'We cannot take the risk of opening the door.'

'Great fuckin' idea. All the cabin doors are wide open. That's where they killed them all already.' She banged on the door again. 'Yoga guy . . . They blew his head right away. I saw it.' They could hear the sound of her crying again.

'Find Dimitri,' said Yuliya. 'He will keep you safe.'

'Don't you get it? They're all fucking dead. I heard it all. Oh, please God, please, please, *please*.'

There was a shocked silence in the room. 'Do you think it is true?' said Yuliya, incredulously. 'Do you think Dimitri is dead?'

Kai left his place by the door and walked over to where Stepan was sitting, still staring at the ceiling as if not able to understand what had happened. Kai reached out and grabbed him by the collar of his T-shirt. 'Let her in.'

Stepan looked up at him startled.

Yuliya barged towards him. 'Stop this.'

Shaking, Kai tightened his grip on the shirt, twisting it so it narrowed around his neck. 'This isn't human. Just let her in. It's a risk, but it's the right thing to do.'

'Please, oh God, oh God.' Marissa's voice again, quieter now. 'Someone's coming.'

They listened. There was the sound of scuffling.

The gunshot's noise was dulled by the metal that lay between them and her.

The four stood in the room in absolute silence, trying to understand what had happened out of their sight.

'It's OK,' said Stepan again. 'We're perfectly safe in here.'

'Did someone just—?' Zina's eyes were wide open, red-rimmed from crying. Yuliya put her arms around her daughter.

'This is a safe room,' repeated Stefan doggedly. 'We are protected. What happens out there is not important. It could be in a different world completely. They cannot get in.'

The four of them looked at each other now. Whatever Stepan said, they weren't protected from the knowledge of what must have just happened.

'If we had opened the door, whoever is out there would have killed us too,' said Stepan. 'It was a simple choice.'

They strained their ears. It appeared to have gone completely quiet outside. The absence of noise was worse.

'I hate myself,' Zina muttered.

'We do what we have to,' said Stepan. 'We are the fortunate ones.'

Minutes passed in silence. They were shut in a windowless room in a rocking boat. Kai pulled himself up onto the top of one of the two bunks and stared at the plain metal ceiling.

'Who is it, *milyy*? Who is trying to kill us?' said Yuliya, standing below him.

Stepan sat opposite him at the other end of the small room looking up at his wife. 'Who do you think?' There was a note of weary exasperation in his voice.

'Oh, Stepan. No.'

'What, Dad? What are you talking about?'

Yuliya looked at her husband sourly. 'Your father is an idiot.'

'What? I don't understand.'

The boat rolled heavily, in a swell. Kai steadied himself against one of the bunks.

'What is it, Stepan? What did you do?'

Kai looked at the mother and daughter, still clinging to each other, staring down at their father. 'What is it, Dad? Were you trying to take over one of their companies?'

'Whose companies?' asked Kai.

'No.' Stepan leaned forward, laid his head on his hands. 'Of course not.' He sighed.

He looked up, and started to speak in Russian. He spoke for two or three minutes. The two women listened, mouths open, as if horrified.

'What is he saying?' demanded Kai at one point, but everyone ignored him. They were too engrossed in what Stepan was saying – and obviously horrified, too. 'Who is out there? Tell me. What is going on?'

When Stepan finally stopped, Yuliya shouted at her husband in Russian, spittle flying in his face. He yelled something back. Each raised their voices until she slapped him hard on the side of the face; this time he didn't retaliate. '*Kretin.*'

Stepan looked hurt, affronted. 'I was doing it for us. For everybody.'

Kai turned to Zina. 'What is it? What did your father say?'

Zina said, 'He says perhaps they are not trying to kill us.'

'Who? . . . Don't be ridiculous. Everyone on this boat is dead.'

'But not us,' said Stepan.

'Who the hell is *they*? Who did your father piss off? Will somebody please explain something to me?'

Nobody answered. Kai swung off the bunk again and put his eye to the hole in the door. He could see no one there at all. The boat seemed lifeless now.

THIRTY-TWO

Erin hit the water hard. She continued swimming straight down as she heard bullets slice the surface above her. The deeper they went the more muffled the noise became.

At the point when the pain in her ears was too much to bear she swam up again, but at an angle, as far away from the boat as she could, holding her breath until the desperation for air grew difficult to fight, trying to calm herself enough to last a few seconds more.

She broke the surface as gently as she could, gasping for breath. It took a second to orientate herself. Someone up on deck was shining a torch down at the water; Aleksander, she guessed. It had been him on the bridge.

'*Ty vidish yeyo?*' His voice again; talking to an accomplice. He was not alone.

She dipped down below the surface again. Stayed below a second time for as long as she could. It was her best chance; emergency drills had taught her how hard it was to spot bodies in moving water, even in good conditions. In darkness it would be almost impossible.

The fourth time she came up they had given up looking.

She lay on her back in the water, arms out, trying to get her breath back. Though the sea was warm as bathwater, she was still shivering from shock.

Dimitri had tricked them. He had pretended Tommy was the assassin when all along it had been him, and she had helped him deliver Tommy to the police. She wondered if the whole story about him escaping from prison had been concocted by Dimitri to drive them away from shore, into this trap.

What mattered most was that Aleksander had had two clear days to disable the Ship Security Alert System. It was no surprise that the main power had been cut; it would have been easy for Aleksander to do.

There were at least two of them. They must have overwhelmed the rest of the crew quickly. She guessed that they had murdered poor Marius first, then worked their way through the ship to find anyone else who was still awake. She had escaped only by chance; she had not been in her room when they had come for her.

She hoped some, at least, had made it to the citadel. If they had, they would be safe there until help came.

The death of Marius shocked her most. She was not a woman who made friends easily, and Marius had been the closest thing she had had to one for the last few years. He was a decent man. The people who had attacked this boat had not been after him; like the rest of the crew, he had just been in the way.

She looked at her watch and was shocked to see it was only

seventeen minutes past midnight. The whole attack had only lasted a few minutes – but it had felt like a lifetime.

Though she was grateful for it, it puzzled her that the boat was stationary. They could, she guessed, restart the engines now and move on. If they did, she needed to be close enough to board before the boat moved. Out here on her own she would be a dead woman.

Cautiously she swam a little closer, taking care to make no noise. With the lighting dead, *Zinaida* loomed ghost-white in the darkness. She approached with trepidation but she knew she needed to get back on board if she was to survive.

About ten metres off the stern, quietly paddling, she heard a single gunshot from somewhere deep in the yacht and flinched. It was the horror of knowing that someone else was probably dead. She wondered if there was anyone left alive, apart from her.

When she checked her watch next, she saw she had been in the water for half an hour. There had been no more shots.

In the darkness she could see that the port-side sea door to the toy garage was open, which was strange. Had the attackers taken the launch and escaped?

She had not heard any boat leave, but *Zinaida* was completely quiet now. With no power, she had drifted side-on to the wind, which had made her rolling worse.

It was time to move. Erin swam the final few metres to the boat, put her hands onto the ladder that rose up to the swimming deck and rested there for a moment before lifting herself slowly out of the water.

There was a towel hamper by the ladder. She reached in,

201

took two, laid one at her feet and stripped down to her bra and knickers. Wet clothes would drip, leaving a trail by which she might give herself away.

She threw her shorts and T-shirt into the bin, followed by the wet towels.

On a yacht like this, where style ruled over function, the flotation rafts were well hidden in case they spoiled the line of the boat, but there were two on this deck in a locker under the stairway, each with a life cell – a waterproof case containing a hand-held VHF radio, flares, drinking water. Attached on the outside of each case was an emergency beacon – an EPIRB – which would be activated the moment it hit water.

She opened the locker. It was too dark to see inside, so she felt her way. The life cell was exactly where it was supposed to be, but as her fingers groped they found nothing. The EPIRB that should have been attached to the side of it was missing.

Her chest tightened. She had personally checked all this equipment two days before they had sailed. She felt for the second case; there was no beacon there either.

She remembered Aleksander asking innocently, the day they sailed, for a list of all the electronic emergency equipment; she had given it to him willingly, pleased to see him doing his job so conscientiously. He had taken them all.

She felt like crying. All this had been planned so meticulously. He must have disabled the VHF radio and the Ship Security Alert System. She had not only helped Dimitri deliver Tommy up to the police, she had told Aleksander the location of all the EPIRBs and given him free access to all the electronics on the bridge.

If Marius had not succeeded in getting an emergency signal out before he was killed, then nobody would know what had happened to them. The only sign that something was wrong would be that anyone monitoring their movement via AIS would have seen the yacht stop, mid-ocean. There was nothing particularly suspicious about that. No one could know that the boat had been hijacked and its crew and passengers – possibly all of them – murdered. She had always wanted to be alone at sea, cut off from the world, and now she was – and it was terrifying.

There were always satellite phones. She did not own one, but other members of the crew often did. Marius kept one on permanent charge in his cabin behind the bridge.

She would have to go there again; to the very place she had escaped from just half an hour earlier. She looked up again at the steps she was about to walk up, and then at the communication masts rising up from above the bridge, then back at the water, puzzled. She frowned. Something was not right.

THIRTY-THREE

The night was going to be a long one.

Stepan and Yuliya got onto the bunks, taking the lower ones, and tried to rest. After a while, Kai gave up his watch at the spyhole and climbed into the bunk above Stepan's. There was nothing to see out there, beyond the darkness of the corridor. After the half-hour or so of gunfire, the boat seemed eerily quiet.

'I don't suppose there's anything to drink in here?' Zina asked.

'Water,' said her mother. 'Drink it. It'll do you good.'

Zina wrinkled her nose and started opening the cabinets at the back of the room. 'What kind of panic room doesn't have a bottle of vodka in it?'

Nobody found her flippancy amusing. After a while she gave up looking for anything stronger and took out a bottle of water and a packet of Reese's Peanut Butter Cups. She opened the sweets and offered them round. She tried one herself, then spat it out into her hand, then picked up her water and went to swill out her mouth with it.

'Shit,' she said.

Kai sat up. 'What?'

'I dropped the bottle. It's gone everywhere.'

She sat watching the bottle rolling back and forth slowly on the floor, emptying its load, not bothering to pick it up. 'What time is it?'

Yuliya looked at her watch. 'Almost one o'clock now. How soon do you think they will be here to rescue us, Stepan?'

'Soon, angel. Soon.'

'Do you think Dimitri is dead?'

'I don't know, angel.'

Kai noticed that the boat seemed to be moving more now. It was making him nauseous. He did not like being in confined spaces at the best of times, and now, as he looked down from the bed at the water Zina had spilt, he noticed how it moved one way across the metal floor, then flowed back in the other direction. Watching it didn't help. He turned away to face the wall.

'Do you think they've gone?' asked Zina.

'Maybe,' Stepan answered. 'They know they can't harm us. They must be aware that people will be on the way to help us. They have done their job. Why would they remain here?'

Kai thought about this. 'Did you hear another boat?' he said, turning back.

'Probably they have taken the launch. It would be a quick way to get away.'

'I didn't hear any engines,' Kai said again, and found himself looking at the water pooling on one side of the room again.

'It doesn't matter whether they are here or not. As I have told you, we are safe.'

205

The water seemed to be gathering more on one side of the room than the other.

'We should sleep,' Stepan said. 'Everything will be OK.'

It wasn't an illusion. The boat was tilting gently to one side. Kai watched the water a while longer until he was convinced.

Zina stood up again. 'I can't sleep. I'm too wired.'

'Listen,' Kai said, after another minute. 'Something's not right.'

The first time he said it, nobody paid him any attention, so he repeated himself.

'What?' demanded Zina, finally.

'Why is the water staying on one side of the room?'

Yuliya sat up. 'What do you mean?'

'Look.' He pointed at the water her daughter had spilt on the floor.

Stepan sat up too; Yuliya leaned out into the middle to get a better view. 'Maybe it's the wind,' said Yuliya.

'What are you all talking about?' demanded Zina.

'I've been watching. It wasn't like that ten minutes ago.' Kai lowered himself to the floor and went to look out of the peephole again, but there was still only darkness.

'The boat is tipping,' said Yuliya.

'Yes. I think it is.'

'Why?' Zina's mother asked.

Kai looked at Stepan and watched him frowning as he processed this fact. From the looks on the others' faces, they had all come to the same conclusion, but nobody wanted to say it out loud, so he said it in the end. 'Maybe we're sinking.'

All four of them were watching the water now. Where earlier it had been moving across from one side of the room to the other, it was now firmly pooling on the side opposite where Zina had been sitting.

'No one,' said Kai. 'I've been looking. There's no one out there.'

Stepan had been trying the intercom to the bridge again, but there was no answer.

'Fuck,' said Zina.

'They're sinking the boat so we have to come out,' said Yuliya.

'I suppose it's possible,' said Stepan.

Zina let out a sob. 'You said we were going to be OK, Papa.'

Kai banged on the door. 'Hey. Is anyone there?' He remained by the door for a while, but nobody appeared. When he turned, Stepan and Yuliya had got up and were sitting on the couch opposite where the water had pooled, arms around each other, watching the puddle.

'What must we do, Stefan?' Yuliya asked.

'We must negotiate.'

'With who, exactly?' Yuliya said.

Stefan stood, went to the communications panel and called the bridge. 'We need to talk,' he said, but there was no answer.

'I am ready to talk,' he said again. Still no answer.

'Who is it out there anyway? Maybe they don't even speak English,' said Zina.

'*Estoy listo para hablar*,' said Stepan. Then he tried again in Russian.

Only a faint hiss came back. Kai wondered if they were completely cut off from the bridge or whether there was simply no one there.

'Hello?' Stepan was saying. 'Hello?'

After a while he gave up and sat back down on the sofa; he seemed smaller now, more hunched. Yuliya put her arm around him again.

Zina folded her arms. 'Do something, Dad.'

Eventually Stepan lifted his head, looked at Kai. 'You were the one who wanted to open the door,' he said.

'Yes.'

'I will open the door for you then. You find them and talk to them.'

'Me?'

'Tell them I will give them whatever money they want.'

Kai's eyes narrowed. 'Why don't you do that?'

'Because me and my family, we are the bargaining chips. If we give ourselves to them, they don't have to give us back anything. If you go, you can talk to them. They are not interested in you.'

'I'm worthless, is that what you mean?'

'Not how I would have chosen to express it, but . . .' said Stepan simply.

Kai strode back down to the end of the room and put his hands on the cold metal of the door.

'They're not interested in me?'

'Don't take it badly,' he said.

'They weren't interested in Marissa either, but they killed her all the same.'

Stepan gave a small, considered nod. 'You can just choose to die in here with the rest of us. There, you stand some chance.'

Kai looked at him. 'I don't think so.'

Stepan seemed to think about this for a while. 'I can give you money, obviously.'

'Obviously.'

'Please, Kai,' said Zina.

'What? You think I should go as well?'

The boat rocked in a wave. They all stopped talking, waiting for it to centre itself, but instead it seemed to hang more to one side, if only by a fraction. It was no longer just the spilt water that showed how lopsided *Zinaida* was now. Kai could feel the ship's lack of balance.

He turned. With his back to the door he slid down it until he was sitting. 'I've seen what happens to people on the outside of the door. Once I was out there you would never let me in.'

'Of course we would. You are different,' said Stepan.

'Right,' he said. 'I take Zina with me. Just to make sure you do.'

'Kai!' protested Zina. 'You shit. Why would you do that to me?'

Kai pushed himself up onto his feet and sighed. 'Open the door then.'

'You're going to go alone?'

'Stay in here and suffocate with you lot or go out there and probably be shot?'

'Maybe you'll be lucky,' said Stefan.

'Yes. Maybe I will.'

Stepan stood up, stepping forward with his hand extended to shake. Kai looked at it a while and then took it in an oddly formal gesture.

'Are you ready?'

Kai nodded.

'I will only open the door quickly. And the moment you are gone I need to lock it again. Do you understand?'

'Yes.'

Kai looked around. Zina and Yuliya were staring at him,

big-eyed. The chances were that he was walking out to his death. It wasn't really bravery. The idea of being stuck in a sealed room as a boat sank terrified him more.

'Right,' said Stepan, and he leaned past him, his hand over the electronic keypad.

'On three,' said Stepan. 'One.'

Zina had looked away, as if she couldn't actually look him in the eye.

'Two.' Stepan started punching in the six digits.

Kai readied himself. For all he knew there was someone tucked out of sight on the other side of the door just waiting for this moment.

'Three.' Stepan completed the code.

'Go.'

Kai pressed down the handle hard. Nothing. It seemed to be stuck.

Stepan looked puzzled. 'This keypad should light up when you press it.'

Kai pushed on the handle again. 'It's still locked. Try again.'

Stepan re-entered the code, but the door did not open. Just as when Zina had locked him in here in fun, it would not give.

Stepan pushed him aside and grasped the handle and tried pushing it down himself hard, pulling it up and pressing it down, but it stayed firm.

Kai watched the blood leaving Stepan's face as it dawned on him. 'That is not possible,' he said. 'It is designed so that cannot happen.'

But it had. They had not locked themselves in here; they were the ones who had been locked in. And *Zinaida* was sinking.

THIRTY-FOUR

Something was not right, Erin had noticed. *Zinaida* was not level; she was listing to port. She did not have significant weight aboard her that could cause this by shifting, so it meant just one thing: she was taking on water.

Raising an alarm became even more of a priority. If all the EPIRBs were missing, she had to find another way of communicating, and that meant the bridge; retrieving the satellite phone from Marius's room.

For a second time, she made her way carefully up the port gangway, then ran across the helicopter deck to the next set of stairs. At the top of them, she paused to catch her breath.

She turned her face into the oncoming wind and saw, on the horizon, three lights, one white, one green and one red. The configuration meant a boat heading straight towards them. Her heart leapt.

Rescue. Marius – or someone else – must have been able to raise some kind of alarm before they were killed.

Fixing her eyes on the lights, she watched them, trying to judge the speed of the boat and how soon it was to arrive. The only thing that was clear was that it seemed to be heading straight for them. She hesitated, thinking things through. If there was a boat already heading their way, it was still important to find out where the water was getting in to try and save the ship. But the killers were still on *Zinaida*, and the oncoming vessel would have no idea that they were about to face armed men. She needed to get a signal to them.

She carried on up the gangway until she reached the door to the bridge.

The wind was rising. She looked towards the approaching boat. It was still on the right heading. This was no accidental encounter. It was heading right for them and another disaster was about to unfold.

She peered through the glass of the door into the bridge. Marius's body was still there, face up on the floor, the wound on his neck gaping, but the bridge seemed deserted. Crouching, she twisted the handle and pushed the door back open slowly. Wind rushed through behind her. The far door, the one she had escaped through, was still wide open, swinging in the wind, but apart from Marius, she was alone up here.

She crept inside and closed the door behind her, taking care not to let the wind slam it shut, then turned. The blood that surrounded Marius was no longer liquid. It had become a kind of dark jelly. Against it, his bloodless head looked pale and skeletal.

Pursing her lips, she walked past him to the back of the room, to the corridor that led to his cabin. Somebody had beaten her to it. The charger cradle was empty. The contents of his bedside cabinet drawer had been tipped onto the floor and the drawer was lying upside down on the carpet. She rummaged through the debris, hoping to find it knocked onto the floor, but there was no phone and no way of warning the oncoming boat.

She wanted to scream out loud.

Crew members often had satellite phones themselves too, but the family had insisted on them all being confiscated. Where had Tommy put them all? There was no time to look. The boat would be alongside very soon. Again, she walked past Marius's dead body, noting that the navigation lights approaching from the south were much closer.

The boat must have been moving towards them at a hell of a speed; even in the darkness she could see the white spray around the bow. It was a launch of some kind travelling at around fifty knots or more. 'Shit,' she whispered.

It would be alongside in around a minute and unless she could warn them – or unless somebody else had already done so – it would make an easy target.

She felt utterly helpless.

Opening the door, she made her way back down to the deck below, and then to the helicopter deck. She was about to descend the final stairway when she heard voices below her. Above the wind, she could hear a man talking. She lowered herself to the ground and crawled on hands and knees to the back edge of the deck and peered over.

Aleksander was standing on the sea deck, waiting for the boat with an automatic rifle slung over one shoulder, holding a black plastic bin bag in his other hand. Far from looking worried about the appearance of the boat, he looked pleased. He was beckoning it.

213

It took her a second. This was not a rescue. It was the opposite. They had come to pick up the killers. Aleksander was waiting for them. Dimly, she could make out another figure in the darkness behind him. That would be Dimitri, she guessed.

Erin heard the speedboat's engines slow as it came alongside and bounced gently against *Zinaida*'s stern. It was a large, black open launch, sleek and pointy, with back-angled windscreen, inboard motors and a forward cabin under the bow. The man in the boat held out his hand to Aleksander, who prepared to swing the plastic bag across to him.

But as he did so, something fell out of the top of the bag and dropped onto the deck.

Erin stared down. It was fluorescent orange, torch-shaped. As it rolled in a semi-circle on the deck, both men stared at it, horrified.

Aleksander scrambled to catch the moving object.

It was one of the EPIRBs stolen from the life rafts. If it fell into the sea, the water would immediately activate it. As the ship rolled, so did the orange device, with Aleksander chasing after it.

'*Voz'mi!*' another voice shouted. 'Idiot.'

The EPIRB rolled within a few centimetres of the drop, but Aleksander stepped forward, managed to catch it with his foot. In the light from the launch, she could see the relief on the faces. He picked it up, and next thing he was leaping onto the boat. A second figure emerged from the shadow of the sea deck.

The engine roared into life and Erin rolled back away from the edge to avoid her profile showing against the night sky, shocked. Because it was not Dimitri who had just shouted at Aleksander; nor was it him who had just stepped onto the speedboat.

THIRTY-FIVE

Kai's phone told him that it was three minutes past two in the morning. He looked around the panic room and thought, he would die with these people.

Zina had grabbed hold of her mother on the couch, fingers digging into her shoulders, and was crying. Stepan seemed shocked into inaction, as if he did not believe this could have happened to him, of all people; a man who had made his way to the top of the world.

'And there is no other way out of this room?' asked Yuliya.

'No, Mama. That's the whole shitting point of a citadel,' shouted Zina.

'Ssh, my child.' Yuliya stroked her daughter's arm.

'Are we going to drown, or just suffocate?'

Neither of her parents had anything to say.

'It's all your fault,' she said accusingly, to her father.

'*My ne khoteli, chtoby eto proizoshlo*,' protested Stepan.

'Of course you asked for it to happen. You do all this –' She let her mother go and waved her arm around. 'You distort the entire world and you expect nothing bad to ever happen to you.'

Her father looked baffled.

'You too.' She pointed at Kai. 'It's your fault. You shouldn't have made me come. Why are you laughing?'

This was who he was going to die with, he thought.

Zina was crying louder now. 'It's not funny.'

When he was younger, in his early twenties, when everything was wonderful and people told him he was a genius, Kai had had a recurring dream that he had written a tune and had realised, in his dream, that it was the greatest tune ever written. The flow of the notes and the harmonies that sat naturally around them was utterly perfect. Objectively, it was superior to all other music. Like all the best pieces of music, it did not feel like something he had created himself. It was something that had always been there; he was simply the fortunate person who discovered it.

In some versions of this dream he played it to colleagues or friends, and they had immediately been excited, because they too recognised it as the greatest tune there ever was. They had smiled and danced and hugged him.

Sometimes he woke remembering the tune and rushed to his keyboard to play it. In the light of day it was disappointing to realise that what he had written was just ordinary, of course; there was nothing really special at all to it. On a few occasions he had incorporated the notes he had dreamed into the music he was writing that day, hoping that some of the magic would still be there, but he soon forgot which parts were dreamed and which parts were not.

It was not that the reality was disappointing, he had realised, it was the inability to transcend reality with something greater. His manager, his fans, the musicians who flattered him, had told him he had some great gift, but deep down had always suspected that his talent wasn't greater than theirs; it was just that he was luckier. The magic of his dream was not real. And this was a ship that sank, just like any other.

He turned to Stepan and said, 'You said all this was just a message. Well. It looks like the message is, we are all going to die.'

For a second time since he had joined the boat, Kai marvelled at how calm he seemed in the face of death.

'If my father had not been trying to take over the Russian government, none of this would have happened,' complained Zina.

'Seriously?' Kai looked at her.

'No, no, no,' said Stepan. 'That is absolutely not what we were trying to do. We were not trying to take it over.'

'It sounds like that to me, Dad. Jesus.'

Stung, Stepan stood to address them, as if the point he was making was an important one. 'We were trying to ensure that everything stayed as it was.'

'Right,' said his daughter. 'For the good of the country.'

Stepan put his arm on Kai's shoulder. 'Your boyfriend will understand. The day before yesterday, him and me, we talked about the problem of succession.' He nodded at Kai, as if looking for support. 'He asked a very intelligent question. How do you transfer power if you don't vote in the next leader?'

'Gold star to Kai,' muttered Zina.

'It was exactly the problem that interested us. What if the leader falls ill? What if he just retires? Why shouldn't he? He

217

gets old, like everyone does. How do you ensure that there is no disruption, no power struggle? All we were doing was discussing that. That was our mistake.'

'You discussed this in public?' said Yuliya, aghast.

He sighed. 'No, no, no. In private. I must explain,' he said, addressing Kai. 'Do you know about the Russian constitution?' Kai was shaking his head, but Stepan didn't wait to hear Kai's answer. 'Everyone thinks the power lies simply in one man. It is not that simple. Do you understand?'

'He's a musician, Dad. He sits in his apartment all day playing video games and hoping someone will send him fan mail.'

Stepan ignored her. 'The real power in the Kremlin is invisible. The leader has his advisory council. Everyone knows that what the advisory council thinks is whatever the leader thinks. Do you understand?'

'No,' said Kai.

The boat seemed to tilt a little more. 'Dad,' said Zina. 'Shut up. None of this matters.'

Stepan ignored her. 'The leader does not have to tell us what he thinks, because we know it already. We have always understood what he wants. He understands what we want, so we think what he thinks. That is how it works in Russia. We benefit. Russia benefits. It's a perfect solution. We just have to do what we think he wants us to do. But there is a problem with this model.'

'It all works until the leader dies, presumably,' said Kai. 'Or is retired. And you don't know what he thinks any more.'

As if he had forgotten their predicament, Stepan nodded enthusiastically. 'Exactly. As long as he is there, it works. Without him, we fear it will descend into chaos and fighting between ourselves. We are businessmen. Some of us are even old enough to remember what it was like under Yeltsin.'

'Ssh,' said Yuliya.

They were all quiet. 'What, Mum?'

'I thought I heard something.'

They were quiet for a while listening, Kai heard nothing.

Stepan gave up listening and started talking again. 'Two months ago, a few of us met informally to discuss it. We had a kind of code. We called it The Farm. Let's go for a weekend on The Farm, we said. It was just six of us. Kazanova Mihailovna . . . some others who you will probably have heard of. But, of course, we couldn't tell the others that we were making a plan . . .'

'Because it would look like you were plotting a coup,' said Zina.

'By meeting, we felt we were investing in a kind of futures market – to begin to discuss what the structure would be if the centre was absent.'

'Kind of ironic you're talking about taking power, Dad, when you don't even have the power to get out of this . . . coffin.'

'He found out,' said Yuliya. 'Didn't he? That's why we're here.'

'Maybe. Or someone else did. You see? We think what he thinks. One of our group may have felt it wise to tell the President. Or maybe someone just decided to act on his behalf. I believe the second of these is more probable. We are him. He is us, after all. It began two weeks ago when one of us farmers was taken to hospital with heart problems.'

'Kazanova Mihailovna. I heard she was unwell,' said Yuliya.

'Yes. Exactly. Except there was nothing wrong with her heart,

219

it turns out. She is better now, but the doctors think she was possibly poisoned. In the tests they discovered traces of a natural plant toxin called gelsemium which suppresses the heart rate. Then on Monday somebody came for me.'

'In Paris?' Yuliya said.

'Poor Martin dropped by unexpectedly. He was in Paris with a girlfriend. I think the killers must have mistaken him for me.'

'You were there too?'

'The killers came in over the roof, I think. I was changing clothes in the bedroom because we were going to go out for lunch. One moment he was there, and then when I came back from the bedroom he was gone. I heard screaming from the street below and when I looked over the balcony . . . I left as soon as I could without being seen and waited in a cheap hotel in Le Bourget for what seemed like half of my life until Dimitri could pick me up and fly with me to St Thomas.'

'Let me get this right. Your own country is trying to kill you?' said Kai, incredulous.

'Only the best for Dad.'

Stepan shrugged. 'We do not know who it is. It may be the Kremlin, it may be a colleague of mine. The message is loud and clear. They do not think what we think. The point is, we know now. We understand. This is how power is communicated now. There is no one to disagree with or to blame, because the leadership will deny ever knowing about this. But the message is absolutely clear, even though it came from no one. Their method, you see, is not one of plausible deniability. It is the opposite. It is one of implausible deniability.'

He looked around as if expecting applause for his clever analysis of their situation.

'Don't you see it?' He looked around at them. 'It is obvious that the Kremlin, or someone who thinks like the Kremlin, is behind this. So we are afraid of them. That is all they need to know. Others will receive the message. It is not important whether we live or die. It is all about the message. Our duty is to show we have received the message.'

'It's not important whether we live or die,' said Zina.

'Ssh.' Her mother tried to calm her.

'I hate you,' said Zina. 'You think you understand everything, but really you understand nothing. You're just an idiot who has a lot of money.'

'Quiet,' snapped Yuliya. Kai thought she was going to upbraid her daughter for disrespecting her father, but she was holding up a single finger.

'My family is a sick joke.'

'Quiet.' Kai added his voice to Zina's mother's.

'Listen,' she said. They all stopped talking and looked around.

At first Kai heard nothing. He saw Zina's mouth fall open, her eyes widen, then he heard it too. It was the unmistakable noise of another boat's engines.

'They have found us,' said Stepan triumphantly. 'I told you we were safe.'

Zina stood quickly, and started going through the cupboards at the back.

'What are you doing?'

With a tin can in her hand, Zina strode down to the other end of the room and began to bang it loudly on the door. 'Help!' she shouted. 'Help us!'

The metal made a harsh thunk each time it hit. Yuliya joined in the shouting. 'We're in here. We are in here.'

Stepan joined them, shouting as loudly as he could. 'I am Stepan Pirumov,' he shouted. 'I am Stepan Pirumov.'

After a while, Kai shouted, 'Quiet,' and they stopped, looking at the walls around them.

They listened straining for any response. 'Can you hear anything?' he asked.

Zina started her banging again, while the other two set to shouting as loudly as they could.

'Stop it,' Kai shouted once more. 'Listen.'

Again, they heard the engine noise of the other boat. It seemed to be getting quieter, as if the other boat was not coming towards them at all, but travelling away.

THIRTY-SIX

Erin watched the black launch's wake make a straight line away from *Zinaida*, bow thumping on the rising waves, shocked by who she had just seen boarding it.

She breathed a sigh of relief. The killers had left them, but the yacht was sinking fast now.

As the speedboat pulled away, she heard something else. A banging sound from within *Zinaida*. Someone was alive, she guessed, and trapped. She was not alone on the sinking ship. That made her happier than she would have predicted; she was not alone.

Even if she wanted to, she couldn't just launch a life raft on her own now. There was someone else to think about. Besides, the rule was never abandon ship unless you had to. Your chances were always better on board a boat as long as it was still afloat.

Sinking any boat was not hard; you just had to know what the easiest method to take water aboard was. If she wanted to sink *Zinaida*, she knew how she would do it.

Any diesel engine needed cold water to cool it so there were always pipes that ran to the engine room. All you had to do was open the sea cocks and the water would come gushing in. Sinking a boat this way took time; it was like filling a bath slowly. In the sea, she had noticed the sea door to the garage was open. That was to speed the process up. Once the water level reached the open sea doors, it would quickly flood into the bilges and they would be lost.

Able to make noise at last, she clattered down the gangway to the sea deck and down again to the landing on level two. She was right. There were two doors into the garage, one from the engine room landing, and the second from a private staircase that descended from level one. The floor was already awash with water pouring into the hull from the garage deck. She realised with a lurch that there was very little time now to save *Zinaida*. Whoever it was who was making the banging noise would have to wait.

The level two bulkhead door to the garage deck opened outwards. Leaning through, she grabbed the handle and tugged it towards her; at first it was tough work, forcing the door against the water, but finally it started to move, and when she had got it closed far enough for the pressure to mount behind it, it slammed shut with a dull clang.

One door down; another one to go. She ran, splashing, into the dark corridor that led to the stairs up to level one, tripped on something soft and fell down hard in the darkness.

In horror, she realised she had fallen onto the wet lukewarm skin of a dead person. She wailed out loud.

One of her many dead crewmates, she guessed. She thrust herself away from the body. There was no time to think about what she had just done or who it might be.

Scrabbling upright, she continued onwards, up the stairs to L1 and then back down again to the second garage door. She had guessed right. They had left this bulkhead open too, but this time they had wound a rope around the handle to keep it open. It was too dark to see the knot; instead she had to feel for the end of the rope, follow it all the way back to the knot and gradually start to loosen it, water sloshing past her bare ankles into the boat.

It seemed to take an age to even start to shift the tight rope; all the time her fingers worked, she was imagining the boat rolling over into the sea as it took on water. Being caught here in the heart of the boat didn't bear thinking about. 'Come on!' she screamed at herself. 'Come on!'

She mustn't panic. With knots, force didn't help and this was not a knot tied by an experienced sailor. It was a mess, so she pulled cautiously until it finally began to untangle.

When she had sealed the second door, she returned the way she had come, back towards the engine room, pressing herself against the wall of the corridor to avoid the body she had tripped over earlier.

She had dammed the main flow, but there was still plenty coming in from elsewhere. The electrical room was already deep in water, and behind it, the engine room lay below, though it was so dark in there, it was impossible to see anything.

This is where the long hours she had spent aboard the *Zinaida* paid off. She knew this ship well. Before entering the engine room, she shut her eyes and tried to remember exactly where the water pipes that let in water lay – one on each side of the engine room – then she headed down the gangway.

The warm water was already up to her groin. She remembered that the pipes ran at floor level. Only able to feel her way, she took the shallower starboard side first, ducking down into the water, finding it, then finally finding the pipe end. She was right. They had removed a steel cap. Water was gushing in through it with such force that she couldn't simply insert some kind of bung. She remembered the round, red valve handle was at the rear corner of the engine room. Again she worked her way back along the pipe until she found the tap with her fingertips. It was too low in the water for her to reach it without submerging her head, so she took a gulp of air and ducked under the surface to twist it. It was positioned awkwardly, so close to the steel wall that she could only make little turns on it. She came up, took a gasp of air, and then returned to her twisting until it wouldn't move any more.

Wading forwards again, she put her hand over the open end to check she had stopped the flow, then made her way round to the deeper side of the engine room to repeat the operation. This time it took longer. Here the valve was further below the surface. It took four lungfuls of air before she started to feel the valve tighten.

As soon as she was sure she had shut it, she crawled up the stairs, waded through the electrical room and emerged onto the deck to catch her breath. She lay for a minute on the flat deck, grateful to be alive.

She had slowed the boat's sinking, but *Zinaida* was already dangerously low in the water. It was tilting as much as ten degrees towards port, she guessed. With the swell and that much water in the bilge, she might still be unstable.

*

226

Next, she had to free whoever was making that banging noise. She checked her watch. It was twenty past two in the morning. There were a little over two and a half hours of darkness left before twilight.

Pulling herself to her feet, she looked out over the water and was surprised to see the black launch standing off about three hundred metres away, navigation lights clearly visible.

With a shock she realised that they were waiting there until *Zinaida* sank, to check that their work was complete. They were not done yet.

They had disabled her electronics and removed the EPIRBs. There would be no emergency signal when she went down.

Something that had happened earlier tonight had puzzled her; now it began to make sense. If Aleksander had been a traitor, then nothing he had said was reliable. The false AIS trace that Kai had spotted hours ago on the bridge had not been a mirage or a fluke of atmospheric conditions at all. There had been another boat copying *Zinaida*'s identity; and it had almost certainly been that speedboat.

It was a kind of maritime identity theft. They were spoofing *Zinaida*'s position; presumably they had activated the signal by accident when Kai had spotted it, and then switched it off again. When the real *Zinaida* sank, they would simply switch on their own signal again and sail away. To anyone watching marine traffic movements, it would look like *Zinaida* was fine and sailing on to its destination. Nobody would be concerned.

That's not what they wanted though. Aleksander had taken all the emergency beacons and presumably deactivated any of the ones left aboard the ship. Somewhere out in the Caribbean, they would switch the signal off entirely and possibly throw an EPIRB or two into the sea as well. It would look like *Zinaida* had sunk, but in a totally different place. Even if they sent divers to look for their remains, they would not find them. Nobody would ever discover where she had sunk, or why.

They were still out there, waiting until their ship had gone down. And they would be back soon to discover why she hadn't.

THIRTY-SEVEN

'There's someone out there,' said Kai. He had his face against the peephole.

'Who is it?'

'I can't see, it's too dark.'

Dim green light appeared on the keypad next to the door.

'Dad. I think the door's working again.'

They looked at each other in the bright light of the citadel. Zina was still clutching a dented can. For the first time, Kai read the label: *Dinty Moore Beef Stew*.

From the far side of the door came sound. Someone was banging on the outside.

'Who is it?'

There was no answer.

'It might be them,' said Yuliya, but Stepan had already stepped forward and was entering his code into the keypad.

'Quick,' said Stepan. He turned, reached into the cabinet, pulled out a can of his own and held it, ready to throw.

When Stepan pushed the door open, there, standing in the light from their room, small in the doorway, stood the first mate. She was in her underwear and there was what looked a bloodstain darkening her bra.

Erin looked back at them, two of them with cans of beef stew in their hands, raised like weapons.

Stepan was looking past her anxiously, trying to see if there were more people.

'Are you wounded?' Kai asked her.

Erin looked down at herself and for the first time noticed the blood. She thought of the body she had fallen on. 'No. That's not my . . . I'm fine. Come on. Please hurry. We don't have much time.'

'The door was locked. How did you . . . ?' demanded Yuliya.

'Somebody had overriden safe room mode.' They had been locked in all this time, Erin realised. It hadn't been their citadel, it had been their prison.

'Just you?' Stepan said. 'What about the others?'

'The others are dead,' Erin answered. 'All of them, I think. I'm sorry. I couldn't do anything.'

'What about Dimitri?' said Yuliya. 'Where is he?'

'I think he was the first to die.'

Yuliya shook her head and said, 'Impossible. How do we know you are not one of them?'

Erin stepped back to let them out. 'Go and look for yourself. Dimitri's in his cabin. It's L27. I think they may have drugged him, then cut his throat.'

230

Yuliya let out a sob. Still standing in the doorway, Stepan put his arm around his wife.

They emerged hesitantly, the family walking cautiously, looking around. 'Just you? On your own?'

'Just me.'

Stepan looked incredulous.

'Where is Marissa?' Kai demanded, gazing around, disorientated. 'We heard the shot. She was here. I heard her out here begging for her life.' He inspected the gloom of the space on the other side of the door, puzzled. 'She wanted to get in but this bloody family wouldn't let her. They shot her.'

'Marissa was pleading to get in?' said Erin. The door had been locked from both sides. The family couldn't get out, but the killers couldn't get in either.

'And they wouldn't let her.'

Erin looked at the family. Zina looked shame-faced; her parents, in contrast, remained stony-faced. 'Well, you're lucky you didn't,' she said.

The second figure Erin had seen stepping out of the darkness onto the speedboat was not Dimitri; it was a woman. Marissa had been one of the killers.

All the time Erin had been trying to stop the boat from sinking, the shock of it had been buzzing around in her head. Things were starting to make sense. Dimitri had said one of the stewards had told him about finding poison gas in Tommy's cabin. Marissa had played him like she'd played the rest of them. Almost certainly it was Marissa who had planted the gas in there to make Dimitri think Tommy was one of the killers. Because of it, Dimitri had trusted her, like they all had, and that would have made it easier for her to get into his cabin; she was probably the one who had killed him. Maybe she had used that same gas to stun him, though she could have just as easily drugged him with a drink, offered with her habitual friendly smile.

'I told you,' said Stepan, triumphantly, when Erin explained. 'I was right. Always.'

'Shut up, Stepan,' said Yuliya, bitterly. 'All this shit is your fault.'

There was no time for this. Erin led them up the spiral stairs to the main cabin, and sat them down on the white sofas. 'I need you to be quick,' she ordered. 'No noise. I need you to stay low and avoid the windows. It will be getting light soon. We don't want the people on that boat to spot our silhouettes. They think you are still in the citadel.'

'Which boat?'

Erin pointed towards the horizon. All they would be able to see was three lights, one red, one green, one white. The boat was sitting in the water a little way off.

'Is that the people who attacked us?' demanded Stepan, peering into the darkness.

'The boat came to take Marissa and the electro-technical officer away. They're the ones who did all this. They're watching to see the ship go down with all of you still aboard. They're expecting us to sink soon. If we don't, they're going to come back to find out what happened. They have weapons. We have none.' The only gun on board she knew of apart from Dimitri's had been Marius Falk's pistol; Dimitri had taken that from him at St Croix. She had gone to Dimitri's cabin to find it; it hadn't been there, but Dimitri had. There hadn't even been any sign of a struggle.

'The servant did this?' said Stepan, appalled. 'The girl?'

'Are we really sinking?' Yuliya demanded.

Suddenly all the family were throwing questions at her. Erin interrupted. 'Everyone stop! Listen to me. Stepan. Do any of you have a satellite phone?'

'In my cabin,' said Stepan.

'Fetch it. We need it. The rest of you wait here. I need to get some things.'

There was a shriek. Zina had spotted the dead man splayed out on the pool deck for the first time. She stood looking towards the stern, with her hands to her mouth. Erin swivelled and watched the other boat anxiously, wondering if they had heard, if the sound had carried over the water, expecting it to rev its engines at any moment and head towards them, but it didn't.

Erin left them to it. She found her wet clothes, stashed on the swimming deck, and put them back on, then fetched a pair of walkie-talkies and some torches from the emergency locker and returned to the main deck where Stepan was standing with his satellite phone. She held out her hand for it.

'It's empty. No charge,' Stepan said. 'Not working.'

'You're kidding?'

'Satellite phone. I must have left it on. The battery runs down very fast.'

Erin felt like weeping.

'What if . . . ?' said Kai.

She turned to him. 'What?'

'I mean, there's still power in the citadel, isn't there?' said Kai.

233

Stepan returned a minute later and handed the phone charger to her. Erin looked at it. 'But this is a hundred and ten volts,' she said.

'Yes. Of course it is.'

'The only circuits working right now are emergency power, which is twelve volts. We can't charge it until we get the mains back on – and the electrical room is half underwater.'

'Give it to me,' Kai held out his hand. Erin handed the phone charger to him and he read the specs. 'It charges on five volts. We could try plugging the phone straight in, but the chances are that twelve volts would fry it.'

Erin nodded. 'Shit,' she muttered.

'I don't believe it,' said Yuliya, looking out at the lights of the other boat. 'That servant girl was trying to kill us?'

'Why don't we get on, like, a life raft?' complained Zina. 'We should leave now. If it's sinking, we can get off this fucking boat. We should get the fuck away.'

Erin turned to her. 'Right now we have no comms. If we get on a life raft, nobody will know where we are. Our chances are still better on this boat if we can keep her afloat.'

'Yeah . . . but—'

'No. Listen,' said Erin, cutting her short. 'Until we can raise an emergency signal we stay on this vessel. Right now I'm in charge of this boat, right?'

Yuliya and Zina looked at Stepan, expecting him to challenge her. Instead he nodded. 'She's right. She's in charge.'

'The problem is, in a little while, that boat –' she pointed out of the window – 'is going to come back to find out why *Zinaida* has not sunk yet. When they do, they'll kill us all. We've only a little time. Sit down, everybody. I want you to listen very carefully to what I need you to do.'

What surprised her was that they all did as she asked; they sat and listened as she gave them orders.

Kai accepted his tasks meekly. He had been totally wrong about Marissa. She would have killed him if he'd let her in.

He followed Zina to the galley. Erin had already warned them about the dead man they would find there. When he shone the torch, he could see the chef face down on the floor. Zina refused to look in his direction.

'How many do we need?' Zina demanded.

'As many as we can carry.'

One of the bottles slipped out of her hands and smashed on the floor, red wine joining the dead chef's blood. 'Fuck, fuck, fuck,' Zina yelled.

'Keep your voice down.'

'The ship is sinking. This whole thing's going to turn over and we'll be trapped.'

'Just take what you can,' said Kai, rummaging around drawers for a corkscrew. He had five bottles cradled in his hands; she managed three. Erin had told them to meet her on the sea deck. When they got there they found that she had inflated and launched one of the big circular yellow life rafts and was sitting in it. 'Is that all you could get?' she demanded.

'You want more?'

'No time. You.' She pointed to Kai. 'Come with me.'

Kai passed her the bottles, then stepped into the small round yellow lifeboat with her. Erin paddled round to the open sea door.

'Any movement?' she asked.

'No,' he said, looking at the lights on the horizon. The other boat was still stationary, as far as he could tell.

The dim green glow that lit the interior of the garage reflected on the water. At the entrance, the tender hung from davits below the low ceiling. At the rear four, jet skis were half submerged in water. Erin got out of the inflatable, stepping into the dark mouth of the garage, then tugging the raft in after her.

'Open the bottles and pour out the wine,' she ordered, walking to the dark rear of the space. 'Keep the corks.'

He did as he was told. He fumbled with the corks, wanting to be out of this space as fast as he could. Zina's words were in his head. *This whole thing's going to turn over and we'll be trapped.* Though he hated enclosed spaces, he had been calmer in the citadel when there had been no chance of escape at all.

At one point he dropped the corkscrew into the black water and had to scrabble at his feet to find it. Eventually all eight bottles were empty.

'Now hold them,' she said. 'One at a time.'

She put a funnel into the neck of the first bottle and lifted a large jerry can. The liquid came out fast, splashing over his hands, making the confined space stink. When the first was full, he stuffed the cork back in the neck, laid it in the bottom of the raft and picked up the next bottle. Erin unhitched the walkie-talkie from her belt. 'Anything?'

Stepan's voice answered. 'They have not moved.'

They set about filling the rest of the bottles and, when they were done, pushed the raft back into the water. Paddling round to the back again, Kai realised there was something malevolent

236

about the look of a boat that had lost its seaworthiness, like the lopsided smile of a mad drunk.

'Still nothing?' asked Erin when they were back at the stern of the boat.

'No. Why are they taking so long?' demanded Yuliya.

A wave slapped against the back of the boat. 'Because they think we're all trapped. Because they think we're all dead,' said Zina.

Erin stepped out of the boat. 'You know what you have to do?'

Stepan and Yuliya nodded. 'OK. Watch them. The moment they move, call me.'

Kai heard a low moaning sound. A rising wind was making the steel cables that ran up to the communications mast sing.

THIRTY-EIGHT

If they were going to stay on *Zinaida*, which was still their best option, there were three priorities. First, to protect themselves from the killers. Second, to get the bilge pump running so they didn't sink. And third, to get some kind of communication system going. The last two required electricity.

Erin turned to Kai. 'So you understand electrics?'

'A little. I work with musical instruments. It's kind of . . . different but . . .'

'Come with me.'

She led the way back inside the boat and down to L3. Only when they were right inside *Zinaida*, within its windowless interior where no light could leak out, did she feel it was safe enough to switch on the torch.

The floor of the electrical room was still awash with water, but at least the level didn't seem to have risen. She stepped inside and shone the light onto the main switchboards. They were made up of a line of panels. Ship electrics were complex. Each panel was a separate cabinet housing the fuses and controls to the ship's various generators, or to its different electrical circuits – those for the engine, the lights, the comms, and for domestic use. She had been thinking about what Aleksander could have done to shut down all but the emergency electrics at once. She had a pretty good idea. For safety, all the cabinet handles were linked to isolation switches, so the moment you opened the door, any power inside would be cut off. But as an extra safety layer, there were sets of interlocked fused isolators that could be removed when major work was being carried out. She opened the cabinet door to the first set of fused isolators but everything looked fine there. The manual switches were still on. A small LED blinked red; she wasn't sure what that meant.

'What?' demanded Kai.

She checked a second box; then a third and final one. The switches were all still on there. They were all up to date and perfectly maintained. She muttered under her breath. It wasn't going to be as simple as she had hoped.

She remembered the power outage in St Thomas. All the power had simply disappeared. What was the red light though?

Understanding dawned. 'Smart controls,' she said, eventually.

'What?'

'What if the power to all these units can be remotely isolated? From a phone.'

'So all this has been switched off from somewhere else?'

'Maybe.' When the power went off in St Thomas, she decided, that had just been a dry run. They had probably hacked the boat's electrics already by then.

'So where's the on switch?'

'That's the problem. Probably on the ETO's phone, or his laptop.' She leaned forward and rested her head on the metal, despairing. Nothing was easy. These people's lives were in her hands and she couldn't even stop the boat from sinking.

'Why don't we just cut out the switches then?'

She looked at him. 'What?'

'All we need is to bypass these cabinets, yes?'

For the first time in what seemed like an age, she laughed. 'You're right.'

'You sound surprised.'

'Actually, yes.' She grinned at him. 'Sorry.'

They found spare wire in one of the cabinets; Kai set about cutting two short lengths from the roll and stripping the ends until he'd made two U-shapes. She watched him work methodically; he seemed to know what he was doing. When he'd completed the first pair of wires he said, 'Right. Which ones do we do first?'

'I don't know which one but the back-up bilge pumps will be running off that, and that's our priority. We've got to try them all.'

Kai used a knife to bare the wire casings at the bottom of the first of the three cabinets. 'So all we have to do is put a wire across there when you say it's safe to light up?'

'We can't do it until the boat has gone. If the lights all come on, they'll know we're here – and know you've escaped.'

A larger wave hit the boat and the boat rolled further than it had before. In the torchlight she could see the fear in his eyes as he wondered if it would just keep tipping, but it didn't. To his credit, he carried on working.

The walkie-talkie buzzed. Yuliya spoke. 'I think they are moving.'

240

'You sure?'

'I think.'

Kai stopped in his work.

'What lights can you see?'

'Green and white.'

'OK,' Erin said. 'That's good. Stay calm. Keep watching. Call me back if you see a red and a green.'

Kai looked at her.

'Maybe they have given up,' Erin said. 'Maybe they're worried about the weather. Maybe they're just going now.'

'You think?'

'We'll leave things until they're safely out of sight, then we can switch everything back on. But we need to have the circuits ready. If it gets any windier, we won't have much time.'

He put his head down and carried on working.

The first time she had ever sailed at night, Erin had been amazed at the simplicity of navigation lights. She had been a teenager aboard the tall ship; they had been heading for the port of Largs. Because she had been the youngest person on board, she was the last to take the helm on night watch, but ended up with one of the busier passages. The Firth of Clyde was full of ships, ferries and trawlers; at the helm, her job was to make sure they didn't crash into any of them. Standing behind the wheel on the wide deck, she had been scared at first; it felt like too awesome a responsibility for a teenager, but she learned fast that with a steady wind, it was simple. Visibility was good. When you spotted lights a long way off it could be difficult to tell what colour they were, but with binoculars you could usually make them out – even several miles away. Just from the configuration, of white, red and green, you were able to work out what kind of vessel they were and what their heading was. From the number of lights you could see, their colours and their layout, you could tell whether it was a tanker or a sailing boat, whether they were under their own steam, under sail or being towed, whether they were moving parallel towards you, or coming at you – and if it was the latter, a simple compass bearing on the lights would let you know within a minute whether you were on a collision course with them or not. The simplicity of it all pleased her. To the untrained eye, they were just lights. To a sailor they were signals that could keep you safe.

They set to work again, Kai preparing the wires while she held a torch for him.

The radio crackled a third time.

'Three lights. White, green and red.'

'Answer this carefully,' said Erin. 'Is the green on the left or right of the white light?'

The voice came straight back. 'The left.'

'Shit.'

Marissa and Aleksander had realised *Zinaida* was taking too long to sink and wanted to figure out why. If the starboard light was on the left, the speedboat was heading straight back towards them.

242

THIRTY-NINE

Kai and Zina hunkered behind chairs on the pool deck to make sure their silhouettes would not be seen against the night sky.

Peering up, cautiously, he could make out the lights of the boat coming towards them.

'Just want to say, I'm sorry,' said Zina.

'What for?'

'In the panic room. I am a fucking terrible person. I hate myself.'

'Quiet,' he said.

The boat came closer.

'It's not me. I promise,' she whispered. 'I was just scared.'

It was a large speedboat, Kai realised. Not the kind of small one you see pulling a skier, but the sort of thing a coastguard might use.

'Please. It's important you believe me.'

When the boat was about thirty metres away it switched on a searchlight, directed it towards *Zinaida*, and dropped the engine

243

speed. Kai heard them talking in Russian. 'What are they saying?' he asked Zina.

'They are arguing. That's Marissa's voice. A woman's voice, definitely. She is asking why the boat hasn't sunk yet. The other guy says they should just leave.'

But the boat didn't leave. It kept getting closer, edging towards *Zinaida*'s stern.

From where he was crouched, Kai could see it more clearly now. Silhouetted by the searchlight, Marissa was standing on the prow, with one hand urging whoever was driving the speedboat to come closer to the stricken hull. She had a gun of some sort slung over her shoulder. They were just metres away now.

On its quietest setting, Erin's voice came through the walkie-talkie in a whisper. 'Wait for it,' she said.

Closer still. She had told them all what they should do.

'Wait.'

Above the searchlight beam, Marissa stood with one leg up on the motorboat's pulpit, ready to jump. Kai could see her clearly now, and the dull black shine of the gun behind her shoulder.

And then Erin screamed, 'Now.'

Kai saw Marissa jerk her head up, as if wondering if her ears had tricked her.

'Quick,' Erin shouted again.

It was Zina who acted first, crouching, throwing the first bottle downwards. Her aim was poor. It hit the side of the speedboat's hull without smashing, dropping into the water.

Marissa shouted, '*Eti ublyudki sbezhali!*'

Kai joined Zina, throwing his first bottle. This one shattered

244

on the deck behind Marissa, spilling its contents. It took a second for Marissa to figure out what was going on. A third bottle followed, thrown by Zina.

What sounded like a gunshot came from the helicopter deck above them; Erin saw all three on the speedboat crouch instinctively at the noise. A massive red ball of light exploded above them with a loud bang.

The fireworks had started.

From above them, they heard Yuliya cry out. '*Ubey ikh!* Kill them!'

The smell of petrol from the speedboat's deck reached Kai.

'The cockpit,' Erin was shouting from the helicopter deck above them. 'Get them in the cockpit.'

To disable the speedboat, she had warned them they would have to get the bottles to smash inside the boat. A boat like this was designed to shuck water off its decks but petrol would pool in the cockpit. That was their best chance.

More bangs. Rockets exploded around them, purple and green. From being alone in a dark sea, they were now surrounded by an enormous bubble of colour as the fireworks burst open in the sky.

The attackers were clearly lit up, exposed to the light.

'Go, go, go,' shouted the man in the stern, urging the driver to pull away. Kai recognised him; he had been one of the crew members too. Kai saw him reaching down for an automatic rifle.

'Yuliya, now,' Erin was screaming. 'Now.'

Still at the prow of the speedboat, Marissa had turned and was urging whoever was at the wheel to speed away too. Kai saw the man reach down towards the throttle and thrust it forwards.

At that moment, another of Yuliya's rockets shot down towards the boat and, whether by fluke or design, hit the boat's driver full in the chest. He fell back, screamed. A couple of seconds later the incendiary exploded with a flash inside the open boat and a semi-circle of blue stars blew upwards from the water. The air was suddenly filled with smoke and the smell of gunpowder, sparks crackling and fizzing as they dropped to the sea.

It had been Erin's idea. She had turned several of the hollow metal poles that held the awning into bazookas, securing the rockets at one open end with tape. Yuliya insisted she be the one who aimed them. They were her fireworks, after all. Stepan's job was to stand behind with a lighter, igniting them on command.

Temporarily blinded by the light, it took a second for Kai to realise that, instead of speeding past *Zinaida*, the driverless speedboat had turned straight towards them at speed. The bow glanced hard into their stern side on. There was little to hold on to on the streamline hull, surface slick with petrol. Marissa was knocked straight forwards, catapulting into the water between the speedboat and the superyacht.

Kai watched in horror as the boat motored right over her, bumping angrily alongside the hull until it was free, then screaming off into the darkness beyond the light of the fireworks. There was no kill switch.

Kai leaned forward over the back of the swimming deck, trying to see whether Marissa had survived, and in the same second saw that the boat was circling back, completely out of control. The man who had been standing in the stern had lowered his gun and was struggling to lean past the stricken driver, to try and regain control of the vessel. Even above the engine roar,

246

Kai could hear the driver was still screaming in pain from the injuries Yuliya's rocket had inflicted. The boat was heading back towards them – fast.

'Quick,' shouted Erin.

'What?'

'The bottles. Again.'

Kai looked. Zina was clutching them; there were three left.

'Do it,' she said.

As the boat sped towards them, Kai ran to the side of the boat, checked the angle, raised the bottle and threw his first. It flew up in an arc and splashed into the sea, just before the speedboat collided a second time. This time the bow smashed straight into them, so hard they felt the impact. Nose on, the engines screamed as it pushed against them.

'Again,' Erin shouted.

Fireworks missed the boat, skimming the surface of the sea, exploding into silver moons that spat on the water's surface. Smoke drifted across the water. The only man left standing on the boat raised the automatic rifle up at them, but in the roaring speedboat, jammed against their hull, he was finding standing hard.

'Hurry,' Erin shouted.

The man was firing now. Kai could hear the whizz of bullets speeding past him. 'Another one.' Zina passed the second bottle to him. The neck was slippery with petrol. He misjudged his throw and it smashed uselessly against the side of the boat.

Erin was screaming something, but he couldn't hear what the words were.

Right above them, Yuliya stood with the awning pole on her shoulder. Stepan would be behind with a lighter.

The gun spat bullets.

Her rocket missed the boat completely and was swallowed by the sea before it could explode. Another seemed to shoot up vertically and explode above them, turning the white superyacht a dazzling emerald green for a few seconds.

'Did you get any petrol into the boat at all?' Erin was shouting.

The last bottle in his hand, Kai looked over the edge of the boat, then ducked back as a burst of gunfire shattered the edge of the deck next to him. This was his last chance.

As he glanced up, Kai was suddenly conscious of Yuliya above him again, lit by green light, a huge red rocket in her hand, sparks flying out behind it. She had given up on the improvised bazooka. He watched in horror as she held the body of it as if it were just a toy glider, pointing it nose down, waiting for the fuse to explode. 'Jesus Christ.'

He straightened fast, looked down. The boat was right under them still, pushing against *Zinaida*'s side. As Yuliya leaned over the edge of the deck above, below her Kai let loose the last bottle.

The bottle and the rocket exploded simultaneously. Next thing, they were all inside a vast ball of colour, light and heat. The greens, yellows and blues faded fast, leaving only the orange of flame.

There was the sound of someone screaming. It seemed to continue for a very long time as they lay there on the deck, cowering from the heat.

There was another blast and the screaming stopped.

Kai and Zina stood slowly, faces lit red by the heat below them. The rising smoke turned grey, then a dense black.

'Where are they?' Erin leaned over the side above them. 'Did they go into the water?'

'The boat went right over Marissa,' said Zina, her eyes big. 'I saw it.'

Kai joined Zina, cautiously peering back over the edge, but as the fire caught hold, eating into the glass fibre hull of the speedboat, the smoke became yet more acrid. His eyes watered; his lungs stung. He could see nothing at all.

'We did it,' he said, wonderingly. Fire had consumed the whole of the speedboat's cockpit.

He flung his arms around Zina; she hugged him back.

And then, above, there was a wailing. 'Quick. Come quick.'

Erin turned, disappeared. Above them someone was shouting.

Zina looked around, dazed. 'Dad?'

'*Prikhodi bystro!*'

'Dad!' Then Zina was running towards the steps up to the helicopter deck.

FORTY

Erin switched on her torch and shone it where Yuliya lay. This had been her plan. She was responsible for this.

The woman lay on her back on the flat helicopter deck, moaning quietly. The skin on the right side of her face was burned raw. Pale curls of crisp skin cracked above red wet flesh. Her right arm was black and starting to blister. Blood seemed to be seeping down her T-shirt from underneath her hand.

'*Ona byla zastrelena*,' said Stepan.

'He says she's been shot,' Zina translated. 'She has been shot in the chest.'

Choking black smoke was curling round the edge of the deck.

'Can you hear me?' Erin asked.

'Good fireworks,' Yuliya whispered. '*Oni tebe ponravilis'*, Stepan?'

Erin turned to him and realised there was blood on his face too, though his was from shrapnel lacerations. She shone the torch around; small splinters of metal were scattered over the wood – presumably from bullets that had pierced the deck below them.

'Fetch water,' Erin ordered. Kai disappeared to find it.

Below them there was another explosion from the speedboat, louder than the others and big enough to send debris into the air; a second later it clattered down around them.

Erin stood and went to look over the edge, worried that the burning speedboat would set fire to *Zinaida* too, but the explosion had split the hull of the speedboat in half. She arrived just in time to see the stern disappear, dragged down by the weight of its engines, while the bow pointed upwards and bobbed in the water. A burning life jacket floated on the surface.

She returned to Yuliya's side. Zina was cradling her mother's head, whispering to her in Russian.

Erin took time to look more closely at her wounds. Drops of sweat lined the older woman's forehead. The burns on her face and arm were from the rocket that she had seen her holding – the final explosive that had hit the target dead on. If it was a serious injury to her chest, there was not much they would be able to do. But when she looked closer, she realised that the blood seemed to be coming from the hand that clutched her chest. It took a second for her to realise that maybe Yuliya hadn't been shot in the chest at all. Gingerly she lifted the woman's arm.

Yuliya yelped in pain. The bullet, or a fragment of shrapnel, had not penetrated her torso at all. It had passed right through her palm.

'Hold up her arm,' she ordered. 'It will bleed less.'

Zina took her mother's arm, raising it, while Yuliya keened, wordlessly.

Kai returned with three large bottles of sparkling mineral water. 'Sorry. It was all I could find. The taps won't work.'

Of course they wouldn't. The pumps were all dead.

They worked together. Stepan removed his shirt and they tore it into rags, soaking them and dabbing them on the burned skin. Yuliya groaned and winced as the water touched her skin.

'*Izvinyayus,*' whispered Stepan.

'Best fireworks, hey?' Yuliya said.

Erin realised that Stepan was crying. 'Best fireworks,' he answered. 'They were magnificent.'

Erin dabbed water gently on the woman's forehead and around her eyes.

Yuliya opened them, then closed them again.

Rain started to fall, thick and tropical, sputtering on the flames below.

She turned. 'Kai?' she said. 'Go down to the sea deck. Wait there for a while. See if anyone survived. There may be people in the water.'

'Really?' he answered. 'After that?'

'If they are there, leave them,' said Stepan.

'Go,' said Erin.

Dutifully, Kai disappeared down the steps.

The rain got heavier. It came in gusts. In no time the deck around them was slick with water running off into the sea. She looked up. The wind seemed to be coming from the north-east, which was not good. The depression would be to the north-west of them now, and heading west. That meant the winds would get stronger soon. She would need to get the bilge pump working.

'We need to get her inside,' Erin said. 'Can we lift her?'

'Leave me alone,' said Yuliya, sitting up. 'I can fucking walk.'

Stepan on one side, Zina on the other, they guided her down the external stairs to the Pirumovs' private floor and laid her on a bed inside their bedroom. When Zina closed the door, the silence was a relief.

Erin looked around. When she and Marius had taken their trips together, this was the room they had slept in. He had always wanted to use the best cabin, with the biggest bed. He had lain here, naked on the sheets, looking around him, imagining all this was his. Probably imagining that she was some pretty heiress too.

When Yuliya was comfortable, she went to the first-aid locker on the bridge and returned with dressings. They washed her wound and dressed the burns on her arm and face as best they could, and wrapped gauze round her wounded right eye. The burns were bad. She would need hospital treatment urgently.

'Right,' Erin said. 'I have things I have to do.'

She left the family in the bedroom and walked out onto the helicopter deck. The once white boat looked scarred and dirty. The big deck was covered in blood and debris. On the next deck down, the third mate lay in a pool of shattered glass. She continued down to the sea deck.

The rain was still coming in squalls, but it seemed to be thinning, and the first light was starting to break under a line of black cloud in the east. What had felt like the longest night of her life was almost over. They were survivors. They could reconnect the batteries, start up the pumps; everything would be OK.

She looked around. The swimming deck was deserted. She was annoyed. She had told Kai to stay here as lookout. 'Kai?' she called.

But there was no answer.

FORTY-ONE

Kai felt suddenly exhausted. He had just killed people. This was something that was unfathomable to him.

They had fought a pitched battle with armed killers and won. There should be some sense of exhilaration that went with that; instead there was just confusion.

He was glad to be away from the others so he could process it all. The sea around the stern was full of debris, and, after the brightness of the flames and fireworks, the sky seemed darker than ever now.

The petrol he had dropped on the boat had been what had caused the explosion. There had been two people left on the boat, as far as he could see. A woman had drowned or been carved up by a boat's engine. They were dead and he didn't know how he was supposed to feel about that. What surprised him was that he was not sorry at all, or even repulsed by what he had done. He shivered and peered out into the blackness, wondering if the bodies were out there.

The rain had soaked him, but the water was warm, even in this wind. The drops hissed on the last of the glowing debris of the boat and the blackness became complete again.

Only for a short while. Under the dark rain clouds, a band of dull silver had emerged on the horizon. It was dawn. He was used to the slow arrival of light that came in higher latitudes. Here it was much more sudden.

As he looked he thought he saw something moving in the water, a different motion from the waves.

He squatted low and peered again, struggling to see.

'Hello?' he called, but his voice was cracked and tired. 'Erin? Come. Quick.'

The rain suddenly came down more heavily, muffling his shout.

When the squall abated for a second he saw it again in the twilight. An arm, raised from the waves.

Just five or six metres from the back of the boat, he could just make out the shape of someone struggling to swim.

'Help,' he shouted, trying to call to the others above the noise of the rain on the deck as he watched the man splashing in the darkening water. For long seconds at a time, the man disappeared totally beneath the surface.

Three days ago, in the sunshine of the bay at St Thomas, he had almost drowned himself and had been rescued; now he was watching another person drown. Beside him, dipping into the water as the boat tilted, hung a bright orange lifebelt. He yanked the bright orange ring from its harness and peered out, trying to judge where he had last seen the man.

256

The hand emerged again, clutching at air, and finally, what seemed like an age later, a face. It was closer now.

Kai drew back his arm and flung the lifebelt into the water. It landed well short.

'Wait,' he shouted, and tugged the belt back towards the boat, lifted it, and threw it a second time. This time it fell a little closer. It was not a man at all. It was a woman. Kai watched her splashing towards it painfully slowly, unsure whether she was just a poor swimmer, or whether she had been seriously injured.

It was too dark to see. The swimmer finally reached the lifebelt and hooked an arm round it.

Kai tugged on the thin orange rope, towing her towards the back of the boat. He leaned his weight backwards to haul her in.

A wave broke over her. She emerged from the spray, mouth wide, gasping.

'Pull.' He heard her beckoning to him. 'Please.' He was close enough now to recognise her in the early light. It was Marissa. The woman who had tried to kill them all; who had fooled him by pretending to be a victim once before.

He stopped pulling the rope and called again for help, just as the boat rocked on a bigger wave and, instead of being drawn away from him, Marissa seemed to surf forwards and was suddenly at the lip of the deck. Kai dropped the rope and stood, ready to fend her off if she tried to board before any help arrived.

'Come closer,' pleaded Marissa. 'I'm hurt real bad.'

'Stay right there.'

'Can't you see I'm drowning?'

'Really. I don't care.'

'You bitch,' she said. And that's when he realised that Marissa was not grimacing, she was smiling, teeth perfectly symmetrical and white.

Kai jerked backwards, away from her, and bumped into something – someone. Before he could look around, there was an arm around his neck. He tried to scream but the arm tightened expertly, choking him. All that emerged was a croak.

As Marissa pulled herself out of the water, Kai saw she had the gun still slung across her shoulder. She shook herself like a dog, then stepped forward, her face close to Kai's, and raised her finger to her lips. *No noise.*

The boat had missed Marissa. She was completely unscathed. The other man behind him must have escaped the explosion somehow too.

'Quiet,' said Marissa, and placed her hand on top of Kai's head and rocked it back and forward to make him nod in agreement. 'Good,' she said. 'You understand? Where are they? How many people are still alive? Hold up your fingers.'

Kai tried to shake his head.

'C'mon, Kai. If you help us, we will put you in a lifeboat. I'm not interested in you.'

Marissa and the other man needed to know where the others were so they could sneak up on them and kill them.

'Tell me, please, because you know I will kill you if you don't,' she said.

The other man released his grip slowly so that he could talk, but he had nothing at all to say. They would kill him anyway, just as they had killed Marissa.

Marissa shrugged. '*Ubey ikh,*' she ordered.

258

The rain stopped as suddenly as it had started.

He didn't understand Russian, but he knew what Marissa had told the other man to do. The grip tightened; Kai found he couldn't breathe any more. He would die soon. He kicked and wriggled but the man behind him was stronger and obviously used to killing.

It felt ridiculous to struggle and panic but he was unable to stop himself from flailing his arms and legs.

But instead of tightening, the arm loosened and the man dragged him backwards, into the darkness behind the steps.

Someone was coming down the stairs. 'Kai?' a voice called.

The arm was tight around his neck again, choking him. He kicked out, tried to call out to warn Erin to go back, but he could get no air out of his throat.

FORTY-TWO

Descending the gangway, it was already light enough for Erin to see through the falling rain: a lifebelt bobbing in the water behind *Zinaida*. It wasn't from the speedboat. It was one of *Zinaida*'s, attached by an orange rope. That puzzled her.

Curious, she stepped down onto the swimming deck and as she did so, she heard something moving behind her.

'Kai?' she said again. She turned and peered into the blackness.

It was not Kai who had moved. Marissa was standing in the darkness under the stairs; it was already light enough to see she was holding a semi-automatic rifle and pointing it at Erin. Marissa didn't even have a cut on her.

Behind her, Aleksander had not been so lucky. His shirt had been burned away, much of his hair too, and there were raw red marks across his torso – but he was clearly not too badly hurt because he was holding Kai in a tight headlock.

Kai's eyes bulged from his head, and he was opening and closing his mouth slowly.

'Where are the family?' Marissa demanded.

'Still in the citadel,' she lied.

'Fuck off. I saw them. They were on the helideck a few minutes ago. You're lying.'

'Let him go,' she said. 'He's dying.'

Marissa shook her head and raised the gun up towards her.

She would shoot. Erin talked fast. 'Until someone comes to rescue you, you need me,' she said.

Marissa paused.

'There's a storm coming. This rain is just an appetiser. The main course is on its way. Look.' She pointed. Marissa kept her eyes fixed on Erin, but the menacing black cloudbank to the north-east was showing clearly against the brightening sky.

'Tropical storm. Four-to-five-metre waves on the way.' Erin had the shakes again. She hoped Marissa didn't realise how scared she was. 'The way it is now, this boat will probably go down. Unfortunately you killed all the other crew and I alone am the only person who can sail this boat in this condition. Your own boat is wrecked. Let him go and there is a chance I can save your lives. Kill him and I won't help you.'

Erin was exaggerating. They would feel the storm, but it would not be that bad here. Marissa seemed unimpressed; she had been on boats before. Aleksander, however, seemed to make his own mind up. He loosened his arm just enough.

Marissa seemed to be weighing the situation up. 'OK,' she said, sighing. 'You have a point. I have a job to do. I'm very very tired now. Let me finish all this shit and then we can all go home,' she said. 'To be honest, this whole trip has been a pain in the fucking ass.' She lowered the gun, bent down and yanked a knife from a scabbard tied above her ankle. It had a long blade with the kind of serrations on the top that Erin guessed were there to do maximum damage to anyone whose flesh it entered. She thought of Marius as Marissa handed it to Aleksander, of Dimitri and the chef.

'You stay here with them,' Marissa told Aleksander. 'If they move, kill him first.' She nodded at Kai. 'Only kill her if you need to. She's probably right. We kind of need her.'

Marissa took the gangway two steps at a time, gun slung back over her shoulder.

'What's she doing?' asked Kai, still lying on the floor. His voice was a croak.

'She's going to kill the family now,' said Erin.

'Jesus,' he gasped.

Erin stood there, waiting for the sound of gunshots. 'Let us go,' she said to Aleksander.

'I can't do that.'

'Why are you doing this?'

'It's my job,' he said. 'You have your job, I have mine.'

She turned towards the sea because she wanted to look at it. The sky to the east had turned a rich denim blue. The shape of the waves around them was clearer now.

You could tell a lot from waves. The wind was creating white caps on the crests. That meant the wind was already starting to hit Force 4. But these were small waves still. It took wind a while to create a rough sea and they were just at the start of it. If the wind reached around twenty knots, the waves would gradually grow to two metres. The wind's direction told her the approximate position of the depression, somewhere to the north-east, and also that the depression would be moving closer, and that as it did, the wind would almost certainly get stronger.

These calculations calmed her. Much of sailing was an inexact arithmetic. Rough guesses could save your life.

As she watched the pale crests in the dull early light, she saw something very strange; she didn't understand it at first: about twenty metres away, a small dot of orange leapt out of the water into the air and then splashed back down.

Puzzled, she stared, trying to make sense of what she had just seen, and as she did so, a second popped up closer, and then a third, jumping up like the first, as if it had been trapped somehow under the water and was eager to escape its clutches, shooting out and falling back down again. They were followed in quick succession by more; the sea was suddenly full of them. As they floated, small green lights began to blink in the darkness.

She laughed out loud. They looked like Christmas lights. It was the best thing she had ever seen.

'What this time?' said Aleksander wearily.

Dragging her eyes off the scene, she turned back to the deck. Aleksander had not seen it yet because he was holding the knife to Kai's chest to make sure he didn't shout out and give them away.

'Look,' she said.

Aleksander looked to where she was pointing. A small crowd of small green lights flashing on the stormy water.

'Fuck,' he said simply.

'What's your story going to be now, when the rescue plane gets here?'

Aleksander shook his head. 'This isss a fuck-up.'

'Yes it certainly is,' she said.

Aleksander had put all the emergency beacons in a black plastic bag to keep them dry, and put them aboard the speedboat. They must have been stuck in a locker somewhere when the boat went down. But now the boat had broken up, they had been dragged down with it until they had freed themselves and sprung back to the surface.

'I reckon they'll be looking at multiple reports of *Zinaida* sinking right now. That AIS you set up just disappeared off the map with your speedboat. All these EPIRBs are beaming their location to the Global Maritime Distress communication network. I reckon they'll have search planes in the air out of Honduras in . . .' She looked at her watch. 'Maybe twenty minutes. They'll be here in, what, forty-five? Every ship in the area is already heading our way. They're going to find a yacht full of bodies. What are you going to tell them?'

'Fuck,' he said again. Aleksander, the cocky Pole, looked less certain of himself than she had ever seen him. His name probably wasn't even Aleksander, she realised. He probably wasn't even Polish.

'We're going to talk to Marissa. OK?'

Aleksander lowered the knife. ''Rissa!' he shouted. 'You better come. Something kind of fucked up has happened.'

There was no answer.

He abandoned them on the swimming deck. 'Marissa. *Gde ty?* Stop! *Vy dolzhny eto uvidet'.*'

Erin went to Kai and knelt by him. 'You OK?'

He nodded.

They heard Marissa cursing. Any element of surprise she had hoped for, creeping up on the family, was gone. They heard the two assassins arguing.

Marissa appeared at the top of the steps to the swimming deck. '*O chem ty, chert voz'mi, govorish?*'

Then she, too, saw the lights. Erin watched the woman's face as understanding slowly dawned. Every green light bobbing, disappearing, coming back up on the next wave, was another signal telling the world precisely where they were and beckoning every vessel of every shape and size around them to stop what they were doing and come and find them.

FORTY-THREE

'I have a proposal,' Stepan told Marissa. Stepan and Marissa sat at opposite ends of the long table in the dining room.

They had cleaned the worst of the blood from Stepan's face. He had put on a clean white shirt to replace the one they had torn up to use on Yuliya's wounds. He was trying to look like a man in charge of events again. He was holding a business meeting.

If the scene wasn't absurd enough already, *Zinaida*'s tilt meant that the dining room was at an angle. Marissa sat at the high end of the table, rifle on her lap, Stepan at the lower end. As the ship rolled, each went up and down, like children on a see-saw. Erin sat in the middle, between them, facing towards the bow, as if she was somehow adjudicating.

The table had been prepared for breakfast by a crew who were now all dead. Glasses, plates and gold cutlery lay on the white linen. Kai stood at the door. Like him, Aleksander was merely an observer. He stood next to Kai in the doorway with the knife in his hand, if needed. Zina had remained in the cabin, nursing her mother.

'*Govorite po russki,*' Marissa demanded.

'No. Speak in English, then everyone can understand,' said Stepan. 'English is the language of business. You and me are about to do business.'

'Oh sure,' Marissa scoffed. 'You're not really in a position to offer me anything at all, Stepan, right this minute.' She tapped the gun on her lap.

'You were sent to kill us,' said Stepan. 'You failed.'

'Maybe. Maybe not,' Marrissa answered. 'We still got time.'

Stepan scowled. 'The point is, whoever employed you to do this will not be happy. It has not turned out the way they planned.'

'No. There I must agree. It has not. It has been one royal fuck-up, start to finish.'

'And the reason that person sent you to kill me was because they were not happy with me, either.'

'Will this take long?' asked Marissa, looking at Stepan. 'I just want to finish the job and go home.'

Stepan ignored her. 'It is a difficult situation. Both of us have let the authorities down. Both of us are making them unhappy. A botched assassination attempt makes the person who ordered it look foolish.'

'It doesn't look great,' said Marissa. 'Got to admit that.'

'So how can we fix this?'

Marissa pushed her chair back. She looked at Stepan blandly. 'OK. Tell me. What have you got that is any use to me?'

Stepan leaned forward. A man who held meetings, he seemed

267

to be regaining his confidence. 'When the rescuers come, which they will soon, we tell them we were attacked by pirates. There have always been pirates in these waters. Everybody knows that.'

'That's a movie, Christ sakes,' said Marissa. 'That shit does not actually happen.'

Stepan said, 'You think so? Venezuela is a rogue state, pretty much. There are pirates all along that coast now. There have been other attacks. We will just tell people that they are getting more ambitious now. They attacked us with a speedboat. You fought bravely and defended us.'

Marissa nodded. 'Sure I did. That's me all over.'

'The person who ordered you to kill me will not be seen to have failed. We were simply all victims of a terrible attack.'

'And in return, you won't tell the media we tried to kill you? And in that way you hope the big man in charge will think, *Oh, that's sweet. Stepan doesn't blame me for all this.* And he will forgive you and everything will be fine again.' It wasn't exactly contempt in Marissa's voice, thought Kai, but not far off.

Stepan said, 'I'm not an idiot. I am aware that I have caused a great deal of offence. We will be punished, I know. I will not be in favour. We will lose our fortune. But hopefully not our lives. And we can start again from the beginning. But, yes, I am not going to complain, even though Yuliya is lying in the cabin next door, injured by your man's fucking bullet. If we tell the world this story, at least I may be able to demonstrate that my intentions were always loyal. Which they always were.'

Marissa snorted. 'Yeah. Loyal. Really loyal.'

'It's all we have right now,' said Stepan. 'The rescue boats will be with us very soon. It's the best outcome for all of us.'

Marissa seemed to need a moment to make her mind up. She sat perfectly still as the boat rolled up and down until she finally nodded her head and said, 'You're a clever man, Stepan.'

'Thank you.'

'Pretty fuckin' clever. However, I would expect some compensation.'

'Within reason, I agree.'

'I think we are close to an understanding, Mr Pirumov.'

'I hope so. Because we will not have long to get our story straight. If modern history teaches us one thing, it is that the story is always more important than the truth. I know perfectly well what my story has to be. I hope you do too.'

'Yes, I think I understand very well,' said Marissa. She seemed to consider this for a moment longer and then picked up the weapon that lay on her lap. In a simple, practised movement she flicked a switch on the side, cocked it by sliding back a lever, and then raised it and pointed it at Stepan.

Stepan's eyes widened. 'No!'

But instead of firing the gun at Stepan, Marissa twisted her body slightly to his left and fired.

Aleksander, who was standing next to Kai, snapped backwards, dropping the knife which landed on the floor at Kai's feet, its blade embedded in the floor.

Kai turned to look at what had happened. Marissa's companion lay on his back, a bullet wound just above his left eye. The man's legs twitched briefly, like a dreaming dog's might do, and then he was still.

'A goodwill gesture,' explained Marissa. 'It is important to make absolutely sure of our story. You agree?'

Kai turned to look back at the table. Stepan's face was white. Kai realised he probably looked the same.

'Yes,' said Stepan eventually. 'Received and understood. We have a deal then?'

The next to speak was Erin. 'That was a stupid waste of a human life.'

'Don't,' blurted Kai, terrified for what would happen next if she spoke against Stepan's plan.

'Shut up,' she answered him. 'I have something to say.' All eyes turned towards her. Stepan frowned. She was trying to keep her voice steady, though he could see from where he was that her body was shivering in shock. She continued talking, all the same. 'Aleksander was the one who disabled the electrics, wasn't he? We have no idea how long it's going to take the rescuers to get here. Of all the people we need to keep the boat afloat right now, he was the most important. You're a stupid bloody idiot.'

Marissa looked straight at her. The safety catch was still off on her rifle and she pointed it towards Erin. 'Well, it looks kind of like that is your job now,' said Marissa.

Erin sat there for a moment, shaking her head rapidly from side to side, almost as if she was not in control of it. 'Great,' she said eventually, pushing back her chair. 'Bloody great.' She stood unsteadily, turned and wiped her face with the back of her hand. Kai realised she was crying. 'Kai,' she said, steadily as she could. 'I'm going to need you to help me patch the isolators please.'

Kai knew what she was doing. She was trying to save their

lives. If Stepan wanted to keep the story straight, the story he and Marissa wanted to tell, Erin was an inconvenience, just as Aleksander had been. And so was he. They belonged to an entirely different and much less satisfactory narrative.

FORTY-FOUR

'She wants to kill us, doesn't she?' Kai was shouting to be heard above the noise of the wind. They had left the dining room and emerged out onto the helicopter deck.

The rain was easing off. Glad just to be out of that room, Erin said nothing. Her instinct as a sailor told her that they should do everything they could to keep *Zinaida* afloat before the rescuers arrived, but once they restarted the pumps Marissa would have no need for them.

'What if we lock ourselves into the panic room? They couldn't get us there, right?' Kai suggested.

She was thinking, weighing up the options. None of them were great.

'But Jesus. I'm not sure if I could face being back inside that box again,' he said.

She turned to him. 'You're a friend of the family. Perhaps you'll be all right.'

He rolled his eyes. 'You seriously think so? How long have you

272

worked for them?' She was surprised by the venom in his voice. If they had killed Aleksander, they would think nothing of killing her, but she had hoped he would be safe. 'They are monsters,' he said. 'All of them. Haven't you figured that out yet?'

She led the way down the external stairs, one level after another, until they were at the sea deck again, and then went back through the door into L1 and down the internal stairs. Out of the wind she could think again.

'What about Zina?' she asked.

He blinked at her, temporarily thrown by the question. She was supposed to be his girlfriend.

'What about her?' he said.

'She's your lover. She will stick up for you.'

He looked at her like she was mad. 'She's exactly the same as her parents. She's only sticking up for herself.'

'I'm sorry,' Erin said.

'For what?'

Erin switched on her torch as they entered the dark electronics room. The water sloshed from side to side and it was hard to tell whether it was deeper now than when they had last been in here.

The circuits they had prepared were ready. If Kai was right, all they had to do was fix the wires across from positive to negative and they could eliminate each circuit until they had found the one that would restart the emergency pumps. Kai had left the short wires he had prepared in the base of each cabinet. He picked them up and stuffed them into his pockets, out of sight.

'Right,' she said. 'So we're not fixing the pumps then.'

'No way. The longer we can delay the better our chances, right? What about you? Are you OK?' he asked.

'What do you mean?'

'When Marissa killed that guy . . . What you did was very brave,' he said. He picked up the roll of wire and threw it into the open door of the engine room where the water was deeper. He was thinking clearly, trying to save their lives. 'You stood up to her. I thought she was going to shoot you.'

'So did I.'

He went through the electro-technical cupboards looking for any more wire. There were heavy reels of it. He threw these too behind them, into the engine room's dark water, out of sight. 'This is crazy. Are they really just going to say they were attacked by pirates? Is anyone going to believe them? She's holding the gun she shot at us with. Won't there be forensics?'

'Does he look worried?'

'No.'

'We're at sea and in international waters. Do you know what that means? There won't be any forensics. Or if there are, they'll be on their own terms. This boat is registered in the Cayman Islands and they are billionaires. Whatever they say happened here is what happened here.'

'Jesus. You work under those conditions?'

'That's just how it is. Who knows, maybe they'll set up an investigation to make it look good—'

'Ssh,' he said. 'Someone's coming.'

They both turned.

'Fixed yet?' Marissa leaned into the doorway.

Erin and Kai shared a glance. 'Not yet,' said Erin. 'We still need time.'

Marissa looked down at the water below her, then at the open cabinet doors.

'How much time?'

'Maybe an hour?'

'Seriously? Are you dicking me around?'

'No,' she said.

'I hope not. You have a watch there?' Marissa asked.

Erin looked at her, nodded, puzzled by the question.

'What's the exact time right now?'

It was still early. 'Six fifty-two,' she said.

Marissa lifted the gun and pointed it at Kai. 'I'll give you five minutes and I kill the pretty boy. Tell me when it's six fifty-seven.'

Erin looked at Kai. 'You kill him and you won't get any help from me.'

Marissa shrugged. 'Let's see if that's true in five minutes.'

Erin glanced at Kai. She flicked her eyes meaningfully down at his pockets. He could save himself – maybe for a little while – by pulling out the wires, but she saw him give his head the tiniest of shakes and she understood. They had to take the chance that Marissa was bluffing. Marissa stood and watched them, so she pressed a few buttons to make it look like she was doing something.

'You know, I really think you're dicking me around.'

'Was it you who killed Marius?' she asked, trying to stall her.

'The captain? No. That was not me.' Marissa shook her head. 'Hey? Were you and him close? I heard a rumour but I wouldn't have thought you were his type. I caught him staring at my ass a couple of times.'

'It was Aleksander who killed him?'

'No,' Marissa said, sounding like a schoolteacher exasperated by a child. 'It was pirates. Haven't you learned anything at all today?' She laughed quietly. 'How many minutes have gone?'

Erin checked her watch. It was 6.53. She didn't answer, instead pressed a few more buttons pointlessly. 'Aleksander disabled the electrics remotely. We don't know how he did it. Unfortunately we won't know, now.'

Marissa pointed to her wrist, where a watch would be.

Erin said, 'Maybe you should inflate the life rafts, in case you need to get to them in a hurry. If we don't succeed.'

'Maybe you should hurry the fuck up.'

There was a slap of water against the hull. Side on to the waves, the boat rolled so hard that Kai lost his footing and slipped, falling into the slopping water on the metal floor.

Erin looked up and saw, for the first time, a twitch of anxiety in Marissa's eyes. The instability of the boat was scaring her. She had less faith in *Zinaida*'s seaworthiness than Erin did.

Kai stood, caught Erin's eye. His back was to Marissa. '*What do we do?*' he mouthed.

Erin had given up pretending to fix things; she didn't want to play this ridiculous game any more.

'How long will it take any boats to arrive?' Marissa asked, fingering the trigger of her weapon.

Erin looked at her watch: 6.54. 'The alarm went out twenty-five minutes ago.' Was that all? 'Maybe another twenty minutes still. Maybe longer. There may be a search and rescue plane, but with this weather, who knows? They might not be able to take off. Depends what . . .' Erin stopped. She heard shouting somewhere on the boat. Marissa looked around.

'Guys. Guys.'

It was Zina. 'Hey, Marissa. Come and look at this. They're here.'

'Who?' Marissa said.

'Who do you think? People. They've come to rescue us.'

'You said twenty minutes.'

'There must have been boats closer to us than we thought.'

Rather than relief, Erin thought she saw a flicker of annoyance on Marissa's face. She had had business she wanted to complete before the rescuers arrived – and now they were here. She would kill them now, Erin thought. She closed her eyes, readying herself for the bullet.

But when she opened them, Marissa had gone. Perhaps if the boat was too close she wouldn't want to risk firing a gun.

They emerged out of the room and took the route up the internal steps into the L1 landing.

'This way,' urged Erin. She grabbed Kai's hand and ran up another level to where there were external doors on each side of the boat. Carefully, she opened the door to the port-side gangway and peered out.

She scanned the horizon to the south-east but couldn't see any boats.

'Other side,' she said. They crossed back and opened that door. 'Come on.'

'Nothing here either,' Erin said.

They crouched under the external stairs that came down from the main floor. 'Do you think she did that on purpose?' Erin asked, voice quiet.

'What?'

'Zina. Was she deliberately distracting her so we could . . . ?'

Kai poked his head above the handrail. 'There,' he said. 'She was right.' At first Erin saw nothing. There were no navigation lights; no sign of an armada coming to rescue them. Erin finally spotted a single grey sail outlined against the dark sky, maybe a quarter of a mile away. Even at this distance she could see it was a heavily reefed mainsail, badly set.

'That doesn't look like a rescue boat,' she said, peering at it in puzzlement.

'It doesn't matter. It's people.'

She narrowed her eyes. Despite the small amount of sail it was showing, in this wind she was moving fast. The boat was heeling well to starboard, even with the reefed sail.

Next thing, they could hear Marissa was shouting angrily in Russian. She must have discovered they were missing from the electrical room.

'How long have we got?' whispered Kai. 'How long till the other boat's . . .'

Someone was coming down the stairs from above them, running fast. Erin pushed Kai back into the void below the gangway. Shoes stamped, inches from their face.

At the bottom, whoever it was hurried on without looking back, down the next set of stairs.

Erin recognised him as he descended down the next flight. Her boss, Stepan, was hunting them too. If witnesses were coming, they needed to tidy up loose ends. They were both serious about eliminating anyone who could contradict their story.

The door they had come out of opened. There were new footsteps close to them. Somebody else was coming and this person was calmer, more methodical.

'Come out, come out,' a sing-song voice said, quietly, inches away from where they were hidden. 'I know you're in there.'

FORTY-FIVE

'Stupid place to hide,' said Zina. 'You left wet footprints all the
way up the stairs. Found you easily.'

They both looked down at their wet feet. In the dry interior of
the boat they had left prints leading to the door they had come
through. 'I'm an idiot,' said Erin. It was the mistake she had
avoided making before.

'You have got to move,' Zina was saying. 'They'll find you
easily. In a minute, I'll create a diversion, OK?' Things were
happening so fast, Kai was struggling to take in what she was
saying. 'Find a way to keep out of sight until the boat arrives.
He'll kill you otherwise.'

Before Kai could respond, she turned and followed her father's
footsteps down the gangway.

'Let's get out of here,' Erin said, grabbing his T-shirt and
turning to head back up the stairs they had just seen Stepan
coming down.

It was raining again, a steady diagonal downpour. At the top step she paused, looked around and said, 'Follow me.'

'What does she mean, a diversion?'

Erin didn't answer. She set off at a trot round the curved outside front of the dining room. She was taking a risk. The windows were made of darkened glass. It was impossible to tell whether there was anyone still in there looking at them. All Kai could see was his own reflection in the morning light. The curved pane made him look gaunt, half dead already. When they reached the far side of the boat, she stopped, paused, checked the way was clear and set off once more.

The shouting started again, just as they were at the top of the opposite staircase. It was Stepan's voice, shouting a warning.

Kai caught a glimpse of orange, detaching itself from the stern of the boat.

'Stop,' shouted Stepan. 'Stop, you idiots.'

There was a burst of gunfire. Instinctively Kai ducked, but Erin had grabbed him by the shoulder. 'Come on,' she said, taking the stairs down in twos. 'That's the diversion.'

'What?' He looked, then understood. Not one, but three life rafts were floating away from the rear of *Zinaida*, each like an orange tent on the water. The first was already deflating from where Marissa's bullets had punctured it.

Zina's diversion was a good one. Ducking down at the back of the ship, she had launched every available raft she could, throwing them into the water where they burst open, inflating automatically. Five of them, he counted, six.

The gun fired again. As long as Marissa was distracted by them, they had a chance.

'*Follow me*,' mouthed Erin, and pointed over the edge of the boat. She vaulted neatly over the handrail and landed on the top of the open garage door below, crouching down. From there she couldn't be seen unless someone looked over the railing above.

Kai followed, less elegantly, and slipped on the wet surface. Because of the angle the boat was at, the top hydraulic door was tilted down towards the sea. One leg was over the water before Erin caught him; she had one hand braced on the top edge of the door, the other grabbing his shorts until he was able to scramble back up the slope.

'Keep down. They can't see us here.'

The rolling motion of the boat meant they had to grip the high end of the door to keep themselves huddled close to the hull, out of sight.

There was another burst of fire and then the gun fell silent. Maybe she had figured out already there was no one in the life rafts.

Kai had expected the sailing boat to arrive on the far side. Instead it came up towards the stern, then turned towards the wind and the sail started to flap loudly.

'What's going on?' shouted a voice over the noise. 'Was that gunshots?' The accent was American.

'Shit,' said Erin. 'I don't fucking believe it.'

It took Kai a couple of seconds to work out why she was saying it. They had seen the yacht before.

'Everything is OK,' called Marissa. 'We just lost some life rafts.'

The moment it stopped, the yacht lost headway and the wind

pushed her out of their line of sight again. She was back a minute later, tacking awkwardly into the wind.

'Can you help us? We're lost. We saw your fireworks. Quite a party you had.'

Marissa laughed. 'You're fucking lost?'

'Our radio is down. We have no navigation.'

'Oh my God. You're fucking lost.' Marissa thought this was the funniest thing she'd ever heard. Her laughter was louder than the wind.

Kai understood now. It was the same yacht that had almost rammed them in Christiansted, out here, being battered by the rising winds. They had been hoping for a rescue; instead the first boat to arrive looked to him to be in as bad a state as they were.

'I have a plan,' said Erin, leaning over close to his ear.

Crazy Lady had worked her way to the port side now and was in danger of being pushed against the bigger boat's hull by the wind. The man on the yacht was clearly struggling with the wheel. He looked exhausted and scared.

'It's risky,' she said. 'You want to try it?'

As he nodded, a wave rocked *Zinaida*. He clung on harder.

'We drop into the water and swim to the back of the yacht.'

'We're getting on board that thing?'

'Yes,' she said, and for a second he thought she was grinning, but it may just have been the effort of struggling to stay on the narrow door in the wind and rain. 'Stay close. Don't lose sight. Ready?'

And without waiting for another answer, she let go, slid to the edge of the door and reached out a hand to him.

He took it and and she slid again, dragging him into the water

282

below them. Hitting the surface, his hand slipped from hers and he sank. He came up gasping, looking round for her, feeling like he'd swallowed a lungful.

She was there, next to him. She grabbed hold of him again and spoke when her head was close to his. 'We swim round the boat's bow. We need to get to the far side before she catches the wind again. Understand?'

And then she dived underwater. He looked. *Crazy Lady* lay along the length of *Zinaida*'s stern now, pitching against the waves as the frightened sailor tried desperately to bring her alongside. Kai set off after Erin, struggling against the waves.

Even though *Crazy Lady* looked stationary, it took all his effort to make ground on her in order to make it around her bow. He didn't want to get too close. The boat was moving in the waves, her bow leaping up and down like a chopping blade.

He made it to the far side and spotted Erin again. She had made it; she was already clinging to a rope that had been dragged into the water on *Crazy Lady*'s port side, out of sight of anyone on *Zinaida*. All he had to do was reach her.

He was metres away from her when *Crazy Lady* suddenly pitched away from *Zinaida*, the boom swung across towards her and the sail filled with air.

Before he could figure out what had happened, *Crazy Lady* started to move forward again, into the wind, gathering speed, smashing against the rear corner of *Zinaida*, then ploughing on past the boat. It left Kai alone in the sea, struggling to stay afloat in the waves, alone – completely exposed.

FORTY-SIX

The moment Erin saw *Crazy Lady*, the plan had started to form. If they could get on board the other yacht, they would be mobile; that would give them the advantage because *Zinaida* was not. As long as she could keep the clapped-out yacht afloat until rescuers arrived they would be fine.

The risk was that getting aboard another yacht at sea was never easy, even from another boat; getting aboard from the water was much harder. And getting aboard in winds, trickier still. But the boat was luffing, heading into the wind so her mainsail flapped uselessly, and as long as she was doing that, she was stationary. If the boat stayed like that for the next few minutes, they would have a chance. She had seen Kai swimming at St Thomas. He had been foolish, but he was fit – a strong enough swimmer. They would have to act fast.

She leaned over close and said, 'I have a plan.'

There was no time to do more than explain it. They had to act while the boat was stationary. If she picked up the wind

284

before they could get on board, they would have no chance at all. Besides, the plan was insane. If she thought about it too long she'd chicken out. But it was better than waiting to die on *Zinaida*.

Jacob, the app-developer who had bought the boat as a toy, looked terrified behind the wheel. He was trying to bring his yacht alongside the stern of *Zinaida* under sail, which would have been hard enough for an experienced sailor in these seas. He had probably been expecting there to be someone on board ready to throw him a line. Instead, no one was helping him.

'Stay close. Don't lose sight. Ready?'

She slipped off the open door into the warm sea. The moment she was underwater she swam hard, surfacing only to check *Crazy Lady*'s position and to make sure that Kai was still behind her.

He was, so she dived under again and made it past the sailing boat's bow.

Getting on board a yacht without a ladder in open water without help looked easy – until you were there in the water, looking up at the high gunwales of a boat, maybe a metre out of the water with nothing on a smooth hull to grab hold of. Even if you did grab hold of something, a boat sloped inwards. Your legs had nothing to brace against.

She was hoping for some kind of miracle, and when she rounded the bow she saw it.

When Jacob had taken down his jib, the sheet had not been stowed properly. The rope dangled alongside the boat. His lousy sailing habits were what would save her.

She headed for it, allowing herself to be blown downwind

straight towards it and grabbed it easily. In her excitement at seeing a way to board *Crazy Lady* she had forgotten to look round for Kai.

Swinging from the rope, she twisted her head, but couldn't see him.

'Hey,' she called, hoping to get Jacob's attention. 'Here.'

She would need help being pulled into the boat.

That's when it happened. The boom swung her way and the sail was suddenly plump with wind. She had distracted him. He had let go of the wheel and the boat had turned away from the wind just enough to start her plunging forward again.

For a heavy, broad-beamed boat, the Island Packet picked up speed fast, dragging her along with it. She wound the line around her wrist and looked round just in time to see Kai, a look of panic on his face as the boat moved away from them, leaving him alone in the water.

It had been a stupid plan, made in haste.

'Help,' she shouted. 'Luff up. Luff up.'

Jacob's unshaven face appeared over the gunwale. He looked astonished to see someone clinging on to the side.

'Stop the boat,' she shouted up at him.

It would be difficult to pull her up against the force of water dragging her back; if he could slow the boat she would have a chance of getting on board. His face disappeared again and he must have understood because he steered the yacht to starboard enough to start the mainsail flapping again.

A second time his face popped over the edge. She allowed herself to slip back down the rope a little, playing it out over her wrist, until she was just aft of amidships, where the distance from the water was not so great. 'Give me your arm.'

He leaned over the boat and grabbed her, lifted her enough for her to get a free arm onto a cleat, and she managed to pull her weight aboard, flopping into the cockpit.

Lucy, the young woman she had seen in Christiansted, was curled up in the corner, eyes red from crying. She looked terrified.

Erin stood and looked around. The boat had sailed about fifty metres away from *Zinaida*. She scanned the sea for any sign of Kai. In this kind of water, even this close, a head could be difficult to make out, but she saw him right away. A raised arm, waving.

'Jacob,' she said. 'You see that man in the water? Point at him and keep your eyes right on him. Don't stop pointing at him whatever happens, got it?'

He was docile, at least. He pointed.

Erin looked around the boat, knelt and shouted above the loud noise of the luffing sail. 'Lucy. Where's the lifering?'

The nineteen-year-old blinked, not understanding.

'You must have a ring or a horseshoe?'

'We lost it,' she said.

'What about a life jacket?' A nod. 'Can you get it?'

She nodded again and disappeared into the cabin. 'Still see him, Jacob?'

'Yes.'

She looked around. The boat was a mess of ropes. 'You have a rope locker?'

He looked down.

287

'Keep watching him!' she shouted.

'Under the seat.'

She lifted the fibreglass seat and saw a tangle of poorly coiled lines. By the time she had picked one, Lucy was back with a life vest. Tying the rope to a D-ring, she looked once back towards where Jacob was pointing, took a quick glance to see where the lines for the mainsail were.

'We're going to have to gybe,' she said. 'Keep your head down.' For all she knew, she was talking Dutch to him.

Gybing was not something she would ever want to do in a boat she didn't have the feel for, especially in seas like this, but they needed to make a full turn in order to pass Kai and pick him up, and there wasn't enough time or enough water to do this the right way.

She pulled down hard on the wheel, swinging the boat to port. There was a loud bang as the sail filled again. They turned rapidly round to the left, lurching over hard as the wind tipped her sideways. Lucy screamed and crouched back down into her corner again.

The boat turned slowly at first, but picked up the turn to port. 'Keep pointing,' she shouted, pulling in the mainsail as hard as she could, wrapping it round the winch.

Heading back downwind towards *Zinaida*, she caught a glimpse of Marissa, up on the helicopter deck, still holding the automatic rifle. She must have seen her by now.

The boat slowed, but she still had enough headway to keep turning, and then the wind was right behind them and the boat seemed to slow again.

She hauled the mainsheet as close as she could. 'Gybe,' she

288

shouted. Jacob ducked in time, thankfully, as the boom slammed across, then she loosened the sheet off so the sail pulled out and the boat picked up speed towards Kai.

She would have preferred to pick Kai up on the port side away from Marissa, but the wind direction meant she wouldn't have been able to get close on that heading. The manoeuvre meant *Crazy Lady* was now heading to the narrow space of water between the stern of *Zinaida* and Kai. She was doing everything she had been taught not to do. The best way to pick up a person in the water would be to luff up downwind of them and come up slowly, but that would make them sitting ducks.

Following Jacob's finger, she searched the sea and spotted Kai. They were already close.

'Hold the wheel steady,' she shouted. Obediently, he did as he was asked. Pushing past him, she grabbed the life vest and the line, and leaned over the starboard side of the yacht. When they were five metres away, she waved the vest so he could see it.

She threw it just as they drifted past, moving fast, and was relieved to see Kai catch it.

There was a loud cracking noise.

At first she thought they had hit the back of *Zinaida*, but when she looked round, she realised that Marissa was firing her automatic rifle right down at the boat from the deck above them.

The last thing she saw before she had to turn back to help Kai was Zina throwing herself at the killer, trying to knock her off her balance as another spray of bullets hit *Crazy Lady*.

FORTY-SEVEN

For a second Kai thought *Crazy Lady* was going to sail straight over him, but then she veered to his right, between him and *Zinaida*'s stern.

He saw the sail swing over her head, then Erin was waving something orange at him, and the next moment throwing it. It landed just beyond him, in time for him to grab hold of it. When the boat pulled away it felt as if both of his arms were being wrenched out of their sockets, but he managed to cling on as water forced itself into his nose and mouth and down his throat.

It seemed like an age before the boat slowed and Erin was leaning over, hauling in the rope and pulling him aboard.

He wiped water from his eyes and face, coughing, and looked around him, grateful to be safe. In the cockpit sat a gaunt, thinly bearded man with a sunburned face. There were dark patches under his eyes. He looked exhausted. Squeezed into the corner of the deck near the hatch to the cabin was a young girl, arms tight around her knees.

'What the fuck just happened?' demanded the pale man.

She ignored the question, ordering him to take the helm again and stepped onto the coachroof, setting to work coiling the lines, then tugging on others, adjusting the mainsail, looking up, looking down, looking forward and then back.

Then she was back in the cockpit again making a dozen other minor adjustments to the set of the small, reefed mainsail, looking up at it, tugging on one rope, loosening off another, until she felt that she had got it into some kind of respectable shape.

'What happened?' asked the pale man again. 'I don't understand.'

'It's complicated,' said Kai. Trying to understand it himself would not be easy. For the last six or so hours he had been sure he was going to die, whether by drowning, suffocation, knife or bullet. Finally he was free of the nightmare. Everything would be OK.

He grinned up at her. Erin was in her element on a boat like this, however poorly prepared *Crazy Lady* was for this weather. He looked back; *Zinaida* was retreating into the far distance already and would soon be out of sight.

'Got any food on the boat?' asked Kai. He was suddenly hungry and thirsty. He had been supposed to be eating a luxury breakfast with gold cutlery and drinking champagne on board a billionaire's yacht. Right now just a biscuit would be good.

'We have a lot of stupid stuff,' said the girl. 'The rice got wet. We got a lot of cans of soup, though. And some crackers.'

'It's your fault the rice got wet,' said the man.

'Crackers would be great. And some water.'

'You get it, Jacob. I feel seasick.'

'I'm steering the fucking boat. Can't you see?'

Reluctantly the girl stood and pushed back the hatch, then descended into the belly of the boat. She returned with a drinking bottle of water and a plastic bag. 'It's kind of wet down there,' she said, handing Kai the bag.

Kai peered inside. There were two packets of Cheez-It crackers. He took one and waved it at Erin, who had finished tidying the ropes at the front and was retying a tarpaulin that had been rigged to try and stop water coming in through a forward hatch.

She nodded but carried on with her work.

'You know, there's kind of a lot of water down there, Jacob,' said the young woman again.

'What do you mean, a lot?'

'It's, like, everywhere.'

The ride was smoother than he had expected. Though the waves were growing, they were travelling with them. Kai opened up one of the packets and took a biscuit. It tasted as good as anything he had eaten on the yacht. Satisfied that she had done what she could, Erin worked her way back down *Crazy Lady* and jumped down to join them, taking a biscuit from Kai.

'Thank you, Jacob,' she said, taking the wheel off him. 'I think you saved our lives.'

'I don't get it,' said the owner, sitting down again. 'We were coming to you for help.'

'We were lost,' said Lucy.

'Not lost exactly . . .'

'Liar,' said Lucy.

Jacob ignored her. 'And the wind was getting crazy, and then we saw this bunch of fireworks so we just kind of headed straight towards you. Lucy has been freaking out saying we're going to die. Wait. Did that woman fire a fucking gun at us?'

'Marissa fired at us?' Kai looked at Erin.

Erin said, 'There are bullet holes in the deck there. We've got to plug them or they'll let in water. Your girlfriend Zina stopped her. She kind of rugby-tackled her. She would have killed us, I think.'

'Zina saved us?' Kai said.

'Yes. I think she actually did,' said Erin. 'She created the distraction so we could get away. And she stopped that woman blowing a hole in the boat when she was shooting at us.'

'Really?'

'We owe her our lives.'

'No shit,' he said. 'I didn't realise.'

But Erin had already turned to Jacob. 'No radio?'

'The battery is dead and I can't get the generator working. Besides, it's a pile of shit. The guy who sold me this lied.'

'You surprise me.' Erin looked forward. 'Keep a look out. There will be rescue boats coming from the east – that's the most likely direction. We don't want to go too far south or we'll miss them. And we don't want to miss them. If either of you want to go below and rest, do that,' she said. 'We'll keep watch for an hour. You both look worse than we do.'

Kai examined the couple again. It was true. They did.

'I don't want to.' Lucy shook her head. 'It's all wet in there.'

Erin frowned. 'What do you mean wet?'

'All this fucking water's coming in,' she said. 'That kind of wet.'

Erin frowned.

'Go look for yourself.'

She handed the wheel back to Jacob, stepped forward, pushed back the sliding hatch and looked down. 'How long has it been like that?'

'I don't know,' said Lucy.

'Like what?' Kai stood and joined her and was shocked at what he saw. There was so much water in the bottom of the boat that the boards had lifted off the cabin sole and were floating, banging into each other as the boat rolled. She went back and took the wheel off Jacob. 'You look.'

He stepped forward. 'Jesus. Are we sinking? Is that from the holes in the deck you were talking about?'

Erin said, 'Have you had leaks before?'

'Yeah, a little, but not like this.'

She gave him back the wheel and descended to the main cabin, emerged a while later. 'Do you have a life raft?'

Jacob didn't answer.

'Tell her, Jacob. We were using it as a tender. He rowed it onto some rocks in Puerto Rico. It kind of got shredded,' said Lucy. 'I said we should buy another one but he said he'd spent enough on this boat already. Great idea, Jacob.'

Erin swore. She got up on deck again and looked at the bullet holes, where Marissa had fired down at them. Then she addressed Jacob. 'Turn her into the wind,' she said.

He looked puzzled.

'Turn her into the wind,' she said again. 'We need to luff again.'

He pulled the boat round and, as he did so, she pulled in the mainsail tight. It started flapping again as they pointed straight into the wind, but this time the noise sounded more controlled.

'Do you have a harness?' she asked.

Jacob nodded and pointed to the rope locker. She opened it and spent a while delving around until she found a mess of black nylon, untangled it, then handed it to Kai. 'Put it on. I'm going to need you to help me.

With a bit of help, he managed to get it on, stepping into the leg holes awkwardly. When it was secure she clipped Kai onto a jack stay above the main cabin, then donned the life-jacket harness she had improvised for herself and went out first to unreef the mainsail, raising it higher.

'She's insane,' muttered Jacob. 'There's too much wind.'

'Right. You two.' She pointed to Lucy and Kai. 'I want you to get on this side of the boat.' They moved so they were both sitting up on the bench that ran along the starboard side of the boat; she joined them there.

'Jacob. Listen carefully. I need you to bear away to port by twenty-five degrees. OK? Then I need you to hold that steady. She's going to tip a fair amount, and it's not going to be easy in these gusts, but hold the course for as long as you can. Do you understand?'

He nodded. 'You sure about this?'

She turned away and leaned out over the starboard side of the boat. 'Go,' she said.

As he turned the boat to the left, the side they were sitting on rose right out of the water. Kai's stomach lurched. Within a few seconds *Crazy Lady* had picked up speed and was racing along, smashing into one crest after another, sending spray over the bow and soaking them. To Kai it felt like the boat was going to roll over at any second, but Jacob continued to hold the wheel, looking terrified. The wind roared. The wires that held the mast sang.

'Hold my jacket,' she screamed at Kai.

Kai grabbed it, and Erin leaned right out of the boat, looking down at the hull. The damaged side was now being lifted so high Kai thought the boat must go over at any second. Erin's body was almost entirely out of the boat, way over the water. He was holding on to her life jacket, his weight tipped back the other way, but feeling the force of every wave that hit. When she'd had enough she signalled and he yanked her back on board.

'What?' Kai demanded, as she slumped back inside the boat.

Any smile that she'd had since coming on board had gone. For the first time since she'd been on *Crazy Lady*, she looked as scared as the rest of them.

FORTY-EIGHT

'What?' Kai shouted.

'The bullets went in the deck, but they came out of the hull,' she explained.

Erin had been deliberately sailing with too much canvas, forcing the boat to tip, lifting the starboard side as far out of the water as she could. Leaning over, she could see a line of holes about half a metre below the waterline.

She swapped places with Jacob, taking the helm and looking around. 'How many manual bilge pumps are there?'

Jacob looked blank. One pump handle was visible cockpit, near the hatch on the lower side of the cockpit. To her credit, Lucy did exactly as asked, pulling the handle back and forth, chewing on the inside of her mouth as she worked.

'Kai. Go inside. See if you can see another handle like that. It might be in the head – in the toilet. More likely it's in one of the cabins.'

'Shouldn't we change heading?' Jacob sounded anxious.

'We can't. Don't you understand? If we turn round, the holes in the hull end up below the waterline again. We'll sink in half an hour.'

'But . . .'

It meant sailing away from the rescue boats that would be coming for *Zinaida*. It was worse than that though. To stay on a port tack meant heading east-north-east. That was where the storm was. Jacob had been sold a boat that was already in very poor shape. If they carried on in that direction, the winds would strengthen. She had no idea how sound the boat was or whether *Crazy Lady* would be able to stand up to the kind of winds they would be hitting soon.

'Found the pump,' said Kai, head poking out of the hatch. 'Water's still coming in though on the bigger waves.'

'We have to pump out as much as is coming in,' said Erin.

He disappeared again.

With just the mainsail up, the boat couldn't head too close to the wind, but the wind was their friend right now. It was strong enough to keep them heeled over. If it hadn't been blowing like this, the boat would tilt upright and they would have no chance.

It was hard sailing, keeping the boat as close to the wind as she could. Judging from the froth being blown from the waves she reckoned the gusts must be up to forty knots now.

The sea hadn't had the chance to build yet, but there would be bigger waves to come and they wouldn't survive that. The boat was already plunging into the troughs of the waves. However much she tried to keep the starboard side out of the water, the vessel must be taking on a lot.

Given something to do, Lucy looked less scared, at last. Hair flying around her head, she was pumping the handle for all it was worth.

Looking up, Erin saw the mast bending in what was still a relatively moderate wind. There was too much play in the stays and the crosstrees were badly set. If they carried on in this direction there was a danger of it snapping and then they'd lose all control of her. She had to think fast.

'Have you got any spare sails?' she shouted.

Jacob went to the forward cabin to fetch them. He returned with a spare jib. It was big but there were eyelets at each corner. 'Can you tie a bowline?' she asked.

She set him to work tying the three longest ropes in the locker onto the ring on each corner. When it was ready, she tested the knots, then told him to fetch Kai from the cabin where he'd been pumping. 'How is the water?'

'We're keeping up. We're getting rid of it just about as fast as it's coming in.'

'We're going to try something else.'

Pointing the boat into the wind again, she reefed the mainsail, pulling it down until it was just a small triangle of cloth. Taking the wheel again, she swung the boat around, stern to the wind.

'Can you hold this course?' she asked Jacob.

'Are we going to sink?' He looked scared.

'Maybe,' she said.

She led Kai and Lucy up towards the front of the boat and handed them the two ropes attached to the bottom of the sail while she took the third. 'We're going to try and walk it round the bottom of the boat, from the bow, to try and get your side covering all the holes. Then, when I shout, we pull it tight.'

'Like a bandage?'

It felt a little calmer now, at least, as they were being pushed along by the wind and keeping pace with the waves instead of fighting them.

'We'll only get one chance at this. If we don't do it right and the sail gets away from us, the force of water will pull you in. Keep the sail tight against the hull so it doesn't get away. And we'll have to be fast. We don't have long.'

'Won't it get snagged on the keel?' Kai asked.

'Let's hope it doesn't. Ready?' And to put off further discussion, she positioned them, and passed the bundle of sail under the pulpit.

'Got the ropes? Go!' Cautiously, she pulled the sail down into the water. 'Walk back now. Steady. Not too fast!' she shouted.

Kai followed Lucy back along the boat, letting out rope as the sail slid under the hull, watching to keep pace as best he could with Erin, who was on the other side. The first few metres seemed to go well.

'We're doing it!' Lucy shouted.

By the time Kai realised his leg had snagged in something it was too late. He looked down in horror to see Lucy's trailing rope, one end around his ankle and the other under his foot, and realised he was falling sideways and that the only way to stop his fall would be to let go of the rope.

Instead he crashed down onto the side of the cabin, unable to stop himself smacking his head hard on the edge of it, all the time scrabbling to pull in the slack, waiting for the moment when the sail caught the moving water, either ripping itself out of his hands or snatching him overboard.

He looked up from the deck to see Lucy above him, horrified. But the rope was still firmly in his hands. They were lucky. The sail had stayed tight against the hull.

'Up,' urged Erin, simply.

He stood carefully, and the three of them started to move again, back towards the mast.

'Now,' she called. 'Stop.'

They waited as she tied her own end off, then came to take theirs, seeming to take an age tightening each knot. Kai was last.

'Are you OK?' she asked. Kai looked at his hands, printed white from the rope. He brought a palm up gingerly to check the side of his head where a lump was forming.

'You did well,' she said.

She took the helm again, adjusting the sails to head downwind, and Kai went back down to pump some more and to try and judge if they'd managed to slow the amount of water coming in. Running with the wind, the boat was much quieter.

'I think it's slowed.' Kai stuck his head out of the hatch. 'It would be better if we could see the actual bullet holes from this side. They're behind the seating area.'

'Tear it out,' she said.

'Hey,' protested Jacob.

'Shut the fuck up, Jacob,' said Lucy, who had been pumping patiently all this time.

'You think that I can get this on insurance?'

After half an hour working with kitchen implements and a random selection of tools, Kai had exposed the bare hull in the main cabin. 'I've got an idea,' he said.

He had found a scuba diving suit and dragged it back to the cockpit, along with a pair of scissors.

'What the fuck?' Jacob wailed.

'There's still a little water coming in. I can see four holes. I was thinking I could cut out round pieces and force them through. The pressure from the sail might hold them against the hull and help slow the water. What do you think?'

'Good idea,' said Erin.

'You're enjoying this, aren't you?' Jacob glared at her.

'I think she really is,' said Kai.

It was true. It had already been an extraordinarily long day. For the first time in hours she started to feel that things were really going to be all right.

FORTY-NINE

Kai took the helm for a while.

Jacob sulked. He sat with his knees under his chin glowering at Erin, who had gone back to checking over the boat, stem to stern, making adjustments, trying to get to know what her remaining weaknesses were.

He flat refused to take his turn on the pump. 'I'm not doing that,' he said.

'I don't mind,' said Lucy, even though her palms had blistered.

They were heading south-west now, away from the worst of the weather. Erin disappeared into the cabin and emerged twenty minutes later with some mangoes. 'I found these.' She passed them around. To Kai the fruit tasted like heaven.

'Take a break,' she told Lucy. 'You've done well. It's looking pretty good down there now.'

Lucy beamed and took a chunk of fruit.

Kai took one hand off the wheel and felt the bruise on the

side of his head. Seeing him doing that, Lucy disappeared into the cabin and emerged with some arnica cream.

'Here,' she said, and started rubbing it into his skull gently. 'Is that sore?'

The skin was tender but it felt nice. He caught sight of Erin watching them. From her expression, it was as if she thought they were both making a lot of fuss about nothing.

Around eleven in the morning, sunlight finally broke through from some of the clouds. Erin paused from her work and lay on her back across the cabin roof for a while, soaking up the heat for as long as it lasted.

'So are you going to tell us what was actually going on? Why those people were trying to kill us all?' Jacob demanded.

'Like Kai said, it's complicated,' said Erin.

'How do we even know we can trust you?' Jacob said. 'For all we know they might have had good reason to want you dead.'

Kai said, 'I'm going to tell them. They have a right to know.'

'Fuckin' A we do. You wrecked my boat.'

'Like it was in such great shape before,' said Lucy.

So Kai started to tell them everything that had happened over the last twelve hours.

'You are kidding me. That was Stepan Pirumov?'

'Yes.'

'The multi-gazillionaire Stepan Pirumov?' Jacob whooped.

Kai told them about the assassination attempt, and how all the crew apart from Erin had been killed, and how Erin had saved their lives. Erin heard the story like it was something that had happened to someone else.

'That's horrible,' said Lucy. 'You must have been so scared.'

'So he kind of owes me compensation,' said Jacob.

'Didn't you hear what happened, you numbnut?' said Lucy.

Erin looked at Jacob; he seemed to be thinking all this through.

'Where are we going, anyway?' Jacob demanded.

'I don't know,' she answered. 'Like you said, we're lost.'

That day she taught Kai how to sail.

She explained how sails worked; how they could sail into the wind, how the curve of a sail in the wind could create low pressure on one side of the boat, and how pressure of the water against the keel turns this into forward motion. They turned the boat around, tacked, sailed across the wind, then into it, teaching him how a boat handled on different tacks. He tried to keep up, taking in everything she said. She seemed pleased with how he picked it up. 'Good,' she said.

Lucy scolded Jacob. 'You never showed me any of this.'

'You weren't interested. You just wanted to sunbathe and swim.'

'Fuck you. You just wanted to show off to me.'

Finally Erin set the sails out on either side and tied the boom back, so the wind pushed them over the water. 'It's called goose wing,' she said.

'I knew that,' said Jacob.

They travelled away from the bad weather behind them. The squalls started to die. A pod of dolphins escorted them for a while, about twenty of them behaving as if they were a single creature, leaping through the water one after the other, veering away and then returning to play in their bow wave. Kai watched them with a sense of wonder he had not felt for years.

'Wow,' he said, kneeling in the pulpit at the bow, watching them. 'Oh wow.'

And because she was next to him, grinning like a child, he turned to her and gave her a hug. It felt like a perfectly natural thing to do. The two of them had been through so much together, and now there was this.

In the evening they made beds in the cockpit and took turns helming. On his watch the cloud broke. As a city boy he had never seen this. Above the black of the mast, the sky was alive with stars, planes, satellites and meteors. It bristled with light.

At two in the morning he saw the lights of a distant ship. Waking Erin, she trimmed the sails for a new course to try and catch up with it, but after twenty minutes she said, 'It's moving too fast for us. We'll never catch it. You get some sleep. I'll take over.'

At first light he opened his eyes. She was sitting by the wheel, crying. He didn't need to ask why. For her it had been worse. Her colleagues had been murdered senselessly; she had been the one left in charge, the one who had been responsible for all of them. He got up and put his arm around her again.

The next day was calmer.

'You're, like, a rock star?' said Lucy.

'Used to be.'

'Awesome.'

'Not really. I was just very lucky.'

'I never heard of him and I've got a thousand CDs,' said Jacob.

'There's no such thing as luck,' said Erin. 'There is just uneven distribution of opportunity.'

Erin started to talk too. She told them all about her boat *High Hopes* and how she had once dreamed of doing the Vendée Globe and about how she had ended up looking after her dying parents instead.

'That's tough,' said Kai.

'See?' she said. 'I never got the chance to be lucky.'

Kai nodded. 'I understand.'

'Do you?'

'Sail around the world on your own?' said Lucy. 'I would go mad.'

'It's the other people who drive me mad,' said Erin.

Jacob had rallied. He told them about his dreams of founding a micro-local delivery business. 'Nobody actually wants to go to bricks-and-mortar stores any more. But we still want them to exist. Micro-localism is where the money is going to be. When I get back, I'm going to establish a start-up, get some serious Series A VC funding. There's a lot of money waiting for ideas like this.' Jacob talked in certainties, as if he could will this business into existence. They all listened politely, though none of them really understood what he was talking about. Kai wondered if he had talked about this boat trip to Lucy in similarly certain ways before they'd embarked on it.

'What about you?' Erin asked Lucy.

'I had a plan. Not working out so great so far. I dropped out from my degree during Covid because I was studying marketing and I kind of realised I hated it. So I kind of planned to bum around for a few years. The world doesn't really want young people right now so I don't see why I should struggle to find a place in it. And here I am getting shot at in the Caribbean.' She laughed, a little sadly.

With the wind dropping more, Erin fashioned another harness from ropes and went up the mast, Kai pulling on a halyard to help hoist her. Halfway up, she started laughing. It was weird. He could feel her through the rope, shaking with laughter, giggling like a teenager.

'What's so funny?' he demanded.

'Sorry. Nothing. It's just that I'm happy, that's all.' She looked around for other boats but saw none.

'We'll keep trying,' she said. When he lowered her down, he asked again, what was so funny? But she ignored the question.

The third time she went up, she spotted a fishing trawler to the west and they headed straight for it.

The fishermen were from Guadeloupe and told Erin their GPS position. '*Vous êtes perdus?*' They were about eighty kilometres directly west of Dominica. Delighted with the change in their routine, the fishermen cooked up some snapper for them, lowering it down in a basket, and though Lucy offered to pay, they didn't want any money for it. Jacob refused to touch it because he said it was cooked in unhygienic conditions, but the other three ate it with gusto and declared that it was delicious. The fishermen offered them a safe ride home if they wanted to come aboard, but said they wouldn't be back in port for another four days.

'Four days on that stinking boat,' muttered Jacob.

'Dickwad.' Lucy glared.

Kai turned to Erin, raised his eyebrows. 'Well, I suppose we could still make Dominica in *Crazy Lady* easily enough,' she suggested. 'I mean, the weather's settled now. She's in good enough shape.'

She was trying not to sound too eager, thought Kai.

'What?' she demanded when she realised he was laughing at her.

The wind had moved round to the south-east now, so Erin had Kai set *Crazy Lady*'s sails for a broad reach and told him to maintain a course of 095 degrees to account for wind and current.

Erin found a fishing rod with a float in the mess of the main cabin and got Jacob to cast the float out at the bow. Looking at her watch, she timed how long it took before the float was at the stern.

'We're doing five or six knots,' she said eventually. 'If we carry on at this speed, we'll reach Dominica at three or four in the morning, when it's dark. We'll need to heave to until it's light enough to find a harbour.'

As evening fell, they began to see the lights of other boats. Instead of turning in, they all stayed awake, excited at having made it to land.

At round one in the morning, Lucy spotted a different kind of light; directly ahead there was a glow on the horizon, which became a smattering of lights. A village of some sort, perhaps. After the last two days, land looked beautiful.

They sailed for another half-hour before Erin turned the boat around to the south, and hove to. The boat seemed to stand still in the water, leaving a faintly luminous wake behind them.

'What'll you do when you get to shore?' asked Erin.

'I'm going to phone my brother,' said Kai. 'I'm going to tell him how much I love him. What about you?'

'I have no idea at all,' she said, and for the first time since he had met her, she sounded unsure of herself.

FIFTY

Watching dolphins, he had turned and put his arm around her and squeezed her.

It was a pure joy and relief. It hadn't meant anything, but it felt good.

The next day she went up the mast to look out for any nearby land, or for any other ships. He had tugged her up, winching her to the top with the halyard.

Halfway up the aluminium mast, she realised that there was something strangely physical in this act. There she was, trussed with the ropes she had improvised into a harness; each time he pulled the winch, the ropes gripped her round her thighs and tugged between her legs as they lifted her higher. Every jerk of the winch was like the squeeze of someone's hand. She couldn't help it; she had started to giggle.

'What's so funny?' he had shouted from below.

'It's just that I'm happy, that's all,' she said, and it wasn't entirely a lie. When she had first met him, she had thought he was a prick like all the others. He was not. And he was not a bad sailor, either, considering this was his first time.

The next time he hauled her up, she managed to keep a straight face.

After they had lunched on the fishing boat, the sailing had all been by dead reckoning. They had no instruments. It was about guessing the current and calculating the speed over ground. When Lucy first spotted the lights of Dominica, Erin had patted herself quietly on the back. It wasn't exactly Shackleton, travelling 800 miles in an open boat sailing mostly blind to find the pinprick of South Georgia in the South Atlantic, but it was pretty good navigation all the same. The island of Dominica was less than fifty kilometres long. If she'd been out by a few degrees, they could have sailed right past the island. To a sailor with her experience it was not a difficult task, but it was so long since she had sailed like this.

As dawn broke, the land they were facing turned a lush, rich green. Erin sailed north up the coast until she spotted a bay where she could make out the outlines of hulls and masts. At the north end there was a headland where two outsize hills rose straight out of the water, sheltering the curve of land.

As she approached on a broad reach, passing the hulks of old ships mouldering on the shoreline, she saw a small yellow launch heading out from the beach to meet them.

'Hey,' Lucy said. 'Local welcoming party on their way.'

The man at the helm wore a khaki baseball cap, and when he got close, he waved and shouted. 'You want some help?'

'Ignore him,' said Jacob. 'They're always after money.'

The man stood up in his boat. 'Welcome to Dominica. My name is Andrew. Water taxi service. Customs and immigration. Hotel accommodation. Fuel bunkering. Fishing. Whatever you need, I can supply.'

'Oh God,' said Lucy. 'Hotel accommodation. A shower. Heaven.'

'We also do fishing, snorkelling, horseback . . .' The man who had introduced himself as Andrew stopped, mid-flow. 'Jesus. What in hell you people been doing to your boat?' The sail was still rigged under the hull, protecting the holes. 'Were you caught up in the storm?'

'And some,' said Kai.

'God was on your side,' said Andrew.

'Anywhere around here we can take her out of the water?' Erin asked. 'She's holed below the waterline.'

'Not here. We don't have many facilities on this island. Maybe in Roseau.' Erin recognised the name of the island's capital, further down the coast. As she caught the line he threw over to her, he said, 'Was it rocks?'

'No. Bullets,' Erin said.

'Sweet Jesus. You too? Pirates?'

Before anyone else got the chance to answer, Erin said, 'Yes. That's right. Pirates. What do you mean, you too?'

Andrew shook his head. 'This is going to kill us all round here,' he said, standing in the boat. 'First it was the hurricanes, then Covid, and now this. We never had that kind of thing round here. You heard about the other one on the news?'

Erin and Kai exchanged a look. 'Heard what?'

'Pirates. That crazy big Russian millionaire who was attacked

312

by Venezuelans two nights ago. Terrible thing. We never seen nothing like this round here.'

Kai was looking quizzical, Erin noted, but like her he kept quiet.

Andrew wanted to know everything. 'You see what kind of boat they had? Was there many of them?'

Giving the others a warning glance, Erin told them they hadn't been able to see anything because it was dark.

'Same with the Russians.' Andrew nodded vigorously. 'They attacked them at night, I heard. They killed pretty much everyone on board that boat before they could defend themselves. Scary as hell. Only four survivors. They hid while all the killing and looting was going on. You were pretty lucky, I guess . . .' He shook his head. 'If you call it lucky. They took your money? Passports? Everything?'

Kai exchanged another look with Erin. 'Me and Erin's, yeah.'

'Don't worry,' said Andrew. 'We can fix everything. We can call up the High Commission in Barbados. Everything will be OK.'

They followed Andrew to a mooring close to the shore, where they dropped anchor, then he took them ashore in his launch.

'You got to call up the Port Authority and pay this and that. No problem. We can fix it,' said Andrew.

'For a fee,' muttered Jacob.

'Please, Jacob,' scolded Lucy. 'You're being a fucking baby.' Erin liked her more than she had expected to.

From his pitch on the beach, Andrew drove them in a beaten-up open jeep to a yellow-painted hotel where a Chinese woman

313

on the desk seemed grateful for the unexpected arrivals. She let Kai use the hotel computer, where he logged on to his bank account and transferred some money over to the hotel, while Lucy plugged her phone into a charger and sat staring at the screen waiting for it to come on.

Kai counted out the notes that the hotelier gave him and passed Erin three hundred local dollars.

'I'll pay you back, obviously,' she said.

Kai turned back to the woman behind the counter and said, 'By the way, what day of the week is it?'

The woman said, 'You're here one hour and you've gone local already? Monday,' she added, laughing.

'Can I make a call on your landline?' asked Kai. 'I lost my phone.'

It made Erin a little sad to realise there was no one she had to call, to tell them that she was OK, so she left him to it, stepping back out of the air-conditioned room into the humid morning heat, feeling that she had lost something already.

She walked around a little on her own, looking for a clothes shop. It felt strange to be on land after all this time. The earth felt unsteady under her feet. As a sailor she was used to the feeling, but this time the sensation of being on dry land, among ordinary people, felt curiously alien. They were in a small town with a criss-cross of streets. It was called Portsmouth. 'Like in England,' Andrew had said. 'Only much better.'

Portsmouth was a quiet little place. All these islands had been hit badly by hurricanes a few years earlier. Now after Covid the cruise ships had stopped coming, and their economies were just about holding on. Enjoying the mundanity of it, Erin found a general store that sold some tourist stuff and bought a can of Coke, two pairs of men's swimming trunks that she could use as shorts, and some T-shirts. One said *Seven six seven*, which the woman at the counter explained was the country's dialling code, and another had Garfield saying, 'I hate Mondays'.

She sat on the concrete sidewalk for a while, drinking the Coke and looking at the cars that drove past, feeling the solidity of the land she was sitting on and wondering if it was finally time to go home to England and try and find a proper job.

Now she had clothes to change into, she could shower at least, which might start to lift the sense of sadness she felt for everything that had happened. She made it back to the hotel and knocked on Kai's door.

'I got you this,' she said, handing him the Garfield shirt when he opened the door. 'Special present.' He looked puzzled, though. 'Because you've nothing clean to change into. And because it's Monday.'

'Right. Thanks. It's all just a little strange right now, isn't it?'

'What's wrong?'

'I just spoke to my brother in London,' he said. 'The news back home has been saying we were dead.'

'Oh,' she said.

'He was so upset. He thought I was gone. Everyone did, apparently.'

'That must have been weird for you.'

'They've been playing my old tunes on the radio, apparently. There was an obituary today in *The Guardian*.'

'Congratulations,' she said.

315

'No. It's not that, though. Last night my flat was broken into. I mean, that's bloody sick, isn't it? They think I'm dead, so they guess I'm not going to be in. So they break into my flat.'

And after he had closed the door and they had agreed to meet for a late breakfast, she had stood there a little while in the corridor outside his room, trying to fight the feeling that, even though they were back on dry land and in a safe harbour, something was still very wrong.

FIFTY-ONE

Marley had wept. At first he had refused to accept the reverse charges because he thought the call was a prank. He had been told his brother was dead; it had been on the news, that he had been killed by pirates who had attacked a Russian billionaire's yacht in the Caribbean. He had had to call back a second time. And now Kai was talking to his brother on a hotel phone from an island in the Caribbean.

'It's been huge news this last couple of days. They showed a film of the Pirumov family being taken off a US Navy cutter. All sorts of journalists at our door. All sorts of weirdos.'

'Sorry.'

'Charlie sees them off. Don't worry about us.' Marley told him about the obituaries and how Radio 6 Music had been playing a load of his tracks. 'It's kind of like, you're famous again. Only more than the first time.'

And then he'd told Kai about his flat being broken into. The police had called Marley that morning to tell him about it. 'It happens, they say, when deaths are announced. People know that places are unguarded. Apparently all they took is your computer. What did they want? Is there music on it? I guess it's worth something now, is it?'

Kai was shocked.

'I really don't understand how they said you're dead. The press are saying the attack was the family's own fault. They had had some kind of row with their own security guy and kicked him off the boat. Is that right?'

'Is that what they're saying?'

'So how the hell did you get away?'

He wanted to tell his brother everything, but he wasn't sure where to start.

'It's a long story. Things didn't happen the way they're saying . . . Tell me, Marley. You know about this kind of thing. If Stepan Pirumov fell out with the regime in Russia, what would happen?'

There was silence at the end of the line.

'What's going on, Kai?'

'Just hypothetically.'

'Well, they would crush him. That's what they do. You ever heard of Mikhail Khodorkovsky? In 2003 Khodorkovsky was worth fifteen billion dollars. He made the mistake of publicly calling out another Russian company, Rostneft, for corruption and that company happened to be owned by one of the President's allies and was undoubtedly funnelling money back to the regime. They had Khodorkovsky arrested for tax fraud, sentenced him to seven years in Siberia and redistributed his assets, mostly to Rostneft. Khodorkovsky lives in exile in London now – though he is still alive. That's the way it works. What's going on, Kai? What have you got yourself involved with?'

Just then there was a knock on Kai's hotel door. He was grateful for the interruption because he didn't know where to begin to explain what had happened. 'I need to go. I have things to do.'

'Right. Of course.'

'Wait. I just wanted to tell you I love you, Marley.'

'Of course,' said Marley. 'I love you too, Kai.'

And then, having finally said it, they both felt Englishly awkward. 'Got to go,' said Kai.

'Wait. One more thing. Be careful, won't you?' said Marley. 'Be careful of who you talk about this to, OK? Wait till you're safely back here in England before you tell your story to anyone . . . OK?'

'What do you mean?'

But his brother had already ended the call.

When he opened the door, there was Erin standing in the corridor looking awkward again, with a pair of Bermuda shorts swimming trunks and a Garfield T-shirt. 'Special present,' she said, with a shy smile.

They found a beach bar that was serving breakfast, drank fresh orange juice and ate pineapple, mango and pancakes.

'They just took your computer? Think about it.'

Kai said he thought she was being paranoid.

She had pushed away her plate and was sitting opposite him, gnawing on her fingernails. 'They tried to kill us out there because we were inconvenient to the story.'

'It's not like we're in the middle of the ocean now,' said Kai. 'We're here on dry land.'

They heard a shout. Lucy and Jacob had spotted them. 'Mind if we join you?'

They had changed clothes. Lucy had a pair of shorts and a bikini top on; Jacob was all in black. 'You're on the news,' said Lucy. 'Did you see it? It was on CNN.'

They shook their heads. 'No. We didn't see that.'

'That was crazy, right? You are seriously famous now. And they were, like, playing some of your music. They're saying you're dead.'

'Cash your life insurance in now, pal, before they discover you're alive,' said Jacob, which was the first time they'd ever heard him attempting humour.

'I bought a new phone. I downloaded a couple of your tracks already. They're cool,' said Lucy.

'I should die more often,' said Kai.

Lucy laughed. 'Is it true you worked with Robbie Williams?'

'Once. Yes.' In truth, it was only a remix, and it had only been released to radio, but suddenly he didn't want to mention that.

'I kind of hate Robbie Williams but that's actually really mega. I mean. Kind of weird meeting you like that in the middle of the ocean. So . . . you played Coachella and everything?'

'What are you going to do?' said Jacob, interrupting.

'Neither of us can go anywhere until we've got our emergency passports,' said Kai. 'I was going to just stay here for a couple of days, relax. Maybe go and see the waterfalls.'

'I would love to go to Coachella,' said Lucy.

Kai felt he was coming alive. Nobody had asked him about this kind of stuff in ages. 'I did it in 2009. It was like, M.I.A., Leonard Cohen . . . The Orb. And I was supposed to go back the next year but there was that volcano in Iceland and they cancelled my flights.'

Jacob turned to Erin, interrupting again, as if he resented hearing about Kai. 'What about you?'

'I am really not sure,' Erin said. 'I don't have a job any more. I was thinking it would be a good idea to lie pretty low for a while. What are you doing with *Crazy Lady*?'

'I'm leaving it here,' he said. 'Andrew said he'll fix it up, sail it down to Roseau and try and sell it. You want to buy it?'

She held her hands up and laughed. 'I'm looking for something a little different.'

'By different, she means not a crock of shit,' said Lucy. Even Jacob had the grace to laugh this time. 'We were going to go out and have a meal tonight. Maybe have some cocktails.' She was looking right at Kai as she spoke. 'Apparently there's this cool place at the north end of the bay. You want to come?'

'Yes,' said Kai. 'I would really like that.'

'I'm not really one for bars right now,' said Erin. 'I'm still feeling pretty raw.'

'Oh come on,' Lucy goaded her. 'We owe you. It'll be fun. You need to relax a little.'

Kai smiled. It was true. It would be good to let go a little after what they'd been through. It felt good to know that people were talking about his music again; to know they were playing it on the radio. He was on a beautiful island and he was alive. Maybe when he went back to London he could hook up with some of the old guys. Maybe he could get things going again. Do a few interviews. Get back into the limelight.

Lucy was talking to him about the tracks she had downloaded.

Everything was going to be great again. Everything was going to be just fine.

FIFTY-TWO

When Kai said, 'I should die more often,' Lucy laughed, like he'd said something really witty.

There wasn't anything funny about it, thought Erin. They had both almost died for real. But Lucy was young and pretty and fun, and had none of the weight of the world on her, and Kai was obviously loving the attention. She was even younger than Zina had been.

Jacob wasn't enjoying the conversation either, she noticed. It might have been that he didn't like the woman he had brought sailing fawning over another man, but Erin thought he looked like he was antsy about something. 'I have to go back to the hotel and make some calls,' he said eventually.

After they'd gone, Kai said, 'Maybe my career's not dead, after all. Maybe this is all it needed, a little kick-start like this. I should get in touch with my manager.'

'A little kick-start like this?' she said bitterly. 'I don't really think everyone sees it like that.' She thought of the head chef from Puerto Vallarta, his throat cut in the kitchen, the security men, the second chef from Bremen, the Swedish steward, the chief engineer from Lagos, the fitness trainer from LA. They would all have friends, lovers, relations. And Marius too, of course.

Kai squirmed. 'We've been through some really awful things. I wouldn't pretend otherwise. But the whole point of life is you have to try and take the positive from it, don't you think?'

She said, 'Well, I'm very happy for you, Kai, that you feel you have a positive to take from it.'

And when he smiled at her she wished she had made the irony a little more obvious.

She lay on her bed. Exhausted, disconcerted, lulled by the hum of the air conditioner, she fell into a deep dreamless sleep.

At six, Kai knocked on her door and it took an age to remember where she was.

'We booked a cab,' he said. 'It'll be here in ten minutes.'

It was a mistake going out, thought Erin; she was not in the mood. Her head was still sluggish and her throat felt sore. A ten-minute taxi ride up the coast, the bar turned out to be part of a large and very corporate tourist hotel that lay the other side of Cabrits, the small hilly peninsula on the north end of the bay that she had seen when approaching it that morning. Jacob and Lucy had clothes they could change into. She felt like a slob in her baggy T-shirt and shorts. On Kai, the Garfield T-shirt looked like an ironic statement. Hers just looked like a hand-me-down.

On the patio bar, where a gas flame burned in a stone bowl, the waiters brought tables to set in front of their stone benches.

Lucy started the evening off by ordering mango daiquiris, so Erin decided she might as well get hammered.

Like a storm that appears first as just a dark dot on the radar screen, the evening had a kind of inevitability to it. The food was expensive and Jacob was a bad drunk and started trying to pick a fight over politics.

'Society is split between makers and takers,' he started lecturing them. 'In America we have stopped even noticing the scale of the corrupt elites who exist on our tax dollars.'

Nobody bothered to argue with him, which irritated him even more.

'People who make money are the people who keep our society dynamic.'

'Like Stepan Pirumov?' interrupted Lucy. 'Who almost had us killed?'

'Keep your voice down,' cautioned Erin.

'Maybe,' said Jacob. He had had enough of them and walked off to sit at the bar, leaving Lucy next to Kai – and she started to ask him about other famous people he'd met. Kai warmed to the subject again, talking about gigs he had played, and Lucy said 'wow' a lot.

'London was really buzzing back then,' he was saying. 'There was a whole generation of new clubs arriving and the dubstep thing was still new and fresh.'

Erin didn't have a clue what he was talking about. She enjoyed dancing as much as the next person, but the club scene had never been that big a deal for her.

'You worked with La Roux? Get out of here. I loved La Roux,' squealed Lucy. 'I can't believe I'm on this shitty boat in the

325

middle of the sea and I bump into this guy who worked with La Roux.'

Erin felt like she was some elderly aunt who had gatecrashed the young persons' party. After the horror of two nights before, it seemed ridiculous to be sitting in this bar. She asked, 'Do you want another daiquiri?' She signalled a waiter. If she drank something, maybe her throat wouldn't hurt so much.

'Oh my God,' Lucy said. 'Erin's picking up the pace. Sure. I'll have one.' When Kai had gone to the bathroom, Lucy asked, 'You have a boyfriend back in England?'

'Am I supposed to?' Erin answered frostily.

'I don't know . . . You seem like a really amazing person.'

'Amazing people don't necessarily automatically want or need boyfriends,' she said, and then thought how trite that sounded.

'Sorry,' Lucy said. 'I didn't mean anything by that, you know. I was just making conversation. Am I pissing you off?'

'Why would you think you were pissing me off?'

'Have I done something to annoy you?'

'Of course not. Sorry. This is all just too weird. I don't feel great.'

The drinks arrived. Lucy picked the strawberry out of her glass and chewed on it thoughtfully. 'I just want you to respect me, that's all. Like I respect you.'

Kai returned with a bottle of beer and looked at them both. 'Everything OK?' he asked.

'I was just thinking. Maybe I can come and see you DJ some-where?' Lucy started saying.

'I thought you said your career was over,' Erin said.

Kai winced.

Lucy said, 'They're playing your music on the news. People are going to want to know who you are. You have to seize the opportunity.'

Erin rolled her eyes. 'Seriously. This is an opportunity?'

'Well, Jacob says it is,' she answered. 'He thinks Stepan Pirumov should invest in his start-up in exchange for him keeping quiet about what really went on.'

'He's not serious?' Erin said. 'I didn't realise I was supposed to see this as an opportunity,' she added darkly. 'I lost my job, my friend, my colleagues. What do I get? Where exactly is my opportunity.'

Kai said, 'Look. Sorry. We didn't mean to upset you. I'm probably a bit full of myself. I talk a lot of shit sometimes.'

Erin stood up. 'Maybe I drank too much. I'm going to walk back to the hotel.'

'It's still early,' protested Kai. 'Don't go.'

'You young things enjoy yourselves,' Erin said. 'Right now I need to be on my own for a while.'

'Wait. Come back.'

She turned to give them a wave before walking back into the hotel, but they weren't looking at her. Lucy had leaned against Kai and had taken hold of his arm proprietorially.

Once outside, she took off her deck shoes and walked barefoot on the warm tarmac, past Cabrits and back to their bay. When the road ran close to the shore she cut through a sandy gap between the beach bars and strolled along the sand, feet in the water.

She was better alone. She didn't understand people at the best of times. They were all too self-centred, wrapped up in their own fantasies.

Halfway round the bay she lay down, listening to the noise of the waves. She had a headache now and felt hot and cold, all at once. All the tension of the last few days seemed to have left her depleted. After a while she realised she was getting bitten by sandflies, so she got up and wandered on.

The hotel was on a road that she was amused to see was named Moo Cow Trail. She was just rounding the corner where the road turned away from the sea when a small white minivan passed her and stopped. She watched Kai get out and pay the driver.

Lucy emerged from the sliding door, a little unsteady on her feet. On the concrete hotel steps she turned and put her arms around Kai then leaned in to him and kissed him.

He stood, his arms around her for what seemed like a long time.

Not wanting to be seen by either of them, Erin turned back towards the beach and stayed there for a while longer, risking the sandflies before heading back to the hotel, up the silent stairs to her room, where she lay on her bed with the air conditioning on, her head pounding, unable to sleep.

FIFTY-THREE

Kai and Lucy left Jacob at the hotel bar. He had found some fellow Americans who were on a scuba diving vacation and started drinking whisky with them, talking shit.

In the darkness of the back of the minivan, Lucy had put her hand on Kai's knee, then slid it down between his bare legs, then moved it up towards his shorts. 'Ow,' she said, withdrawing her hand, giggling. 'Fuck.'

'What's wrong?'

'I caught my blister on your seam.' Instead she leaned back and kissed him on the ear and said, 'Think of it as commitment-free sex. I'm going in the morning,' she said.

At the hotel, after he had paid the taxi driver, she walked up the hotel steps first, then turned towards him, put her arms around his back and pulled him close to kiss him.

She was young, she was beautiful. He was famous again.

*

But he woke alone on Tuesday morning and went to the window and looked out over the bay. He had not slept with Lucy. She had kissed him standing unsteadily on the steps, but he had not returned the kiss. She was drunk. He just stood there with her arms around him, holding her up, while she said, 'You're pretty cute for an old guy.'

'You should go to bed.'

'Yeah. I should.' she laughed. 'Don't you want to?'

Eventually he had walked her to her room and pushed her inside gently. 'Go to sleep, Lucy. You have to be up early in the morning.'

'It was only going to be a pity fuck anyway,' she had said. 'Loser.'

'Yep,' he had said, and closed her door.

Downstairs at the restaurant he ate breakfast alone. Erin probably wasn't up yet, he thought. He wanted to apologise for being an arse last night. He had just been happy to be alive and in the company of someone with whom he could pretend that he was still a star, but that was all bullshit and he knew it.

He was eating a third slice of toast when Andrew appeared carrying a briefcase. He said he had been in touch with the High Commission in Barbados to start the application for their emergency passports, but it would be a few days before they could leave the island and in the meantime they would need to report to the local police. 'Everything has been arranged,' said Andrew. 'There's an officer from Roseau going to be here tomorrow afternoon to talk to you both. He needs to take a statement about . . . the events.'

When he'd gone, Kai called Marley again. 'When are you coming home?' his brother asked.

330

'It'll be a few days before I'm allowed to travel. I don't mind. It's quiet here. It's a beautiful little island. Maybe I'll rent a little apartment for a few days, do a few hikes.'

Kai heard the sound of London traffic in the background. He didn't mind being away from all that for a while. 'It's just that there have been journalists calling to write stories about you. I have to keep putting them off. I don't want to say anything until you're back.'

'I'm sorry. It must be quite a nuisance. But I can't travel until I get a passport.'

'And two men came this morning before I left for work,' said Marley. 'They were very insistent.'

'Jesus. I'm so sorry. I had no idea.'

'The thing is, Kai, I don't think they were journalists.' He had lowered his voice, presumably to hide his concerns from whoever was with him. 'They wouldn't tell me what newspaper they were from. From their accents I think they may have been Russian. They wanted to know where you were and of course I wouldn't tell them. How did they even know you're alive? And then they sat outside in their car for an hour just waiting, as if they thought you were hiding in the house or something. In the end, I called the police. Of course the moment they saw the police car arrive they drove away.'

The call rattled Kai. He wanted to tell Erin about it, but she didn't seem to be up yet.

He left the hotel, bought a used phone from a store up the street, then walked on a little further to the north end of the bay where there were a few beach boutiques. Like Erin, he discovered that buying a new set of clothes in Portsmouth was a challenge;

331

he ended up with a selection of brightly coloured Hawaiian shirts, some shorts and a pair of sandals.

'No sign of the other guest yet?' he asked the woman on the front desk when he walked back into the hotel.

'They all checked out,' she said.

'Not Lucy and Jacob. I meant Erin Wade.'

'Her too. She checked out six o'clock this morning. All settled and gone.'

Kai was shocked. She hadn't mentioned anything about this last night. 'Did she leave a note for me?'

'No, sir.' When he looked puzzled, she made an elaborate show of checking his cubbyhole and around the reception desk just to prove it. She had gone without even saying goodbye to him.

Kai was another asshole, it turned out.

Erin didn't have a passport, and though she had a little of Kai's money left, it was not much. The sensible thing to do would be to head out, down to Roseau, either to find out how to get a passport herself, or to see if there were any yachts there and try and hitch a ride. Instead she walked north, in the opposite direction. Right now she just wanted to disappear, to become invisible. The violence of the last few days had left her hollow.

She was the far side of Cabrits, past the hotel they had gone to last night, when a red pickup pulled up. There were two men inside; they grinned at her. 'Need a ride?'

She shook her head. 'No, thanks. I'm fine.'

'Where you goin'? We can take you there. You look tired, lady.'

'I'm just walking. Go away.'

'Suit yourself.' They drove on.

The morning's breeze vanished. She was hot. The road turned inland and she found herself heading up a steep hillside, sweating as she walked. When the road split, she took the tracks that led back down to the coast. By nine she was following steep hairpins, to a small bay with grey sand and a few huts and houses.

Down at the bay she swam in shorts and T-shirt. The water was murky, stirred up by the winds of the last few days, so warm that it failed to cool her. She dropped underwater and swam, eyes stinging from the salt. All her life she had dreamed of getting a boat of her own. All that seemed stupid now. Maybe her parents had been right after all. She might have been happier if she had just got an ordinary job and settled down.

She broke the surface and looked back at the small, scrubby bay. It would be easy just to swim out as far as she could and not come back, but she felt too exhausted to even do that.

She swam back and lay on the beach, dozing in the shade of a fig tree, flies buzzing gently over her. Though it was hot, she was again shivering.

After an hour, she got up and looked around. Her throat hurt even worse than it did last night. One of the shacks rented out paddle boards and kayaks, and under the shade of its metal room sat a thin woman in a blue skirt and flip-flops who was watching her, a bored expression on her face. 'Do you sell water?'

'Sure,' the woman said, with a smile.

The woman pointed to a small handwritten menu, pinned to a post. 'Got food too.'

Erin found herself ordering some lunch there, though she wasn't hungry. The kitchen was at the back of the beach shack.

The woman cooked up some fish and rice, singing along to a local radio station while Erin sat at the table, head back against the wooden wall.

When the food came, Erin couldn't eat it.

'Is there somewhere to stay around here?' Erin asked. She suddenly felt too weak to stand.

When she looked up, the woman was looking at her, a worried expression on her face.

FIFTY-FOUR

Kai spent Tuesday on the beach on his own, swimming and then hiking on a couple of the trails at Cabrits. Erin didn't appear; she had completely vanished.

On Wednesday, a police sergeant in a khaki shirt and peaked cap with a shiny black brim arrived soon after lunch; he shook Kai's hand formally, then looked around. 'My name is Alvin Royer,' he said. 'And where is Miss Erin Wade?'

'I'll be honest, I don't know,' said Kai. He told the officer that she had checked out the previous morning but left no forwarding address.

Sergeant Alvin Royer tutted. 'She should have remained here. This is a very serious business. You should have insisted she stayed. Was there any reason why she left?'

They sat in the hotel's empty restaurant and, though it was air-conditioned, the sergeant seemed to sweat through the khaki of his uniform. Droplets of moisture gathered on his forehead and his upper lip beneath a thin fluff of moustache. He placed a plastic folder on the table in front of him, removed several witness statement sheets from inside and started by taking Kai's details, spending a long time noting down his address, telephone numbers and email address, writing each sentence with great care, then stopping to check it before moving on to the next.

Finally, he said, 'So tell us about the night of the pirate attack. Where were you in the ship when it started?'

He told them about being in the room with Zina when the lights had gone out.

'Are you able to describe the pirates in any detail?'

Marley had suggested that he keep the truth of what had happened on *Zinaida* to himself until he was safe at home. Erin had thought the same. But this was a policeman. Kai was not comfortable lying. If they wanted to see the killers caught, there could be nothing wrong with telling a police officer about what had really taken place.

'Mr Smith. I asked you. Are you able to describe the pirates?'

'No,' said Kai finally. 'Because there were no pirates.'

The policeman looked puzzled.

Kai continued. 'The attack was supposed to look and sound like we were under attack from another boat, but there was no other boat.'

The man leaned back a little, frowning. 'That's not what I heard at all,' he said, picking up one of the papers in front of him. 'I have read witness statements from four other people who describe the assault in very clear detail.'

'It's not what happened,' said Kai.

'It is what the newspapers are saying as well.'

'But it's not what happened,' Kai repeated.

Sergeant Alvin Royer seemed to think about this for a while, then sighed. 'OK.'

Kai explained everything that had taken place after the lights first went out on the yacht. It took an age. Every now and again the policeman stopped and shook his head, as if not believing any of it. Several times he read Kai's version through. 'This is what you are saying? You are absolutely certain?'

Eventually the sergeant sat back, folded his arms and said, 'You say there were no pirates, but as a matter of fact the American coastguard ship has already recovered one of their bodies. It was very badly burned but he had credit cards with him that appear to identify him as a member of a well-known Venezuelan criminal gang. Are you trying to say he was on board your yacht as well?'

Kai was temporarily thrown. 'Hold on. No, no. He must have been the man who arrived in the speedboat.'

'The pirate boat,' said Sergeant Royer, looking at his notes. 'Which you say wasn't there.'

'No. As I said, the speedboat arrived after the attack. It was an assassination attempt by members of the crew itself. The speedboat arrived later to take the attackers off our boat.'

The man sniffed, wiped sweat from his upper lip and dutifully wrote this all down too. After a while he stopped and read the pages back to himself, chewing on his lower lip. Eventually, when he'd finished, he said, 'If Miss Wade was here to confirm this account, that would obviously be very useful, especially as it differs in material detail from what the other survivors have already said.'

He appeared to believe none of it, but he got Kai to sign the pages, each of them separately, then placed them very carefully inside the coloured plastic folder, stood up again and shook Kai's hand.

'What will happen to the report?' Kai asked.

'We will pass it on, obviously. I'm sure it will be helpful.'

That evening Kai dined alone at a small beach hut, drinking the local beer and eating vegetables and rice, and thinking about what the policeman had asked him. *Was there any reason why she left?*

When he got back to the hotel he asked, 'Any messages?' The woman at the front desk shook her head. 'Very sorry, sir,' she said.

On the Thursday he had still heard nothing from Erin. He put her name into Google, which came back with several social media profiles, but none of them were hers. When he got back from a morning swim, the woman on reception called out to him, 'You have a message. That one woman who was here with you. She called you one hour ago. Left you a number.'

She was beaming from ear to ear. He smiled back at her. But when he took the paper he saw that the number had an American code.

'Is that not what you were waiting for, sir?'

'Not exactly.'

He wandered up the beach and found Andrew, who was about to take a group of white-haired American tourists on a tour up Indian River. The tourists were all wearing T-shirts that read *Babs 65th Birthday Tour.*

'You've heard nothing from Erin, I suppose?' he asked.

'Not a thing. She got to be on the island still. Unless she hitched a ride on another boat maybe.'

338

'Where would she do that?'

'I don't know. Maybe out of Roseau?'

He found a place in the shade and dialled the number the woman at the hotel had given him. When she answered, Lucy was crying.

'What's wrong, Lucy?'

She blurted out. 'Jacob's dead.' Between sobs she said, 'They shot him.'

Kai's skin went cold. 'What? Who shot him?'

She talked fast, not always coherently. It took a while for him to piece the story together. According to the Sarasota Police, it was probably mistaken identity. Jacob had been stopped at traffic lights in North Sarasota when a white pickup had pulled up alongside him; a man had leaned out of the window and shot four times with a handgun. The first bullet had hit him between the eyes.

'Don't you see? It wasn't mistaken identity. He was asking that fucking family for money to keep his mouth shut. I know he was. He is always such a stupid fuck.'

'You don't know that,' said Kai. 'People get shot all the time in America.'

'You're such an idiot. I'm scared. The thing about Jacob is that he is so arrogant. I mean was. He thought he could cut some kind of a deal with them and probably told them he was going to go and tell the newspapers everything you said about how the attack had happened. He wanted them to buy him a new boat and set him up with a new business. He thought this was basically the best thing that had ever happened to him.'

'He had definitely been in touch with the family?'

339

'Didn't you hear me? He called up some company in Russia that Stepan Pirumov owns and was talking to their public relations department like he was some big shot – and like, a day afterwards he's dead. What shall I do, Kai?'

He didn't know what to tell her. 'Just keep your head down. Go somewhere quiet. Stay there for a couple of weeks.'

'I'm fuckin' scared.'

'It's not you they are after, Lucy. Jacob was making himself conspicuous. That was his mistake.'

It was the best advice he could give.

'One thing,' he said. 'When you left on Tuesday morning, did you see Erin?'

'Erin? No. She checked out way before us. Must have been early. We never got to say goodbye. A shame. She was a cool lady.'

Erin lay on a bed on her back, soaked in blood.

She was so ill she could barely move.

Though she could tell it was daylight outside, the room she was in was dark, and she couldn't remember how she got here.

Her head was pounding and her throat was like sandpaper. It took all her effort to twist her head to one side.

Beside her lay Marius Falk, breathing heavily. His white shirt glowed in the darkness, but around the neck it shone scarlet. It took Erin a while to realise that it was his blood she was lying in. She wanted to cry out loud, and when she finally managed to, she woke.

The room was the same as in her dream; she didn't recognise it. She had no idea how she had got here.

She was scared and alone in a bed in a strange room, soaked in sweat.

On the hotel's computer, Kai logged into his Apple account and retrieved his address book. Then he walked down to the beach and sat at a small bar that seemed to have opened for him alone, ordered a bottle of the local ginger beer and sent a text on his new phone.

This is Kai, he wrote. **We need to talk.**

The phone buzzed immediately. **It's true!!! You're alive.**

Then it buzzed again. **Sorry for this. Need 2b sure. How do I know it's u?**

He thought for a minute, took a sip of his beer, then wrote: **U have a mole on your left shoulder blade. It's the shape of Africa.**

There was a long pause. **I'm sorry for everything. My family sucks.**

'Suck' didn't come close. He sat looking at his phone for a long time. The bar was directly on the water.

He wrote: **Thanks for what you did on the boat. You saved our lives.**

Beyond a flimsy fence, water broke on grey rocks. He had finished the beer and peeled the label from the bottle when the phone buzzed again.

I love you. Where are u?

He stared at the message for a while. The woman who ran the bar asked if he'd like another bottle. He nodded, and drank it watching a gaggle of grey pelicans floating in the bay. They looked like creatures from another age. The woman brought him a bowl of nuts to eat and moved the umbrella, saying, 'What's wrong with you? It's a beautiful day and you look like you're going to a funeral.'

He nodded. 'Kind of,' he said. In their time together, Zina had never told him she loved him. He picked up his phone and texted: **How do I know it's you?**

He waited for a while, but there was no answer. He watched the pelicans until something disturbed them and they took off heavily, flapping inelegantly over the water, then he switched off the phone, removed the SIM card and threw both over the rocks into the sea.

FIFTY-FIVE

That afternoon, Kai settled up at the hotel. The hotelier was helpful. He accepted Kai had no credit card until his bank sent him a replacement and allowed him to pay the hotel an extra thousand pounds using PayPal; in return they handed over three and a half thousand Caribbean dollars, which would keep him going for a while. With the money he bought some insect repellent, some cheap phones, some bread and some nuts, some boiled sweets, a few bottles of water and a shoulder bag, and then he rented a small motorbike from a shop near the university campus.

For a while he studied the map the rental office had given him. It had been years since he'd been on a motorbike, so he took it slowly at first, riding north round the top of the island, up the mountainsides and down towards the east. Locals were used to the island's narrow roads. They drove fast on them, leaning on their horns to warn you they were approaching. The afternoon weather turned grey and heavy, and it had started to drizzle by the time he arrived in the hamlet of Atkinson.

There he rented a green-painted wooden bungalow that had been built in a cleft of the hillside. It had a sloped tin roof, shutters on the windows, and a small verandah.

'Air conditioning a little faulty in this house. Don't you want the one down the hill, closer to the beach?' the young woman who ran the rentals asked him.

'This one's perfect,' he said.

On the third day the fever lessened.

The woman in whose room Erin had lain was called Pam. She was the aunt of the woman who had run the kayak hire stall in Toucari Bay, which is where she passed out. Pam was tall and thin, like her niece, and kind.

In the late afternoon, she got up and joined Pam on her verandah, dressed in a pair of Pam's pyjamas, legs rolled up the bottom because they were too long for her. Pam gave her a slice of pawpaw with lime squeezed over it. It tasted delicious and slipped down her throat easily. 'You were very sick,' Pam said. 'A throat infection. Your temperature was a hundred and three. I gave you some tablets.'

'I'm so sorry to cause you all this bother.'

Pam said, 'I live here on my own. It is no trouble. It is quiet here since the hurricanes. Nobody comes here any more.'

The house was a little way up the hill and Pam's verandah looked out over the blue bay.

'You have friends on the island who are missing you?' the woman asked. 'I looked for your phone, or receipts, so I could try and contact someone, but I couldn't find anything that showed where you came from.'

'No. I have no friends.'

The woman laughed, as if Erin had told a joke. 'Of course you have friends,' she insisted.

Erin finished the pawpaw and Pam offered her another slice.

'I need to get to Roseau,' Erin said.

'You have friends there?'

'No friends. I'm alone,' she said.

'You're not well still. You should stay here a few more days until you're better.'

Erin shook her head. 'No. I need to go. It's time I got home.' Pam nodded and said she knew someone who was driving there in the evening. She would ask if Erin could ride with them. When the ride came it was the same red pickup she'd refused to get into a few days before. The back was loaded with bright green bananas, piled up into a huge neat rectangle. Before she left, Pam gave her the bottle of antibiotics she'd been giving her. 'Keep it.' When Erin tried to offer her money, Pam refused it. In the end Erin pressed a few notes on her, and then got in next to the two grinning men.

Andrew came to visit Kai after dusk in his pickup, bringing some cold beers. Kai walked down the slope to talk to him. 'You were right. A guy came to the hotel asking after you and the lady,' he said. 'He asked the woman what clothes you were both wearing. He was enquiring about *Crazy Lady* too.'

'What did he look like?'

'You people all look the same to me, honest to God. He looked like you. Fair hair. A little slim. He had a rental Hyundai out of Roseau.'

'Russian?'

'Most likely. They said he spoke with some kind of accent. But then, everybody does, don't they?'

They were closing in, thought Kai. If they had his computer, they probably had logins to his bank account by now. They would be able to see his transactions.

'No sign of Erin?' Kai asked.

Andrew shook his head, swatted away a fly that had landed on his steering wheel. 'No doubt she got the same idea as you. Ride all this out somewhere until the storm has passed.'

Kai opened one of the beers Andrew had brought him. 'Where on Dominica do you hang out if you want to crew on a yacht?'

'You wouldn't. You'd go down to Martinique; that's where all the rich people with yachts are. We've been trying to get them to come here for years.'

'Could Erin have made it there?'

Andrew shook his head. 'She don't have a passport, so how's she going to get there? On the island, if you want to find a boat to crew, the best place is right where you come from. More yachts come to Portsmouth than anywhere else on the island. After that, Roseau.' He started up his engine. 'You stay safe. If I hear anything, I'll let you know.'

Kai sat in the chalet with the lights off. It was quiet here after dark, apart from the noise of birds, bugs and frogs. When the light had gone, few cars passed on the main road behind them.

At around nine in the evening, he heard footsteps on the path below the bungalow; someone was moving outside. He tensed; carefully he got up off the bed.

346

The steps got closer. To Kai, it sounded like whoever it was was trying to walk as quietly as they could. Barefoot, he crossed the wooden floor. Taking a kitchen knife from the small drawer by the cooker, he stood behind the door, listening to the creak of feet on the small run of steps that led up to the verandah. Whoever it was was coming this way. He gripped the handle of the knife tight.

And then a quiet knock on the door. He waited a while, heart beating, before he said, 'Who is it?'

'Is everything all right, sir? I saw no light so I thought the electric might not be working.'

He relaxed. It was the woman who looked after the place. 'Everything is fine. Thank you.' The footsteps retreated and the noises of the night filled the space they had left.

He slept only lightly, trying to keep an ear out for any other noise. Just before dawn broke, he took one of the cheap phones he had bought before setting out and texted Zina's number again.

This is Kai. I need to talk.

The message came back within a minute. **Talk.**

Your not Zina. I need to know who u are.

It took a little while before the phone vibrated again. A new message: **Hi cute face.** Kai stared at the phone. Sitting in Zina's cabin, pretending to be stoned on cocaine, Marissa had called him that.

Marissa?

Wassup boyfriend?

Where is Zina?

Do not worry. Ur girlfriend is fine.

Kai wondered if Marissa had tricked Zina out of her phone, or whether she had given it to her willingly. The next message he wrote was: **I just want to get on with my life. I want to be sure I am safe.**

There was a pause. Somewhere a cockerel started crowing.

R u with erin?

He thumbed the keys. **No. Just me.**

The phone vibrated again. **U r safe I promise u have no reason to fear.**

So I can go back to live my life as normal?

Of course. We all wish you well.

He left the phone on inside the drawer of a small bedside table, packed his shoulder bag with a few provisions, and then walked up into the forest behind the shack. This was the lushest place he had ever been to. He did not have to walk far to be swallowed up in the thick green vegetation. To a city boy, it was alien, but beautiful.

About fifty metres into the forest he found a small clearing. A few years ago a hurricane had come straight through the island, tearing down most of the buildings and many of the trees. There were tree trunks everywhere, and still enough gaps in the vegetation through which he could get a clear view of the chalet. He picked a log to sit on, chewing a breakfast of bread. Butterflies sat on leaves the size of dinner plates, opening and closing their wings.

As the sun moved higher, pools of rich light burned around him, adding colour to more shades of green than he had ever seen in his life.

An iridescent blue hummingbird appeared, hanging in the air less than a metre from his face, unbothered by his presence.

All of this was awesome. Taking in the movement and colour, heat and beauty, he realised how dead he had felt, these last few years.

All this time he had spent in his flat in London, waiting for something to happen to him. He had grown lazy. He had stopped noticing the world around him and that had made him dull. It was hardly a surprise that people had stopped being interested in him.

By midday, though, he had eaten his small stash of food and was hungry, hot and thirsty, and his early morning enthusiasm was wearing thin. Though he had insect repellent, blackflies had bitten him several times on the back of the neck and on his ankles, and the bites were starting to itch.

He stood and was about to give up his vigil and return to the bungalow when he saw a car pull off the main road and drive a little way up to the chalet. It was grey.

The car paused at the bottom for a second, then continued up the road. It parked a couple of hundred metres down the slope, tucking in beneath some palm trees. Even from here he could tell it was a Hyundai.

FIFTY-SIX

A pale man with fair hair got out of the car. He wore a jacket big enough to conceal a weapon and carried a smartphone, whose screen he checked several times before heading up the hill in the direction of Kai's bungalow. He moved slowly and cautiously, as if hoping to arrive unnoticed. The man caught sight of the motorbike parked outside Kai's dwelling and seemed to inspect it closely before straightening up and continuing up the slope.

The position Kai had chosen meant he couldn't see the man when he approached his bungalow's front door, but a minute or so later he appeared again, climbing the slope to get access to the back of the bungalow. Kai watched him creeping up to a rear window, peering through it, trying to figure out if there was anyone inside.

Again he disappeared from sight, and this time did not re-appear. Kai guessed he had gone inside the bungalow now.

He would find it empty.

When he didn't reappear, Kai guessed he was hiding inside, waiting for him to come back.

Kai opened the bag of boiled sweets and ate a couple, washing them down with lukewarm water, and rubbed the bites on the back of his neck. They didn't seem to itch so much now.

When he had waited long enough, he took out another of the phones he had bought in Portsmouth and texted Zina's number again. **You lied.**

The message stayed unanswered.

He sent another text. **Tell your man with the blond hair I'll call the police in ten minutes unless he's gone.**

There was no answer to his text this time either, but the man emerged a few minutes later and stood in front of the bungalow holding a phone to the side of his head, looking around anxiously, as if trying to find Kai somewhere in the thick vegetation around him. Though he was too far away for any sound to carry, Kai was pretty sure he knew who the man was speaking to on the phone. His movements were no longer cautious. He was angry.

The man stopped by the motorbike again, seemed to look at it a second time, then stamped down the hill to his car, started the engine and drove off, spitting gravel behind him. Kai remained hidden for another twenty minutes, until he was sure the man was gone.

The cabin had not been disturbed. The man had only been inside for a few minutes. Packing his few clothes quickly into the shoulder bag, Kai left the bungalow, got onto the motorbike, then stopped.

Why had the man been looking at the bike?

He got off again and started to inspect it more closely. It took him a little while to see what the man had done. Attached to the bike's steel frame, just under the vinyl seat, was a small black box a couple of centimetres long. He pulled at it and it came away. There were two magnets on it that held it in place.

Leaving the bike, he wandered down the road to a small market at the bottom of the hill where women were selling melons, plantains and yams. As he haggled over mangoes, a small rusty white minibus pulled up and a couple of passengers got out. He attached the GPS tracker to the back, childishly pleased with himself.

He was exhilarated by a sense of victory. He had outwitted Marissa's man. He had won some time and a little knowledge, at least. He knew what the man who was trying to kill him looked like; he would recognise him if he saw him again.

He found himself imagining telling Erin about what he had just done, and then realised with a lurch that if this man was looking for him, he would be looking for her too.

The thought shocked him. She had disappeared. Maybe Marissa's man had already found her. He could not stay here any longer. It was not safe. Getting back on the bike, he took the road to Roseau that ran across the middle of the island, winding up into the mountains.

Riding this road on a motorbike was harder than he had imagined it would be. The rain from the storm had washed away large pieces of road, creating red mudslides, sometimes ripping away the tarmac, leaving a narrow single carriageway. Taxis, lorries, cars and buses had to queue up on each side before taking their turn.

The motorbike's small engine struggled on the steeper hills, and traffic built up behind him on the winding bends where it was impossible to pass. Vehicles blared their horns as they revved behind him. The journey should have taken him an hour and a half, but it took him that long just to reach the midpoint, Pont Cassé, where, somewhat absurdly in the middle of nowhere, was a rather grand roundabout where four roads joined.

He paused by the side of the road to check his map. Directly to the south was Morne Trois Pitons, the mountain range that dominated the south of the island; the lush slopes rose steeply above him, disappearing into a rain-heavy mist. There were two ways to reach Roseau from here. The smaller road was the more direct one, wriggling down the mountainside for fifteen kilometres in a series of tightly wound hairpin bends. There would be less traffic here. He was tired of being honked at.

The first few kilometres were easy, but then the bends started to get tighter, and he became conscious of a car close behind him, approaching his rear wheel. He was going to pull over to let it pass when he caught a glimpse of it in his rear-view mirror.

It was grey.

He sped up until there was a straight enough stretch to take a proper look backwards.

A grey Hyundai.

He twisted the throttle, heart thumping, regretting his stupidity. It had been arrogant of him to think he could outwit these people. He had found one GPS tracker, but that didn't mean there hadn't been a second. He had not outwitted them; he had just made them angry.

Maybe they hadn't even needed a tracker. Dominica was a small island. His map showed there were not many roads. The killer could have just been waiting at Pont Cassé on the off-chance that Kai would pass that way, and now he was right on his tail.

Downhill it was easier to move quickly on his motorbike but the bends became more lethal. The rain had dislodged stones and earth, making braking and cornering on two wheels hazardous.

At a sharp left his rear wheel skidded round to the right and he almost lost control, having to accelerate forwards towards the sheer edge to keep upright, leaving plenty of road to his right for the car to move into – and it did. He was now riding between the front wheel of the car and the drop. All it would take was a simple nudge to knock him sideways into the ravine below. Braking at this speed to let the car move ahead was too risky on the loose surface; he could lose balance with the slightest skid. Instead he dropped a gear and screamed the engine, pulling ahead again.

He was an idiot. He had dropped his guard and allowed the enemy the element of surprise that he had denied him earlier.

He swung into another bend, and another, hoping that some fat truck would be coming the other way. On a bike he could squeeze past it and get far enough ahead to think.

No trucks appeared. Instead the car gained on him again. He slowed for another corner, accelerated out of it, spun around a right-hand blind turn where the road clung to the edge of the hillside.

To his horror, right in the middle of the road, stood a black and white goat, looking blankly towards him.

If he had been going slowly, he would have missed it easily. Instead he panicked, swerved left and, just as he did so, his front wheel hit a large loose stone, the shock propelling the back wheel off the tarmac. The bike swung round in the air, so that when the spinning rear wheel hit the tarmac again, instead of being in line with the front wheel, it was well to his right. There was only one possible outcome. The bike tipped violently sideways.

He was already too close to the edge. Instead of hitting the ground, he fell into empty air, toppling down the steep slope below. The machine sailed away above him, while he fell vertically down into the branches of the small trees that clung to the hillside.

He hung for a second awkwardly, caught by the vegetation, dazed and disorientated. Then he felt another crack and he plummeted again onto wet soil.

Blinking, he heard the motorbike below him, still crashing down the slope. And above he heard the car braking to a halt.

He lay still on his back, head down the slope, looking up at the small tree that had broken his fall, trying to figure out if he was hurt. His ears rang. Though the shoulder bag slung across his shoulders had bruised his collarbone, there seemed to be no blood.

Footsteps approached the edge of the road above him. No other cars came past. There was no one to call out for help to. If he was killed now, nobody would find him here; he would simply have disappeared. He wondered again what had happened to Erin.

He lay absolutely still, trying to quieten his breathing, praying that the undergrowth would be thick enough to hide the bright print of his Hawaiian shirt.

It wasn't, of course. Against the light he saw the shadow of a man above him.

'*Sa ki non'w? Es'ou blessé?*' came a voice.

It took him a second to realise that the man above him was not speaking English, or Russian either.

FIFTY-SEVEN

Kai squinted up. The man on the roadside, three metres above him, was not fair-haired or thin.

'American? German?' the man said.

Kai scrambled to his feet.

It was not the killer. It had just been a local in a grey Hyundai. The man found a way down towards him and looked him over. 'You are lucky,' he said, extending a hand to help him back up the muddy slope.

Kai laughed. 'So people tell me,' he said.

'Luckier than him,' he said when they were finally at the top, pointing back towards the bend in the road. Kai looked. A dead goat lay on the gravel.

'Do you need to go somewhere?' He said he ran a building material supply company in Roseau, and didn't mind driving him there if that's where he wanted to go. Kai got in willingly. The motorbike, if he could find it, would be a write-off.

The man's encounter with the goat had not deterred him from

driving at speed round blind corners. He talked incessantly all the way down the mountainside. His business had thrived since the hurricanes, he said. The island was gradually building itself back up again. 'They knock us down. We keep getting up,' he said. 'Like you.' He laughed. 'And what business are you in?'

'I wish I knew,' said Kai. The man thought this was hilarious.

He dropped him at the heart of the old town, recommending a tourist bar that was run by his cousin, close to the seafront. 'Stay lucky,' he said.

'I sincerely hope so,' said Kai.

Roseau was a ramshackle town. At its centre were a few old remnants from its English and French colonial pasts, crowded by low concrete buildings whose walls were blackened from the damp air. As an act of defiance, locals painted walls blue, yellow, orange and green, and painted their tin roofs red.

His first task was to find somewhere to say. Big hotels would demand a passport, and he didn't have one. Airbnbs would mean he had to use his bank account, which meant that the booking could be traced by anyone who had access to his bank logins; he guessed that someone who could trace his calls so efficiently would probably have hacked his bank account by now. He found a small bed-and-breakfast that took cash a little way down the coast and booked a room, then walked back to the old town, stopped inside a general store and bought a roll of sticky tape.

He found the café the driver had recommended. It was called The Ruins because it had been built into the ruins of an older, large colonial building. Taking a seat with a clear view of the door where he could see anyone coming in, he ordered a fruit juice, some salad and some red beans.

It would be evening in Moscow. When he had drunk a little juice, he took out another new phone, put in a SIM card and texted Zina's number again.

This is Kai. What now?

The food came. He ate cautiously. He had decided he would stay only thirty minutes after sending the message, then move again if he had not heard back. It was easy to trace the location of a mobile phone; he had already proved that in Atkinson.

He was about to leave when the phone buzzed.

We can help you. Do you want money?

He dialled the number. To his surprise, Marissa picked up.

'I don't want money,' Kai said. 'I just want you to leave me alone.'

'Sure.' The voice was no longer so sing-song American; that had been an act. But it was obviously Marissa. 'I understand. You're a man of principle, not a greedy man. We'll leave you alone, my word of honour. You did good, with our man this morning. It was very clever.'

'Fuck you. You're not going to let this go, are you?'

'One thing,' Marissa said. 'I understand you have applied for an emergency passport.'

'You know that, too?' He watched the door more cautiously now. He had not intended to get caught up in a conversation with her. The killer could be tracing the call's location now.

'We could supply you with one ourselves. A new name, a new identity. Maybe that would be for the best. What about an

American passport? Or maybe even a Russian one? We can do that shit, you know?'

'Wouldn't you need my photograph for that?'

'It appears we have several already.'

A young man came and took his plate, wiped his table with a cloth. 'Of course,' said Kai. 'You have my computer.'

'Yep. Think about it. We can help you out.'

'You haven't exactly earned my trust.'

'That was a mistake,' said Marissa. 'I apologise. We're just anxious to put all this shit behind us.'

'How do I know you're telling the truth?'

'You don't. But, really, you don't really have many other options, do you?'

Kai ended the call. He pulled the tape from his pocket, and, when he was sure no one was watching, taped the phone to the underside of the table, then he paid the bill and left, walking up the street away from the café, to the doorway of a disused shop where he could lurk in the shadow, but still keep an eye on the place.

He waited an hour but the man who had tried to kill him in Atkinson did not show up. He stayed another hour, just to be on the safe side, and then another, though his legs had started to cramp from tiredness, but nobody who looked like they worked for the Russians appeared.

Eventually he gave up and walked away. He took a circuitous route from the old town to his guest house, checking over his shoulder every now and then to see if anyone was following him, looking with suspicion at every car.

The B&B was a squat concrete house, with concrete balconies.

The rooms were basic but clean. He showered for the first time in a couple of days, and felt just as sweaty as soon as he'd dried himself.

He slept fitfully. Just after he had dozed off he was woken by a helicopter flying low over the town. The weather broke some time after midnight and he lay in bed listening to the thick tropical rain on his windows.

Marissa had offered him a passport and money. With that he could disappear into thin air and start a new life.

The rain had cleared the air. He stepped out onto the road that ran south of the main town, looking for somewhere to have some breakfast.

There were about fifteen yachts moored on buoys in the bay. As he watched, a yellow inflatable with three people in it detached itself from one of the boats – a large, two-masted yacht – and motored to a jetty further down the bay. There seemed to be a few tenders moored there.

He walked cautiously, keeping an eye out for the thin man with fair hair. There were other tourists around, but not many. In his bright Hawaiian shirt he felt he stuck out like a sore thumb.

The jetty was in front of a place called the Anchorage Hotel. He walked inside and saw the group he had seen leave the yacht ordering breakfast, so he found a table, ordered a coffee, then approached them. He said he was looking for a friend of his, and described Erin.

'We only got in last night,' they said. 'You should speak to that couple. They've been here a week.'

They pointed to a lean, suntanned middle-aged pair who were drinking coffee by the swimming pool.

'Erin?' said the man. 'There was an English girl here two nights ago. She looked very poorly and she did not say her name.' The couple were French, in their sixties. He had made a fortune as a dentist and now they spent three months a year on board their own yacht. They both wore sporty sunglasses up on the top of their heads, tucked into greying hair. 'When sailors get together, we tell each other stories,' the man was saying.

'Very nice girl,' said the woman, with a perfect-toothed smile. 'All she wanted to talk about was boats. We sail across from Europe every year. She has done the same crossing a few times I think. She really knew her shit,' she said. 'But we were very concerned. She looked very exhausted.'

It was Erin. He was sure of it. Which meant she was alive. 'Dark hair. About this tall?' He held his hand in the air.

'Absolutely. You know her?'

Kai nodded. 'She saved my life.'

'At sea?'

'Yes.'

The woman laughed delightedly. 'Tell us the story. We adore this.'

Kai hesitated. 'It was complicated. Maybe another time.'

The woman said, 'My husband thought she seemed a little . . . *distraite*. Maybe worried.'

'A little sad, perhaps too,' he said. 'She seemed a little lost. I was worried about her.'

On the jetty, he found a couple of young women in bikinis sitting with their long legs in the water, leaning back a little to catch the sun, confident of their own beauty. A boy who was trying to sell them bracelets was shooed away. 'Pest,' one said.

361

They looked just as irritated when Kai walked up towards them, but their aloofness vanished when he mentioned the woman he was looking for.

'She was definitely calling herself Erica,' they confirmed. 'Not Erin. She was weird.'

'I thought there was something off about her.'

'Me too.' They were Americans on a yacht charter holiday. 'She asked us if she could hitch a ride down to Martinique. Fuck off. You don't just roll up and ask someone that.'

'She could be a drug courier for all we know,' said the other. 'She looked like she was on drugs.'

'Kind of like begging us, you know? It was sorta ugly. Creeped me out.'

'But you haven't seen her since . . . ?'

'Thinking about it, a couple of days. Maybe some sucker gave her a ride. Is she in trouble?' they asked, eager to know.

Back inside the Anchorage, he discovered the hotel owner had met her too. He thought maybe she had gone down to Scotts Head. 'It's a fishing village, down in the south of the island,' he said. 'Is there a problem? Because, there was another gentleman here asking after her yesterday afternoon. Is he a friend of yours?'

'What nationality was he?'

'I don't know. I didn't ask?'

'Was he English?'

'Oh no. Definitely not. He didn't speak English well at all.'

'Blond hair. Like mine?'

'Yes. Exactly.'

Kai's optimism vanished. He hoped she had made it off the

island after all. He had managed to trick the attacker once. She might not have been so lucky.

He walked back along the road to his guest house.

The honk from a car behind him made him jump. He moved closer to the side of the road, looked round.

In front of staring pedestrians, the driver jumped out and threw his arms around Kai. Kai was bemused, until the man shouted, 'Sweet Jesus. I thought you were hurt.' It was the man in the grey Hyundai who had driven him to Roseau.

'Me?'

'I thought the shooting was you.'

'What shooting?'

'My God, my God. You didn't hear the news?' the driver exclaimed. 'There was a man shot outside The Ruins yesterday evening. White guy just walked up to him and shot him, walked off again, just like he had done nothing at all. My cousin said the man who was shot was wearing a shirt just like this.' He tugged on Kai's Hawaiian shirt. 'Blood all over the street. I saw that with my own eyes. I thought it was you, my friend. And I had recommended you go there. I thought it was all my fault. I was upset to think you were hurt.' And he hugged him again.

Kai was shocked. 'What happened?'

'No one knows. Just a random attack. Man came out of the café and some lunatic foreigner shot him.'

He had left the phone in The Ruins to try and draw the killer out a second time. It had worked too well; but the killer had shot the wrong man.

'Is he OK?'

'Helicopter came last night and took him to hospital on one of the other islands.'

A man had been shot. All this was his fault. All that talk of a passport had been a ruse to put him at his ease. He had made up his mind; he couldn't just drift. Waiting for the killer to come to him was no longer an option.

FIFTY-EIGHT

'How many car hire companies are there on the island?' he asked the man.

Dominica was small. If it was impossible for him to hide, it would be for the killer too.

'You want a car? My cousin has a rental company,' the driver said. 'Get in. I'll take you there.'

He drove Kai to a small lot. Half a dozen cars were parked behind a chain-link fence. The cousin was washing one of them down with a hose. She did not, though, own any grey Hyundais. Andrew had said the rental was a car from Roseau. 'Is there anywhere local that rents cars like that?'

'Tropic Cars in Canefield,' said the woman. 'It's close by. They rent at the airport. They have Hyundais.'

Kai thanked her and her cousin, and walked from there to the market, where he caught a local minibus to the airport, which turned out to be a small single strip of tarmac that ran alongside the sea. The Russians were not going to stop until he and Erin were dead.

The office of Tropic Cars was an air-conditioned room by the roadside just south of the runway. Inside a man in a pressed white shirt sat at a desk; he had a name tag that read: *My name is Victor. How can I help you?*

'A man in a grey rental Hyundai helped me when I had a terrible motorbike accident at Pont Cassé,' Kai improvised. 'I was too shaken up at the time to ask his name or where he was staying but I wish to thank him. Do you know where I can find him?'

It was a small island. It seemed that people trusted each other here. The man tutted about the state of the roads on the island and the terrible habits of their drivers, flicked through his computer and said, 'Yes, Mr Dudnik is staying at the Garraway. You know it? In the French Quarter at Roseau, just by the cruise-ship berth.'

'Mr Dudnik?' It was that easy.

'That's right.' The man beamed, pleased to have been helpful.

The Garraway would have been modern once; a five-storey concrete building with metal framed windows. Now, though it had been covered in a fresh coat of mint-green paint, it looked careworn. The lobby was a hotch potch of dark wood and white painted bamboo furniture.

'Yes, Mr Dudnik is staying here,' a woman at the desk confirmed. 'Would you like me to call up to his room?'

'No, no,' said Kai hastily. 'Is he in?'

'I don't know, sir. I can try . . .'

'No, no, no,' Kai said again. 'It's fine.'

The rain started as he left the hotel. He wandered up the road, unsure what to do next. The rain soaked his skin and matted his hair. A little way up the street was a small bar and grill, empty but for an elderly woman sitting on a stool, reading the newspaper.

'Do you serve coffee?' he asked.

'Of course we do,' she said, but made no effort to try and serve him. He sat down at a table, dripping on the ground, pulled the last of his cheap phones out of his bag, and inserted a SIM card. Then he delved into the bag again and found the business card the police officer had given him.

'Mr Smith?' said Sergeant Royer when he answered. He sounded irritated. 'Where have you been? I have been looking all over for you.'

'I'm sorry. I had to leave the hotel.'

'You have no documents. You must stay where we can find you. It is not legal. I'm very disappointed with you, Mr Smith. I have wasted my time looking for you.'

'I'm in Roseau. I have important information for you.'

'Where exactly? And your companion, Miss Wade? Are you with her? We have not been able to locate her either.'

'I'll explain everything. It's just—'

'Please, Mr Kai,' the policeman interrupted. 'I need to warn you. You may be in some danger. We believe a man injured last night was attacked in a case of mistaken identity. We believe you were the intended victim.'

'I beg your pardon?'

'There is evidence that someone may be trying to harm you.'

'Yes. I know,' said Kai.

367

'You know? So we need to make sure that you are safe.'

Kai felt an enormous weight lifted from his shoulders; he was no longer alone. 'That's why I was calling you. I know who attacked that man last night,' said Kai.

Sergeant Royer paused. 'You do?'

'Yes.'

'Mr Smith. Please listen to me, very carefully. I would obviously be very interested in discussing what you know,' said the policeman. 'But not on the phone. It may not be safe. Do you understand?'

'Yes. Perfectly,' said Kai. 'Shall I come to the police station?'

'Absolutely not, sir. Are you somewhere out of the public eye right now? Then stay where you are,' said the policeman. 'I will come to you.'

Kai gave him the name of the bar and grill he was in, and Sergeant Royer promised to be there in fifteen minutes. Before he ended the call, Royer said, 'Please. Promise me, sir. This time, stay exactly where you are. Understand? Remain inside. Don't show your face on the street outside, OK?'

He hadn't realised how alone he had felt until ending the call. Outside the rain was thick, coming in waves, hitting the tarmac so hard it was difficult to hear himself think.

'So, you want coffee then?' asked the woman, above the noise.

He dug in his pocket and pulled some dollars out of his wallet.

'Everything OK, sir?' she asked.

'Yes.' He nodded, and smiled at her. 'I think it is.'

Sergeant Royer was true to his word. He arrived almost exactly fifteen minutes after Kai had made the call, but not in uniform;

he wore a plain pair of chinos and a white shirt, and stood by the door for a while, shaking out his black umbrella.

He said something to the woman on the stool and she sucked her teeth, but went to the door and put a *Closed* sign on the door.

'Hello, Mr Smith,' he said, peering out of the glass in the door. 'No. Don't get up. We must stay here for now. We need to make sure it is safe before we leave. We are expecting someone who can escort us safely away.'

When he seemed satisfied, he pulled up a chair and sat at Kai's table. '*Kafé bwézilyen men*,' he ordered the woman. Unsmiling, she shuffled away to the kitchen.

'Miss Wade is not here?'

'I was hoping you could tell me where she was. I think she is in danger.'

'Sadly, no. We have not heard from her.'

The woman returned with two cups, glared at Sergeant Royer as she put his cup down, and walked over to her stool.

'So,' said the sergeant. 'You were telling me, you also believe the man shot outside The Ruins last night was mistaken for you?'

'How old was he?'

'Mid-thirties, perhaps.'

'And he wore a shirt like this?'

Royer nodded. 'Exactly.'

'Two days ago a Russian man came to that hotel in Portsmouth – after I checked out. He was asking people if they had seen me, and what I looked like. He knows I was dressed like this.'

'It is unbelievable,' said the sergeant. 'Why would someone want to kill you?'

'Because of what I told you. It's all true. The killer is staying at the Garraway Hotel under the name of Dudnik. I believe he's also on the island to kill Erin Wade. He may have killed her already.' Saying it out loud for the first time felt bleak.

'So you absolutely don't know where she is?'

'Of course I don't,' snapped Kai.

'No, no. I understand.' The man pulled out his phone, checked it, put it back in his pocket.

'How long is this escort going to be? Where are you going to take me?'

'Don't worry, Mr Smith. We are going to take you somewhere safe. You have nothing to worry about at all.'

The phone in his hand buzzed. The sergeant looked down at the screen, then looked around. '*Ki koté backdoor?*' he said to the woman.

She nodded towards the kitchen. Sergeant Royer stood, took Kai's arm. 'Come on. We have to go now. Quickly.'

It was only then that Kai registered that the policeman was not just in a hurry. He was anxious, too; he was pushing his shoulder now, marching him past the cooker, attached by a pipe to the gas bottle, past the piles of yams on the table and the headless fish lying in the plastic bucket, to the red door at the back of the room.

Kai realised, too late, who would be on the other side of it.

FIFTY-NINE

The knife was in the bucket with the fish.

Kai dropped his arm down, grabbed the handle and swung round so the blade faced Royer.

'What in hell you doing?' the policeman said with a look of horror on his face.

For a second, Kai doubted himself. 'Who is out there?'

'Help, of course.' He frowned. 'People have come to help us. Relax. Jesus Christ. You insane?'

Kai wondered if he was just being paranoid after two days being chased across the island. He had been mistaken once before, on the motorbike. He kept the knife steady in front of the policeman's chest.

'Put that down,' the sergeant said, his hands up, palms forward. 'Please. You are making a big mistake.'

'Why aren't you in uniform?'

The sergeant hesitated. 'Come. Please.'

'Why did you come alone?'

371

'I was in a hurry. I am here to help you.' Kai scrutinised him. The man's eyes kept flicking to the back door.

'Let's leave by the front door instead.'

'No, no, no.'

'We're going out that way.'

'The street is not safe for you.'

'Why not?'

Instead of answering, the sergeant made a sudden lunge for the knife, making Kai jump back.

There was suddenly blood on the floor and a look of horror on Royer's face. Kai glanced down at the blade in his hand; there was red on it too. Instead of grabbing his wrist, Royer had grasped at the moving blade. 'You stupid—'

Kai looked back up in confusion and saw the rear door opening, dropped the knife and started to run back the way they had come – 'Wait!' – out of the kitchen and into the restaurant where the woman who had served him coffee was holding the door open, eyes wide. Outside the door, the rain was thick. 'Out,' the old woman said, hurrying him out of there. 'Out. Quick. Run.'

In panic, he threw himself out into the street without looking where he was going and collided with a man riding a bicycle, sending them both sprawling onto the wet tarmac. Kai got up in time to see the woman closing the door behind him, and trying to hold it shut, then there was a second face behind the glass. He had been right. It was the same blond man he had seen breaking into his bungalow in Atkinson. Dudnik. It had been a trap. Royer had betrayed him.

Disentangling himself from the bicycle, he stood, leaving the rider dazed on the ground, and set off running up the hill, past the old low houses, looking for somewhere he could hide.

'Stop him,' someone shouted. 'Police. Stop that man.'

The rain was flooding down the narrow street, pouring out of the storm drains on either side. It ran from his hair down his face, blinding him. At a crossroads a motorbike loaded with bags on each handlebar roared out of nowhere, banging against him, skidding. The biker cursed, but Kai didn't stop, running on up the hill round the bend, past a squat grey cathedral.

A car came hurtling towards him from the other direction, sending him leaping onto the pavement, and just as he jumped, something stung him hard on the hip. At first he thought he had run into something, but when he looked back, there were no obstacles at all in the way. Instead he saw a single man running purposefully up the hill behind him. The man paused, raised both hands and Kai saw he was holding a gun.

Before he could fire again, a lorry passed between them.

Now he was running again, zigzagging to make it harder for Dudnik to aim. He rounded another corner and found himself suddenly in a crowd. Panting now, he pushed himself into them.

'Hey.'

'Watch it, mister, what is the big hurry?'

He was stumbling, but the throng around him was thick. He was the only white man there, as far as he could see, but the further he could get into the middle of it, the harder it would be to spot him.

'He's bleeding,' someone said.

A child screamed, pointing at him.

The crowd around him parted, pushing each other back. He

found himself in a circle of people, all staring at him. The expressions on their faces were of fear and horror. Kai looked down. There was blood on his right leg. He must have been grazed by a bullet; only now he had seen the wound did he start to feel the pain.

'Help me,' he said, turning slowly, but nobody moved. Looking down, he put his hand on his leg where the bullet had hit him. When he lifted it and held it in front of his face, he saw blood mingling with rainwater.

As the crowd pushed further back, keen to be as far away from him as possible, he saw why they were all gathered. A little further down the road, six men in black suits were holding a coffin, covered in damp flowers.

This was a funeral. He hurried on, towards the coffin.

'Man's hurt,' someone shouted, but nobody came to help him.

Ahead of him, the pall bearers were marching slowly. Eyes forward, they had not registered what was happening behind them. Kai grimaced and ran on, hoping that he could conceal himself again where the crowd was thickest.

Pressing together as they passed slowly through gates into a cemetery, Kai was swept along with them. Laid out on the hillside, family plots with concrete crucifixes and white headstones were surrounded by low white walls. The funeral party spilt into the graveyard, and he realised his mistake. As the crowd entered, they thinned out, dividing to avoid stepping on graves, taking the thin pathways between the plots. He had followed the throng of umbrellas into an open space where the only things to hide behind were memorials to dead people. Most of the gravestones here were low and small. He slumped down behind the largest grave he could find, suddenly exhausted. Above him, a white painted Jesus, crucified on a large wooden cross, gazed down at him with bright blue eyes and a look of pity.

A woman in a purple straw hat approached him, leaned down. 'Are you OK, son?'

'I am hurt,' he said.

Now he could see a man at the gate he had come through, looking around the white headstones by the east side. It was Dudnik.

The woman was trying to help him stand. 'Out of the way,' he shouted. He got up and started walking again through the rain, aware now of the pain in his leg.

'Wait,' the woman called after him. But safety was in the crowd, not here in the open. The umbrellas had gathered together again in the south corner of the cemetery. He needed to reach them.

He didn't look round to see if Dudnik had spotted him. There was no time.

He limped across the soggy ground.

Maybe after all he had always just been lucky. He had almost made it, too.

He was fifteen metres away when a man pushed through the crowd and shouted, 'Armed police. Stop that man.'

He wiped rain from his eyes and saw Sergeant Royer. His white shirt was translucent with water. He had a kitchen cloth wrapped around his wounded hand.

Behind Royer stood a uniformed officer with a pistol in his hand, raised.

'Get back. He is dangerous. This is the gunman we have been looking for.'

There were screams. The people with the umbrellas scattered, leaving six men by an open graveside holding the coffin.

'He is armed. Shoot him,' shouted Royer.

The man at his side hesitated, unsure of what he was being asked to do.

'Shoot him,' screamed Royer again. More policemen were arriving, guns drawn. Royer grabbed the weapon off the other officer and held it in his left hand, steadying it with the injured right, squinting down the barrel.

Pressed back against the edge of the cemetery walls, the crowd stood and watched in horror, cowering.

Kai stood, looking round, desperate.

There was a single shot. And Kai fell.

SIXTY

Two weeks after the Russian man fell from the window of the balcony next door to his Parisian apartment, David Bullimore is in his rooftop hot tub, naked. His clothes, neatly folded, are in a pile on a chair next to the speakers, which are playing Pink Floyd's *The Division Bell*. The band are no longer in fashion, but to David, they represent the pinnacle of British musical achievement, though he thinks they were weaker after the departure of Roger Waters.

He installed the stereo for moments like this. He has switched on the coloured lights and they pulse to the sound of the rock music. The music and the warm water calm him a little; he hopes that the familiar songs will reassure him that all is well in the world.

He has not been himself. Though the gendarmes left the street after the second day, when they finally accepted that it was not Stepan Pirumov who lay dead on the ground, but a less important person, the whole episode had disturbed him. He had watched the news and seen his neighbour on the television looking tired and scared. It was a terrible thing. Not only had a young man committed suicide in his apartment, but a few days later Stepan Pirumov and his family had been attacked by some kind of criminal gang in the Caribbean. The world is a shocking place, full of sudden reversals. No one is safe any more.

Perhaps, after all, he should install security in his flat.

The music doesn't stifle the anxiety in the way he hoped it would. If anything, the tolling bell at the end of the last track sounds particularly sinister and makes the water pulse with red light.

But when the sound dies away, to be replaced by the ordinary sounds of the Parisian street below, he hears a child's voice singing. It is beautiful. The words of the song are indistinct but it's definitely not French. Realising that the voice is not coming from the street but somewhere much closer, he sits up, puzzled.

He stands, grabs a towel and wraps it around himself. From the edge of his rooftop he can see onto next door's balcony. To his surprise, he sees that a small, fair-haired boy is playing with a furry toy, singing to it. He doesn't ever remember seeing children in Stepan Pirumov's apartment.

The boy sings:

> *Căţeluş cu părul creţ*
> *Fură raţa din coteţ*
> *Şi se jura că nu fură*
> *Şi l-am prins cu raţa in gură.*

David Bullimore is glad to see that it is occupied again, at least. The boy sings the verse again. This time a woman joins the boy on the balcony, offering him a glass of milk. She is thin and very beautiful.

The boy stops. The woman picks up the song, singing it hesitantly.

> Little curly-haired puppy,
> You swore you wouldn't steal,
> But you stole the duck from the coop
> And I've caught you with it in your mouth.

The boy laughs as she sings, and she reaches down to pick him up.

And as she turns, with a shock he recognises her. He is sure the singing woman is the Romanian who used to clean his flat.

He changes his mind at once.

Of course it could not possibly be her, standing in that rich man's apartment, singing as if she owned the place. That would be ridiculous. Besides, the woman he sees standing on the Pirumovs' balcony looks younger and is more good-looking than Mihaela ever was. She is wearing the kind of clothes a cleaner could never afford, too; a chic silk chemise and khaki trousers that fit her perfectly. He stands there, towel around his waist, looking down. Apparently unaware she is being watched, she exudes a kind of enviable contentment.

Something of her happiness seems to rise up towards him. Unseen by her, he begins to smile. Their strange song has calmed him much more than the rock band's music; this simple children's song seems more honest and pure than any of the thousands of records he has, neatly stacked in alphabetical order.

This is an awful world in which people die unfairly and in terrible violence, he reflects, but there is something about this woman, standing on the balcony, singing with her child, that reassures him there is still unfathomable joy in it too.

SIXTY-ONE

When Andrew told her that Kai was dead, she cried.

Erin had arrived that morning, dirty and tired, finally walking back into Portsmouth. She had been sleeping rough in the hills after failing to hitch a ride on a boat from Roseau. When he caught sight of her, Andrew had hurried her out of sight into one of the cabins near the beach where he kept some of his boating gear. He brought her fresh water and some packs of sweet cakes from a local shop.

'Police just shot a man in cold blood,' Andrew explained, looking down at the wood floor. 'That's what they said on Facebook right now. Up in the Catholic cemetery in Roseau. They haven't given any names yet, but they are saying it was an Englishman who had arrived at the island illegally.'

'Kai,' she said.

Andrew sat with his arm around her in the dark room as the rain hammered down and told her about everything that had happened since she checked out of the hotel; about the man who had come looking for them.

381

'He was Russian, you said?'

'That's what Kai thought. There was a Russian man and he was looking for you both.'

'Why did Kai even go to Roseau then? He must have known it was dangerous.'

Andrew kept his eyes firmly on the floorboards. 'He was looking for you, pretty sure. My fault, I suppose, because I told him you had gone there.'

That didn't help. She cried some more.

Exhausted, she spent a couple of hours sleeping there on her own until there was a small knock on the door. 'Me,' said Andrew. He had brought some more water, and some fried cod.

Erin took the food gratefully. 'Was there any more news?'

He nodded uncomfortably.

'They confirmed it was him who was shot?'

'They gave his name as Mr Kai Smith. He was shot dead by Roseau police at the Catholic cemetery this morning. That's all they're saying.'

She left the cod for later. She couldn't eat now. She felt utterly empty. 'He must have been desperate,' she said.

Andrew sat on a wooden stool and wiped his forehead. The afternoon's storm had not cleared the air. It was raining still, though the wind had dropped. 'Best if you're gone soon.'

She nodded.

'Sorry. But you know how it is. I got a business here. I can't afford to be mixed up in all this.'

'I understand.'

Andrew had told her how she was going to do it. *Crazy Lady* was in no state to sail. Andrew had put a solar-panel-powered pump on her to keep her afloat, but even from the beach you could tell she was low in the water again. Instead, Andrew told her to take an ancient Westerly 22 that he was looking after for a tourist who had abandoned her here when the Covid epidemic had started back in 2020.

'I'll tell people you stole it. Take it down to Martinique – Fond Lahaye, just north of Fort-de-France. Moor it there. I'll tell people that it's been spotted down there, take a motorboat down in a couple of days and pick it up. It will be fine for me, that way.'

The rain was still rattling on the cabin's tin roof.

'You must go.' He gave her a bottle of fresh water and then reached inside his wallet and pulled out a hundred local dollars. 'It's not much, but . . .'

'I'll pay you back. I promise.'

'Sure. When you get home, tell all the people about us here. If we're going to bring this place back alive, we need the yachts to come back. That will pay us back even more.'

It was generous of Andrew to let her take the boat – it would do his reputation no good for him to have this one stolen – but it wasn't just generosity that was making him do this. He needed her gone now. Dominica was a tiny island. He could not hide her here for long. She guessed he was spooked, too, by what had happened. The same people would be coming for her.

'What's the weather going to be like?'

'Fair. There will be a light east wind, maybe eight, nine knots. I will have to report her stolen soon after you're gone. You understand that, yes?'

'When?'

'I'll call the police at eight in the morning. Otherwise they may suspect me. I can't afford that. I would lose all my business. Bad enough for business having a boat stolen, you understand?'

They sat together a little while longer until he said, 'I have to go. You leave after it gets dark, right? After everyone here's gone home, so no one sees you.'

She shook his hand to thank him for everything he had done.

After he had gone she did the mental calculation. On a beam reach with a light wind she would still probably have enough time to get ashore before he called the police.

The rain had cleared by the evening. She waited until the coloured lights had gone out at the bars nearby, then took the oars and rollocks and pulled the small dinghy down to the water's edge and rowed over to the Westerly.

The mainsail was already rigged and ready to for her hoist. She pulled up the anchor, hand over hand, as quietly as she could, and sailed out of the bay, setting a course for the south-west to take her away from the island. The cabin stank of mould from being left in the bay for too long, but she found a genoa in the sail locker and hoisted it up, and was soon making good speed, towing the dinghy behind.

It felt good to be free of the island and on the move again. On Martinique there would be sailors at least; people she could talk to about boats.

It was simple sailing. The sea was still a little rough from the night before, but the wind was steady and the stars had come out. Polaris was clearly visible, low in the inky sky behind her. Occasionally, in the darkness, she passed close to a trawler.

At around four in the morning she saw the first lights of Martinique, the small villages clustered at the coast under black silhouette of the volcano of Mount Pelée. When dawn finally came up, revealing the huge primitive outline of the peak, she was close to the coast.

At around 6.30, still on a reach with the west wind in the sails, a pod of dolphins arrived to escort her in. She remembered Kai's pure joy at seeing them that day aboard *Crazy Lady* and felt like he was there on deck with her, watching them.

When she dropped anchor at Fond Lahaye, she was still crying.

SIXTY-TWO

It was around nine when she reached the small beach, pulling the dinghy up as far as she could. If Andrew was lucky, it would still be there when he came to collect the Westerly.

The morning sun was hot; she walked the busy road down the coast towards Fort-de-France.

Martinique was a richer island than Dominica, with expensive resorts tucked into the bays along the coast. She walked into the first hotel she came to, down a long palm-lined avenue, into an open white reception area staffed by a pair of women in identical red jackets and asked, 'Can I get a taxi?'

The taxi took her on the short drive into the port. She bought some lunch from a local supermarket with what was left of Andrew's money and wandered down to the marina on the east side of the docks, among bright white hotels.

There, sitting on the edge of a jetty, she ate a sugar bun, drank cold Fanta and surveyed the scene.

The monied people were here, sunning themselves on their

decks, shading beneath their biminis. She was back among the wealthy.

She wandered down the pontoons, wondering where to start.

Boat people were easy for her to talk to. 'Beautiful boat. How close to the wind can she go? Who was she designed by?'

It was as simple as that.

She asked owners about sail configurations, what kind of speed they got out of their yachts, where they had been. Boat people loved to tell stories. All she had to do was start a conversation. And once it started, she told them lies about how she had become stranded here and that she was looking for a ride home.

Most of the boats were unoccupied. A few had people aboard. Some looked like they were being used, but the owners had gone ashore. There was not much point sitting in a hot hull on a day like this. She hung around through the afternoon, wondering if she should try another of the marinas that lay around the bay. At around four she saw two men, both in striped T-shirts, walking down one of the pontoons. They let down a plank and climbed aboard a long, fat, expensive-looking boat.

'Is that a Dufour 390?' she called to them. 'I sailed one of those to Copenhagen once.'

'You're kidding me? We just picked this one up and were having a discussion about how to set up the jib.'

They were a couple, she guessed. The taller one reminded her of her uncle Ben. She wished he was here now, she thought. She would have liked to throw her arms around him and tell him she loved him.

'I remember the genoa tracks make it difficult to pull the sail in when you're close to the wind.'

'Exactly,' the one who reminded her of her uncle said.

'You tried a barber haul?'

'A what?' The men looked at each other. 'How's that going to work?'

'Come aboard,' the other one said. 'Show us what you mean.'

So she spent a little time standing on the cabin roof, talking them through how to rig a tweaker. 'You'd need a block here,' she told them. 'And then . . .'

They poured her a cold wine and sat together in the shade of their bimini. She told them the same lies she'd told everyone else. 'I came out here on a yacht delivery,' she said. 'Now I'm looking for a passage back to the UK. You heard of any boats heading that way?'

They hummed and hawed for a while. 'Honey, we'd take you there ourselves. That would be an adventure, wouldn't it? But we're heading in the other direction. We're going to head through the Panama Canal and make it out to the Pacific.'

'What about that guy we met last week who's moored at Etang Z'abricots?' the other man asked.

'Maybe. German guy. He's been living aboard but is trying to sell up. He's got some health problems. Heart maybe, I think. He's been trying to find a buyer for months but got nowhere. When we were talking to him he said he was going to give up on selling it and get a delivery company to get it home. You should talk to him. Maybe he'd even pay you to do it.'

'You think?'

'Drink up,' they said, 'we'll take you to him. There's a bar there that makes the best caipirinhas.'

They took their tender round to the far side of the headland on the north side of the bay, Erin sitting in the bow, welcoming the spray in her face, and motored into a small marina.

'There he is.'

It was a Dehler 38; sleek and crisply maintained. Moored stern on, there was a sign on the back that read *For Sale: All offers over $200K considered. Urgent reason for sale.*

The cabin door was open and there was someone inside. 'Great boat,' she called. 'You must get some speed out of her.'

A pale-faced man in his late sixties emerged from the cabin. 'Want to buy it?' The accent was German, she guessed.

'Flat broke,' she said. 'I heard about your situation. I'm very sorry to hear that.'

'Shit happens,' he said. 'All my life I'd been planning for this. Now I can't do it any more. I'm too sick. I have to go home.'

'That's very sad,' she said. 'You sailed here alone?'

'*Ja*. Single-handed,' he said proudly. 'Right across the Atlantic. Took me just seventeen days. Best time of my entire life, but unfortunately it almost killed me.' He laughed, wheezily.

'Which keel do you have?'

He smiled. 'See? I knew you know boats the moment I saw you. The competition keel.'

She whistled. 'You must be a good sailor to handle her single-handed.' Erin looked over the boat admiringly. The Dehler was a high-performance boat, built for racing; the kind of boat

389

that responds to the slightest tweak of the sails, especially with the kind of keel he had fitted.

'Thank you,' he said, pleased by the compliment. 'I just wish I had done this twenty years ago.'

'So that's the bigger mast?'

'Yes, yes. I could not resist. You have sailed one of these?'

'No. But I always wanted to.' The two men had retreated to a bar that seemed to be called Baywatch; they waved at her from their table. 'My friends over there said you might be looking for someone to sail her home,' said Erin.

'Indeed. I was told you were coming,' said the German.

'What did you say?'

'I knew you were coming. I was waiting for you.'

She blinked at him. 'Sorry. How did you know?'

'A man was here. He said you would probably be asking around.'

She squinted at him in the reddening light. 'You must have the wrong person.'

'I don't think so. Your name is Erin, that's what the man said. Is that right?'

Instantly anxious, she looked around. 'What man?'

'A fair-haired guy. This morning he came here. He said you would come too, soon. He was very keen to find you. Wait here,' said the German, and disappeared back into the interior of his boat.

Erin stood on the pontoon rotating slowly, looking all around, trying to see if anyone was watching them.

The German emerged again. 'Here. He left his name. Dudnik. He's staying in one of the hotels in the seafront. He told me to call him up if I saw you.'

'Dudnik. That's a Russian name, right?'

'Yes. Naturally.'

She turned away, feeling like she had been punched hard in the stomach. She was going to have to run again. If the Russian had followed her here, he could have followed her everywhere.

'Wait,' the German shouted, standing in his cockpit. 'He told me to tell you something. I wrote it down.'

The two men at the bar were looking at her, worried. 'Hey, what's wrong? Did that guy say something?'

'High hopes,' the German shouted.

At first she didn't catch the words against the tinking of the halyards on the aluminium masts around them.

'High hopes,' he called again.

She stopped and turned. 'What?'

'That's what he told me to tell you. He said he had high hopes. Something like that.'

'High hopes?'

'I know. It's a strange thing to say, don't you think?'

'He's alive?' she said.

'Of course he's alive,' the bemused German said. 'Why wouldn't he be?'

He arrived five minutes after the German had called him, running down the pontoon towards her.

She was running towards him too, then throwing her arms around him.

'What is this? A party?' said the men at the Baywatch.

'I thought you were fucking dead,' she said. 'Andrew told me you had been shot.'

And he was saying, 'Why did you just run off like that from Portsmouth without even leaving me a note? It was dangerous.'

She pushed him away. 'Why did you go and sleep with a nineteen-year-old airhead? You creep.'

Kai cocked his head to one side: 'Wait. You snuck off because you thought I'd slept with another woman?'

'She's not a woman. She's . . . nineteen.'

'I didn't even want to sleep with her,' protested Kai.

'You just did it as a civic duty, I suppose?'

'I mean I didn't sleep with her. Jesus. She was very drunk. I took her to her room and left her there, honest to God, and when I got up in the morning you were gone. You just crept off.'

The men pulled them both towards the bar, bought them drinks. The German joined them.

'Are you, like, boyfriend and girlfriend?' demanded one of the men, handing them both cocktails. ''Cause you're really acting like it.'

'Dudnik?' she was saying.

'Yeah. That's my name,' he said. 'For now at least.' And he produced a red passport and showed it to her.

392

SIXTY-THREE

When he opened his eyes in the cemetery, he was not dead. He had not been shot. He heard screaming all around him and sat up and looked around.

The funeral party had scattered. Dudnik was nowhere to be seen.

Royer was holding a gun in his left hand, and though he was running towards him he was not aiming the gun at him, but past him. When he reached Kai he said quietly, 'Don't say anything. Not a word. Keep quiet. Jesus Christ, what a mess.'

Then he continued on towards one of the gravestones behind Kai. As he stood and looked, Kai saw two shoes, soles facing him, and then realised he was looking at the body of a man, prone among the gravestones. He stumbled over to where Royer was standing.

Dudnik was dead. Royer had shot him. A single bullet that had penetrated his left eye.

'Total mess,' muttered Royer.

'He paid you money to let him kill me,' said Kai.

'Keep your voice down.' Other policemen were moving towards them now.

Rainwater was pooling in the ugly wound already, sending a thin red trail down the side of his face and onto the white marble he had fallen on. 'Why did you shoot him, not me?'

'What would it have looked like, do you think, if I had killed the man who didn't have the gun? What would it have looked like if I'd just stood there and let him shoot you? I had no choice. Now keep your mouth shut. OK?'

'Check his pockets,' said Kai.

'Why?'

'Get his documents – anything that will identify him.'

'Why?'

'Get them.'

'Fuck you. I only got the one good hand. You do it, and be fast.'

Kai knelt in the puddle of water next to him and pulled out a single key on a brass fob from his trouser pocket; a red passport was inside the man's jacket; a small billfold with credit cards was in his rear trouser pocket.

When the uniformed constables approached, Kai straightened.

'Who are these men, sir? What has happened?'

'Secure the crime scene,' Royer said loudly, 'I'm taking this man away for questioning.' Grabbing Kai's arm before the constable had a chance to say anything more, he pulled Kai away from the body and marched him, limping, through the crowd of muttering onlookers and out onto the street he had been running down minutes before.

The rain kept falling.

The police station turned out to be just on the far side of the crossroads, but instead of going in through the gate, Royer pushed Kai into a white Suzuki jeep parked on the pavement outside and started the engine.

'Where are you taking me?'

'Away. Anywhere but here.' He pulled out into the traffic, honking on his horn.

'Wait,' said Kai. 'The man who was calling himself Dudnik paid you to turn me over to him, didn't he? You were going to let him kill me, but you couldn't let that happen in front of all these people.'

Royer didn't answer.

'I hope he paid you well.' At least, thought Kai, Royer looked embarrassed, though he didn't know if that was because he was ashamed about what he had done, or just about being caught out. 'I won't tell anyone. I promise. You don't have to worry. But you have to do one thing. And then all this finishes. And everything will be OK.'

'This is a mess.' Royer was zigzagging past parked cars now, on the road down towards the waterfront.

'Bloody stop for a second and let me explain.'

Royer pulled up hard, throwing Kai forwards in his seat. 'What?' he said angrily.

Kai pulled the dead man's passport from his pocket.

'Give me that,' said Royer, snatching at it.

Kai yanked it away and tucked it back into the pocket of his shorts. 'You tell people that the dead man's name is Kai Smith. You already met him. Say that's who you think you shot. You give the ID. Tell people you think he was the one with the gun.' If Stepan Pirumov wanted him dead, then maybe that was the best way. He would die – again. 'I will take Dudnik's passport, settle the bill at the hotel, and leave on the next ferry out of here, and I promise to get as far away from here as I can. Planes are too risky. As far as Dudnik's employers know, their plan succeeded. I'm dead. You don't have to worry about any of this ever again.'

Royer stared at him for a long time.

'You want me to tell people you are dead?'

'Exactly.'

The rain slowed. Around them drains clogged with plastic bags spilt water onto the street. Royer leaned out of the window and spat on the wet pavement. 'There is a ferry this afternoon. I will personally escort you there and make sure you get on it,' he said eventually.

The key fob announced that his room number was 301. The room was easy to find. Nobody challenged him. In the hotel room he cleaned up the blood on his leg, then looked around. There were two bags, packed and ready to go. In one he found clothes. He changed into fresh trousers to cover the wound, then searched the drawers, looked under the mattress and finally on top of the wardrobe, where, pushed right to the back against the wall, he found a third bag. He put on a pair of dark glasses he'd found on the night stand and took all three downstairs.

'I want to check out.'

'It's afternoon, sir. You'll have to pay an extra night.'

Kai had a lie prepared to explain why he, not Dudnik, was paying the bill, but the man at the front desk didn't question him, ask who he was, or why he was checking out early. Dudnik – if that was his real name – had probably been discreet, not wanting to be recognised. Or maybe the man on reception didn't really care as long as Kai was paying.

There was more than enough money to settle the bill in Dudnik's billfold, so he settled in cash and met Royer outside.

'All good?' he said.

Royer drove him to the terminal. 'I'm taking two bags,' Kai said. 'The third one has a rifle and ammunition in it. I'm going to leave that with you.'

'Understood,' said Royer.

A gun would make it hard to get through security at the port; Kai had never fired one in his life, and he didn't want to start now.

'And that's it. You never come back here?'

'Did he pay you well?'

Royer didn't answer. Kai got out. At the ticket office, he looked back; Royer was still watching him as he pushed through the turnstile. The ferry, a large, double-hulled high-speed boat, arrived twenty minutes later, disgorging cars onto the jetty.

Kai walked aboard, not turning back to look at the island.

'The Russian is dead?' said Erin incredulously.

'Yes. And until Marissa and Stepan and the rest of them discover that, they think I'm dead too. For now at least. It will give us a few days. It's our chance to escape.'

'How?' said Erin. 'I don't have a passport.'

'But I do.' He had gone through customs and immigration on the dead Russian's passport and had got away with it. They

397

had looked enough alike for nobody to take a second look as he had boarded the Express des Îles.

'I don't understand.'

'How much do you think that German will take for his boat?'

'What are you talking about?'

One bag in the hotel room had been full of Dudnik's clothes. Another had been full of guns and ammunition. The third had been full of US dollars. Kai didn't have time to count the notes until he reached his hotel room in Martinique, but there was just under five hundred thousand dollars in there. He had sat in his room, making piles of notes. It took him almost an hour to count them. Presumably, he guessed, it had been a down payment on their lives. *There is no such thing as luck*, he had told himself, looking at all the money in the black bag, *there is just uneven distribution of opportunity*.

'Hey,' said the two men whom Erin had befriended. 'Stop acting so fucking serious, you two. What are you drinking?'

SIXTY-FOUR

Mihaela loved her new apartment on the Rue Guénégaud, where she lived with her boy, Florian.

When the man had stood behind her, a knife to her throat, she thought her life was ending. She had been so terrified she had wet herself on David Bullimore's parquet.

But the man behind her had been just as scared as she was, it turned out. He had just escaped from the apartment next door; it was his friend who had been thrown from the balcony.

When the man realised that she was no threat to him, he had pulled the knife away from her face and slowly released his hand from her mouth. 'Help me,' he had pleaded. 'There are men who are trying to kill me.'

It was supposed to be him lying on the pavement below. He had been sure of it. She had recognised him as David Bullimore's rich neighbour.

The man was desperate. 'I need to get to Le Bourget. There is a plane waiting for me. The killers will be outside, watching.'

'Catch a bloody taxi,' she had said, still angry he had held a knife to her throat, ashamed that she had been so afraid.

'I cannot. They will see me. Do you have a car? I will pay you anything. I promise.'

'Anything?'

She had made him wait, pacing on the parquet, while she cleaned up last night's mess. She moved the Mashad rug to cover the wet patch on the floor, then dressed him in Kiki's faux fur coat and Uma Thurman wig, and, despite his protests, marched out of the back door with him, arm in arm. Clutching her waist on the back of her battered Piaggio, he rode, zigzagging through the Paris traffic, all the way to a cheap-looking airport hotel at Le Bourget, Kiki's wig flapping in his eyes.

Stepan stuck to his agreement. She would have full use of his apartment rent free, with a generous stipend so that she could look after the place well for him. He would not be needing it, after all. It was only for a year, but she was happy; she had just one apartment to clean. For that one year of her life, she and Florian would live like the rich and never regret a moment of it.

Once, not long after she moved in, she thought she saw David Bullimore looking down at her from his rooftop, but she simply pretended she hadn't seen him. That was a different life completely.

In late July of the year that Mihaela and Florian moved into the apartment in Rue Guénégaud, *The Guardian* and the *New York Times* both published the true story of what had happened to Stepan Pirumov and *Zinaida*. The newspapers refused to name their sources; they simply stated that they had been contacted by two witnesses to the events who wished to remain anonymous. The newspapers had confirmed the identity of both witnesses, but had agreed to keep their names secret. Teams of journalists had managed to corroborate much of what the two people had said.

Alongside the account of the attempted assassination of Stepan Pirumov, they published the full name of the chief steward whom witnesses had identified as Marissa. Those witnesses alleged it was she who had murdered Captain Marius Falk and all the other members of the crew, acting with another man named Aleksander. Journalists identified Marissa as Masha Voronin, a former Senior Lieutenant in the GRU. According to the *Washington Post*, she had crewed on many superyachts in the last few years, often those owned by the powerful. It speculated that she had been spying on behalf of the Kremlin for several years. Shortly after returning to Russia from the Caribbean, Masha Voronin had died in a house fire, caused by what local police claimed was an electrical fault.

The newspapers named the second attacker, Aleksander, as Russian citizen Konstantin Petrov, an electronics specialist for the GRU. Petrov's body was never recovered. A security guard named Thomas Scadder had indeed been wrongfully imprisoned on St Croix; there had been no gunfight at the police station, and there was no record of any officer calling a security guard on *Zinaida* to tell him otherwise.

As a further corroborating detail, they referenced a story that had been published earlier in the month in the Polish newspaper *Rzeczpospolita* about how the body of a Polish electro-technical officer, who had been booked to work on *Zinaida*, had been found in woods near John Paul II International Airport in Krakow.

Stepan Pirumov appeared on CNN denouncing the story as fake news, concocted to try and undermine confidence in the Kremlin. 'The story is ridiculous,' he said, 'and offensive to the memory of those who died.'

The Kremlin said the accusations that it had somehow been behind the attack on the boat were amusing but hardly logical. 'Pirumov is an old and dear friend of us all,' one of the leadership's inner circle told reporters. 'He suffered a great deal at the time of the attack and it is terrible that these journalists are trying to make him suffer more now in an attempt to smear the Russian people.' The President himself made no comment.

Reporters noted that Pirumov looked pale and gaunt, and that he had also recently resigned unexpectedly from the position of chief executive in several of his companies. He claimed it was so he could spend more time with his family, who had become precious to him after the incident aboard *Zinaida*. As part of his withdrawal from the companies, he had sold off the majority of his shares. A report by the investigative website Bellingcat traced the buyers of the shares and found they had all gone to individuals with close links to the Kremlin.

Three months after the attack, the Seafarers International Union put out a press release listing the names of all the crew who had died on *Zinaida*. Several bodies had never been recovered; they were presumed to have been lost overboard. Among the names listed was Erin Wade, First Mate. The note next to her name said simply: 'Whereabouts unknown.'

Reports that the musician Kai Smith had been killed in a shooting incident in Dominica turned out to be false; the body of the

402

man who had been shot remained unidentified. An examination confirmed it was definitely not Smith's.

People waited for the real Kai Smith to reappear, but he didn't. In the late summer, someone set up a Facebook group called 'Kai Smith Is Missing'. People speculated about what had happened to him. '*Bermuda Triangle. It makes people disappear*,' someone wrote. That October someone else posted a video of a DJ at a beach club on the V&A Waterfront in Cape Town playing an impromptu set, claiming that the man on the turntables was Kai Smith. At first fans agreed that it looked a lot like him, though this man was bearded and perhaps more muscular than Kai had ever been. Cynics soon posted videos of friends who looked a little like Kai Smith mowing the lawn, or skateboarding. 'I Found Kai Smith' briefly became a meme. A video of a cat with shaggy pale hair a little like Kai's emerging cautiously from a cardboard box had over two million views. Within a couple of weeks, the joke was old.

That December a tourist fishing boat operating off the Maldives reported that an unnamed yacht had responded to the Mayday signal it had sent out when its engines failed in high winds. The yacht stood by for two hours until the Maldives Coastguard arrived, but sailed away as soon as the tourist boat was safely under tow. Photographs that the trippers took showed the yacht to be a Dehler 38. It was crewed by a woman and a man, but the quality of the photos was poor and it was impossible to make out their faces clearly. It was also impossible to work out what the yacht that had come to save them had been called because their AIS seemed to have failed, making the boat largely invisible to radar except simply as an unidentified vessel.

After a brief bout of interest in the musician, people forgot him again and his tunes lapsed from popularity.

A few fans remained faithful. One, a thirty-year-old record collector from Brighton, posted a photograph of himself in the Facebook group Kai Smith Is Missing, standing next to a man who looked much like Kai only a little older. '*Never guess who this is? This is Kai's brother Marley Smith. Lives close to my mum who knows them from dog walking. Marley says not to worry about Kai; says they message every week, but Kai just wants time to himself.*'

The majority of the few people who replied below didn't believe the poster: '*Total BS. Kai is dead. Everyone knows that.*'

In December the luxury yacht broker Edmiston announced that they were handling the sale of the superyacht *Ella*, looking for offers in the region of 85 million euros. In the yacht's description, it boasted that the boat had been extensively refitted, but nowhere did it mention that the boat had previously been known as *Zinaida*.

Because in 2021 the appetite for superyachts still seemed insatiable, *Ella* sold quickly to another Russian, though for much less than the Pirumovs had paid to have her built. The following March she was impounded by Spanish authorities at Port Vell Marina Barcelona at the start of the Ukraine War.

Earlier that year the *London Evening Standard* had reported that the billionaire industrialist Stepan Pirumov had joined the ranks for Russian exiles living in London. Despite the sale of *Zinaida*, he was reputedly broke. Among the list of properties he was selling was a recently vacated luxury apartment in Paris's sixième arrondissement. The article was accompanied by several photographs, some of Stepan and Yuliya Pirumov in the days when they had been part of the inner circle, contrasted with photographs of them peering from the windows of a small flat in London. There was one photograph of a beautiful young woman smoking a cigarette at a party. It was captioned, *Stepan's estranged daughter, artist Zina Pirumova, at the Vauxhall Gallery*. Zina Pirumova had her own exhibition there.

On Dominica, Andrew came into some money. With it, he bought a brand new Toyota Land Cruiser and had the name of his business painted on the side. When people asked where he'd got the money from, he told them he'd won it on the lottery; everyone on the island knew that Andrew disapproved of gambling because of his religious faith, but they knew better than to ask more.

That spring, a yacht sailed into Marina Verolme, a small marina near Rio de Janeiro, to repair some damage it had sustained in high winds east of Patagonia.

It was crewed by a couple; a man with straggly fair hair and a beard, and a woman with short dark hair. They both spoke English, though the man had a Russian name. The mast and rudder had been damaged in a knock-down, the woman said, and they had lost their wind speed and data system.

They stayed in Brazil for ten weeks waiting for parts to be shipped from Germany. The boatyard's owner insisted they stay at his uncle's house in the nearby town of Garatucaia while the repairs were being carried out, and over the weeks they became friends with the family – though the pair of them liked to spend a lot of time alone on the beach together; they kept themselves to themselves. The two foreigners fitted in easily, even though the man did not eat meat, which the boatyard owner thought was ridiculous, until one evening the man with the Russian name cooked the whole family a *feijoada* using only vegetables. It was not that bad. 'Better than my wife's,' joked the boatyard owner, though his wife did not find that funny.

The boatyard owner found people who could help them mend the boat, and the couple worked away with them in the boatyard. When it was finally finished, the couple paid in US dollars and stocked the boat up with dried and canned food, preparing for a long voyage. Early that morning, the boatbuilder's whole family came down to the dockside to wave them off on the tide, because they had liked the couple so much and because they didn't have many visitors like that in this part of the country.

'Come back,' they said, hugging them.

As he watched them both handling the boat expertly out into open water, the boatyard owner said, 'They seemed pretty happy together. Very, cool. You know? A good, strong relationship.'

His wife looked at him sourly, thinking he was making some kind of accusation against her by the comment. 'She was strong,' she said. 'I liked that. And he respected that. But you are wrong. They weren't even lovers. They were friends. Good friends. You don't often see that between a man and a woman; a real mutual respect. It was nice. It happens when a man properly respects a woman.'

The man shrugged. 'They were lovers,' he insisted. 'They lived with us for weeks. How can you not understand that?'

His uncle agreed. He said, 'If they weren't even lovers, how come she was pregnant?'

The boatyard owner's wife snorted. 'Pregnant? Where did you get that bullshit from? If she was pregnant, she would have told me.'

'You don't have to be told. I could tell. She had that glow. And one time I found her being sick in our toilet.'

'That was because of the vegetable *feijoada*,' the boatyard owner's wife said. Her husband laughed.

'That's why they have to go,' said her uncle. 'They were going back to her home in England so they could have the baby.'

The boatyard owner's wife said that was bullshit. 'They were going to sail to Australia, she told me, just yesterday.'

The family continued arguing, because that was how they liked to talk to each other.

The wind was light, coming down from the hills behind them. And as they watched, the boat ran up another sail. It was a fast, well-practised move; the sort that shows how well a crew are working together. The huge yellow spinnaker seemed to shake itself out over the bows for a couple of seconds, then, with a snap, they were too far away to hear, and the wind filled it, making a perfect big-bellied curve that seemed to be pulling the boat behind it, faster now, eastwards and out towards the Atlantic.

THANKS

This book was inspired by a sailing holiday I took with my brother Christopher. Thanks for inviting us to join you.

Thanks to Anna Cartwright, Dirk Weise and Nic Compton for checking many of the details of the manuscript.

I'm hugely grateful for the team at Quercus and riverrun who had such enthusiasm for this book; especially to Jon Riley and Jasmine Palmer. Huge thanks too to Elizabeth Masters, Ana McLaughlin, David Murphy, Hannah Robinson and Ella Patel, and to copy editor Nick de Somogyi for ironing out so many wrinkles. Again. I'm aware of how lucky I am to have these people in my corner.

Karolina Sutton of Curtis Brown for her insight and support. And Jane McMorrow for patiently letting me talk through the plot again and again at strange times of the day. Colin Scott likewise, and Roz Brody, Mike Holmes, Janet King and C.J. Sansom for their enduring support.

And finally to Elly Griffiths, Val McDermid and Sara Paretsky, and so many of my colleagues, for their generosity towards me and for leading by example.